4—

D0041077

The Wake
of the Lorelei Lee

L. A. MEYER

The Wake
of the Lorelei Lee

Being an Account of
the Adventures
of Jacky Faber
on Her Way to Botany Bay

HARCOURT
Houghton Mifflin Harcourt

Boston   New York   2010

All rights reserved. For information about permission to reproduce selections from this book, write to Permissions, Houghton Mifflin Harcourt Publishing Company, 215 Park Avenue South, New York, New York 10003.

Harcourt is an imprint of Houghton Mifflin Harcourt Publishing Company.

www.hmhbooks.com

The text of this book is set in Minion.

Library of Congress Cataloging-in-Publication Data
Meyer, L. A. (Louis A.), 1942–
The wake of the Lorelei Lee : being an account of the adventures of Jacky Faber on her way to Botany Bay / L.A. Meyer.
p. cm. — (A Bloody Jack adventure)
Summary: Now rich, Jacky Faber has purchased the *Lorelei Lee* to carry passengers across the Atlantic, and believing she has been absolved of past sins against the Crown, she docks in London, where she is arrested and sentenced to life in the newly formed penal colony in Australia.
ISBN 978-0-547-32768-6 (hardcover : alk. paper) [1. Sex role—Fiction.
2. Prisoners—Fiction. 3. Seafaring life—Fiction. 4. Orphans—Fiction.
5. Australia—History—19th century—Fiction. 6. Sea stories.] I. Title.
PZ7.M57172Wak 2010
[Fic]—dc22
2010008686

Manufactured in the United States of America
DOC 10 9 8 7 6 5 4 3 2 1
4500248881

As always, for Annetje . . .

*. . . and for Katy Kellgren and the fine staff at
Listen & Live, who so eloquently brought
Jacky to life in the audio world.
Thanks, also, to Elaine Jimenez and her troops
on the Bloody Jack Boards, they who keep
Jacky's flame glowing.*

Prologue

She is beautiful.

She is trim in the waist and young—only sixteen years old—and frisky as a new filly.

I have been all over her, trying to find her wanting in some respect, but found nothing to diminish her in my eyes or in my heart.

I have swum with her in the harbor and felt her bottom and it was smooth and sound. I have thrust my knife into her knees and into all her cracks and crevices and found nothing but good, solid bone.

I have been with her at sea and found her there to be the most amiable of consorts. She was as spirited and wild as any mermaid as we splashed headlong through the waves, a bone in her teeth, and her tail to the wind.

She belongs to me and I love her and her name is *Lorelei Lee.*

PART I

Chapter 1

April 1807
Boston, Massachusetts
USA

"*Must* you have your grubby hands on her chest, Davy? *Must* you? I swear you are just the *dirtiest* little monkey!" Davy Jones is leaning over the bow and has a grimy paw on each of the girl's breasts.

The rogue grins hugely, but does not change his grip. "Gotta hold on to somethin', Jacky. We wouldn't want to drop her in the drink now, would we?"

"You drop her in, Mate, and you're goin' in after her. Tink, take a strain. John Thomas, swing her in and hold her. There. Good."

"She's in place, Skipper."

"All right, pound 'er in."

Jim Tanner swings the heavy mallet and drives in the thick pegs that will hold the girl in place on the bow, under the bowsprit. Then we all step back to admire the figurehead.

My, my . . . Look at that, now . . . She is absolutely beautiful.

I had hired a master woodcarver to carve her because my ship lacked such a figurehead, and I felt we needed one to guide us on our watery way; and a real master he turned out to be. She is carved of good solid oak and positively glows in her new paint—luminous pink skin with long amber tresses that wrap around her slim body. Her back is arched to match the curve of the ship's stem; her breasts thrust proudly forward, peeking out through the thick strands of her hair. She smiles—her red lips slightly parted, as if her voice were lifted in song—and her hands hold a small golden harp, a lyre, actually, which conveniently, and modestly, covers her lower female part. When we'd discussed the sculpture, the carver, Mr. Simms, thought it would be just the thing if the piece looked like me, and I agreed. The *Lorelei Lee* is my ship, after all, and so I posed for him—in my natural state, as it were. All who know me know that I am not exactly shy in that regard. Plus Master Carver Simms is an old man, so what's the harm? I must say Mr. Simms succeeded most admirably in capturing my particular features, and I am most pleased with the result.

And, oh, I am so very pleased with all the other parts of my beautiful ship, as well.

She is called a brigantine, having two sturdy masts, square-rigged on the foremast, with three fore-and-aft sails off the front and the mainmast rigged with a fore-and-aft spanker as mainsail. She is, in dimensions and sail rig, much like my first real command, HMS *Wolverine,* which was a brig; but in elegance and spirit, she is much more like my beautiful *Emerald,* who now sleeps beneath the sea. I like saying *brigantine* better than *brig,* as it sounds more elegant. And, oh, she is elegant. I fell in love with her at first sight, lying all sleek next to Ruffles Wharf, looking as if she wanted to shake off the lines that bound her to the land and go tearing off to sea. It was from there that we did take her directly for her sea trials, and she performed most admirably, running before the wind like a greyhound, dancing over the waves and pointing up into the weather like she wanted to charge directly into the teeth of the gale itself. Glory!

I had purchased the *Lorelei Lee* from a Captain Ichabod Lee, who had named her after his daughter. I decided to keep the name, the mythic Lorelei being something like a mermaid who sat on a rock on the Rhine River in Germany and lured poor sailors to their doom with her singing. So it seems appropriate, somehow, my having been something of a mermaid myself in the near past, as well as my being a singer of songs, though I wish no doom on any poor sailor.

How could I afford such a splendid craft, you ask? Hmmm? Well, that's where the mermaid bit comes in. Earlier this year I had been sent by British Naval Intelligence on a treasure hunting expedition, diving on a Spanish wreck off Key West in Florida. It was entirely against my will, but my will or wishes don't seem to matter much in this world. The wreck was the *Santa Magdalena,* and she had yielded up much, much gold and silver, so much so that it didn't seem quite fair that King Georgie should get all that loot and that I should get none. No, it did not. I, who was the one who risked life and limb and peace of mind by diving down into those horrid depths to bring up all that gold from the *Santa Magdalena.* No, I did not find it fair at all, not by half, so I squirreled away a few of the gold ingots—well . . . actually about fifty of them—in the hold of my bonny little schooner, replacing part of her ballast, and after the diving was done, hauled it all up to Boston.

And speaking of ballast, I have in my hold right now the selfsame diving bell we had used to get me down two hundred and fifty feet into the Caribbean Sea. I had the thing on my little schooner the *Nancy B. Alsop* when we were detached to return to Boston, and since no one was here to claim it, I stashed it, under cover of night, of course, deep in the hold of the *Lorelei Lee*. It's as good a ballast as any dumb lead bars, and who knows, it might prove useful someday.

So anyway, we got back to Boston, revealed the golden stash to the astounded Mr. Ezra Pickering, my very good friend and lawyer, and he set about converting the gold into cash, lines of credit, and whatnot, hiding it all very cunningly in various dummy corporations and holding companies, so that King Georgie wouldn't find out and perhaps be a bit miffed. Clever man, that Ezra.

Hammers have been pounding since the day of the *Lorelei*'s purchase. We have constructed four relatively spacious cabins, two on either side, aft, on the mess deck, just under my cabin. Forward of them we have twelve regular-sized cabins (big enough for a bed, dresser, and dry sink), again on each side, making a total of twenty-four. Then we have three levels of open hammock spaces, two hundred hooks in each. The upper level, being a bit airier than the lower, will be more expensive, of course. It's all in what one can afford. Hey, I have swung my hammock in many a dank hold, and what was good enough for me will be good enough for them. I intend to give everyone, regardless of berth, plenty of fresh air and as good food as I can manage. We can carry three hundred passengers, as well as thirty crew.

And, yes, of course, the fitting out of my beautiful cabin continues, the design of which is being directed by my very good John Higgins, second in command of Faber Shipping Worldwide. Never let it be said that Jacky Faber goes any way but first class when she can afford it, and Higgins does not spare the expense.

There will be separate facilities for families with young children and a separate dormitory for young females traveling alone. After they are established in the New World, men will be sending back for their wives and sweethearts, you may be certain of that.

"One thing is for sure, Sister," I had said to my friend Amy Trevelyne when she had come onboard several days ago to view our progress in outfitting the *Lorelei*. "My ship shall never become a floating brothel."

"Are you not the one, dear Sister, who once admonished me to never say never, as it has a way of coming back on you?"

"Well, it won't happen this time, Amy," I'd answered with the sure and smug certainty of the truly stupid. "And furthermore—Hello, what's this?" A cheer had gone up from the dock.

We looked over the rail and found that the new figurehead of the *Lorelei Lee* had chosen just that moment to be delivered.

"Isn't she fine?" I exulted, drawing in a deep, satisfied breath and regarding the richly painted figure glowing in the sun and smiling up at us with what, to Amy, would be a very familiar wolfish grin.

Amy's mouth fell open upon seeing the sculpture, unable to speak. I gave out an evil chuckle and put the backs of my fingers under her fallen chin and gently lifted it back to its proper place.

She regained the power of speech and cried despairingly, "Oh, Jacky, no!" as she had said so many times before.

So anyway, here I am with this fine ship all outfitted and ready to go, awaiting word from my darling Jaimy, back in London, that my name has been cleared of all charges against it and that I am back in the good graces of the King, upon which word I shall immediately set sail for Merrie Olde England and—*finally!*—marriage to Lieutenant James Emerson Fletcher. *Hooray!*

Chapter 2

The final carpentry changes to the *Lorelei Lee* being completed, Amy and I are off in the *Morning Star* for a weekend at Dovecote, her family's seashore estate in Quincy and one of my favorite spots on God's green earth. Because there are no classes on Saturday and Sunday, we have Joannie Nichols with us, as well. She has been granted this treat in return for her not complaining too bitterly about being left behind on our first crossing of the Big Salt. *"Now, Joannie, you know that school is still in session and that you must attend. I hear from Mistress Pimm that you are doing quite well and that cheers me greatly." "Yes, but—" "But nothing, Joannie. When our* Lorelei *returns, school will be out for the summer and we'll all ride back across together. Agreed? Good."* Her temper is somewhat soothed by this delightful little outing on this perfect spring day. Her very good friend Daniel Prescott, now thirteen, is proudly at the tiller, and she revels in showing off to him her new ladylike ways, as he delights in demonstrating to her his skill as a true nautical coxswain. All is well.

· · ·

After a lovely sail across Massachusetts Bay on this beautiful, soaring day, we bring the *Star* up to Dovecote's dock and tie her securely to it. Then we are off—Joannie and Daniel to explore the farm with all its charms, and Amy and I to get settled in her room. I know full well that the kids are planning to spend the night together in my little cuddy cabin on the *Star*, and I trust they will be good, because by now Joan Nichols has been apprised of Mistress Pimm's requirement that her girls maintain their "innocence," else they will be asked to leave the school, and Joannie is, by and large, a sensible girl.

After we have stowed our gear, Amy and I agree that a brisk morning ride on this glorious April day—*Ah, spring, how I love thee!*—would be just the thing to start what will probably be our last weekend together here at Dovecote for quite a while. We don our riding gear while two fine horses are saddled, then we are off.

We gallop down the main road to the columns at the entrance to the estate, and then back by the sea, and then to a place we call Daisy Hill, where we walk the horses to let them catch their breath. I rejoice to see Millie, the black-and-white collie who is, without doubt, The World's Best Dog, scampering about, merrily chasing the first butterflies of the season—she who was my boon companion on the road to New York, which fair city I never actually reached, and who later saved my very life.

"Is it not just the most wonderful day, Sister?"

"It is indeed," says Amy. "And it is so good to have you back, even if it is only for a short while." She gazes about at the soaring clouds and lifts her face to the fresh breeze from the sea. Yes, spring is always most welcome in frosty New

England. Amy sits her horse sidesaddle, while I, of course, sit athwart on a regular saddle. She is demurely dressed in a dark brown riding habit, while I have on my scarlet jacket, white trousers beneath, and Scots bonnet on top. Amy's parents are away, so I don't have to be especially proper, which is good, 'cause it ain't really in my nature to be especially proper.

Millie again has a flock of sheep to herd, which pleases her greatly, but right now the sheep are in the fold for shearing, so she contents herself with herding whatever poor beasts she can find to do her bidding. She cocks her head, smiles her doggie smile, then, barking, she disappears over the hill.

We sit for a while on the top of Daisy Hill, looking out over the deep and, for now, quite calm blue sea . . .

. . . and then I give a shudder.

"Are you cold, Sister?" asks Amy. "We can go back."

"It is a mite nippy, but, no, a goose must have just walked over my grave," I say, laughing over the old saying that people use when they shudder involuntarily for no apparent reason.

Then, what should appear over the crest of the hill but a flock of agitated geese, honking and squawking and crossing right in front of me, followed closely by herd dog Millie.

Amy gives a bit of a gasp and I let out a nervous laugh.

"Well, at least I know where my grave will be. Funny, I always figured I'd be buried at sea."

"Don't joke about things like that, Jacky."

I look at the ground beneath my mare's feet and think on this as the geese disperse and head back down to the barn.

"I'm not joking," I reply. "But I thought you were a Person of Sweet Reason and not in any way given to superstition, Amy dear."

"I am not, but still, no sense tempting Fate."

"It is not the worst place in the world to end up," I reply, looking out over the broad ocean. "Such a beautiful view it would be."

Then I hear the sudden pounding of hooves, of a horse being ridden hard and very nearby.

What?

I twist around in my saddle and see a man dressed in a scarlet jacket and white britches explode from a copse of trees and bear straight for us. I reach for my shiv that I keep up my sleeve, but he is on me too fast and I cannot get it out.

Scarlet? British? Still after me? No, it cannot be . . .

The man wears not a hat, but a kerchief tied across his face. *A highwayman, a robber, here on Dovecote? No, it is not possible . . .*

I hear Amy shout in alarm and then he is on me. He bumps my poor little mare and reaches around my waist and hauls me off her and over in front of him. I squeal and pummel him with my balled-up fists, but to no avail. He pins my arms to my sides and holds me tight.

What? Am I to be kidnapped after all that has happened?

I twist and struggle but cannot—*damn!*—free my arms. But I find I can lift my left hand, and with it, I reach up and pull down my assailant's kerchief. My mouth drops open in delighted astonishment.

"Randall!" I gasp. "How—"

But I don't get to say more because the rogue's mouth comes down upon mine, stifling my cries of delight. I give up the fight and put my arms around him and hug him tight.

"Well met, Lieutenant Bouvier," says the grinning rascal when our lips part.

"Oh, very well met, Lieutenant Trevelyne! So *very* well met! When . . . ? How . . . ?"

"Later, Jacky my love. Right now I'm hungry for a bite to eat, a bottle of good wine, and another of your sweet kisses."

As he plants another one on me, Amy picks up the reins of my former mount and prepares to lead her off down the hill.

"Good to see you, Brother," she says simply. "Jacky, I assume you'll be riding back to the house on your present perch. Ah, I thought so."

Well, I can't say nay to that, no I can't. Nor do I want to.

Lunch had been prepared and laid out on the large table in the grand dining room. If it had been just Amy and I, we would have taken our dinner in the kitchen, but that would not do for the young lord of the manor, oh, no. He must have the finest upon his return to the ancestral manse. Bottles of the best wine are cracked, several geese pay the price of being geese, and there is jubilation all around the household—the young master is back!

"So, Randall," I say, seating myself next to him in a chair he has pulled out for me. "It appears you have joined the English army. I can scarce believe it." His jacket is of the deepest scarlet with white turnouts and cuffs and a high— *red leather?*—collar. He does look awfully good in it.

He tilts back his head and laughs. "No, my love. Although I have enraged Father many times in the past, for *that* he would surely put a bullet between my eyes." He beckons for Blount, the butler, who usually acts as Randall's valet when he is home, to refill his glass. I take a small sip from mine. It is always best that I keep a clear head when I am around this rascal, else I should end up on my back, with a heavy bit of explaining to do later. Well I remember that time under the rosebushes.

"No, once again, I am following your lead, Jacky," he says, leaning back in his chair and tapping his empty wineglass with his knife. "I am going to sea." The attentive Blount once again fills his goblet.

I give a small gasp of surprise. "To *sea*? Randall, you don't know the first thing about seamanship. What captain would take you on as an officer?"

"Not a sea captain, maybe, but perhaps a seaborne colonel," he says smugly. "You are gazing, in what I plainly see is open and frank admiration, at Second Lieutenant Randall Tristan Trevelyne, United States Marine Corps."

What?

"I would have thought we were done with uniforms, Randall, after all that we had witnessed at Jena." I see now that there are gold fouled-anchor pins on his collar, with the initials USA embossed upon them.

He loses his smile at that and merely nods. I know he is thinking of that awful day in Germany. I'm sure he had made many friends in Napoleon's army, and I'm equally sure he saw some of them die, as did I. Randall had always wanted to see what war was like, and he found out then, for sure—thirty thousand young men lying dead on the plains of Jena and Auerstädt. He gives his head a shake, and the smile—though a bit forced, I think—is back.

"Thank you again for saving my life, Randall," I murmur, lifting my glass to him and recalling that time when I lay helpless upon my back about to be gutted by a Prussian bayonet.

"Think nothing of it, my dear," he says, leering at me over the rim of his wineglass. "But you must know that I shall expect repayment in full—if not in kind, then in deed." He takes another pull at his wine and continues. "I am assigned to the frigate *Constitution*, which lies at Long Wharf in Boston Harbor, and we leave next week for some exercise or other. Therefore, that means I do not have much time to complete the seduction of Miss Jacky Faber, so we must get down to it with all possible speed, such that the, um, deed can be done with all possible dispatch. As you naval types would put it, 'Not a moment to lose!'"

"You might have even less time than that, Randall," I counter, grinning my foxy grin at the rascal. "I intend to ship out for London the moment I receive a letter from Lieutenant James Fletcher, my intended husband, informing me that the coast is clear for my return and our eventual marriage."

"Umm. Him again," says Randall, dismissing Jaimy with a shake of his head. "Well, we shall see about that."

"How did you get your commission, Brother?" asks Amy, to change the subject. Discussion of my eventual seduction and ravishment not being a comfortable topic for her.

"The Commander-in-Chief of the newly formed Marine Corps, Colonel Burrows, was in Boston when I debarked, so I secured an interview. I showed up, resplendent in my French Cavalry officer's uniform, told him of my experiences in the Grand Army of the Republic, and within an hour I was being fitted for this uniform, commission as Officer and Gentleman in hand."

"Why are you here, Brother"—Amy had given a ladylike snort at the word *gentleman*—"and not resident at some house of ill repute in Boston?" she asks. "I believe Miss Bodeen's is still in operation and should suit your needs quite well."

"Surely not to see you, dear sister of mine," retorts Randall, not in the least abashed. "Actually, after being fitted, I sought out Ezra Pickering, to determine if he knew anything as to the whereabouts of our gadabout young warrior goddess. He informed me she was here, and off I galloped. I *do* have to accomplish this seduction, you know. I feel it is my duty as a rakehell, a cad, and a scoundrel."

"How is Mr. Pickering?" asks Amy, again trying to steer the conversation in a more seemly direction.

"He is well," answers Randall. "And actually, he is quite an amusing fellow—for a lawyer—and excellent company. We had a fine lunch together at the Pig and Whistle. I hereby give you my permission to marry him."

Amy chokes at that. When she composes herself, she hisses, "Aside from the fact that I am not yet ready for that sort of thing, Randall, what makes you think that I would ask your permission?" Amy's back is ramrod straight.

"Because, *ma chère soeur,* when Father is not here, I am in charge of you and what you will or will not do. Surely you know that?"

Amy says nothing, but only sits and fumes. What he has said, of course, is, unfortunately, the absolute truth.

He continues. "Pickering seems quite taken with you, as a matter of fact. Poor man, I cannot imagine why," says Randall. He tosses his napkin onto his plate, places a cheroot between his teeth, and leans back as Blount offers a burning match to light it. Puffing mightily and sending out a cloud of vile smoke, Randall looks about him, then says, "But maybe *this* is what he is taken with." He gestures all about him at the fine dining room, the ballroom beyond the French doors, taking in with that gesture all the rich grandeur that is Dovecote.

Oh, Lord, that cuts it.

Amy leaps to her feet. "That is despicable! How could you possibly impugn the name of a fine gentleman like Ezra Pickering with a slanderous statement like that! You—you . . ."

I spare Amy her sputtering search for the proper epithet by jumping to my own feet and putting my arms around her outraged self and exclaiming, "Please, Sister, it is only Randall being Randall. Let us rejoice in his safe return and not take all he says to heart. Please, Amy, sit back down. He did not mean that. Please. Randall, be good."

She reluctantly sits, and so do I. Randall eyes me through the smoke of his cigar.

"So," he says, "Jacky Faber, the young snippet I first met as a simple chambermaid now owns two ships and a shipping company. How did you manage that?"

"Hard work and sound investments," I primly reply, wanting to quickly get off this particular subject. Since the purchase of the *Lorelei Lee*, Amy, too, has wondered at Faber

Shipping's sudden rise in fortune. But I have put her off with the same sort of weak explanations, as we can't have her putting my gold-hoarding scam into print for all of England to read, now, can we? I can see it now: *The Rapture of the Deep, Being an Account of the Further Adventures of Jacky Mary Faber—Urchin, Orphan, Thief, Sometime-Sailor, Sometime-Soldier, Sometime-Spy—She Who Stole Even More of the King's Treasure and Deserves to Hang for It.*

No, we cannot have *that*.

"And a good bit of simple larceny, too, I'll wager." Randall laughs, and I notice that Amy does not contradict that, but only slides her eyes over to look at me.

"Ahem. Well, enough of that," I say, pushing on. "Again, Randall, I must ask you, after what we have seen of the horror and carnage of war, why would you once again put a uniform on your back and go to live the ofttimes rough and sometimes murderous military life?"

He considers this, putting the heel of his left boot on the table. Eventually, he says, "What else am I going to do? I am not a scholar wishing only to sit in a garret to pore over the dusty pages of academe, the words of long-dead men. My time at Harvard has proven that. No. Nor do I wish to study the Law—Good God, I leave that to Ezra and his ilk. Take on the vestments of Divinity? Could you imagine the Very Reverend Randall Trevelyne? The heavens would open up, and destruction would reign upon the entire world at that outrage."

I myself have to laugh outright at *that* image. "Yes, floods and plagues and clouds of locusts would surely follow your ordination."

"Ummm . . . right. So, being too big to be a jockey, too small for a prizefighter, and detesting farming, it is the life of a soldier for me."

"What of politics? Have you not considered that? Would it not suit your rascally nature, Randall?" I tease.

"Hmmm . . ." He muses on this possibility. "After I distinguish myself in the Marine Corps, it is not impossible that I could become Governor of this state. Or even President. I would not mind having a horde of sycophants licking my boots. Actually, that is quite an attractive notion. Thank you, Jacky, I had not thought of that."

Amy gags at the notion of his being the governor of anything, and I laugh and rise. "Come, Randall," I say. "Let us see how politic you can be. I want you to stand and embrace Amy and say, 'How good it is to see you, Sister.' And Amy, I want you to hug him to you and say, 'Welcome back, Brother. I am so glad you have come back to us safely.' If either of you refuse, then I shall speak to neither of you and will immediately head back to Boston and you will be denied my company, for whatever that is worth." And that is just how politic *I* can be.

They do it, and I think that despite all of their posturing, they are sincere in their expressions of affection, each for the other.

Chapter 3

"Come on, Amy! Let us go! The horses are saddled and ready!"

Amy Trevelyne sighs, then puts up her pen. She has been taking down yet another of my rambling accounts. This time I'm telling her about the rather riotous trip I took last summer on the Allegheny, the Ohio, and the Mississippi—rivers that course through the great American frontier wilderness—and I have become restless in the telling of it. It is too nice a day to be indoors, even if it is in Amy's pretty little room. Her scribblings are sure to end up in yet another lurid book recounting my misadventures as I stumble through this life, sometimes properly clothed and well-mannered, though mostly not. But it is all to the good, I figure, as it makes her happy. And thanks to Amy's generosity, the proceeds from sales go to help support my London Home for Little Wanderers.

It is Saturday, the second day of our stay at Dovecote, and, since we must return to Boston tomorrow to get Joannie back to the Lawson Peabody in time for Monday's classes, I intend to make the most of this fine day. I have been informed by Amy that a spot on the fallow fields of the south forty acres has been leased to a religious revival, and I insist that we go see it.

"But, why, Sister?" she asks. "That sort of thing always seems so . . . primitive."

"Aw, Amy, it's just a show like any other, and maybe it'll be fun. They are sure to have some rousing hymns. And it will be good for my Immortal Soul, which certainly could use a bit of a wash."

She sighs, then says, "I am sure you are right in thinking that. Very well." Amy does a lot of that—sighing, I mean—especially when I'm around.

We do not take Joannie with us on this outing, as she has not yet had many equestrian classes and could not keep up with us. Besides, she seems quite content to gambol about the place with Daniel. Narrowing my eyes, I warn the both of them to be good, but I suspect the hayloft will get a long visit this afternoon. This being April, I am sure the river is still too cold to swim in, but I suspect the two scamps have brought their Caribbean swimming suits with them and would like nothing better than to take a dip for fun and to scandalize the other kids on the farm. So maybe they'll brave it, because it is so nice and sunny and warm.

So with good mounts under us and our riding jackets on our backs, Amy and I pound away in search of Redemption.

Randall has begged off, too, saying he'll be damned if he'll waste one moment of his remaining time ashore listening to religious claptrap. He rides with us to the gates of the farm, where he splits off, heading for a nearby tavern in hopes of finding some sport. As that inn has a bit of a notorious reputation, the rogue will probably find it.

"I will be back for dinner, ladies," he says as he prepares to ride away. "Make sure a place is laid for me. Tallyho and all that."

Before he goes, he leans over and gives my right thigh, just above the knee, a bit of a squeeze and says, "Till later, my sweet little Tartar, and we will take up where we left off."

"It is probably too much to expect to see him come back sober," growls Amy as we watch the dust settle behind him. "But let us now go see this . . . er, show."

We give heels to horse, and with a *whoop!* from me, we are off.

Coming up over a knoll, we see the revival spread out below us. There are hundreds of people seated on makeshift benches and hundreds more standing around behind them. All are swaying to the cadence of the hymn that is being sung by all.

> *Bright morning stars are rising,*
> *Bright morning stars are rising,*
> *Bright morning stars are rising,*
> *And day is breaking in my soul.*

"Coo!" I exclaim, after I have sung along with the very familiar verse, as we on the *Belle of the Golden West* used to include this song as part of our Sanctified Act. "I did not think so many people lived around here."

"They do not," said Amy, by way of explanation. "You can see by the small family tents and covered wagons spread all about that they have come from all around. Their fields have been plowed, but it is still too early to plant, as there might yet be a frost and all the seed would be lost. So it is a time for socializing, and this is one of the ways they do it."

All the young folks, the boys and girls, down there sparkin', glancin' about at each other, maybe bein' so bold as to hold hands and to meet behind the tent, finally daring a kiss or two. Ah, yes, I know this scene quite well—as ancient as the world and as new as tomorrow.

> *Where are our dear brothers?*
> *Oh, where are our dear sisters?*
> *They're down here in the valley prayin',*
> *And day is breakin' in my soul.*

"And then in the fall, after the harvest, we will have the big County Fair, and the same sort of thing will go on."

"Well, Amy. You've got to get the boys and girls together. Otherwise, everything grinds to a halt. Is it not so?"

"I suppose. The world must go on, in its sometimes tedious way."

"It is not all that bad, Sister Melancholy, as the world does have its charms," I say. "Come, Sister, let us get closer."

> *Oh, where are our dear fathers?*
> *And where are our dear mothers?*
> *They've gone to heaven shouting,*
> *And day is breaking in my soul.*

We ride down amidst the outlying wagons and buggies as that great old chestnut of a hymn winds down, and pull up at the fringe of the crowd. I take my long glass from my saddlebag and train it on the stage. It is about four feet high, twenty feet wide, ten deep, and has a backdrop of red curtains, which are closed. There is a short stairway up the center. *Hmmm . . . This is quite a production for this sort of thing, I'm thinking.* These revivals can be, and usually are, as simple as a preacher standing up in the back of a buckboard, with the crowd standing about him.

The stage holds a high lectern and two preachers, each in long frock coats and high white collars, who take turns standing at the podium to thump the Bible and harangue the congregation, which seems to thrive upon the verbal abuse being thrown at it. Arms wave in the air and shouts of *Hallelujah!* and *Praise God!* are heard, and some people have fainted. We are close enough now to hear snatches of what is being bellowed out by the larger of the two men of God.

". . . and cast out Satan, yes, cast him out, oh my brethren! Listen not to his forked tongue, nor to his honeyed words, words that may sound sweet but are covered with flies and maggots, words that will condemn you to eternal damnation should you heed them!"

"He's pretty good," I observe. "Giving 'em their money's worth, that's for sure."

"Humph," says Amy.

"And speaking of money, that part should be coming soon."

Yep.

The preacher holds out both of his arms and closes his eyes, seemingly deep in silent prayer. The crowd goes quiet. Then he makes the pitch.

"My friends, our time here together is drawing to a close. It is my fondest hope that you have been spiritually nourished by this gathering of kindred spirits. As you go forth to continue

to live your good, Christian lives, I will ask you to file up the center aisle and testify to your reborn faith. *And if you can, offer some token of your favor, your wish that Brother Lempel and myself might continue our ministry. Any amount is welcome, and you will be blessed, oh so blessed for it!"*

I notice now that a waist-high board fence cunningly encircles the main congregation, forcing all to go by the collection plate on their way out, or be seen putting a leg over the fence in order to avoid the tithing. *Pretty crafty,* I think as I chuckle to myself, but it turns out that there are even craftier things to follow.

"*. . . and to receive your most welcome offerings, I give you . . ."*

At this, the curtains open.

"*. . . the Angel Evangeline, the very embodiment and soul of purity and of grace."*

The congregation gasps and so do I. A girl, an impossibly beautiful girl, floats forward from between the red curtains. She is dressed in a long flowing white dress and has two gossamer wings attached to her back that flutter in the slight breeze. Her golden tresses pour out from under a golden starry crown to which is attached a halo that rides a few inches above her sainted head.

"Hey, what's going on here? That's from my old act with Reverend Clawson back on the Big River," I say, cutting my eyes to Amy's. Amy raises her eyebrows and nods. I had only recently told her of that part of our river journey. "But that ain't Reverend Clawson up there, and for sure that ain't me in the angel rig."

Stunned, I swing the glass around to look more closely at the two preachers. *Ha!* Of course, they ain't preachers at all. At least not the ordained kind. I see with a great deal of glee—*Oh, Glory*—that beneath some wigs and fake facial hair it is none other than my old associates of the stage, Mr. Fennel and Mr. Bean, master thespians, entrepreneurs, scam artists, and impossible ham actors. Upon my return from the Mississippi, I had renewed my acquaintance with the two, performed in several small parts in some of their Boston theatricals, and had related to them my experiences on the river over many tankards of ale at the Pig. 'Tis plain they took my account of our Sacred Hour of Prayer act very much to heart, because here it is again, with them in starring roles, but with one very big difference . . .

I twist the barrel of the long glass to focus it on the girl's undeniably beautiful face, beatific and radiant. Long golden curls, huge blue eyes—*Oh, my God, it cannot be!* I look again . . . *But it is* . . .

He is calling the congregation down now.

"Come down, Christian Soldiers, and testify! You must affirm your faith in the Blood of the Lamb, and renew it every blessed day. Cast out sin, oh my brothers and sisters, come on up. Come up and testify, yes, testify before the Lord God to your rock-solid faith! Come up, come up! Can you shout 'Hallelujah'?"

"Hallelujah!"

"Again, Brothers and Sisters! Let the host of heaven hear you!"

"HALLELUJAH!"

The very valley rocks with the sound.

"RIDE ON, KING JESUS!"

"HALLELUJAH!"

And come up they do—up the center aisle—testifying, waving their arms, and speaking in tongues. They approach the glowing angelic presence to place their offering into the basket she holds out before them. Fathers lift up small children so that they may drop their pennies into the basket. Mothers, tears streaming down their faces, put in their butter-and-egg money. The Angel Evangeline beams her beatific blessing down upon all. The smaller one of the two preachers concludes the service. The larger one, seemingly too overcome with emotion to continue, sits in a chair to one side of the stage, his face buried in his hands.

"Let us leave this now holy place with the words of that great old hymn 'Down in the Valley to Pray' on our lips," says the smaller of the two preachers, whose voice lacks the power and timbre of the bigger man's basso profundo, but still rings with religious fervor and conviction. *"Go with God, and praise be to His name."*

> *As I went down in the valley to pray,*
> *Studyin' about that good old way,*
> *And who should wear the starry crown,*
> *Good Lord, show me the way.*

The crowd's common voice is raised in the song and I join in, too, for I do know who wears that particular starry crown. Plus, I like the tune. And yes I, too, am a sinner.

> *Come on sinners and let's go down,*
> *Let's go down, oh, come on down,*
> *Come on sinners and let's go down,*
> *Down in the valley to pray.*

"Can we go now, Sister?"

"Go, yes, but not back to Dovecote just yet. Follow me, Amy, and you'll get an interesting surprise. You might even write about it someday." Wondering, she spurs after me, and I head down toward the stage as the crowd disburses all around us, they all going in the other direction, while I head through the throng, around to the back, where sits the tent, which has, as I suspected, a back flap, now shut.

I leap off my horse and tie the reins to a wagon wheel.

"What are we doing?" asks Amy, remaining in her saddle.

"You'll see."

At that moment, both Mr. Fennel and Mr. Bean come around the corner, giving instructions to a stagehand for taking down the stage and breaking down the benches and stowing all in the waiting wagons. Upon seeing us, Mr. Bean says, "I'm sorry, ladies, but the service is over . . ." and then, "Uh, *oh*," as he recognizes me.

"Why, it's our own dear Puck!" cries Mr. Fennel, full of false bluster. "How good to see you again, Jacky."

"Mutual, Reverends," I say, enjoying their discomfiture. "May I present Miss Amy Trevelyne, owner of this property upon which you have been . . . performing." I give them a big smile.

They look at each other, fearing trouble.

"Yes, well . . ."

"Do not worry, she will not peach on you, will you, Amy? Good." Amy slowly shakes her head but gives a profound sniff. Her moral sense is plainly offended by the discovery of this little scam. She, of course, has now recognized the pair, having been with me to watch them on the stage many times. She still has not seen fit to dismount, preferring to look down upon them with some disdain. Amy may be a poet, a freethinker, an Abolitionist, and a republican, but she is still an aristocrat.

"As a matter of fact, you are invited down to the big house for dinner, libations, and conversation," I say, over-reaching myself, thinking that I'll apologize to Amy later for this breach of manners. "We must catch up on things, mustn't we? Oh, yes, and please bring the Archangel Evangeline with you. I will go invite her now."

With that, I turn and dive through the tent flap.

The girl has shed the angel costume and stands there in her simple shift. Even without the stage prop she is an absolute vision of loveliness—golden curls, ample chest, nipped-in waist, and slim but well-turned bottom. Startled, her amazingly blue eyes open wide, and her full, red lips form a perfect little O of surprise.

"Don't be alarmed," I say, extending my hand. "You see, I know you, Polly Von."

Chapter 4

Polly Von had wandered into our kip one day, about eight years ago, thumb firmly stuck in her mouth, and we took her in. Where she came from, we did not know, but she turned out to be a real asset to our gang as she became our very best beggar, looking like the dirty but perfect little angel that she was. I figure now she was actually quite close to me in age, but I had grown up fast in those days—in my mind, at least—while she remained charmingly child-like. She had fashioned a doll from some scraps of rags and would sit cooing to it in the evening, when all were back in the kip under Blackfriars Bridge and snugged up in the straw. Right now, she stands before me dressed only in her linen, regarding me with hooded eyes. I hear Amy enter the tent behind me, and Polly's eyes narrow with even more suspicion.

"It's me, Polly. Mary Faber, your old mate from the Rooster Charlie Gang. Do you remember?"

"Mary? Little Mary?" she asks, incredulous and confused, looking me up and down. I know it will take some time for this to sink in, since when last she saw me, I was barely dressed in a torn shift, and now I stand before her in my fine riding habit, looking every inch the nob.

The suspicion falls from her face and she laughs, then says, "I kin no believe it!" and she holds out her arms. We embrace and then put each other at arm's length again to look each other over.

"Coo. Look at ye now, Mary, a proper toff!"

"Ow, not s'bad yourself, dearie," I says, myself slippin' easy back inta the old way o' talkin'. "A rum bint, f'sure, and lookin' t' be workin' a jolly scam."

"'Ere, sit yerself down and we'll 'ave a bit o' a gam. D' ye ken wot become o' our other kipmates? I dinna know."

"Ahem," says Amy, from beside me, the Lawson Peabody Look full upon her face. "If you two were to speak English, I might feel more welcome here in your company."

Abashed for my rudeness, I say, "I am sorry, Sister. May I now present Miss Polly Von, my very dear mate from my Cheapside days. Polly, Miss Amy Trevelyne. She is our hostess here on her family's farm."

Polly jerks a bit at that information, but guarded nods are exchanged and we sit in the several chairs that are there. Polly places herself at a crude dressing table, which has a mirror mounted on it, and begins wiping the stage makeup from her face.

"So, Mary, tell me, about . . . them, and how you come to be here," she says, facing the mirror. I know that this will not be easy for either of us.

"Well, you know that on the night that Charlie was killed I went to see Toby Oyster and his gang who lived under the grating on West Street and convinced him to join his crew with what was left of ours."

She nods.

"And then . . . then I took off, dressed as a boy, joined the navy, and had a great deal of luck," I say, feeling the pang of guilt I always feel in recalling that.

"I remember your leaving," she says, looking over at me. "You must know that was a hard night for us, Mary . . . to lose the both of you."

I look down, unable to hold her gaze. "Right. I know. I am sorry. I have tried to make it up . . . to atone for that. But you . . . you must call me Jacky now, as I am no longer Mary."

"All right . . . Jacky. So tell it."

She nods gravely when I tell her what had become of Judy Miller and expresses surprise to find that she will be dining with Joannie Nichols this evening. Joannie was part of Toby's crew and so would have known Polly quite well.

When I tell of Muck's demise on the deck of the *Wolverine,* she smiles, showing rows of perfect, white teeth—*serves the bastard right*—but when I tell of Hughie's death upon the *Bloodhound,* a tear courses down her cheek. I do not know if it is a stage tear or a real one, but it is a tear all the same.

"Poor Hughie," she whispers. "He was always a good boy, and he always looked after me."

"Yes, he was just the best boy," I say. "But now tell us about you."

She collects her thoughts and begins. I've noticed that Polly, as a young woman, has developed a very breathy way of speaking. I suspect that men like to hear her talk.

"The gang was run in the same way as before, with Toby in charge and Hughie as the muscle. At least it was till a press gang took him. Coo, Mary, you should have seen it. It was a true battle royal it was—Hughie roarin' and swingin' his fists, and all of us throwin' rocks and the press gang goin' down, one after the other. But a few of the bleedin' coves finally got up behind him with their clubs and brought him down."

She takes a breath, then goes on.

"After that, we had to be really careful in dealin' with the other gangs, not having Hughie to back us up, but we got along, and . . . after we grew up a bit . . . Toby and me came . . . together, like. He took me as his miss." She cuts her eyes to us at this, as if daring us to make comment. When we don't, she continues.

"And we were like that till one day we were out in the town, arm in arm, and far, too far, from the kip, and yet another press gang come down upon us and took Toby away, and I ain't seen him since." She sighs. "But I was done with that, anyway. On my way back to the kip, I walked by a brothel and stood outside it for a while. From inside there was the sound of laughing and singing and the smell of good food. I stood there a while, considering. Then I went on down the street and I come upon a theater, where Mr. Fennel and Mr. Bean was putting on a theatrical, and I went in and asked them for a job and they took me on. They was good to me and didn't . . . bother me . . . in that way, and here I am." She stands and bows to an invisible audience. "An actress," she says with a certain amount of pride.

I clap my hands and say, "Bravo, Polly, I am so glad!"

And I am glad, considering how she could have ended up . . .

"She is indeed very beautiful, Jacky, but she seems to have all the morals of an alley cat."

"*Meeeoooow,* Sister," I purr back at her, holding up my curled hands as if there were claws at the ends of my fingers. "I am shocked at what you say, Amy. Christian charity and forgiveness and all."

"I am not being catty." She sniffs. "I am merely stating my impressions."

We are back in Amy's room, combing up and dressing for dinner.

"And what do you imagine would have become of *me,* my dear Sister who says she loves me no matter what, had I not been very, *very* lucky? Hand me the powder puff, please. Thank you. Remember, both Polly and I, and Joannie, too, came out of that very same stew, there under Blackfriars Bridge. And believe me, Sister Amy, had it come right down to it, I would *not* have chosen death over dishonor."

"I don't want to imagine that happening to you, Jacky. I don't." She looks down at her hands, clasped in her lap, and is silent for a bit. Finally she says, "Oh, I know so very little of the world, Jacky. You must forgive me."

"Aw, g'wan wit' ye, Amy," I tease, knowing how irritated she gets when I slip into the Cockney way of talking. But this time it gets a slight smile out of her. "Now 'tis time for us to go down and receive our guests, poltroons and rascals though they may be.

Around the perimeter of Dovecote's great banquet hall lie easy chairs and couches covered in soft leather and fine cloth. Between them are delicate end tables, placed there for the holding of teacups and wineglasses. Above all hang large paintings in fancy carved gilt frames, depicting fox hunts and bucolic landscapes and champion horses. On a previous visit to this room, I recognized the Sheik of Araby pictured there, with a tiny jockey in green and white silks on his back, winning the Great Invitational Race at Dovecote Downs, an event famous in legend and song. Ahem . . . Oh, well. Nothing is more fleeting than fame, and I should remember that.

When Amy and I come in, we find Joannie and Daniel already seated side by side on one of the couches, being, as far as I can see, good and well behaved. I also see that the long dining table has been set for eight, and the great chandelier has been lit.

Amy and I take chairs near the kids, and the butler, Blount, comes in carrying a tray that bears glasses of sarsaparilla, the root beer made from the sassafras plant that grows abundantly wild around this region, and which I dearly love. He gives each of us a glass, and we murmur our thanks.

Each of us, 'cept for Amy, says, "*Ummmmm*," as we taste the brown, gently fizzing brew. Putting down my glass, I look upon the youngsters.

Joannie, a student at the Lawson Peabody School for Young Girls, my own dear Alma Mater, is decked out in the school's uniform—black dress, black stockings, and white shoulder shawl—and looking quite presentable. Hands in lap, ankles crossed. I approve.

Daniel fidgets a bit, but he is being as good as he can manage. I know he wishes nothing more than to be back on the *Nancy B.* and up in her rigging, with Joannie by his side, and well I know the feeling. Instead, he is being sent, entirely against his will, to the public grammar school on School Street. He doesn't want to do it, but if he is to keep up with somebody like Joannie, he's just got to. *"Right, Daniel Prescott,"* I had said, sticking my finger in his face. *"You stay here as a deck hand while she goes off to that fancy school? All right. Then one fine day, she will go off with her hand on the arm of some nob and where will you be? On your knees, scrubbing some deck and feelin' real resentful, is where. Feelin' real sorry for yourself, is what."* He takes my advice to heart. Since he has been good in school, mostly—keeping up on his assigned studies and only one or two fights in the schoolyard—we have bought him a respectable suit of clothes in which he is a bit uncomfortable, with its high, tight collar and all, but he'll get used to it. And I think he looks right good in his rig.

After having given us our glasses of root beer, Blount retreats to stand by the sideboy to wait for his next call to duty . . . which comes very quickly.

The young master of the house, Randall Trevelyne, looking splendid in his uniform, enters the room and throws himself down in the armchair next to me, then puts his booted feet up on a hassock. He seems to be in a surly mood. Without a word of greeting to any of us, he holds up a cheroot for Blount to light. That accomplished, he accepts a glass of wine from the butler and then deigns to survey the scene.

"Who are the brats?" he asks, sounding bored and not really very interested in the answer.

"Good day to you, too, Mr. Trevelyne," I toss back at him, miffed at his rudeness. I then introduce the young ones. They rise, and Joannie does a very presentable curtsy and Daniel manages an acceptable bow. Randall nods curtly in return but does not get up.

I tell Randall of Joannie's and my common origins and recount the bravery shown by both Joannie and Daniel in various encounters with pirates, nefarious British officers, and large reptiles on the *Nancy B*. Daniel blushes modestly at the retelling and Joannie takes his hand.

"All very charming, I'm sure," says Randall. "And so where did you come from, boy? Another of the Holy London Orphans? I hear we are to meet yet another of that benighted crew this evening. Could it be that the Sanctified Kip Under the Blackfriars Bridge might actually have been a fancy finishing school, rather than the foul pit described by some? Hmmm? Maybe someone should design The Old School Tie? I suggest green and black diagonal stripes—green for the moldy garbage in the streets of your youth and black for the mud and stench. You could all get together annually and have festive reunions—picnics on the banks of the Charles, and such."

You watch it, Randall, you arrogant . . .

"Beggin' your pardon, Sir, but no," says Daniel, to his credit. I reflect that the boy is coming along just fine. "I was a captive of river pirates at Cave-in-Rock when Missy and her crew on the *Belle of the Golden West* stormed the place, killed the outlaws, set me free, brought me back to health, and gave me a berth. So here I am."

"Of course, the Goddess of War happens upon the scene, and all is made right," says Randall, glowering through lowered brows at me.

I look away. "Things happen, Randall."

"Right. And is that what I think it is?" he asks, his gaze now on my chest.

"If you think it is the Legion of Honor medal, then you are correct." Figuring it was a good day for grand uniforms, I had decided to counter Randall's scarlet Marine rig with my own blue naval lieutenant's jacket, with gold braid entwined. If we had been in the same service, I would outrank him, which fact I will delight in so informing him later. And, yes, I did pin the medal to my own chest. Sin of Pride, I know, but it is such fun to needle him.

"And just where did you steal *that*?"

I puff up in mock outrage. "Actually, *Sir*, Napoleon gave it to me."

"Napoleon, as in Bonaparte?"

"Yes. It was right after I left you there on the plains of Jena. In his carriage. I rode with him for a while. Then he sent me on to Paris with a letter to his empress, Josephine."

Amy looks over at me, mouth agape in a very unladylike way. I hadn't yet related *that* particular story to her. I have been a spy, after all, and certain things have to be kept under wraps, at least for a while.

Smiling slightly, Randall shakes his head and sinks back into his chair, seemingly abashed. "Then I am in rare company, indeed," he says. "A young woman who sits in the lap of an emperor, and a boy and a girl who stand up to pirates and alligators. How can I possibly measure up?"

"There are some medals on your own chest, Randall," I say, to soothe his male pride a bit.

He looks down at them. "Well, Murat thought I was valuable to him."

"You should be proud, then. Marshal Murat is a great general and a fine man." Both Randall and I had participated in Murat's now famous cavalry charge against the Prussian ranks at Jena, me *most* unwillingly.

We hear the distant ringing of a bell, and Blount leaves the room.

"I do believe your somewhat questionable friends have arrived," says Randall, as I rise to greet the newcomers.

"Randall, you will be civil," I hiss at him, eyes narrowed. "You, too, Amy. Now get up, both of you."

The two young aristocrats heave well-bred sighs and get to their feet to greet our dinner companions—my two fellow actors and one fellow orphan.

Mr. Fennel and Mr. Bean come into the dining room and there are bows and curtsies and hearty greetings all around—*our Puck, our Titania . . . and you, Miss Amy, the very image of noble Portia . . . And is this gentleman not the personification of the fiery Hotspur, Mr. Bean? Oh, yes, he is, Mr. Fennel, if we could only beg him to take a turn upon the boards!* The two rogues certainly know how to work a room, that's for sure; and Randall and Amy, in spite of themselves, are soon smiling and laughing.

Then, another enters the room, having taken some time in having her cloak hung in the anteroom so that she could enter the hall alone. She, too, knows how to make an entrance. And a radiant entrance it is. Smart . . . and, I perceive, a very cunning girl.

"Randall," I say, taking his hand and leading him to her. "May I present Miss Polly Von, a dear friend of my youth. Polly, Lieutenant Randall Trevelyne."

Eyes hooded, Polly drops down in a deep, deep—and, I must say, very well executed—curtsy, and when she rises, a stunned Randall Trevelyne drops my hand and reaches out his own for hers . . . and I have a feeling that it will be henceforth reaching for hers, not mine.

As she comes up, she lifts those baby-blue eyes to his and murmurs in her breathy voice, "So pleased, Mr. Trevelyne, so *very* pleased to meet you."

It is said that boys fall in love with their eyes, because they can be initially struck to their very core by a girl's mere physical beauty, while girls tend to fall in love with their ears. The outward handsomeness of the lad notwithstanding, a girl most of all likes to hear the words of love everlasting, of how he will be kind and gentle with her and protect her from harm and want and always hold her in the highest respect and esteem.

Me, I fall in love both ways. While my eyes do like to look upon a handsome, smiling, well-turned-out young man in tight britches, my ears also like the words of everlasting love poured into them, as well. Yes, a soft, kind word whispered in her shell-like ear can cause the sometimes outwardly formidable Lieutenant Jacky Faber to fall, and fall hard.

And I know, looking at those two standing there, their eyes only for each other, that Randall Tristan Trevelyne, Second Lieutenant, United States Marine Corps, has fallen, and fallen hard, on this particular field of battle.

Chapter 5

We have returned to Boston. Joannie has been stuffed back into the Lawson Peabody—*"Promise me I'll go on the next cruise, Jacky!" "Yes, dear, I swear by my tattoo. Now, you be good and study hard"*—and Amy Trevelyne spent last night with me in my beautiful cabin onboard the *Lorelei Lee*. We know I will be gone soon, as all the refitting and preparations for departure are done, and we want to spend my time remaining in port in each other's company. Plus, she wishes to take more notes on my travels. We have risen, washed and dressed, and eaten breakfast.

As we sit sipping our tea, I look about my new cabin. It is huge compared to my tiny but cozy cabin on my little schooner *Nancy B. Alsop*. We sit in the warm glow of polished wood as sunlight pours through the semi-circle of windows set into the curve of the stern of the ship. Mementos and trophies from my previous voyages surround us— my Jolly Roger, with its grinning skull and crossed bones, is draped in one corner, and my guitar leans against the opposite bulkhead. The Lady Gay, my very fine fiddle, lies in her case on a shelf made just for her. In a special rack rests my sword and harness—Bardot's sword, given to me as he lay upon his deathbed following that terrible battle. I've had the blade shortened to fit my size and strength, and made some alterations to the grip, as well, and named the sword Esprit. Every time I put it on, or even just glance at it, I think of my bonny light horseman, who in battle was slain, and heave a great sigh for the loss of such a good friend.

We sit at the table that runs fore-and-aft down the middle of the cabin. It is a long table that will seat eight and was designed and built by Ephraim Fyffe, newly married to my dear friend Betsey. Like all my tables, both here and on the *Nancy B.,* there have been depressions routed out to hold my fine Delft china plates and crystal glasses in place in the event of a heavy blow. Down below, the other tables are similarly routed out, to hold securely the more common pewter plates and cups, which I think all using them will appreciate. Tucked under this fine polished table lurks a black-painted nine-pound Long Tom pointed aft and ready in a moment to be run out through its gun port to trouble any pirate or other brigand who would seek to chase us. A similar gun rests up forward, its muzzle just below the tail of the figurehead. This gun in here has been named (by Davy, of course) Kiss My Royal Ass and the one up forward has the name Stinger painted in red on its butt. I have seen a good bit of the oceangoing life and I believe in being well armed. Out on the deck are six twelve-pound cannons on each side, with cannonballs stacked neatly beside them, and a full powder magazine below. Since I will henceforth be involved in only honest commerce, I shall expect others to be honest as well, by God.

There is a light knock on the door, and Higgins says, "Excuse me, Miss, but Mr. Pickering is here. Are you decent?"

Amy folds her hands and puts them in her lap, hooding her eyes and looking down demurely. I know she will be glad to see the young lawyer, but she will not show it outwardly. If pressed on expressing her feelings for him, she will invariably say, "I am not ready for that sort of thing as yet."

I look at her and reflect that it may be possible that her reserved way with males might be a better way than my usual manner of working the brutes—which seems to be to hop immediately into the lap of the nearest likely looking gent in a grand uniform or a fine cut of clothes and who looks like he might provide a bit of fun. She certainly has Ezra Pickering well in hand.

"As decent as I ever get, Higgins," I call. "Send him in."

The door opens and my very good friend, lawyer, and Clerk of the Faber Shipping Worldwide Corporation enters the cabin, wearing his habitual half smile, which widens upon seeing Miss Amy Trevelyne seated there.

"How good to see you, Ezra," I say. "Will you take tea with us?"

"Alas, no, Miss Faber," he says, turning to Amy. "Will you join me for a promenade about the deck, Miss Trevelyne?" he asks, bowing to her and reaching out his hand. "It is a fine day, and I believe Jacky will be wanting some privacy."

I lift my eyebrows in question as he reaches into his vest and pulls out a letter, which he hands to me.

Reading the address on the envelope, I let out a squeal of delight as I see it is from Jaimy. Amy rises and takes Ezra's hand, and they both go out, leaving me to tear open the letter and throw myself across my bed.

Lt. James Emerson
Onboard HMS Dolphin
Bournemouth, England
March 17, 1807

Miss Jacky Faber
c/o Pickering Law Office
Union Street
Boston, Massachusetts, USA

Dearest Jacky,

I have wonderful news!

It appears that the petition for pardon on all the charges against you is virtually certain of passage. Hoorah! Only a few more signatures and formalities and the deed will be done and you will be free—free to sail back to England and to all of us here who hold you so dear.

I was delighted to hear of your purchase of the brigantine *Lorelei Lee*—a very colorful name, to be sure, but totally befitting your nature. How you managed to afford such a purchase, I shall not ask. That notwithstanding, I am somewhat comforted in my worry for your safety in crossing, yet again, the broad Atlantic, by the fact that you will be traversing it in a much larger, sturdier craft than the *Nancy B.* Still, I will continue to worry until such time as I see you again running toward me, arms upraised, illuminating some dismal dock in London with your shining presence.

Ian and Mairead McConnaughey were delighted to receive your last letter and have left for Waterford to recruit the Irish crew you requested and begin booking passengers for your venture in transatlantic passenger service. Things are hard in Ireland right now, and I am sure you will not lack for a full manifest of human cargo.

All is well at your little orphanage and your grandfather looks forward to your return to the ancestral soil.

Captain Hudson, Lieutenant Bennett, and all aboard send their regards and best wishes. Dr. Sebastian is off on a scientific voyage to the Greek Isles and reports that he regrets he will miss both the spirited company and the artistic skills of his lovely fellow naturalist.

Again, I apologize for the brevity of this letter, but, as you well know, I am a perfect scrub with a pen and there is much to do to prepare for your greatly anticipated arrival.

Till we again meet, I am
Yr Most Humble & Obedient Servant

Jaimy

I tuck the letter under my pillow, wipe the tears of joy from my eyes, and go back out on deck.

"Send for the Captain ashore," I crow. "We leave on the morning tide!"

Chapter 6

Miss J. M. Faber
Faber Shipping Worldwide
15 Battery Street
Boston, Massachusetts, USA
April 22, 1807

Lt. James Emerson Fletcher
Onboard HMS Dolphin
London, England

Dear Jaimy,

Oh, Jaimy, I got your wonderful letter and there is so much exciting news to tell!

You'll remember, dear one, in my last letter to you, how I managed to buy the beautiful ship *Lorelei Lee*—yes, Faber Shipping has made some very good investments, plus the rum and molasses runs have been very profitable. And Solomon Freeman's fishing and clamming operation has been turning a tidy profit as well. He has added two more fishing smacks to our little fleet and crewed them with responsible men—Jemimah Moses's grandson Caleb, a strapping lad of seventeen and newly bought out of slavery, being one of them.

So now that I have my lovely *Lorelei* all fitted out, we're ready to embark on my Irish emigration scheme to ferry men from Ireland to work in Boston on the landfill project. The town has decided to fill in the Millpond and the Back Bay so as to give the town some growing room, and the workers will pay the price of their passage by having it deducted from their wages, gradually, over several months. Yes, it is rather like indentured servitude, but not nearly so harsh. If a man is industrious, sensible, and sober, he should be able to repay Faber Shipping within several months. If not, he will face the wrath of John Thomas and Smasher McGee, our Enforcers, who can be quite persuasive, believe me.

I have written to Ian and Mairead McConnaughey to request that they go find Liam and ask him to put together my Irish crew and begin signing up passengers. We shall sail out of the *Emerald*'s old home port of Waterford on the southeast coast of Ireland, and make that our European base of operations. As I've often said, Faber Shipping WORLDWIDE.

As things have gotten so much more complicated, we have taken offices on Battery Street, at the end of Long Wharf so that we will be close to the commerce of the harbor. Chloe Cantrell runs the office and handles all the paperwork, as dear Ezra Pickering is prospering in his law practice and so cannot be expected to give all his time to my poor enterprise.

Oh, what a thrill it gave me to see the sign, Faber Shipping Worldwide, go up over the entrance, all gold and gilt, outlined in black on a deep red background. I painted it myself, and it gave me great pleasure in doing it. Sin of Pride, I know, but I can't help it; it looks so grand.

Amy Trevelyne is well. She has just completed an account of my journey down some big rivers in America, which she calls *Mississippi Jack, Being an Account of the Further Waterborne Adventures of Jacky Faber, Midshipman, Fine Lady, and the Lily of the West.* A bit wordy in her titles, I feel, but let it go . . . I must say, Jaimy, that you come out well in that one . . . mostly, you dog. I hope you'll be glad to hear that Clementine Amaryllis Jukes Tanner is with child . . .

I put up my pen for a moment, imagining Jaimy mentally counting back the months upon reading this. Don't worry, you bad boy, it's been well more than nine months since you last . . . saw her.

Ahem! Enough said about *that.* Best keep that book from your mother, though, as she might not be as forgiving as I.

If you hope to see our brothers Davy and Tink upon my arrival, I'm afraid you will be disappointed—as former British sailors, it would be best that they not venture out onto the high seas, where they would be in danger of impressment. Nay, they shall remain in Boston and crew the *Nancy B. Alsop* on the Caribbean molasses and granite runs. Plus, Davy and Jim want to stay close to their wives, and Tink wishes to see a certain Concepcion down in Havana. Of all our friends, only Higgins shall accompany me on this voyage, for I have hired a full crew from a disabled merchant ship stranded in Boston. They were desirous of passage back to London and so I got them for a song—and you know how I dearly love a bargain. When we return, I hope that Ian McConnaughey will have assembled that Irish crew in Waterford with as many of my old *Emeralds* as he can find—and wouldn't it be prime if he found our old sea-dad Liam Delaney free to be master of the *Lorelei?*

My, this is turning out to be quite a long letter. My hand is growing quite cramped. But the thought that you will hold this paper in your hand and read it gives me the will to push on.

All here are well and send their love. I'll tell you more of that later, when I see you in person (oh, blessed day!). We leave right after I post this letter on the Fast Mail Packet.

Yours forever and ever,

Jacky

The lines are off and the *Lorelei Lee* is free of the land. *Oh, Jaimy, I am so very hopeful of happiness!*

Chapter 7

Lt. James Fletcher
Onboard HMS Dolphin
London
April 26, 1807

Miss Jacky Faber
c/o Ezra Pickering
Union Street
Boston, Massachusetts, USA

Dear Jacky,

I write this in great haste and I do not have time to tell you exactly what has happened, but suffice it to say there have been changes in the Admiralty and great aspersions have been cast against your good name—and mine.

Please, I beg you, do not depart Boston just yet, as you would be in great danger should you arrive here now.

I have to make this letter short, for I must post it immediately and make myself ready. I have received word that I am to be arrested within the hour.

Hoping to God that you have not yet left, I remain, etc.

Jaimy

Chapter 8

"Land ho! Dead ahead!" comes the call from the lookout high up in the mainmast. There is a great cheer from those on deck at the sighting of their homeland— soon all will see wives, families, sweethearts, or at least enjoy some gentle company in familiar and cozy inns.

I had been standing on the quarterdeck, talking to Captain Browning about the weather and the trim of the sails and whatnot, when I heard the call. I added my yelp to the general cheer and dashed up the ratlines to my foretop to gaze out over the bow of the *Lorelei Lee*. It is indeed the Isle of Wight and we are back on home ground. I take a deep breath and note how I can feel my heart thumping in my chest. *It won't be long now, girl . . .*

I sink down and sit with my back to the foremast, and with my eyes on my native land, I pull out my pennywhistle and play upon it—"Rule, Britannia" seems appropriate— and let my mind think on James Emerson Fletcher, whom I might well see very soon.

In my last letter to the lad, I didn't tell Jaimy about Randall. Jaimy always looks calm and composed, but I know he has something of a temper and more than just a little streak of jealousy as concerns me and my somewhat numerous male . . . er, acquaintances. But he need not worry any longer about Randall Trevelyne, at least not now. Ever since their first meeting, he and Polly Von have been keeping constant company in Boston, enjoying the charms of the city—and each other's as well. I had put on a show at the Pig and they were there. I played a slow tune on my fiddle, and they danced together there in front of me. It was lovely to see—Randall in his fine uniform and Polly in her Desdemona dress from the Othello production that Fennel and Bean were about to mount, their having made enough money out in the sticks, putting on the revival shows, to do such a thing.

Watching the two of them dance that night, did I feel a slight pang of my own jealousy?

Yes, I did.

Did I have any right to feel that pang?

No, I did not.

But I did, all the same.

Little Mary Faber, that feral child of the streets, who remains a part of me, pops up and asks, *Why can't we have all the pretty boys, Jacky? Why not?* But I push her back down and tell her to be quiet. No, I am promised to just one.

I had the darling couple over for dinner on the *Lorelei Lee* several evenings after we all got back from Dovecote. Amy was not there, being back at school, so it was just the three of us. They were both gracious and exclaimed over the intricacies of the ship and the richness of my cabin and the bounty of my table—*a long way from gnawing on cheese rinds pulled from the garbage, eh, Polly?* 'Tis a pity that Second Lieutenant Randall Trevelyne must sail soon, but that is the way of things, ain't it? Same as it ever was, you find what might be the love of your life on one day, then you have to ship out the next—*anchors aweigh, me boys,* and all that. Boys go; girls stay and are left crying.

But Polly will be looked after in Boston. I have seen to it.

As the land gets ever closer, I swing back down and remount my quarterdeck.

"We should be at Sheerness by tomorrow, Miss Faber, and London the next day," says Captain Browning, smiling at the thought. It has been a very pleasant crossing, but all anticipate the joys of the land. The captain turned out to be a thoroughgoing seaman, and good company as well. He made some excellent suggestions for changes in the *Lorelei*'s sail set, which increased her speed and stability significantly, and which pleased me greatly. We had discussed changing the rigging of the sails on the mainmast from fore-and-aft to square sails, but I felt it best to leave her a brigantine. If we were to change her to a brig, she would be less maneuverable than in her current condition, and there have been times in my life that I have felt a pressing need to get away *very* quickly.

Higgins comes up from below and joins us in gazing upon Merrie Olde England. Back in Boston, I had told him that he did not have to accompany me on this trip—his being a rich man now, and all, and my being in safe and capable hands—but he replied that there was his dear old dad in Colchester, whom he'd like to see. I can understand that . . . and . . . some friends up in Brideshead whom he wished to revisit. Hmmm . . . don't know about that, but it ain't my business. "Besides, Miss, you might insist on being married, and I must be there for that. Remember, I am expected to be Best Man at that blessed event."

Back in the present, I say, "Captain Browning expects we will dock tomorrow, Higgins. Is it not exciting?"

"Indeed, Miss. Well, we'd best start getting you cleaned up and back in proper attire."

As I follow my very dear Higgins down into my cabin, anticipating a good hot bath and some serious pampering, I see a boat being put into the water. It will carry Captain Browning's purser, a Mr. Blake, into Bournemouth, where he will disembark and make his way to London overland, to ensure that we have a fine berth waiting for us when we get there, and to announce our arrival, so that all who wish to greet us shall be able to do so.

Oh, Jaimy, please be there!

Chapter 9

We are warped into our berth on Whitten's Dock, and there are many there to meet the *Lorelei Lee*—yes, very many, but, no, not the one I so desperately want. No, there is the Purser, there are wives and sweethearts of some of the men aboard, there is Captain Browning's wife and family, but there is nothing . . . and no one . . . for me.

Hearing me sigh, Higgins, who stands beside me, says gently, "Perhaps the *Dolphin* was called out to some light duty and will be back shortly."

I put my hand on his arm and nod. *Thank you, Higgins, for trying to make me feel better.*

Captain Browning's wife is welcomed aboard for a joyful reunion with her husband, introductions are made, refreshments are served, and then heartfelt goodbyes are said. Finally the entire crew, which had been paid off yesterday, disappears into the streets of London—some in coaches, most on foot. When all is said and done, it is only Higgins and I who stand in the quiet on my deck.

This morning I had donned my white Empire dress, which I had bought in Paris last year—high in the waist, puffy in the sleeves, and low in the bodice—thinking it might please Jaimy. Now it just makes me feel foolish . . . and exposed. The very wise Higgins has my cloak over his arm, ready to ease my mind.

"I sure hope Ian McConnaughey succeeded in putting together a good crew, and that crew is nearby," I say, a mite uneasy in the silence after all the hurly-burly. I don't like having my ship completely unmanned and unguarded. *Where, then, are my bully boys?*

"I am sure he has, Miss, and . . ."

It is then that we both see the one coach still left on the wharf.

What . . . ?

It is soon made plain.

The doors of the coach open and Messrs. Carr and Boyd, black-suited agents of British Naval Intelligence with whom I am very well acquainted, appear and stride up the gangway.

Oh, Lord, what now?

Higgins and I exchange glances but say nothing as the two approach us.

"Good day, Miss Faber," says Boyd, his fingers to the brim of his hat. "If you would come with us, please. The First Lord sends his compliments and requests your presence."

I was not able to don my forearm sheath for my shiv, but I know that Higgins does have his two small pistols tucked into the waistcoat he wears under his outer jacket, so that does gives me some comfort.

"Your cloak, Miss," says Higgins, holding up the garment. "And we shall be off with these two fine fellows."

"Ahem . . . Beggin' yer pardon, Mr. Higgins," says Mr. Boyd, "but just Miss Faber will come with us for now. The First Lord will call for you later."

Higgins's face darkens. "I do not like this," he whispers into my ear.

"They probably just want to thank me for all my fine service in dropping several million pounds sterling in gold into His Majesty's coffers," I say, with a bit of a shaky laugh. "After all, Jaimy did say everything was well now twixt the Crown and me. And I now count the First Lord, Sir Grenville, to be my faithful friend, and even the stern Mr. Peel, as well. So all should be fine."

"We shall see, Miss," says Higgins. He places my cloak around my shoulders and pulls the hood up over my head.

"Thank you, Higgins," I say. As he fastens the clasp under my chin, I lean into him and whisper, "If I don't come back by nightfall, contact my lawyer. Immediately." With a mutual squeeze of hands, we part.

Down the gangway, across the wharf, and then I am handed up into the black coach. Carr and Boyd climb in beside me and we are off.

I decide to not worry about the future and to fully enjoy the ride back here on my home turf, so I chatter merrily as we ride along, pointing out this and that. "Oh, it's so good to be back, lads!" I babble. "There's good old Admiral Benbow's Tavern, and there's the dome o' Saint Paul's, and . . . wait a minute . . ."

Alarmed, I stick my head out the open window.

"Hey, we're crossin' Paternoster Street . . . This ain't the way to the Admiralty, mates! It's on Whitehall, next to the Horse Guards, you know that! Wait . . . What's going on here?"

They say nothing.

Sensing a trap, I pull the latch on the door next to me, ready to leap out, but the latch doesn't work; it just hangs there, limp and useless, connected to nothing. The coach lurches to a stop at the corner. A hopeless feeling is flooding over me.

"Lads, what are you gonna do to me?" I cry, trembling, my helpless hands clasped in my lap. "What will it be, a knife thrust to my belly, a bullet in my head, a . . . ?"

Mr. Carr looks me in the eye for the first time since I have known him and says, "We are sorry, Miss." Mr. Boyd nods. *Uh-oh . . . I do not like the looks o' this, no, I don't.*

Then the doors are pulled open. Carr and Boyd get out, and four men get in and array themselves about me. Two of them—big hard-faced blokes—sit to either side of me, and them I do not know. But the other two I do know and they sit opposite me, grinning. One is that damned Bliffil, who I could have expected to be here, but the other . . . I sit rigid, astonished.

Flashby?

How is it possible?

"You are surprised to see me, you conniving little thief," he says, with a broad smile. "I thought you might be, since you undoubtedly considered me as good as dead, didn't you? Devoured by alligators on Key West—was that part of your plan, your very nicely placed little trap? Oh, it was an excellent ruse, I must say. Yes, it was—and yes, those brutes got most of the pirates, but they didn't get me, because as you can plainly see, I am not dead. But you, Jacky Faber, will very shortly be as cold and dead as a stone."

Flashby leans forward and grasps me by the neck with his left hand and brings the back of his right hand hard across my face.

Oh!

"I managed to get up into a tree with those monsters snapping at my very heels. Over the treetops I saw your ship sailing away with what I knew to be your ill-gotten gains." Flashby is not smiling now. "I imagined you laughing as you did so. Laughing at me, yet again. It merely hardened my resolve to survive such that I might bring you down some day, you insufferable piece of gutter trash. And now I have you well in hand."

I throw my chin into the air. "You may rest assured that Lord Grenville will hear of this outrage, you miserable traitorous cur. And Mr. Peel. And the rest of my friends at the Admiralty, too. I shall tell them of your perfidy in joining with the pirate El Feo to cheat His Majesty of his rightful treasure!"

"Tell them all you want, since they are no longer at the Admiralty. That tedious bookworm Grenville has gone back to his dusty library. Peel is off on other duties. Dr. Sebastian is on a voyage to the South Seas. Baron Mulgrave is now the First Lord, and all he knows of you is what I, and Mr. Bliffil here, have told him. You have no friends. Do you understand?"

I do not have to reply. I am lost and I know it.

"Here, dear, let us have another," says Flashby, and he brings his hand across my face again.

Oh, God, it hurts, it hurts!

I begin to sob in pain and desperation.

"That's it, bitch, cry," he hisses. "Think of it, a week in that tree with all those monsters below, roaring, snapping their jaws, never leaving, day or night." He hits me again, and I try to hide my face, but the two men who sit beside me grab my shoulders and hold me up such that my face can receive the blows.

Flashby is not yet done talking. "Think of it. A whole week of living on bugs and slugs, licking the dew off the leaves in the morning for water. Think of that, brat!"

He hits me again. I flinch and taste blood in my mouth.

He continues. "How did I get out of that? A good fifty of the alligators waiting below to taste the Flashby tenderloins? Well, I shall tell you. Not all the pirates were immediately ingested by the reptiles. No, there was one in my tree with me, and in a nearby tree were three more, all of us in a similar fix. Mr. Bliffil, would you like a stroke?"

"Indeed I would, Mr. Flashby," says the vile Bliffil, reaching out and lifting my chin such that he might deliver a crushing, closed-fist punch to my cheek.

No, no, not again, not Bliffil . . .

"That's for shaming me on the *Dolphin,* snot. And here's another."

His fist slams into my face again and my head begins to loll upon my shoulders. I'm losing . . .

"We slept in the crooks of the tree, my sole companion and me. His name was Javier, I believe. A youngish man and not a bad sort. One morning I woke up, licked the leaves, and looked down upon the monsters slumbering below. Next to me, Javier was also asleep. I looked out across the trees and saw that our small boat was still anchored there in shallow water. I thought, I considered, and then I lifted my foot and shoved Javier out of his perch. He screamed as he fell and hit the ground. When I saw that the reptiles were upon him, I dropped out of the tree and ran for the boat. I gained the shore and found that the pirates in the other tree had seen what I had done. They'd taken it to heart and had thrown out the smallest of their number, shrieking, into the jaws of the beasts, and then had pounded down to the beach in all the confusion. We got in the boat, made it back to Cuba, and here I am. Are you not glad?"

Another fist slams into my face.

They take turns beating me till we reach our destination, and by the time we are there, I am bleeding from my nose and mouth and there is a cut above my left eye, put there by Bliffil's ring.

Dazed, I realize that we have clattered through a very familiar courtyard. We pass what I know to be the gallows and stop in front of a barred gate.

"I do hope you will enjoy your stay in this fine establishment." Flashby grabs my hair and lifts my hanging head so that I might hear his words. "But take heart, as I am sure your time here will be short—about as short as a hangman's rope. Take her."

The two thugs on either side lift me up and haul me out of the coach, then stand me up, weaving on my pins, before Flashby.

"Mr. William Brunskill is the hangman here, and he favors the short drop—only twelve inches or so. Thus, you won't die right off. You will gasp for breath and struggle in vain, yet no breath will get past the rope, and I shall watch you twist and turn until the life finally goes out of your wretched body. I'll be there and I shall watch your worthless form being taken down and thrown into the lime pit. And I will spit upon it, you may count on that!"

I am spun around.

"Take her!" yells Flashby. "Take her and throw her in the Condemned Cells, for that is surely where she will spend her last miserable days. Do it now!"

The two guards slam me hard against the outside wall for good measure, and then I am dragged through clanging gate after gate into the very bowels of the place, until . . .

I am thrown into a dark, dirty cavern. My face meets the grimy floor and the blood oozing from my face mixes with the dirt. I rise up on my forearms to look about me. I see smoked-stained curved vaults overhead and stone ledges below, and over all, the stench of an uncovered privy pervades the dankness. Haunted eyes from the forms huddled in rags upon the ledges stare down upon me. I hang my head in deep despair.

I am in Newgate Prison.

Chapter 10

It's been three whole days and nights since I was first thrown into this vile hole, and because I have seen no one except my cellmates, I know that I am to be allowed no visitors. Oh, I'm sure that Higgins is out there doing his best, and I do have other friends, so there is a small glimmer of hope—a very small one, to be sure. But it is there and I nurture it, trying to stave off the Black Cloud and not fall into an abyss of self-pity. But it is hard, so hard . . . However, if I am to be hanged, I shall want to go to my end with some dignity, if only a shred, so I try to keep up the spirits.

Remembering how we had cared for our clothing back on the *Bloodhound,* I soon doffed my white dress and rolled it up, inside out, to keep it as clean as possible. I do have my cloak to wear over my undergarments. If I am to be hauled before some court, I will not want to look like a low beggar. There were already some stains on the front, blood that had spilled from my split lip, but I couldn't help that— and maybe those stains will gain me some sympathy. We'll see.

I look up at the narrow slits of light high above and reflect how me and the gang used to be able to get into Newgate Prison to deliver messages and small parcels of food from friends and family of the confined. But that was only into the other parts of the place, where they kept debtors and suchlike. We were never able to get right into the Condemned Cells, nay. They were locked up tighter than a churchman's purse. Oh, we could pass a note through the bars sometimes, but that's about it.

In spite of my present condition, I smile as I think back to those days when I, for a shilling a week for milk money for my baby Jesse, would slip in and out of Newgate on errands for the prison reform crusader Elizabeth Fry and her Quaker do-gooder cohorts. I knew her then as Miss Gurney, before she married Preacher Fry, and a fierce one was she. It is rumored that because she had some influence, she being from a banking family and all, she connived one day to arrange for certain ladies of the court—handmaidens to royalty and wives of judges and such—to be gathered in their carriages for a gay Monday outing, and while enroute they were driven to the gallows at Newgate at just the right time so that the shocked ladies within could witness, up close, the last twists and struggles of a sixteen-year-old girl. The poor condemned one, hanged for stealing a hairbrush, had been counseled and comforted by Mrs. Fry during her final terrified days. Most of the fine ladies lost their fine breakfasts on the floor of their carriages that fine day, and many an influential courtier and many a stern, bewigged judge was denied access to his lady's bed that evening and many more . . . *until something is done, Sir! And I mean it!*

But, alas, I can't slip in and out of Newgate now, not like I once could, oh, no.

There are three girls in here with me, all condemned to hang the Monday after next.

The youngest of them is Mary Wade, a small scrap of a thing and all of ten years old, condemned to death for the stealing of a shawl. *"This rich girl come down to the market and I was so cold and she had this purty thing 'round her shoulders and I didn't think. I just grabbed it and ripped it off her and ran . . . There was another girl in my gang wi' me and when we was caught, she peached on me to get herself off. Now I gots to choke for it. 'Tain't fair . . ."*

Then there's Molly Reibey, age fourteen, convicted for stealing a horse. *"It was a joke, a lark, but then my uncle who put me up to it said he didn't have anything to do wi' it and there I was on this horse . . . and . . . people said I was there in town tryin' to sell it . . . and I was taken and tried . . . and here I am. Didn't do nothin' wrong . . . just a joke, just a prank . . . and now I'm gonna die for it . . ."*

And there's Esther Abrahams, a very beautiful girl of sixteen who was apprenticed to a milliner who accused her of stealing a piece of black lace. She protests her innocence—*"I didn't do it, I didn't"*—for all the good it's gonna do her. She is cultured, and has some social graces . . . and she's a Jewish girl, too, which probably helped her get condemned.

Sometimes I think certain house mistresses accuse the young help of petty crimes just so they can be rid of them. Why? Perhaps a husband's wayward glance at a comely servant, or for mere convenience, I don't know. Sort of like drowning unwanted kittens, 'cept you don't have to watch their struggles as they die—unless you want to. It sickens me.

My face is still swollen a bit, but I feel around my teeth, and though my lip is split, I feel no other damage—prolly afraid of hurting their knuckles, the bastards—and though I wish to see those two rotters in hell, I realize, with a sinking feeling, that the truth is I'll prolly get there 'fore them. Well, if that's the case, then I'll stoke up the fires, by God, to make sure that things are really hot for them when they come.

Idle, stupid thoughts.

On the second day, I am amazed to see that Elizabeth Fry herself is granted entry into our cell to lend solace to the doomed girls within. Just how she managed that, I do not know, but she seems to have her ways.

"Missus Fry," I say. "Do you remember me?"

She squints at me in the gloom and then takes my hand.

"Yes, I remember you, child . . . Mary, is it . . . ? With the baby? Our messenger several years ago?"

Again I nod, the tears welling up at the kind touch of her hand.

"I am sorry to see you in here, Mary. Are you . . ."

"Condemned? Not yet, Mrs. Fry, but it seems certain . . ."

"Are you right with God?"

"I don't know, Missus."

"Then come and pray with us."

And I do.

This evening, it being Sunday, we are taken out and herded into the chapel room, where we stand in the balcony and are made to look down upon the condemned who are scheduled to perish the next day. They are down below, bound and arrayed around an open coffin and treated to a sermon concerning their very soon demise. They have been on bread and water the past three days and have nothing to look forward to except a grisly death to end their suffering. All males, this time, they make great lamentations, but the preacher above has no mercy, condemning them to hell for their crimes. It is such a cruel world.

Next Sunday it will be the girls' turn to be down next to the coffin.

Maybe me, too.

Chapter 11

As dawn breaks on Wednesday, the four of us lie huddled under my cloak in a corner of the cell, the past night being chilly and damp. We take some comfort in each other's nearness, as well as from the warm cloak, and so we make no move to rise. What is there to get up to? A mean bucket of the slops they call food? Some hard crusts of bread, so hard they make your gums bleed? Nay, no need to get up for that.

There is a jangling of the lock and the door to our cavern of despair opens. Thinking it is the arrival of the breakfast gruel, we moan and stretch in our bed of stone.

It is not, however, that.

Two men, dressed somewhat better than the usual prison wardens, come into the cell, and one says, "Mary Faber, come with us."

"Why?" I ask fearfully.

"Today you shall be tried at Justice Hall for the crimes laid against your name. The court and the jury will be seated within the hour, and you will stand at the bar for judgment. Surely you have something to put on to make yourself more decent, girl." I stand before them in my undergarments.

They wait for me while I put myself back into my once white and stainless dress.

When I have done it, I go to each of the girls in turn and hold their hands and kiss them on the cheek. "Be brave, Sisters, and please, keep my cloak . . . I'm sure to be back with you shortly."

If not, at least they shall be warm until the day when . . . oh, God . . .

I turn to the two men.

"I am ready," I say. I thrust out my crossed wrists to be bound, as I know they will have to be.

After that is accomplished, I am pulled out and sent down a hall. There is bedlam all about me as I go—some jeering, some shouting defiance, some offering comfort, some quite mad.

We come to a low archway and duck down into it. Lighted by small slits in the masonry high above, it opens out into a long, bricked passageway. I know where we are going—to the Old Bailey itself and prolly to my doom. After we have walked maybe a hundred yards, I lift my hands to my face and I pretend to cry. That is not at all hard, since I really feel like doing it.

But I am not crying. What I am doing is feeling for the cut above my left eye, put there by Bliffil's fist in the carriage that day when they first brought me to Newgate.

Flashby had slapped me around some, yes, but it was Bliffil who used the knuckles, pounding me again and again, and eventually opening up a cut above my eye. *"Here's one for getting my nose broke and here's another for . . ."* At last

Flashby restrained him—"*Come on, old boy, we want to see her hang, don't we? Let's not kill her here, as there's scant sport in that, eh? Believe me, we'll have courtside rooms at Newgate for that special hanging, eh what? With some fine sporting ladies to keep us company and a few jugs of good whiskey. I know just the rooms, and I shall hire them. We'll stand there with a whore in each hand and watch her dance her last. We'll send off the little slut with a shot of whiskey and a curse. Won't that be fine?*"

And Bliffil did stop beating me at the prospect of that fine day, and I was allowed to slump back between the guards and pass out.

So now, today, I lift my hand to that same cut above my eye. It had essentially healed, but I shall not let it rest. During my time in the condemned cell, I had taken the fingernails of my right hand—since I used them to pluck my guitar, they were quite long—and I filed them to points on the rough rocks of the cell wall, thinking to give myself some sort of weapon in the absence of my shiv. Now I turn the sharpest one on myself and dig it into the cut above my eye.

It hurts, but I am gratified to feel the warm blood once again course down over my cheek.

Having accomplished that, I walk the rest of the way down the passageway between the two court bailiffs. In another hundred yards, we emerge into a courtyard surrounded by a high circular wall on one side and the front of the Old Bailey on the other. I blink in the sudden light and then notice two men standing there, waiting for me. One is my London lawyer, Mr. Worden—*it is so good to see a friendly face!*—and the other is a man I do not know. Both wear long black robes, high collars, and short white wigs.

"Good Lord!" exclaims Mr. Worden upon seeing my face and general appearance. "What did you do to her?"

"We did nothing, Sir, but bring her here," replies one of the guards, a trifle uneasily. "As we were ordered."

"It looks, Sirrah"—Mr. Worden glares down his long nose at the two—"that you worked her over very thoroughly, very thoroughly indeed!"

"No, Sir. Any damage that was done to her was done by others."

I'm standing there with head up and face bloody.

"Very well," hisses Mr. Worden, giving it up. "We have custody of her. You may go." The bailiffs go to the entrance of the court and wait.

"Miss Faber, may I present Attorney Farnsworth," says Worden. "He is a barrister and he will argue your case before the bar."

"Then I place my fate in your hands, Sir, and thank you," says I, lowering the eyes and doing what I can in the way of a curtsy. He bows back, plainly appraising me.

"We must get her cleaned up," says Mr. Worden, sounding a bit flustered. I know that he is much more at ease handling financial cases than he is capital crimes. "We can use the lawyers' washroom."

"Hold on, Mr. Worden, I do not think we should do that at all," says this other bewigged gent next to him. "I think we should present her just as she is."

"But she is a mess."

"All the better," says Farnsworth, in a deep, mellifluous voice. "The winsome, woeful waif—a poor orphan of the storm . . ."

I perceive with some satisfaction that Barrister Farnsworth is a cunning man, one after my own heart.

"We have but a short time to go over this case. Are you ready to tell me all?"

"I am."

"You must tell him the complete truth, Jacky," says Attorney Worden.

"I will," says I, and I do, in the next hour, relate all that has happened since first I set foot on the *Dolphin* until I very recently stepped off the *Lorelei Lee*. I leave nothing out. Never any sense in lying to your lawyer.

After I am done, he nods thoughtfully. "Hmmm. Much to consider here, but we will do what we can."

A man dressed in a black coat with a red sash and carrying a long golden scepter appears in the arched doorway leading into the Old Bailey.

"They are ready for her," he says. "Bring her in."

I am led down a short hallway, through a set of large brass-bound double-doors and into the Hall of Justice.

There is a common gasp as the crowd of spectators sees my face and condition. As I proceed to the bar, at the front of the huge room, I try to hold my head up in a semblance of the Lawson Peabody Look and I affect a slight swoon and lean against Mr. Farnsworth. The court goes into an uproar.

"Good God! Look at that!" and *"Oh, the poor thing!"* and, as my wrists are encased in the iron shackles that are attached to the bar, I hear a great, stentorian bellow: *"This is an absolute outrage! I demand an explanation!"*

In spite of my confusion, I'm thinking that I recognize that particular bellow. I look around, and there . . . there is good Captain Hudson of HMS *Dolphin*. Tears come to my eyes as I see him stand and point an accusing finger at the witness box, where sit Lieutenants Flashby and Bliffil and a few other blokes who surely mean me no good.

Oh, my! If Captain Hudson is here, then Jaimy . . . But I see him nowhere . . . *But there is my dear Higgins, oh, yes, how good to see you, I cannot tell you how good!*

There is a loud banging, and it comes from the Chief Justice's scepter being pounded vigorously on the floor.

"Quiet! Quiet in this court!" he thunders, having quite a strong voice himself. "Quiet or I'll have you all thrown out!"

"I'll not be quiet, by God!" roars out yet another. "I demand satisfaction from those who did that to her!"

"And just who, Sir, are you?" demands the Judge.

"My name is Lord Richard Plantagenet Allen, and I am the twenty-first earl of Northcumberland!" he thunders. "And I will not be silenced."

Oh, Richard, my bold cavalry captain! Can it really be you?

"Oh, yes, you will, my lord, as I am Chief Justice of His Majesty's Court at Sessions and, as such, speak for King George the Third! Now sit down, Sir, or be forcibly ejected from these premises!"

Several men, probably Richard's brothers and cousins, sensibly haul him back into his chair. I look over at him and give him my most heartfelt look of thanks for his concern.

Now that things are quiet, I look around to see how things lie.

I stand at the bar, and before me is the witness box. Those who would testify against me sit in that box, while those who would speak in my behalf are called from the general court. Above and behind them are seated five judges, resplendent in red robes and long, luxuriant white wigs.

To the right is the jury box, where sit those who will judge my guilt, and all about and below me are the tables where sit the lawyers, scribbling away at papers.

There are high windows all around, and a large mirror is placed such that it bounces the light from outside directly on my face, the better for the jurors and judges to see my expressions and so judge my guilt or innocence. I blink in the glare, and my blinking probably signifies guilt to those who wish to condemn me.

"Very well, then," says the Chief Justice. "State your name, and how you come to be bleeding in my court."

"My . . . my name is Mary Faber, and I was beaten by those two men over there when they took me to Newgate, and the wounds keep opening up."

The Judge looks over at the witness box. Flashby gets up and says, "If it please your Lordship, the accused was unruly and attempted escape."

"Ummm," says the Judge. "Well, the sight is disgusting. Call for the Matron to bring some bandages to bind up the wound. Meanwhile, swear everyone in."

The Bible is brought around, and all concerned place a right hand upon it and swear to tell the truth, so help them God. A woman comes up to me and wraps a bandage around my forehead and neatly pins it up.

"King's Counsel, read the charges and let us get on with this."

A man wearing a wig somewhat bigger than my lawyers' wigs gets up and intones, "The Crown against Mary Alsop Faber, also known as Jacky Faber, also known as Jacqueline Bouvier, also known as La Belle Jeune Fille Sans Merci. The accused is charged with Piracy on the High Seas, Treason, and Theft of the King's Property, and . . ."

I hunch my shoulders to look as small and helpless as I can and listen as the charges are read.

The King's Counsel finishes the quite lengthy list of my various crimes against the Crown, and then he says, "The Crown calls its first witness, Lieutenant Henry Flashby, Royal Navy."

Flashby gets up and stands before me and the court and tells his lie. *"I did hear this girl plot with the Spanish pirate Flaco Jimenez to steal a good portion of the King's gold. I attempted to thwart the plan, but—"*

"That's a lie," I shout. "It was *he* who was in league with the pirates under the leadership of his comrade El Feo! These are all lies! He is bearing false witness against me! I may die because of his falsehoods, but he will surely go to hell for it!"

I am restrained.

Then Bliffil stands up and does the same, the lyin' bastard. And he wasn't even there.

Barrister Farnsworth does his best to refute these accusations, but to no avail.

The trial drones on and on. All that old stuff about the *Emerald* and my privateering on her is brought up again, and I answer to that. *I was given a Letter of Marque and I assumed it to be genuine!*

Things don't look good. In fact, they could not look worse. I'm certain that on the Monday after three Sundays have passed, I will feel the rough hemp on my throat, and that will be it for me. Why do we even bother with all this? Just take me out and hang me and be done with it.

And then . . .

"There is the matter of the brigantine vessel the *Lorelei Lee*. Shall we discuss that little item? Just how did you acquire it? Hmmmm?"

"Sir, that ship is owned by Jos. W. Lawrence and Associates, Incorporated, of Boston, Massachusetts—"

"Yes, Miss Faber, and we also know that Lawrence and Associates is a wholly owned subsidiary of Laurentian International, which, in turn, is wholly owned by Faber Shipping Worldwide, Incorporated, the majority shares of which are owned"—here he pauses to point his finger at me—"by *you*, Miss Faber."

Damn!

He is relentless.

"Do you mind telling the court where you got the money for that ship? Hmmm?"

"I made some very good investments."

"Oh? And in what, might we ask?"

"In rum and sugar . . . and other things."

"Other things . . . like in gold? The King's gold?"

"That was Spanish gold, and not the King's! And don't forget *I* was the one who dove down more than two hundred feet in the Caribbean Sea to bring up millions of pounds for King George's treasury! Don't forget *I* was the one who swam with sharks and eels and monsters of the deep to enrich my country in her time of need! But was

I granted a share of the prize? No! You should be pinning medals on my chest, rather than treating me so shamefully!"

"I believe, Miss Faber, that the shame is all yours. The Crown rests."

Captain Hudson is then called in my behalf and gives testimony about the battle. "She did attack a Spanish First-Rate man-of-war in her tiny schooner in an attempt to save my ship HMS *Dolphin,* which was foundering due to a fallen foremast. She managed to disable the Spaniard by destroying his rudder, allowing us time to cut off our mast and return to the fight. Quickly gaining the weather gauge, we pounded the Spaniard and he soon struck his colors." He turns and points to me. "My lord, this girl, by her brave action, did save my ship. Of that I am certain."

Lord Allen gets up, resplendent in his scarlet uniform, and swears to the sterling nature of my character. A letter from Dr. Sebastian is read, and then Mr. Farnsworth gets up and delivers a long, impassioned plea on my behalf . . . but I know it ain't gonna do any good. Those new charges on top of the old ones of piracy and stealing the *Emerald* will be enough to seal my fate, I just know it.

The Chief Justice gives the case to the jury.

It doesn't take them long. They confer for a mere ten minutes and then they have a verdict. A note is handed to the Judge. He reads it and then addresses me.

"Mary Faber, you have been found guilty of all the charges against you, and we all know what the sentence should be in this case . . ."

I'm waiting for the blow while the Chief Justice is conferring with the other judges on that bench.

". . . but in consideration of the service you have heretofore rendered the Crown, and to avoid the surely endless appeals to keep you from the hanging you so richly deserve, it is the order of this court that you are sentenced to Transportation for Life at the penal colony in Australia. You are to be remanded to the Hulks on the Thames to await transport to New South Wales."

He brings his scepter down.

"Take her away."

I almost swoon as I realize . . .

I am not to hang.

Chapter 12

As I was taken in chains from the courtroom, I took a last tearful look at Richard Allen's face, then mouthed a silent *Thank you* to both him and Captain Hudson . . . and to Higgins. I was not able to say a similar farewell to my other friends there assembled, for I was quickly hustled out and thrown into an open wagon and hauled off toward the Woolwich docks.

After a jolting ride in that cart filled with similarly shackled unfortunates, we came to the place where, once again, I laid my eyes on the Hulks, lying down on the banks of the Thames. Before we even got near, the stench of raw sewage hit my nose and I could not keep from gagging. There were four massive Hulks moored there, each one containing at least four hundred prisoners. The Thames, large as it is, doesn't move fast enough to clean up after that multitude. There is a low, greenish, miasmic fog over the river.

Steady down, girl. You'll just have to get used to it.

Dismasted and shorn of all rigging, these sad remains of once proud fighting ships had been decommissioned and refitted as prisons to hold the overflow of England's jails—some convicts awaiting transportation to the penal colonies while others were serving out their whole sentences aboard these stinking, rotting derelicts. I knew that the *Bellerophon,* a bold eighty-four-gun First-Rate of the Line of Battle, which fought so valiantly at Trafalgar, broadside to broadside with the best of Napoleon's fleet, was one of them, and it saddened me to think on that.

Me and my mates from the Rooster Charlie Gang had come up to Woolwich one summer day many years ago, hitchin' rides on the backs of hay wagons, to see if there was anything shakin' in the neighborhood that might lend us some sustenance. But lookin' down at the poor convicts toilin' away on the mud, dredging out the channel, we knew there was nothin' for us here, so we went back to our kip in Cheapside and, for once, were glad of our state, which was sure better than *that* . . .

. . . than *this* . . . And I thought Newgate was bad . . .

I am taken aboard and tossed into a cell, and metal shackles are put around my ankles. After giving me a kick or two and warning me to be good or else, the jailers leave and lock the door. I look about me and take stock.

The room measures about fifteen feet square and there are barred windows high up on two sides, which I suspect were once gun ports, and rough benches line the walls. There is a table in the center. There is no privy, but the place still stinks worse than any latrine.

There seems to be about twenty or so females in this particular cell, all seated on rough benches that line the walls, intent on sewing the fabrics spread out in their laps.

'Tis plain that, while the male convicts are sent out to do the muddy river work, the females toil here, making the rude garments the prisoners are given—after their own clothes rot off their bodies. From their general pallor, I assume they seldom, if ever, see the sun.

With my iron hobbles rattlin' on the deck, I shuffle over to the bench and sit down. The relief that had flooded over me after my deliverance from the noose has somewhat ebbed, and despair, once again, slips in. I know that I, too, could rot away in here for years and years, or at least until the typhus takes me off.

"Welcome to Haitch Hem Hess Bedlam, dearie. Yer sure t' love it here." The woman next to me laughs. "And what be yer name, then?"

I tell her.

"Well, yer name be all that you got o' yer old self down 'ere, dearie, so 'ang on to it as best ye can. In a couple o' years ye might be forgettin' it, and then you'll be like poor Edwina there."

At the end of one of the benches sits an old woman, her head nodding, saying over and over, "Eat cher puddin' girl or you'll get a whack . . . eat cher puddin' girl or . . ."

I notice that about half the women wear the ill-fitting prison garb, and the other half got the remnants of their former clothes still clingin' to them. My companion sees me lookin' at the others.

"Y'see, dearie," she says, givin' me a companionable elbow in me . . . my . . . ribs, "Y'can tell who's bin 'ere a long time by how they look and what they're wearin'. See, over there? That's Elizabeth . . . Elizabeth Drury."

I look over to see the woman, bent over and sewin' at the same sort of garment she's got on herself—rough cloth coat, rough cloth waistcoat, rough cloth skirt, her own clothing long since rotted off in the rank dampness of this place. The men outside got clothes made similar, 'cept they got trousers instead of skirts.

"She's been 'ere since '04, and 'tis wonder that she's still alive, poor thing, and 'as still got a part o' her mind left. 'Bout every summer, gaol fever comes through and takes about half o' us off, but she's still 'ere, bless 'er. Bless us all," she says, smoothing out the cloth in her lap. "I was named Margaret Wood at me christenin', but you can call me Maggie. Settle in, dearie. They'll soon be puttin' needle and thread inta yer hand and . . . Ooohhh, look! 'Ere's the grub!"

There's a rattle at the door of the cage and men enter, carrying what is sure to be Missus Wood's much anticipated dinner. Cloth, needle, and thread are put aside, and the women flock to the table. I go to join them, and sit next to Maggie.

It is burgoo, of course, and particularly foul, bein' of a milky-lookin' mush, which sure ain't never seen no real milk and what's got a scum of brownish fat curdled up on top. I give it a bit of a sniff . . . *No . . . I can't . . .* The biscuit that is put next to it is moldy green on both sides and soft . . . squishy soft. I can do weevily biscuits, but not that. I push both bowl and biscuit toward Maggie.

"Thankee, dearie! But y'know you'll come t' eat it bye and bye, Missy, count on it," she says, munching contentedly on my discarded biscuit. "Else you'll die."

After the so-called dinner, the lights go out and I curl up alone on a bench and go to sleep listening to the moanings of the lunatic Edwina and the howlings of many others like her, echoing throughout the length of this miserable Hulk.

Lord, help me . . .

Chapter 13

It's been a week since I was brought here, and things sure ain't gotten any better. I have been given needle and thread and simple trousers to sew together. The cloth comes to us already cut—they don't trust us with scissors, and that's a wise move on their part for I'm about ready to slash the throat of any number of our jailers, heartless bastards that they are. There ain't a good one among the filthy bunch, and I don't care if I hang for my thoughts, I don't. I've already been struck by the rod several times for mouthin' off to the guards, and Maggie told me to watch my gob if I wanted to live through this. Don't care . . . they can all go to hell.

And yes, I have even learned to eat their slops. I have cursed myself ten times over for not wearing my money belt on that day that I was taken—could've bought some decent food from the corrupt jailers, I could.

I'm wishin', too, that I'd kept my cloak that I'd left back in Newgate, because nights here are damp and my dress is thin . . . my once elegant white Empire dress, now even more bloodstained and filthy. Recalling Newgate makes me think sadly of Mary, Molly, and Esther. *Poor girls, you've got to be off and gone by now, your Monday appointment with the gallows certainly having been kept . . .* Ah, I can't stand to think on it, but I can't help it. *I do hope you died quick and clean, but I fear from the slightness of your forms that your deaths were slow and obscene. I don't pray for much anymore, in light of all the vileness and evil I have seen, but I have prayed for your souls and hope that they now rest easy wherever they may be.*

I stick mostly to myself, seldom talking to anyone but Maggie. Most of the rest of them are a pretty rough, surly bunch. Well, I can be rough and surly, too, as several have already found out. Jacky Faber may not have 'er shiv, but Little Mary's fingernails are still sharp. She may be little, but she is strong . . . in body, anyway. But in mind . . . when I think on the fact that I could be in this hellhole for years and years . . . I dunno . . .

It's mid afternoon and we are sitting silently sewing when we hear a commotion outside. Maggie gets up and stands on the bench so as to be able to peer out the barred window.

"Coo, come look, dearie!" she says.

"Wot, Mag?" I ask, getting up on the bench.

"Sumthin's happenin'!"

I'm too short to see out merely by standing on the bench, so I leap up and grab the bars and pull myself up to look out. Chin on bottom sill of the window, I see crowds of women being herded aboard our Hulk—women who ain't bein' particularly quiet about it, neither.

"Oo the 'ell you think you are? I runs a respectable house and I always has! Getcher hands off me! And getcher hands off my gels!"

And . . .

"*I'm a good girl, I is! That sheriff is a lyin' bastard! Let me go!*"

And . . .

"*Ow! You watch it wi' that stick, you filthy bugger! Ow!*"

There must be at least fifty of them, dressed in a wild assortment of clothes—from the garish and bawdy, to the clean and respectable, and to what is plainly prison garb. *What's goin' on here?*

I watch until I hear a rattlin' of keys behind me.

Uh-oh, prolly gonna smack us for slackin' off on the sewin'.

I drop back down and quickly snatch up my cloth and needle and sit. *Ain't no one bein' bad 'ere, guv'nor . . .*

The door opens and two of the guards—and a particularly nasty pair they are—come into the cell.

"Mary Faber, whichever one o' this gang o' sluts ye be, stand up," says the viler of the two, the one known as Toad.

I stand up and say, "Wot?"

"Ah, 'tis our little bint w' the fancy dress," he says, coming over to stand in front o' me. "Sit yer ass back down."

He puts his fist on me chest and shoves me backward, and I fall on the bench.

"Wot's goin' on, Toady?" I ask.

"Jes' shut yer gob. Get 'er hobbles off, Frogger, and be quick about it."

The other bloke, known to all and sundry as the Frog because o' his general appearance, crouches down at my feet and unlocks the shackles from my ankles. Before he brings them up to put on my wrists, he runs his hand up my leg. *Way* up my leg . . .

"Fancy drawers on this one." The Frog chuckles. "Fancy dress, too."

"Come on, Frogger. Later for that. There's money to be made."

"Aye, and I knows 'ow I'll be spendin' my money. I'll be buyin' pretty little things, I will." He gives me a poke in my ribs and a big leerin' wink. It makes me sick to my stomach to see it.

"First the money," says Toad, seemingly the more practical o' the two sods. "And then the quim. Get 'er up. Let's go."

I am taken and hauled out the door. It is a bit of a relief to be able to walk free for a change. I look about for a chance to escape in my current condition—if I could make it to the side, I could leap over and swim away. I believe I could manage it even with these heavy irons about my hands, but I am not taken topside, no. I am taken into what I suspect is the guards' mess room . . . and there . . . lookin' glorious . . . there stands . . .

Higgins! Oh, thank you, God! Higgins!

I go to rush to his side, but I am held back by my fetters, grasped firmly by the Frog.

"Nay, you sit down there," says Toad, pointin' to me and to a spot at the table. "And you, Sir, can sit yerself across from the tart. Keep your 'ands clear so's we can see 'em. Don't pass 'er nuthin' or else I'll toss you out, nob or not, and she'll taste me cane again. And maybe taste a few things more . . ."

I sit, and so does Higgins.

"You've got fifteen minutes," says Toad, and he takes himself to the other end of the table and sits down, his gimlet eye on the both of us.

I clasp my hands on the tabletop and cry, "Oh, Higgins, you can't know how good it is to see you!" Then I start in to blubberin'. "Don't look at me, Higgins, or get close to me. I am filthy and unclean."

"It is not your fault, Miss. I know that. However, we have some things to cover in our allotted time and we should get to it," says Higgins. "But first you must have a bite to eat." He unfolds a waxed parchment upon which lie several strips of beef smothered in a rich brown gravy. The aroma of finely roasted cuts of tenderloin hits my nose like a hammer. *Oh, Glory!*

I gasp and reach for a piece, but Frogger comes up beside me and stays my hand.

"Nay, this warn't part of the deal." And with that, he reaches in with his filthy fingers and scoops up three of the pieces and shoves 'em in 'is mouth. The Toad, seein' the fun, nips alongside and scoops up the rest, then drops 'em in his gob, leavin' only a few streaks of the gravy on the paper.

I look at it, all forlorn, and am thinking about licking it out.

"No," says Higgins, knowin' my inclination. "Don't give them the satisfaction. It cost us a good bit of our declining fortunes in the way of bribes for me even to get in here, so let it go. You will be gone from here tomorrow and that will be the end of your stay in this . . . place."

Gone? Oh, joy!

I lift my eyebrows in question.

Higgins folds his hands on the tabletop and says, "I have already given you the good news, in that you will be delivered tomorrow afternoon from this place, which, by the way, does bear a distinct resemblance to the sixth level of hell. But I also have some other news that you might find hard to swallow. Are you ready?"

I sit up straight and nod, hands and shackles in lap.

"First, you are to be taken from here, along with about two hundred and fifty other women and girls, and put on a ship bound for the penal colony in New South Wales, Australia."

"I knew that, Higgins, as that was my sentence for my supposed crimes against the Crown of England," I say, feeling that my crimes were not all that horrid as to warrant a life sentence to God knows where. "But why are they so interested in transporting us worthless females?"

He takes a breath, then says, "Speaking plain, you are being brought there as breeders, pure and simple. England, having lost the American colonies, needs another place to expand—a place to put their overflow of petty criminals, revolutionaries, and troublemakers of all kinds, and maybe a place where honest folk could thrive, too. There are a lot of men there right now, and if you toss in a lot of women, then you will have a multitude of children and then maybe you might even have a country someday.

"Even as we speak"—Higgins's voice is muffled by the scented handkerchief he brings to his nose to disguise the stench of the place—"England is combing the prisons, brothels, and slums for women to fulfill just such a noble purpose."

"A far-seeing race is us Brits," I say. Me, I can usually see only as far as my own nose and my immediate needs, which, of course, are always considerable.

"Indeed, Miss, we are a race blessed with foresight. Legend has it that when College Hall at the University of Oxford was built, in 1379, acorns from the oak trees that were used to make the high vaulted beams of the ceilings were planted in a special grove, to insure that in four hundred years, when the original beams would need to be replaced, ample wood of the same stock would be available. Now, *that* is foresight," he says, and then stops talking for a few moments. "But I digress."

I know you do, Higgins. You are avoiding something. I wait for more bad news, which I know is coming.

"Ahem. Yes, Miss . . ." And here he pauses again. "You know you are to be transported, but you do not know this . . ."

"Yes?"

"Your ship, Miss . . ."

"I know, the Crown has taken her. She is no longer mine."

No longer my fine, fine treasure . . .

"Yes, but not only that—"

"What are they going to do to her? Burn her? Turn her into a garbage scow?"

Higgins takes a breath, and then goes on. "No, Miss. The *Lorelei Lee* has been sold to the East India Company, and they have been contracted to transport a certain group of female convicts to the penal colony in New South Wales."

It hits me and I gasp. "What? I am to be taken in bondage to Botany Bay on my own goddamned ship?"

"I am afraid so, Miss. I perceive that the Admiralty has a fine sense of irony. That and the fact that you outfitted the ship so perfectly to carry a large number of passengers. There is a good deal of irony in that, also."

I hate irony.

I fume as I ponder this. Then I think more on it and say, "This might be a good thing, Higgins, for it will give me a measure of comfort to be on her, if only in a reduced capacity . . . and I will have my ship back, I will . . ."

"I am happy that you view it so, Miss."

"All right, then," I say, collecting myself from the last blow. "But I know there is something else, isn't there, Higgins? Something you haven't told me . . ."

He looks down at his hands and nods, but says only, "Several things . . ."

"Jaimy."

There, I have spoken his name and let it hang in the air. Why did I not ask of him before? Because I was afraid to hear the answer . . .

"Where has he been? Why has he not come to see me? Why was he not at my trial? Why . . . ?"

Higgins takes yet another deep breath. "Steady, Miss, for I must inform you that he is being held in the naval prison at Portsmouth, awaiting court-martial."

I bury my face in my hands and bawl. *Oh, Jaimy, no, not you!*

Higgins's strong hands grasp my shaking shoulders and hold them tight till I subside a bit.

"Wh-wh-what is the charge?" I manage to stammer.

"Conspiracy to Defraud the King of His Rightful Property."

What?

"Lieutenant Flashby has made sworn testimony to the effect that Mr. Fletcher colluded with you in the misappropriation of gold from the *Santa Magdalena*. Lieutenant Bliffil adds to the lies, contending that he heard the two of you laying plans for the theft."

"The lyin' bastards! Jaimy knew nothing of my scheme! Bliffil wasn't even there! And I didn't even have any idea of the project until we were well into the salvage of the *Santa Magdalena*! When is the court-martial?"

"In two weeks."

"When does the *Lorelei Lee* leave?"

"In about a week."

"So am I to leave and cross the Southern Ocean never to find out Jaimy's fate? How can I live with that? How could they be so cruel?"

Oh, Jaimy, how much better your life would have been had you never met me!

Higgins considers this and then says, "If convicted, his punishment would not be as harsh as yours, I do not think. Remember, it is Flashby's word against his, and Mr. Fletcher has an excellent service record. He is highly regarded by every captain he has served under, and those who can be made available will testify to that. Captain Hudson, for sure. Furthermore, he is an officer of the line of battle, while Flashby and Bliffil are merely intelligence officers. The admirals and captains who sit in judgment will also be much scarred and battle-tested line officers, and their sympathies would lie with Lieutenant Fletcher, one of their own."

I clench my fists and think hard on this.

"It may be," I say, thanking Higgins silently for, as always, softening the blows that come at me. "But only if Jaimy can hold his temper when that damned Flashby stands up and tells his lies. I can tell you it was hard for me to take, that day in the courtroom, and I was . . . well . . . sort of guilty. It will be harder for Jaimy, who is totally innocent. He had nothing to do with it—I didn't even let *you* in on it till afterward, when the expedition was done and we were about to head for Boston."

"Yes, Miss. I know."

If only Jaimy can hold his temper!

"We have but a few more minutes, Higgins," I say, trying to calm myself but beginning to tear up again, for I know he will soon be gone and I will be back in the cell. I must now ask him to do some things, to put some things in order.

"Please, Higgins, if you would, go back to Boston and take over the helm of Faber Shipping. I hereby give you all the remaining shares in the corporation. I will sign a paper to that effect. So many people now depend upon that business, little as it now is. Get Ezra to—"

"I'm afraid I cannot do that, Miss."

"Oh," I say, confused. "Why not?"

"Because I have taken other employment."

I gasp and lower my head. *Oh, Higgins, I cannot bear to lose you!* I collect myself and say, "Of course, John, you must do what's best for you now that my silly house of cards has collapsed, probably for good and ever. Give me your hand in farewell, dearest friend, in hopes that we might meet again in gladder times. Oh, I so wish it!" Tears pour from my eyes as I squeeze his hand and press it to my wet cheek.

"You may have my hand, Miss, but do not despair of seeing me." Through the blear of tears I see the glint of his teeth in the gloom.

"What . . . ? Why . . . ?"

"I have signed on as steward to Captain Augustus Laughton of the *Lorelei Lee*. I have met the captain and I've found him to be an affable man."

Apparently my face betrays incomprehension, so he goes on to clarify things.

"You see, Miss, I am going with you."

My mouth is agape.

"But why, Higgins?" I manage to gasp. "You are a rich man now. You could set yourself up quite comfortably. Why would you do this? You musn't! I have left nothing but confusion and waste and destruction in my wake!"

He smiles his perfect smile. "Yes, but much joy and excitement, as well. I'm afraid I can never go back to being a simple valet to a rich man. It would be just too . . . boring. No, Miss, you have led me onto the path of adventure, and from that path I cannot retreat."

Once again I place my face in my hands and sob.

"Besides, if they have arrested you and Mr. Fletcher, it is possible that the judiciary will soon cast a wider net, and it is possible that it will be my turn next. I fear that I, too, would not be able to give a court a plausible explanation for my sudden wealth." He pauses, looks about, and sniffs. "I also know that I could not abide a less-than-clean prison cell. I fear the men's prison is not any better than this, and I believe I would find neither the accommodations nor the company all that . . . charming."

"Who shall run Faber Shipping?" I ask, still astounded.

"I have written to Mr. Pickering, informing him of the recent events. We both know he is a very competent man. He will handle things."

I ponder this. "You must get another letter off to Ezra before we go. Tell Davy and Tink to lie low, very low. They are to do the Caribbean run only and must stay close to the shore. No telling what lies Flashby has told about them, too, and Davy is still technically in the British Navy. Give everybody my love and tell Amy not to worry."

"Yes, Miss. Although that last request is a vain one."

From his tone, I suspect he has already done all that. Though my mind is spinning, I manage to clear it enough to ask, "This Captain Laughton, is . . . is he a good man?"

"Yes, Miss, I found him to be so. Furthermore, I have gone into what will now be his cabin, where I managed to retrieve your seabag and most of your clothing, and I've stashed it in my quarters below—your violin as well."

The Lady Gay! And I thought I'd never see her again!

"Hmmm . . ." I muse, calculating. "Then, Higgins, if you would, and if we have any money left, please go out and buy me as much sheet music for fiddle and guitar as you can—Boccherini, Bach, Vivaldi—anything you can find, and lots of spare strings for each instrument, too."

Higgins nods in agreement and then voices some thoughts of his own.

"I think it would be best if we were to pretend not to know each other till we see how things lie. Also, it'd be better if you are known as Mary Faber, as that was the name under which you were tried and convicted, and that is the name that will appear on the ship's manifest. Your notoriety as the infamous Jacky Faber might not work to your advantage, you know. When Captain Laughton was conversing with me, I got the distinct impression that he has yet to be apprised of the fact that not only will he have La Belle

Jeune Fille Sans Merci onboard, but also the former owner of his ship."

"*Hmm*. Wise counsel, Higgins, as always. I will—"

"Awright, time's up," says the Frog. "Ye got one more minute to get yer business done, guv'nor, then getcher self gone." He stands, leering at me, grinnin' a snaggletoothed smile. "Me and 'er, now, we got some business of our own to git on, a little later."

I stiffen and he turns away, laughing.

Higgins takes my hand and whispers, "Don't worry, Miss. When I found out where you were to be taken after the trial, the first thing I did was to bribe the Supervisor of this Hulk to ensure that you would not be . . . bothered in that way. That . . . man . . . will not disturb you, rest easy."

I squeeze his hand. "In spite of all that has happened, things are looking up, Higgins, and I thank you for it."

"No thanks are necessary, Miss."

I look over at the snickering Toad and Frog, and oh, how I wish I had John Thomas and Smasher McGee here, by God, and Davy and Tink, too, and then we'd see just whose food those bastards would take!

"Those two," I say, with a nod toward the Toad and the Frog. "If we have a spare bob or two . . . ?" Then I run my finger across my throat.

But Higgins merely smiles and nods . . . and rises. I kiss him on the cheek. He picks up his hat, cloak, and walking stick, then leaves.

I am taken back to the cell, where my ankles are re-shackled, and I sit and seethe.

The Frog and the Toad may very well pay dearly for their meanness in some dark alley this night. As for the others—all the ones above these two weasels; all the ones with power—King George and his goddamned Crown . . . the judiciary . . . the Admiralty and all its minions . . . all of those bastards . . . to them I say . . .

You may yet regret the day
you sent Jacky Faber in chains
to Botany Bay.

Chapter 14

It being June, the dawn comes early.

I rouse myself and stretch, waiting for the guards to come open our door and let us shuffle down to the privy, which is, of course, the derelict's old head—that place at the bow of the ship with the open holes to the seas or, now, to the Thames. Some fetid water will be placed in buckets for us to wash as best we can. Bits of harsh soap are provided. We must dry with the hems of our garments.

That done, we shuffle back to our cell, and I am shocked at the sight of three ghosts seated within, and . . . *oh, what a welcome sight it is!*

On the bench, huddled under my cloak, which I had thought was lost forever, sit Mary Wade and Molly Reibey and Esther Abrahams!

Oh, thank you, Lord!

"Jacky! We thought you was dead!" says Molly, who rises, amazed, upon spying me.

"And I thought you hanged!" cry I, equally amazed. "Come, embrace me and tell me how you come to be here, alive and whole!"

I hug each of them in turn, as we had grown quite close when we shared not only the hell of the Condemned Cell at Newgate but four very doubtful futures as well.

Mary Wade gulps and tells their story in a rush of words and gasps.

"Well, they puts us on bread and water, and then three days later, on Sunday night, they made us go to that awful sermon . . . with the open coffin and all . . . and then in the mornin' they come got us and led us out to the gallows. I saw it high above me with the nooses hanging on this long piece of wood, and I'm so scared I wets me drawers. And . . . and they took some coves up there and slung the ropes around their necks and put hoods over their faces, but they didn't take us, no. They led us to the side, and then the traps fell and them poor blokes was hanged; and after they stopped kickin', they flung us girls in a cart and hauled us 'ere."

She looks about her in wonder at how her fortunes have changed. "And 'ere we are."

"Here you are, indeed, Mary, and I am so very glad of it!"

"And when they led us away, the people that was there reached out and tried to touch us." Mary has this faraway look in her eye, and no wonder, considerin' the hell she's been through. "They was yellin' and grabbin' at us . . . I don't know why."

I had heard of things like this before, and I take her by her thin shoulders and hold her and say, "You managed to cheat the hangman, Mary, and they wanted to take some of your luck for themselves. That's what it was."

"Oh," she says, looking around at our dismal prison. "Luck? I dunno . . ."

"Aye, 'tis a pit," say I. "But cheer up, ladies, for this afternoon we're gonna board a fine ship!"

Leaving them wondering at this, I go to the bars and stick my face through.

"Hey, screws!" I call out. "Get the Matron! We got three fine new girls here what's got to use the privy and wash up, 'cause we're a-goin' sailin', we are!"

I'm gratified to see that the guards who answer my call are *not* the Frog and the Toad.

Maybe it was just their day off, or maybe they was sick . . . But maybe it was a day of reckoning . . . *Take that, you sods . . . You mess with Jacky Faber and you might live to regret it.*

There is a great hubbub as we are taken up out of the dark and into the sunshine on deck. *Oh, the wonderful, glorious warm sunshine! How I have missed it!* I hold my face up to it as we are pushed along, and I revel in its warmth. And then we are pulled over the deck and down the gangway, across the wharf, and pushed onto great rough open carts. We all still wear the heavy wrist shackles and are bound together in a line to keep any one of us from suddenly darting off and disappearing into the alleys of the city. Big thick and sturdy draft horses are harnessed to the wagons, and as soon as we are somewhat settled, the driver gives a flick of his whip and we are off.

We roll down from Woolwich and plunge into the heart of London, through Cheapside, the mean but familiar and somewhat beloved streets of my youth, then down to the Lower Docks on the Thames.

People on the streets jeer and throw things at us as we roll along. I pay it no mind, but I notice my companions' heads begin to droop in fear and shame.

"Heads up, girls," I chirp, to cheer them up. "Never let them see you cringe and cry, as it only makes 'em happy. Here, do this—chin up, eyelids at half-mast, lips together, teeth apart. Like this . . . that's it."

They manage a reasonable version of the Lawson Peabody Look. "And remember, you're as good as any of those sods over there and prolly a damn sight better."

There is a cart behind us containing a very unruly gaggle of girls, and standing at the head of the bunch is the woman I saw shouting curses at the guards as she was brought aboard yesterday. More garbage is thrown, but she and the other women in the wagon give as good as they get.

"Back off, ye curs!" she cries at the mob. "Or you'll get what for!"

With her shackled hands she picks up a stone that was thrown and pitches it back at the crowd.

"You tell 'em, Missus Barnsley," shouts a woman behind her. "The filthy buggers!"

"Roight, ye'll miss us when we're gone, you sods!" crows another of the girls, whipping around and pulling up her skirts and bending over, exposing a considerable span of knicker-clad buttocks to the roaring crowd. "'Ere's one fine arse ye'll n'er see no more!"

"Coom, Rosie, gi' us one more kiss 'fore ye goes!" shouts one rounder, who clutches the side of the cart and presents his pursed lips to this Rosie but only gets a rap on his knuckles from her wrist irons.

He yowls and falls back into the laughing mob.

After about an hour of this, we arrive at the docks, and there . . . there . . . lying like a jewel, is my *Lorelei Lee*, all glorious in the summer sunlight. Tears come to my eyes . . . *Oh, I thought never to see you again!*

The carts come to a stop, and we are pulled roughly to the ground and shoved in a line snaking up toward the gangway. We pass underneath the figurehead, and several of the girls exclaim in wonder at it. Too late, I try to cover my face.

"Coo, Jacky, that looks just like you!" says Mary Wade.

"Does it? Strange, that," I reply, and say no more.

We are pushed into a line that heads up the gangway. There are maybe twenty in front of us. We are one of the first carts to arrive, which I think is good, as we might be better able to grab the choicer berths.

As we get to the top of the brow, I see that, incredibly, it is Higgins who sits at a table, open ledger in front of him, pen in hand. When each girl stands before him, he asks her name, checks it off the list, and then writes her name on two small wooden disks, to which are attached strings and pins. He is dressed in what would appear to be a standard white steward's uniform, except that it is made of the finest cloth and sports several special touches here and there—a bit of lace at the cuffs, some trim on the collar.

When I stand before him, he looks up at me and tonelessly asks, "Name?"

"Mary Faber," I reply, standing there in my once proud Empire dress—I would have looked grand in this dress at one time, but now it looks like a dismal rag, nothing more than a shift.

"Very well," he says, and writes "Faber" on each of the two disks. "You will pin one of these to your dress and one to the hammock you will be issued. If you cannot read, just memorize how your name looks, so you will be able to find it again. Do you understand, Mary Faber?"

I hang my head and nod, all forlorn.

"Good. Now get in that line there, and you will be examined by the Surgeon Superintendent, who is in charge of the cargo. Next."

I shuffle along in the line that leads down into the fore hatch. Before each of us get to the hatchway, however, a seaman unlocks the shackles from our wrists—*Oh, it feels so good to have those horrid things off*—and throws them in a pile.

"Be good, girls," he says. "They can go right back on if you ain't. Now git along."

"What's gonna happen, Jacky?" asks Esther fearfully, in her breathless voice.

"We're gonna be checked for head lice . . . and crabs—body lice—and signs of the pox, or other diseases like that," I say. "It won't be pleasant, but you'll get through it. I've had it done to me before, and it ain't so bad."

I hear Molly Reibey sobbing behind me. *Chin up, Molly, there's worse things.*

Don't think about it. Enter the makeshift surgery. Hop on table, drop drawers, and pull up skirt. Most times I revel in being a girl, but sometimes I don't. A grunt from the surgeon's assistant, and I am done and back in line again.

Some of the women are given potions, some are directed toward washtubs. Mary Wade gets her head ducked into a pail of soapy water and scrubbed for head lice. Hope I didn't catch any from her, but hey, I've had 'em before.

After that fine time, a grinning sailor raises his cap and motions for us to go below. *Hmmm . . .* In a situation like this, I'm used to being thrown down into the hatchway and not treated at all nice. Maybe it's a good sign. Who knows?

We are then led into the hold and given hammocks and told where to hang them. Then we are left on our own.

"Come on, girls, follow me," I say, as I lead them through the central passageway and up onto the top level of the main hatch. "Your new home, Sisters. This is the best spot down here."

In outfitting the *Lorelei*, I had taken a page from my time on the *Bloodhound,* that vile slaver, and raised the two hatch tops eighteen inches and installed rows of open windows all around. Sturdy flaps hinged at the tops could be lowered and dogged down during rough weather or high seas. I did it so as to provide fresh air and some light to the passenger decks below. I'm powerful glad I did, too, seein' where I am now.

"Come, girls, over here. See, here's how you hang your hammock. That's it. Now pin on your badge."

One hook goes to a ring on the outer bulkhead and the other to a similar one on a heavy beam that goes all the way around the balcony, encircling the open dark hold where the stores are kept. There are three more sleeping decks below, which, though they receive air, get very little light. We're lucky to be some of the first aboard and so able to grab these berths.

"How do you know so much about this place, Jacky?" asks Maggie, who has tagged along with me and the others.

"I've been to sea before, Mag, is all, and I know how things work out on the briny," I say. "Now, in the morning, you'll take that outer hook off and put it on the bulkhead one so the hammock will hang against the wall, out of the way," I say, showing them. "Neat, eh?"

It should be, as I designed this whole setup.

That done, I go to the window and gaze out at the hubbub on deck. Mrs. Barnsley is being processed and not being at all cooperative. Now that I have seen her close up, I recognize her as one of London's reigning madams, running what was probably the biggest brothel in the city. But not anymore, she ain't. Her whorehouse wasn't far from our old kip, and Rooster Charlie and the gang would go by there sometimes to see what we could scare up in the way of food and handouts. And sometimes she would come down to our turf to scout out the orphans in our neighborhood—recruiting, like. In fact, when I was newly orphaned, at the age of seven, only to be thrown out into the mean city streets to die, the girl what stole my clothes on the Dark Day, who I later found out was named Betty, ended up at Mrs. Barnsley's. She might even be one of this bunch. If so, I do not think I shall renew her acquaintance.

Aside from running her house of ill repute, Elizabeth Barnsley had her hand in many other illegal scams. Sort of a female Fagin, she was. *Hmmm* . . . She must have stepped on the wrong toes to end up here. Or forgot to pay the usual bribes.

After Higgins finishes with her, she goes raging and squalling into the medical inspection line, just like the others.

"Next," says Higgins. "Name."

"Rachel Hoddy, damn yer eyes!"

Badges given, and the line moves on . . .

Violetta Adkins . . . Ann Bone . . . Mary Chafey . . . Elizabeth Gale . . . Sarah House . . . Ann Marsh . . .

. . . and on . . .

. . . Hannah Pealing . . . Susannah Pickett . . . Ann Poor . . . Mary Talbot . . .

I spot a sailor standing nearby and I shout out, "Hey, Mate, when do we get under way?"

He slides his eyes over to mine, and instead of telling me to shut my gob and go to hell, he answers, in a pleasant enough voice, "Soon as they gets done loadin' this lot and Captain Laughton comes aboard."

I decide to press my luck and keep my eye out for a kick. "Is he a good captain?"

He barks out a laugh. "*Good* captain? Aye, girl, a sailor would kill to become one o' 'is crew, they would . . . and t' get on *this* particular cruise"—the sailor looks out over all the girls coming aboard—"he would murder 'is own mother!"

A seaman standing next to him nods in gleeful agreement and . . . *Good Lord, I recognize him!*

I duck down so that only my eyes show above the sill. *Who would have thought that, and him of all people!*

It appears that all of the women have been processed, for I see that Higgins has risen from the table and, cargo manifest in hand, goes to stand by the rail. Several seamen gather up the table and chairs, to take them below. Beneath me I hear the confusion as the women are being settled in their berths. I do not envy the sailors assigned to that task.

An officer mounts the quarterdeck and dispatches the Messenger of the Watch. The boy scurries below, and presently three more officers come on deck, two young and one somewhat older. They go stand next to the gangway. From his bearing, the older man will be the First Mate, and I think the Officer-of-the-Watch there is Second. The young ones are probably Third and Fourth Mates. A man who is not dressed nautical also comes on deck. He must be the Purser.

A sturdy and rough-looking sailor in Master's garb, plainly the Bo'sun's Mate, stands ready with his pipe.

"He's here!" comes the shout from the foretop. I cannot see it, but I sense that a carriage has arrived at the foot of the gangway. There is the sound of a coach door closing, and a mighty cheer goes up. It rings from every deck, every spar, every ratline on the ship.

Hoorah! Hoorah! Hoorah for Captain Laughton!

Presently a head, wearing a captain's elegant hat, is seen above the rail, and then the rest of Captain Augustus Laughton appears and steps onto the deck of the *Lorelei Lee,* to even more cheers.

There he is, good old Gussie, bless 'im! Hoorah! Hoorah!

Any thoughts I might have had of rallying a disgruntled crew to mutiny and so reclaim my ship have just been banished. 'Tis plain they love him. Oh well, there will have to be another way . . .

Captain Laughton is a big man, wide of girth. In doffing his hat to acknowledge the cheers of his crew and the salutes of his officers, he reveals a bald head, fringed with gray hair. His nose is bulbous, his lips thick and sensuous, and his eyes merry.

Putting his hat back on, he speaks first to Higgins. "They are all aboard and accounted for, Mr. Higgins?"

"Yes, Sir," says Higgins, with a slight bow. "The ladies are being accommodated below." I notice that Higgins has already acquired a "Mister" before his name, though he is but a steward. Higgins does have his ways.

"Good. I hope they are comfortable." He turns to his First Mate. "Are we ready to get under way, Mr. Ruger?"

"Yes, Captain. The tide is right and the wind is fair for the channel."

"Very good, Mr. Ruger," says the Captain, as he mounts his quarterdeck. He turns and, in a great stentorian bellow, shouts, "All men to your stations! Topmen aloft to make sail! All others on deck, hands on the buntlines!"

Men scurry to take their places, but they do not yet raise the sails, for it turns out there is one more man to come aboard.

Another cheer breaks out as the man comes across the brow, carrying a long, thick staff. The crew calls him something, but I cannot make out what it is. He is dressed in a black Royal Navy Master's uniform and is very tall, and his face is clean-shaven, with craggy features—those features one can see, anyway, as he has a white bandage tied across his eyes. He is obviously blind, and he uses the staff to tap his way aboard. He does not bend his back, however. It is held ramrod straight.

Behind him, a young sailor carries what is apparently the man's seabag, and over his shoulder is slung a large drum. The sailor proceeds quickly to the foot of the foremast, drops the seabag, and sets the drum up on a tripod. The man in black follows his assistant to the foremast—I suppose by ear—and puts his hand out to touch the drum, which sits about waist high to him. He positions himself with his back to the mast, and two bass drumsticks are put in his hands. He faces aft expectantly.

"Shantyman!" bellows the Captain. "Get us under way!"

The Shantyman begins beating the drum head with a slow, steady *boom . . . boom . . . boom . . .*

And then he lifts his chin and sings, in a deep, rich, powerful voice . . .

> *London girls ain't got no combs,*
> *Haul away, haul away!*
> *They comb their hair with codfish bones!*
> *Heave away, haul away!*

The land lines are thrown off and the sails begin to rise. The men on the lines come in singing on the *heave away!* and *haul away!* lines, grunting as they put their backs into the work, as the shanty makes it easier for them to pull together.

> *Liverpool girls ain't got no frills,*
> *Haul away, haul away!*
> *They tie their hair with codfish gills!*
> *Heave away, haul away!*

The sails are up and they begin to fill. The Captain barks orders to the helmsman and to the men aloft trimming the sails. *Goodbye, London. Goodbye, Jaimy. Goodbye, all I know and love.* We heel over on the starboard tack and the *Lorelei Lee* turns her head from the land and points her bold bow south to the sea.

> *So heave away, my bully, bully boys!*
> *Haul away, haul away!*
> *Heave her up and don't you make a noise.*
> *We're bound for South Austral-ia!*

PART II

Chapter 15

Before we leave the calm waters of the Thames, we are fed dinner—deck by deck we're called down to get in line at the galley. I had reclaimed my cloak from my Newgate pals so's I can go through the line with the hood pulled over my face, as if in shame. In reality, I do not wish to be spotted, having already recognized one seaman I know and . . . *Good God, there's another . . . and there, standing behind the pots o' burgoo, yet another!* I pull the hood lower and get through the line undetected. *Never expected to see those three again, and I don't know how delighted I am to see 'em.* Oh, well, a mate's a mate, no matter what.

On the mess deck we're each issued a tin mess kit—spoon, cup, and bowl. *"Take 'em, ladies, fill 'em up wi' the Lorelei's good grub, and when you've dropped it all down yer pie hole, well, you takes yer u-ten-sils over to that soapy tub right over there and washes 'em wi' that brush hangin' there and then stashes 'em in yer hammock, neat as y'please . . . Awright? . . . Good . . . Next . . . Hello, ladies . . ."*

I sit at one of the long tables with my back to those blokes dishin' out the grub. It's pretty good burgoo, I must say—oatmeal mush with peas and some pieces of meat, and a nice biscuit, besides. And some weak tea for your cup, too. Can't complain, no, and sure better than that swill dished out to us on the Hulk. *It should be good,* I growls to myself, *considerin' what I paid for them stores . . . No, no, stop that . . . You've got to quit saying that, girl . . . Until you take her back, she is not your ship anymore, and her stores are not your stores. Best to get over all that and stick to your watching . . . and planning . . .*

Figurin' we're about to start rockin' and rollin' real soon, I get my gang back to our kip to rig their hammocks.

Sure enough, when we hit the open waters and commence to rock and roll, the conversation turns from excited talk about our new surroundings to moans and groans of the deepest distress.

In the waning light, I go down to get two of the buckets, placed about in convenient spots, and hand one to Maggie. Thinking that I would be carrying a large number of landlubbers, and knowing the effects of seasickness on unseasoned sailors, I had purchased them for just such a purpose—to be put under the mouths of those who are spewing out their innards and praying for a quick death—for no one wants to clean up another's undigested meal. I hold one such bucket under the face of Esther Abrahams, who is not having an easy time of it. *It's all right, Esther, you'll get over it, soon, I promise . . .* Maggie, who is a tough one and has seen much more trouble in her day than this, holds her pail under the nose of Mary Reibey, though she herself is a bit green about the gills. We get everybody into their hammocks and reasonably comfortable and then I climb gratefully into mine. It has been a long and spiritually wrenching day.

Swinging there, I think of Jaimy. *God, I hope and pray that they are fair to you—you who are so noble and upright but, because of me, are in a lot of trouble. I'm so sorry, Jaimy. I just thought things would work out different . . . Please, if you can find it in your heart, forgive me.*

Goodnight, love.

When morning comes, the ocean is as slick and calm as a lake, with a soft breeze from the northwest, putting the *Lorelei Lee* on a sweet quarter-reach, her sails full and stiff and a neat bone in her teeth, and leaving a fine wake. Because of the gentleness of the day, most of the cargo has recovered from their bouts with the *mal de mer*. I noticed that the flaps did not come down last night—this sure ain't the *Bloodhound . . .*

We have breakfast—burgoo again, and good—and then, after all are fed and the mess kits washed and stashed, a sailor sticks his head in the hatch and booms out, "Awright, ladies! All of yiz topside now! The Captain wants to talk to yiz, and it ain't good to keep the Captain waitin'!"

I gather my little brood and, followed by all of the others, we tromp up the gangway and out onto the deck, blinking against the bright sunshine.

"Get yerselves up on the hatch top," says this seaman, who I now see is the Bo'sun, complete with whistle and knobby and all. He also has a sturdy rod stuck in his waistband. "Line up as best you can . . . That's it . . . Be quiet, now . . ."

Hmmm . . . So far we've been called girls, women, and la-dies. We ain't yet been called bitches or whores or bints or any of them hundreds of other names they got for us . . . Hmmm . . .

I get my girls, in a line, to the front edge of the hatch and look up to see Captain Laughton on the quarterdeck, flanked on either side by his officers, four of them in blue uniforms, one in a gray suit, and one, standing at the end of the right flank, in white. On the left flank there is yet another man, clad in the scarlet uniform of an army officer. The Shantyman stands behind the Captain, his face to the wind, and appears to be looking up at the sails, though he can't possibly be. The ratlines and rigging are filled with grinning seamen, laughin' and pokin' each other in the ribs. *Ain't the Royal Navy, that's for sure.*

"Good morning, ladies!" booms out the Captain, after all are up and generally quiet and presented in some order. "I trust you spent a restful night on the *Lorelei Lee*?"

Mumbles and low grunts are heard in acknowledgment.

"Good!" he continues. "Now, I have brought you up here to recite to you the rules of conduct on this ship! First of all, I shall introduce my officers. On my left here is First Mate, Mr. Ruger, and my Second, Mr. Seabrook. There, in the red, is Major Johnston. He is to take command of the garrison in Botany Bay, and you all will undoubtedly see much of him after you are landed in that place. On my right is Third Officer, Mr. Gibson, and Fourth, Mr. Hinckley. At the end there is Purser, Mr. Samsock, and Ship's Steward and Assistant Purser, Mr. Higgins.

Assistant Purser! Higgins, you have been exercising your charms! Bravo!

"If I, or any of these men speak to you, you are to consider it the Word of God. Do you understand?"

Another murmur of sullen assent from the assembly.

"If you do not understand, you may gaze upon that man there." He gestures toward the man who had brought us up from down below. "That is Bo'sun's Mate Roberts, and he wields a stout rod that your buttocks would not like to meet, believe me on that. Behave yourselves, ladies, and we shall get along.

"Ahem!" He clears his throat loudly and then goes on. "Now you know us, and now we shall know you. Mr. Higgins, read the manifest!"

Higgins steps forward and reads from a sheet of paper.

"The cargo manifest of the *Lorelei Lee*, ship of the East India Line, embarked June 17, 1807, and bound for the colony in New South Wales, Australia. To wit:

Fifty-one girls, aged ten to nineteen,
one hundred and sixteen females, aged twenty to twenty-
   nine,
forty females, aged thirty to thirty-nine,
fifteen women, aged forty to forty-nine,
and eight, aged over fifty."

Higgins folds his paper and says in conclusion, "Two hundred and thirty total. Additionally, twelve children under ten. All declared to be fit and in good order."

Higgins, having recited all that, steps back.

"Very good, Mr. Higgins," says the Captain. "Now listen to this, all of you. You are being transported to the penal colony for having committed various crimes, and for the purpose of populating a continent. Here are the rules:

"Number one, obey all rules.

"Number two, stay off the quarterdeck, the place where I am now standing. Other than that, you may have the run of the ship."

What? I can't believe it!

"Number three, don't touch anything and stay out of the way of the seamen when they are performing their duties. When you hear the Bo'sun blow three times on his pipe, you will hurry below and stay there.

"Number four, there shall be no thievery or fighting aboard this ship. I have mentioned the Bo'sun's rod and I will now warn you about the ship's brig—it is very low in the bilges and not a pleasant place. So, ladies, be good."

Captain Laughton pauses to take a breath and to look out over the multitude, patting his broad belly and looking very satisfied. Then he goes on.

"I intend for this to be a happy ship. You shall all be fed very well, as I want to deliver you plump and healthy to your new home. It will take us between five months and a year to get there, and you should know that the East India Company will receive an extra fee of ten and six for each of your dear bodies received intact, and we intend to collect that bonus. If you are delivered bearing a child within your womb, we shall get twelve and six, a child at your breast, fourteen and six. If you are the mother in either case, you shall receive a shilling for your trouble."

Another pause, while Captain Laughton takes a drink from the coffee cup offered up by a small boy by his side.

"Ah, that is good," he says, smacking his ample lips. "Furthermore, I now announce that every man aboard may take a wife . . ."

There is a tremendous roar from the men in the rigging.

Hooray! Hooray! Hooray for Captain Laughton!

He listens to the cheers for a few moments and then makes a cutting motion with his hand and there is dead silence. They may love him, but his authority is absolute and they know it.

"With the following caveats. No woman shall be forced, and no one under the age of sixteen will be allowed to participate . . ."

Another roaring cheer.

". . . whether female or male."

This occasions some heartfelt groans from the four ship's boys sitting overhead in the foretop.

The Captain, hearing those groans, looks up. "Cheer up, my lads. It will be a long voyage, and you may yet come of age during it."

Much laughter from the crew.

"Now, to continue," says Captain Laughton. "We must talk of serious matters. To wit, your lodgings."

I wonder at this, but I do not wonder long.

"You will have observed that this ship is admirably fitted out for the carrying of passengers, and, as such, there are some quarters more desirable than others. Of the three decks in the main hatch, it is plain that the top one is the most desirable—more light, more air, quicker access to the deck." *The one that I and my girls have claimed,* I think with a certain trepidation. "And, there are ten cabins up forward . . . small, yes, but private."

What is he getting at?

"After we leave Gibralter, we shall auction off the four hammock levels to the highest bidder," announces the Captain with a greedy little smile. "We shall work it out, ladies."

Guffaws all around from the ship's crew . . . but not our Crews.

A voice speaks up. It is Mrs. Barnsley. "But, Guv'nor, 'ow the hell are we to make any money out 'ere?"

"Well, Mistress," says Captain Laughton. "There are many jobs to be done on this ship—laundry, sewing, cleaning of the heads, and kitchen help—all jobs my seamen don't particularly like doing, being seasoned sailors and all. There's money to be made, you see."

"Me and my gels don't do that kind o' work," retorts Madam Barnsley, puffing up. She is a large, florid woman who wears a crown of fake blond curls under her mob cap. To me, at the moment, she rather resembles an irritated hen.

"Ah," says the Captain. "I have been informed as to the nature of my cargo, and I perceive you to be Mistress Elizabeth Barnsley. There are several other of your profession aboard as well. Am I right?"

Madam Barnsley gives a curt nod.

"Well, then, Mistress, I am delighted to inform you that we will be making a port visit to Gibraltar in a few days to take on fresh water and a few more passengers. There are many men there, and you—Mistress Barnsley, and others of your . . . profession—will be permitted to ply your trade there."

There is a common gasp of astonishment, mine included.

"But you must know that I will take twenty percent of your commerce to my own coffers."

"Twenty percent!" retorts Mrs. Barnsley, a stern businesswoman and one not used to having terms dictated to her. "That's robbery!"

"Twenty percent, Mrs. Barnsley," says the Captain. "Else you and your 'gels' will stay below, entertaining each other, during our port visit to that *very* active town."

I see Mrs. Barnsley gritting her teeth. "Twenty percent, it is, Captain. For now."

"Good," say Captain Laughton. "Now our business is done. It is Friday, so all hands commence ship's work. There will be holiday routine tomorrow afternoon, good food, and a ration of grog on Sunday, with singing and dancing on the fo'c's'le. Turn to."

With a final cheer, the men in the rigging swing down to the deck, eyeing the lot of us as possible wives, and the women, not knowing what else to do, retreat below to their berths.

When all are back at their various levels, I lean over the edge of the balcony and call out, "Ladies, we've got to talk."

In the gloom below, Mrs. Elizabeth Barnsley's angry red face appears.

"What you want, girl?"

"I think we've got to organize. In teams, like, so we can better our condition."

She looks up at me.

"And just who the hell are you?"

"Mary Faber. And I've been to sea before, so I know how things work."

"So what? All I noticed was you grabbing the best deck for you and your gang."

"Yes, but . . . I can—"

"What you can do is shut up. You and your gels is nothin' but Newgate trash . . . thieves and such. That's all you are. Me and my gels has been workin' an honest profession. Ain't never stole nothin' . . . Just give o' ourselves for the joy o' our gentlemen. That's all we did."

What? Trash?

"Aye, I've noticed you've claimed the nice deck, but we'll see who's sleepin' there after Gibraltar, sweetie, and I'll wager it'll be me and my gels, not yours. Now, get yerself off, twit."

Well, I guess Plan B ain't gonna be workin' neither.

Chapter 16

The Shipping Gazette
Edition of June 23, 1807

Excerpts of the Court-Martial of Lieutenant
James Emerson Fletcher, Royal Navy,
held this week at the Naval Base at
Portsmouth,
Vice Admiral Wm. Chamberlain, Presiding

Dear Reader,

The following is an account of the more cogent aspects of the testimony of evidence presented against Lt. Fletcher and his replies thereto. He was charged by this Court of the Crime of Conspiracy to Defraud the King of His Rightful Treasure, in Collusion with the already Condemned Mary Faber. Your Reporter was present during the entire proceedings.

All were sworn in, the charges were read, and Lt. Henry Flashby, Royal Navy, was called forward to give testimony.

King's Counsel, the Honorable David St. George:
"State your name."

"Henry Flashby, Lieutenant, His Majesty's Royal Navy."

"And were you not on His Majesty's Ship *Dolphin*, during a mission to the Caribbean Sea this past year?"

"I was."

"And in what capacity?"

"As Intelligence Officer, to oversee the execution of the Mission."

"Which was . . . ?"

"To recover gold from a sunken Spanish galleon."

"Did the mission succeed?"

"Yes, to a degree."

"To what degree?"

"To the degree that the female diver on the wreck, Mary Faber, known to the criminal world as Jacky Faber, did not allow the King the full measure of the recovered gold, gold sorely needed to fund the Treasury in this time of war."

"What do you mean?"

"I mean that she set aside a large amount of the gold for herself . . . and her friends, of whom Mr. Fletcher is one."

At this point, Attorney Joseph Williams, Barrister and Counsel to Mr. Fletcher, leaped to his feet and made objection to the implied insinuation.

"My lord, the Witness is making allegations against Mr. Fletcher that cannot be proved!"

Admiral Chamberlain:

"Objection denied. Come, come, Mr. Williams, it is common knowledge that the female has already been convicted and condemned for her crimes, and also that the

Defendant has had a long-standing relationship with her. Let us proceed. Mr. St. George."

"Lieutenant Flashby, just how did the female in question manage this theft of the King's property?"

"It was my theory, as a trained Intelligence Officer, that she had secreted great amounts of the gold from her ship, under cover of darkness, to an island known locally as Key West, and had it buried there."

"Ah, just like the pirates of old, eh?"

"Yes, Sir. I attempted to intervene, but was deceived by the female and subjected to grievous personal harm."

"Your Honor, I object. This is nothing but supposition."

"Pretty reasonable 'supposition' I must say, considering the girl's past history!"

The esteemed Panel took a few moments to guffaw at this.

"Proceed, Mr. St. George."

"Yes, Sir. Now, Lieutenant Flashby . . . what led you to believe that something of this nature was happening?"

"I overheard a conversation between the girl Faber and Mr. Fletcher onboard the *Dolphin*. They thought themselves private on the fo'c's'le, but I was there . . ."

"And . . . ?"

"And I heard her whisper to him, 'Steady on, Jaimy, if there is much gold to be found, then we shall have a good bit of it, count on that! Steady on, my love, and to hell with the King!'"

It was here that Lieutenant Fletcher appeared visibly agitated, and had to be restrained by his attorney.

"You swear that to be true, Lieutenant Flashby?"

"On my honor, Sir."

"Very well, you may step down. Mr. Williams, you may call your first witness."

"I call Captain Hannibal Hudson, Master and Commander of HMS *Dolphin*."

Captain Hannibal Hudson was summoned to give testimony, but even though he pronounced himself fully convinced of the innocence of Mr. Fletcher, he could not provide corroborating evidence and was asked to stand down.

"I now call Lieutenant James Emerson Fletcher, to speak in his own defense."

This was later to be seen as a not particularly wise move on the part of the defense, as Mr. Fletcher seemed to be in no mood to be amenable.

"Your name, Sir?"

"James Emerson Fletcher, Lieutenant, Royal Navy."

"You have pled innocent of all these charges."

"Yes."

"How do you refute them?"

"By calling that goddamned Flashby a bald-faced liar, Sir!"

"Please, Sir, restrain yourself, or I shall find you in Contempt of Court!"

"Contempt of Court? Why, Sir, if you believe the lies of that sniveling coward, then I have nothing but contempt for this goddamned Court!"

Not a wise thing for Mr. Fletcher to say, as it turned out. He attempted to lunge at Mr. Flashby and was prevented from doing that gentleman physical harm only by the swift action of several burly bailiffs.

"I'll kill you, you slimy bastard, if it's the last thing I do on this earth!"
"Order! By God, I'll have order here or I'll slap you all in the brig! Order!"

Mr. Fletcher was again restrained, a look of pure fury upon his face, as quiet was once more restored to the proceedings.

"The evidence has been heard and we are ready to render a verdict. Do you have any final words to say for yourself, Mr. Fletcher?"
"Verdict? Yes, and I know what the verdict will be, and you can all go straight to hell!"
"Sir! Please control yourself!"
"If you are going to hang her, then you can hang me by her side! That is the only request of this so-called court that I will make! Together we shall leave this corrupt world, kept apart in this life yet joined together in death, and damned be to you all!"

It was plain to your humble reporter that Mr. Fletcher had not yet been apprised of Miss Faber's fate—that she had been sentenced not to hanging but rather to Transportation for Life. Had Lieutenant Fletcher but known that and had managed to control his temper and not deliver that vainglorious closing speech, his future might have been much brighter.

"Very well, Mr. Fletcher, you have been found Guilty of Conspiracy to Defraud the King and are sentenced to the following. You are to be stripped of rank, banished from the Service, and Condemned to Seven Years Transportation to New South Wales! Take him away!"

Mr. Fletcher was removed from the courtroom and taken to the Hulks. I thank you for your attention to this article.

I remain Your Humble Correspondent,

Joseph Michael Marks

Chapter 17

Despite Mrs. Elizabeth Barnsley's refusal to follow my advice, the women of the *Lorelei Lee* do form up into groups. In addition to Mrs. Barnsley's considerable bunch—now called the Lizzies, after their leader—there is a large brothel from Liverpool called the Judies, because of the song, and another from Glasgow, called, quite naturally, the Tartans. The Judies are led by Mrs. Berry, and the Tartans by Mrs. MacDonald, both large women of a certain age, and while they are formidable, 'tis plain that Mrs. Barnsley is the top madam and equally obvious that she intends to remain in that position . . . and that she will brook no smart lip from a snip like me, as she has made very plain.

This sure ain't the *Bloodhound,* and these women sure ain't the girls of the Lawson Peabody School for Young Girls.

And so it is, by former affiliation and inclination, that the female Crews are set. There will be minor defections, but things will remain essentially as they are: the Lizzies, the Judies, and the Tartans . . . and us.

My group is called the Newgaters Crew, since most of us came from that foul pit, or from places very similar—convicted thieves, scammers, petty criminals, and such. Knowing that things will get political very soon with battles over turf down below decks, Maggie and I had circulated through the bunch of uncommitted felons to find what we thought were the best of the lot and let them join with us. There were some real hard cases amongst the throng, so we were more than willing to let those join up with the brothel crews. We've got twelve in our batch, counting me, and they all seem like good sorts. The seven new ones in our the group are Ann Marsh, Hannah Bolt, Catherine Wilmot, Sarah Verriner, Phoebe Williams, Elizabeth Parry, and Isabella Manson. I suspect there will be more, but we shall see.

When we're through with our recruiting, I call them all together for a meeting. They sit before me on the deck of the top level.

"All right, girls, listen to me if you will. I'm the one speaking because I have been to sea before, so I know the way of things out here. First of all, you should know what will not be tolerated on a ship. Thievery, is one. I know that some of you have been convicted of this crime, myself included, but don't steal anything else, ladies, for it will get you whipped if not worse. Y'see, a sailor has stashed all of his worldly belongings in his seabag, and since it's stowed right next to his hammock, it's easy prey for a scoundrel, and he pure hates it when somebody steals some of his stuff. So, none o' that. Number two, fightin' and other disorder. This angers the officers above all else. If someone provokes you or slanders your name, you come see me and I'll take care of it. And trust me, I will. Otherwise you will feel the sting of the rod or the lash. I myself have suffered the horrid bite of the whip, and believe me, girls, it ain't at all pleasant. Do you see this whip scar here?"

I yank down the top of my dress to show the welt Captain Blodgett's cat-o'-nine-tails had left on my back.

"Understood? Good."

I continue. "Now. The question of money. You heard what the Captain said about the auction of the living spaces. When we get to Gibraltar, the other three Crews will be making some serious money in their usual way, so we got to be thinkin' about makin' some of our own. Otherwise, if we are found penniless, we will soon find ourselves down on the lowest deck, with the rats."

That gets a common shiver from 'em, they being very familiar with those rodents from their times in the streets, in Newgate, or in the Hulks. And, yes, rats there are on the *Lorelei Lee*. Though she is a young ship, she still has a full complement of the little buggers. I have pictured them climbing aboard on the land lines when we are in port, little seabags over their shoulders, chuckling their ratty little chuckles and lookin' for good berths. Well, can't blame 'em for that, can we? That's all that any of us want. And it could be that they'll come in handy someday. They certainly have before.

"So, what I propose is that we pick up the laundry concession."

This is met with some groans.

"Look. It ain't so bad. In fact, there are some advantages—like plenty of water and soap to keep ourselves, our hair, and our linen clean. There will be plenty of work to be done in *that* regard, especially after the Lizzies, the Judies, and the Tartans have plied their trade in Gibraltar." I hold my nose on that one and get a few laughs.

"And do not mistake me, they will laugh at you for working hard in the laundry whilst they loll about all day . . ."

"Yeah," chimes in Ann Marsh. "But we'll laugh at them for a-gettin' the pox and passin' it on t' their fine fellows so's that they walks with a limp and their noses fall off!"

More laughter, and that seals the deal.

"And I think we might do well with sewing, too. Half the women on this ship are wearin' rags."

"But how do you think we'll be able to do all that?" asks Esther. "The laundry, cloth for the sewing, and all?"

"I got an in with the Assistant Purser, is how," I answer. "Now, if any of you would rather go join the whorey Crews, do it now 'cause I can't have any slackers on my Crew."

There, I have said it: *My* Crew . . . and let there be no doubt of that.

After the girls seem settled, I go topside to see just how far this Captain's pronouncement of "freedom of the ship" goes.

I poke my head up into the light at the top of the hatchway, and so far, so good. I am not stopped and thrown back below. The sailors go about their duties as always, there are officers on the quarterdeck, and work proceeds just as it does on any ship at sea.

I grab a ratline and head for the foretop, my natural place on any ship. I flip up over the edge and, *Oh, Glory! To be here is such a gift!* It is a glorious, soaring, sunlit day. The sails are well set and taut, and the *Lorelei Lee* fairly rips along. She is not my ship now, but still I can revel in this moment. I lean my back against the foremast, as I have so many times before, and let my mind wander back to London.

Ah, Jaimy . . . I do so hope that you are well and have been cleared of all the false charges laid against your good name, and I wish that with all my heart. But, alas, probably I'll never learn the outcome of that travesty of justice.

I, myself, am condemned for life to New South Wales, and it sure looks like I'm gonna end up there, short of shipwreck or an act of God. And . . . Jaimy . . . though I love you, I do not know that I can worry about you forever because the years are sure to dull the edge of my love and my fears.

Y'see, Jaimy, I'm goin' off for the rest of my life, but you have not yet been so condemned. I will always keep you up-permost in my thoughts and prayers, Jaimy, but at the same time, I'm hoping that you will find someone other than me, as I have been nothing but trouble.

Be well, love, and happy . . .

"Wot's this, then? One o' the below-decks-dollies come to visit with a poor sailor, bless 'er." My foretop reverie has been interrupted by the unwelcome arrival of two sailors on the foretop, both big and both ugly.

"Bless yerself, Mate, and leave me be."

"Hey, ain't she a nice little piece, Monk?" asks the uglier of the two.

"Got a mouth on 'er, too," says the other, the very aptly named Monk—I half expect him to start scratchin' at his armpits and begin jumpin' around chitterin'. "She's a bit dirty, but a dip in the dunkin' stool'd take care o' that. Fix 'er smart mouth, too." They hunker down next to me.

"You been taken up by any man yet?" The other bloke grins down on me. "If not, ye are now, and lucky you, as you will soon find out."

"Sod off, Jack," I say, getting to my feet and sticking my nose in the air. "Captain said we didn't have to if we didn't want to, and I don't want to. You heard what he said about forcin' us."

"Me name ain't Jack, little Miss," he growls, grabbin' me by the arm. "It's Suggs . . . Suggs, darlin', to you."

"Yer name's gonna be mud if you don't let me go, Suggs, *darling*. I got friends here." I growl with warning in my tone and shake off his hand.

"Friends? Who you got? You ain't got nothing, girl."

"You'll see . . ."

"Maybe," says this Suggs. "Let's just see you git down." He goes and stands over the lubbers' hole, crossin' his arms and thinkin' to block my exit from the foretop.

I, of course, go to the edge of the platform, leap out, grab on to the fore backstay, and scamper down, hand over hand, dress blowin' about my waist. And any sick-in-the-head bloke what gets some pleasure outta seein' my filthy drawers is welcome to the sight.

Silly sailors, to think you can confine Jacky Faber in the riggin' . . . Ha!

Swinging down to the deck, I give Suggs and Monk up above a two-fingered salute to my brow as I press on. I had thought of givin' 'em the universal single-finger obscene gesture, but thought better of it. Nay, no sense makin' any more enemies than you already have.

As I pass the quarterdeck, I see that the First Mate, Mr. Ruger, has the con . . . and he also notices me as I stride across the deck.

"The first dolly up and about," he says to those on his watch. "It must be a brave, brave girl, indeed!" Chuckles all around.

I thrust my nose in the air and proceed forward.

As I pass the forward hatch, and am hidden from the quarterdeck by the lower belly of the fore-and-aft-rigged staysail, a figure appears by my side.

It is, I am very glad to see, my dear, dear Higgins.

"Well met, Miss," he says. He carries a package under his arm.

"Well met, indeed, Higgins. It is so good to see you."

"We must keep this short. I have here your serving outfit and several changes of linen . . ."

I almost choke with joy.

". . . as well as your pennywhistle. I don't think it wise to bring out anything more, just yet."

"Yes, Higgins, you are absolutely right." I sniffle, then subside. "Now, I have assembled a group of reasonably good girls . . . We are called the Newgaters—"

"Yes, I know how factions are forming in this ship . . . the other Crews and all. I rather assumed that you would be quite busy in your usual ways."

"Good, Higgins, nobody was ever sharper than thee," I say as I take the package from him. "Now, my Crew would like to have the laundry rights."

"Indeed, Miss. I think that can be arranged."

"And I want exclusive rights. 'Course we'll have to do the sailors' clothes, but I don't want anyone from the other

137

Crews barging into the laundry thinking she's gonna dunk her dirty undies into our hot, soapy water for nothing. Nay, ladies, it'll be thruppence a bag, or live in filth."

In outfitting the *Lorelei Lee* back in Boston, I paid special attention to the laundry, knowing that there would be a lot of it on a passenger ship, and so had located it in a spacious room next to the galley. That way the water could be heated on the galley stoves in between the cooking and serving of food and, after being used, could then be tossed out the porthole, that deck being above the waterline. I had also purchased two hundred and fifty net bags—I'd not forgotten my time as chambermaid at the Lawson Peabody School for Young Girls.

"Very well, Miss, I shall facilitate that."

"You are sure you can?"

"Purser Samsock has indicated to me that he would be delighted if I would handle all the tedious everyday concerns, leaving the high-minded and complex Keeping of the Ledgers to him."

"Is he corrupt?"

"I believe that every officer on this ship is in some way corrupt," replies Higgins, with a sniff. "But not in an odious way. The Purser does enjoy his cup, but he seems a pleasant sort, content with his rum, his pipe, and his columns of figures."

I think on this and then whimper, "Can you do it this afternoon, please, Higgins? I am so filthy."

"Yes, Miss. Right after the noon meal."

"Higgins, you are so good to me," I say, and risk a quick kiss on his cheek. "Till later."

• • •

I go back down to my Crew to give 'em the good news. "Yes, ladies, this afternoon we shall wash both our clothing and ourselves! Hurrah! And now I shall go scout out our place of business to make sure it is set up proper!"

I creep down to the galley and peek in, knowin' full well what I will find, and—yep, there they are, all three of 'em . . . I figured they would be . . .

Head up, I stride into the kitchen, and seein' a pot of coffee on the stove and a handy cup hanging on a hook, I take it down and pour myself a cup.

"Here, here! Girl, you can't . . ." The cook's voice trails off upon recognizing me. And then . . . "Oh, my God, it's—"

"Hello, Cookie," I chirp, takin' a big sip of the strong brew. "And Mick and Keefe, too. My, my, it's old home week, ain't it, lads?"

The three stand there, regarding me with open mouths, which, in the case of Mick and Keefe, ain't exactly a pretty sight.

"Wh-why, it's . . . Jacky," says Cookie, the first to recover, the ladle in his hand motionless above a cauldron, one of four that sits on the stovetop, bubblin' and smellin' real good.

"Right, Cookie, your old mate from back on the *Bloodhound*. Ain't life funny sometimes?"

They look at each other fearfully, and well they should. If I informed on 'em, if I told the Captain that these three were involved in the kidnapping of the girls of the very high-toned Lawson Peabody School back in Boston, last year—and one of those girls being the granddaughter of former U.S. President John Adams—they would surely be confined and later hanged for it. That incident has gained wide notoriety, especially since Amy Trevelyne's book on the subject has been circulating freely throughout the English-speaking world.

I let them stew in their guilty juices for a bit, whilst I grab a hot biscuit from a tray and dip it into the burgoo pot, then pop it into my mouth. *Ummmm . . .*

After I have finished it off with much vigorous chewing and smacking of lips, I say to them, "Don't worry, mates. I ain't gonna peach on ye. You was pretty good t' me back on the *Bloodhound,* and I ain't one to forget past favors. Plus, I ain't the peachin' kind, just don't like it, somehow, bein' a tell-a-tale . . . and what's this?"

I feel something furry rub against my ankle.

"And speakin' o' peachin' . . . if it ain't our Jezebel herself!" I sit down on the stool and lift the cat onto my lap to stroke her back. "My! Ain't we lookin' fit and fine, Miss!" Then I ask her reprovingly, "Remember that night on the slaver, when I was hid under the stove, dressed in my black burglar's gear, and these three blokes was tromping about, and you come sniffin' at me? Yes, and you could have ruined everything, 'cept that the Black Ghost intervened just as Cookie was bendin' down to see what you was sniffin' at, and these three fools went howlin' out into the night." I rub her ears and she purrs.

"But you knew, didn't you? You knew it was me who was the Black Ghost all along, and you weren't afraid of me at all. Not like these other silly coves."

The silly coves continue to eye me, and I go on. "Nay, lads, I shan't peach on thee, but in return, you must keep my identity secret, too. I've gone right famous in certain ways, and I don't think it would be good for me to have it known yet just who I am."

Cookie, who always has been the bravest of the three, turns back to his cauldrons and chuckles. "So, Jacky, what's on now?"

"I got me a life sentence to New South Wales, mates, and I ain't at all happy about it. Got the laundry concession here, though, and you'll be warmin' up pots of water this afternoon so's me and me girls can get at it."

Mick and Keefe nod. "Aye," says Keefe. "That's why we're here. Ready to fill up the tubs. That Higgins set us on it."

Keefe, more relaxed now, laughs, then says, "Looks like we're still haulin' water for Jacky Faber."

And it looks like you two are still waisters, seamen rated ordinary rather than able.

"You could do worse, mates. Ain't I took care o' you in the past? You ain't dead, that's somethin'."

Keefe strokes his bristly chin. His long face is deeply tanned and furrowed by long years in the sun, lashed by briny spray. "It was a close thing, Jacky, in that lifeboat when you cast us adrift."

"So, what happened?"

"Well, we rigged up a sail and a rudder, and in a few weeks, we was half dead. And when all seemed lost, we was picked up by a passin' merchant—told him we was the survivors of a wrecked whaler."

"So all of you made it?"

Each face looks at the floor.

"How 'bout Sammy Nettles?" I ask, thinkin' I know the answer.

The three of them exchange covert glances, and I know.

"Don't worry about it, lads. After all, it's tradition."

I ain't a bloody-minded sort, but still, the idea of Sammy Nettles being slowly digested does not overly distress me.

"Well, I'm glad you survived, Jezebel," I say, continuing to stroke the purring feline. "But I ain't surprised. Cats got this way of disappearin' every time you might want to snatch 'em up—like they got this sixth sense, or somethin'. "

"Aye, my Jezebel took one look at the coves in that boat, sized up the situation, and climbed to the top o' the mast and stayed there till we was rescued. She knowed, she did," says Cookie, peering into the pot. "Well, 'tis time to feed the mob."

I rise, letting Jezebel slink back down to the deck.

"All right, lads, till later. Good seein' you again. We'll talk over old times later, the good old days, like."

Mick, he of the pug nose, wide mouth, and thick unruly brown hair, grins and says, "If we fills up the tubs for ye, will you do yer little dance for us again?"

He, of course, has not forgotten the striptease I did for the three of them, me wigglin' down there in the bottom of the hold of the *Bloodhound,* sheddin' clothes in exchange for clean saltwater so's we poor girls could wash ourselves and our things.

I manage a slight blush and laugh. "Nay, Mick, but it's sweet of you to ask for an encore." I reach out and rub his head. "Don't worry, ducks, there's plenty o' quim aboard this barky, and I'm sure you will all get your share. If not, come see me, and I'll fix it."

I go to the door and say, "The tubs—make 'em nice and hot, now, lads, for when I come back."

Giving them a little finger wave, I'm out the door and back to my Crew.

A bath, dear Lord, a bath, and soon . . . Oh, yes!

Chapter 18

James Fletcher, Convict
Onboard a Rotting Hulk
Thames River, London

Jacky Faber
Somewhere in this World
Or the Next

Dear Jacky,

Once again we communicate across the Void.

I do not know what has happened to you—were you imprisoned, tortured, or even hanged? I fear the latter, but I do not know, nor am I likely to find out. Though I am in deep despair, there is one thing that keeps me from willing myself to die—and that is a burning desire to someday track down Henry Flashby and Bliffil, too, and kill them, torturously slowly . . . very, very slowly. The thought sputters like a flame and I nurture it, fanning the flames of hatred and the desire for Revenge. Aye, I shall keep myself alive until I have exacted complete Vengeance on those lying bastards!

After I'm brought out of that so-called court, my hands shackled behind me, my jacket stripped of all evidence of my rank, I am shoved into a cart and taken down to the river. I am wrong in supposing that I will be taken directly to the convict ship that'll bear me away, for I am thrown instead into one of the dank, dark prison Hulks that lie in the mud next to the shore of the Thames.

My restraints are taken off, only to be snapped on again with my hands in front—I suppose so I can feed myself whatever swill they plan to give me, and to relieve myself without help, and such. A similar set of shackles are fastened around my ankles and that is connected by a chain to an eyebolt under the bench that goes around the interior of the foul cell. I suspect the rough bench will be my bed until I am taken from here—and that could be days, months, yes, even years—but I shall endure.

There are two jailers here to manage this cell, which shouldn't take much, since instead of the usual thirty or so, there's only me in here. One of the sorry pair is called Toad and the other Frog.

When being escorted to the privy, I ask the Toad, "Why am I the only one here? Am I that important a prisoner?"

"Nah, you ain't worth shit," says he, giving me a poke with his club to hurry me along the dim passageway. "You're just a bleedin' convict, like any other. Move along." The Frog leads the way.

Speaking of bleeding, both of these poor excuses for men appear to have been soundly beaten recently. There are many bruises about their faces, their lips are split and swollen, and bandages cover some wounds on their heads.

"We 'ad two or three hundred women convicts in 'ere

till yesterday, when they took 'em all off," says the Frog. "Too bad. Sure was a lot more fun than the likes o' you." Both of them leer and chuckle at that. "We're takin' on a bunch o' men today, mostly Micks, I hears."

"Where did they take them? The women, I mean."

"Dunno. Most for the transportation, I reckon. Some for the hanging."

My blood freezes in my veins. "Oh?" I manage to say. "Do you know any of their names?"

The Toad looks slyly at the Frog. "We know lots o' names. Who you got in mind?"

I take a deep breath. "Jacky Faber, sometimes known as Mary."

Another look twixt the two.

"Jacky Faber? Oh, yes, that one—real small, right? Right pretty in a scrawny sort o' way? Well, you'll be glad to know they hanged her ass at Newgate on Monday last."

A coldness comes over me. *Damn them! Damn them all to hell!*

"Fine show it was, too. I was there, front row. She wore a nice little black dress that come up over her legs when they dropped 'er. A good show all around. Cost me two pounds five, but it was worth it, watchin' 'er kick, seein' as how I knows she was the cause o' gettin' poor Toad and me t' get all beat up after we was so good as to set up a meetin' twixt 'er and 'er fancy man . . . 'Iggins 'is name was, warn't it, Toad?"

"'Twas, Froggie, and 'twarn't fair. All I said was that I was gonna take 'er t' me bed soon, and the next thing we knows is some brutes is beatin' us half to death in a dark alley, and . . . *urk!*"

In a blind rage I have slipped my wrist manacles over Toad's head, and I bring the six-inch length of chain that joins the two wrist cuffs hard against his throat and pull back with all my strength.

"Hey, stop that!" shouts the Frog, flailing at me with his club, but I keep the struggling Toad between me and him in the narrow passageway, and the Frog's club does not have much effect on me.

"If they did hang her, then I shall kill you right now. And they will hang me for that, and I will be glad!" I tighten the grip, and the Toad gurgles as he tries unsuccessfully to get his fingers under the terrible chain that is choking out his miserable life. "A few more seconds and you'll be dead!"

The Toad is beginning to sag in my grip, which I make even tighter.

Die, you miserable scum!

The Frog gives up trying to hit me and turns to pleading. "We was only foolin'! All them females was sent for Transportation to Australia! All of 'em! Let 'im go, please! He ain't much, but 'e's me brother! Please, I beg you, Sir!"

I relax my grip, and the Toad slips to the floor, gasping. I continue on my journey to the head, knowing full well that they will beat me senseless when they have recovered. But I do not care, Jacky, for now I know where you are and where you are going . . .

And it is possible that the Admiralty has actually done me a favor in sending me to the same place.

It eases my mind a bit,

Jaimy

Chapter 19

"Come on, my ladies," I say. "It's right down here . . . Duck your heads now . . . Here we are."

Where we are is in the laundry, me and my Crew. There are two steaming tubs waiting for us, and I am hardly through the door when I start stripping off what's left of my poor once-white dress.

This afternoon, after the noon meal had been served and eaten and the galley cleaned up, our laundry tubs were filled with hot water—fresh water, too, as we've got lots of it onboard, and we can refill our casks on Gibraltar before we head down the West African coast. When we run low later, the water surely will be salt.

"There, girls, are the net bags to hold your clothing, and here are the tags to label your stuff so's you can get it back. If we're gonna be washin' clothes for three hundred people, we've got to have a system, like. Here, I've got a pencil—let's get started. Can you read? Don't worry, there's no shame in it. No? Then, here . . . See, Molly, I'll draw a bunny next to your name on your tag so's you can see that it's your bundle. All right. Ann? Ah, good. Then there it is, big and bold 'Ann Marsh'. Now, Esther . . ."

And so on and so on. For those who can recognize their names, I print them on their tags. For those who can't, I draw some sort of symbol on theirs—a star, a crescent moon, a circle within a box, and so on. This will become much more complicated when we start doing washing for all the convict Crews, but I'll work it out.

Enough of that, I say to myself as that hot tub sings a siren song to me.

I doff my dress and toss it into my net bag and then drop down the drawers and shove them in, too. Then the entire bag labeled "J. M. Faber" sinks into the other tub. I am surprised when it does not let out a beastly animal moan as the filthy thing sinks.

Then I climb gratefully into the tub.

Ahhhhhhhhh . . .

The wonderful wet warmth envelops me, covering me up to my neck, and I luxuriantly lean my head back on the edge of the tub. *If you're gonna take me, Lord, take me now, please, for I am in a state of supreme bliss . . .*

After reveling in this fashion for a moment or two, I languidly take the bar of soap that someone—Higgins, I'm sure—has placed convenient to the wash basin, and run it through my hair to lather it up. Having done that, I recover enough of my sense of duty to issue some orders to those of my wondering Crew who stand about me.

"All right, all of you. Reach up under your skirts and drop your knickers. Put them in your net bag. If you've got petticoats and other linen, get 'em off and in the bag. Since you do not have a change of clothes, you'll have to wear your outer dress until your linen is dry, and then we'll reverse the process. Got it?"

I dip my head under the water and run my fingers through my hair to rinse it, and, *Oh, how I wish I had Higgins's gentle but strong fingers to do it for me with me immersed in my own little tub.* Back in Boston I had metal-workers fashion for me a small but very elegant bathtub—yellow copper with pink brass trim and cunning little feet, and just my size. It's kept in a storeroom close to my cabin, or what used to be my cabin.

Oh well, enjoy what you've got, girl, and don't moan over what you haven't.

When I resurface, I see that my girls are getting into the spirit of the thing. There is even some laughter, as bags are tossed into the other tub, and . . .

. . . and then someone is rattling at the door latch, trying to open it.

I had, of course, put my wedges under the door when we entered, to preserve our privacy and to prevent unwanted entry. I mean, Mick and Keefe are in the next space, and I had just paraded twelve females in various states of slovenly loveliness before them, so we must be careful. The door swings inward and so the wedges will do their job. I learned that lesson long ago—it would take a battering ram to open up that door.

There is a loud rapping and a man's voice says, "Open this door!"

"Go away!" I shout back. "There are ladies here! If it's you, Mick, you'd better behave!"

"This is Mr. Ruger, the First Mate. Open this god-damned door! Now! Or I'll have you whipped!" There are some gasps of alarm from my Crew standing fearfully around me.

I wiggle myself around in the tub so as to face the door, cross my arms over my chest, and nod to Mary Wade. "Let him in."

Mary crosses to the door and pulls out the wedges and flips up the latch. The door swings open to reveal the First Mate standing with his own arms crossed on his chest. He is a man of about thirty-five, with dark hair flecked with a few strands of gray and tied back with a black ribbon. He's wearing a black uniform—a jacket with gold trim and buttons, a heavy leather belt, and black trousers. In addition to that, he wears an expression of extreme arrogance, and though he is a good-looking man, I take an instant dislike to him.

I sink down such that only my head, shoulders, and knees poke out of the water, which is now somewhat cloudy with soap, and fasten my gaze upon the intruder. He walks in and stands over me.

"What is your name, girl?"

"Mary Faber," I say, suppressing the "Sir" the military part of me wants to add.

"Is this normally part of the laundry concession?"

"It is when I'm runnin' it," I say. "Which I am."

"Watch your mouth, convict, and stand up," he orders.

What?

"I am the First Officer on this ship and I am ordering you to stand up. If you do not do it, I will have you dragged out of there and taken, in your current state of undress, to the deck and there to be caned."

Fine. I stand up.

As I rise, I place my hands over my sex, as if from shyness, but really so I can cover the blue tattoo on my right hip with the inside of my right forearm.

He grasps his hands behind and walks slowly around my dripping self. He makes some appreciative murmurs, but apparently this is not enough to satisfy him.

"Put your hands down. Uncover yourself."

I stick my chin in the air. "You will not grant me even token modesty?" I burn him with my best Lawson Peabody Look, but seemingly to little effect.

"You are a convict on a convict ship bound for a convict colony. You have very few rights. Drop your hands, or else feel the lash on those buttocks."

I do it, sliding my hands to my hips, where I leave them. The right one continues to cover my tattoo. I'm hopin' this will satisfy him and he'll leave.

It does not.

His hand snakes out and grabs my right wrist and pulls it away from my side.

"Ha. I thought so. Jacky Faber herself," he says with great satisfaction. "When I saw your name on the manifest, I knew it must be you. You see, I read the papers, and I read books, too, even silly penny-dreadfuls sometimes. It will please me greatly to be featured in the next one, in a very amorous context."

Now that I am completely exposed, he drops my arm and takes another leisurely turn about me, chuckling to himself.

"Very nice. Very nice, indeed. It appears the books did not lie," he says with some relish. "You shall be with me, Jacky Faber. You will find it to your benefit."

"I think not."

"I think so. You may report to my cabin."

"The Captain says we cannot be forced, and I hear he is

an honorable man. I assume his order goes for the officers as well as for the seamen."

"We shall see." He lifts his hand toward my breast.

"Do not touch me, Sir, as I have not given permission. Would you disobey your Captain?"

He slowly lowers his hand. "You will change your mind, girl. This will be a long voyage and I am a patient man. I can wait to get what I want."

With that, he turns on his heel and leaves the washroom.

Brows knitted in a deep frown, I sink back into the water, fuming.

"Coo," breathes Esther Abrahams, blond curls about her face, eyes bright with curiousity. "Just who are you, Mary?"

Good question, Esther . . .

Then I pop out of the tub, dry myself, get into clean drawers . . . *ahhhhh* . . . and the rest of my serving-girl rig— black skirt that comes only to my knees, loose white shirt with low bodice, and black weskit laced up tight about my waist and lower ribs. Though it is not anywhere near the finest of my clothing, I have always liked the fit of this outfit. Back in harness, girl, yes, and ready for what comes.

Afterwards, I leave the laundry under the supervision of Maggie Wood, who has become my second-in-command, to go looking for Higgins. I figure it can't hurt, now that my cover has been blown out of the water.

I find him emerging from Laughton's cabin, bearing a tray that holds the remains of the Captain's breakfast. I catch his eye and nod toward the passageway that leads down to the cabins. He nods in response and passes the tray to a waiting ship's boy.

"To the galley, Quist, and pass the word that the Captain will want a table set up on the main hatch to watch tomorrow afternoon's festivities."

The boy scurries off as we go down. Higgins opens a door and we go in. I discover that it is his own cabin, and it is one of the better ones. Trust Higgins to always better his state—bed, dresser, dry sink, porthole, and room to turn around.

"Pretty plush, compared to what I've been livin' in, Higgins." I sniff, with a big pout on my face, suddenly self-pitying and totally ungracious. Then I spy my seabag next to the bulkhead and dissolve into tears. *This had been my ship and that was my seabag and now it's not. I'm sorry, Higgins, I know you do your best for me, and I know I do not deserve it, and I'm sorry, I'm sorry . . .*

He places a hand on each of my shaking shoulders and holds them to calm me. I burrow my face into his chest, sobbing.

"I know you have had a hard time of it, Miss, and I, too, am sorry for that. But you must agree we have found ourselves in much more serious circumstances before." He takes his right hand from my shoulder and places it on my back, gently patting it.

"I know, Higgins"—I snuffle, running the back of my hand under my suddenly running nose—"that I'm actin' like a baby. I'll stop now. And we've got to talk." He releases me and I step back.

He waits, expectant.

"My cover is blown away, burned to the waterline . . ." And I relate to him the incident in the laundry with Ruger.

". . . and he beheld me in my natural state, tattoo and all, so all will now know of my past," I conclude.

"Hmmm . . ." Higgins considers this development. "Well, I was already quite sure your identity would eventually become known, so it's possible that no harm will come of this."

"I don't want him on me, Higgins," I say with a shiver.

"Well, the Captain's order still stands, and I think Mr. Ruger will have to obey it."

Higgins ponders all this some more, and after a while, he says, "Indeed, it could be to your advantage that you come to be known as more than just a common convict. Your notoriety might lend you some protection. I've noticed that Captain Laughton is not a man who worries himself overmuch about ordinary concerns."

"How so, Higgins?"

"Well, for one thing, he has directed that I set up a table for him and his officers for the viewing of the holiday-routine festivities on Saturday afternoon, and that the table is to be laden with the best of our wine stores and other viands . . ."

Grrrrr . . .

"Let it go, Miss. It is only ship's stores, and not worthy of your concern."

"Yes, but it once was mine to parcel out."

"Miss, please . . ."

"All right, I'll be good. What else?"

A slight pause, then a quick clearing of the Higgins throat. "Ahem. The Captain has commissioned me to pick two of the more toothsome beauties from the Crews, as I believe they are now called, to be his . . . companions . . . this afternoon . . . and probably this evening, too."

I laugh. "Poor Higgins, you may now add *pimp* to your list of butlery skills."

Finding that not overly funny, he frowns, and I give him

a poke. "Come on, Higgins, I'll prolly be doin' the same thing myself and real soon," say I, thinking of the hapless Mick and Keefe who couldn't find a decent girl if they were thrown into the same sack with one, as well as the futures of members of my own Crew. After all, we're all being sent down as breeders, so if I can make the pairings kind and pleasant, instead of mean and nasty, then I will bend my best efforts in that regard.

I pop over to sit on the bed and give a bounce or two, then ask, "The man the Captain called the Shantyman. Who is he?"

Higgins goes to the dresser and picks up a brush, and then comes back to stand over me.

"Tsk," he says, applying the brush to my now dry but very unruly thatch. "What am I expected to do with this?"

"What you can, Higgins, and it is so good to feel your hands on my hair again. I cannot tell you just how good." I close my eyes and revel in his touch, forgetting all other troubles.

After a few minutes of vigorous brushing, he begins the tale. "As for the Shantyman, his name is Enoch Lightner, and he was Captain Laughton's Sailing Master when both were in the Royal Navy. At the 1804 Battle of the Nile, they stood side by side on the quarterdeck of the frigate HMS *Falconer*, and during that furious engagement with Napoleon's fleet, Mr. Lightner was struck across the face with a burning blast of powder that blinded him in both eyes forever."

"That is very sad," I said. "But it does happen. What is he doing here now?"

"The Captain and Mr. Lightner were particular friends and, unwilling to see his friend rot away his life in some dismal room, trying to subsist on a meager pension, Captain Augustus Laughton left the Royal Navy and signed on with the East India Company, so that he would be able to bring his former Sailing Master along on his voyages, as a shanty-man, leading the musical chants that help the seamen do their jobs. You already know he has a very powerful voice."

"Very commendable of the Captain. But it must have been pure torture for the poor man, once having been a Sailing Master, to feel the wind on his face and to hear the rustling of the slack sails and not to be able to issue orders for the setting of those sails. I know it would kill me."

"Yes, Miss, but when you consider the alternative—a cold and quiet room for the rest of your days, with no joy, no good company, nothing . . . And unlike the old, retired sea captain of yore, not even the comfort of sitting with spyglass and looking out over the harbor to gaze upon the shipping therein . . ."

"Yes, I suppose, still . . ."

". . . and the man is quite a skilled musician, as you will very shortly see. He plays a variety of musical instruments, and he does not confine himself to sailors' songs. He generally takes his dinners with the Captain and is good company. He does not dwell on his infirmity."

"I shall have to get near him."

"Well, knowing you as I do, I don't think that could be avoided. I also think it wouldn't be a bad idea."

I nod and look over at my seabag.

"Could I have my toothbrush, Higgins? I fear my tusks have grown quite green and mossy. I can conceal it in my vest."

"Of course, Miss," he says, putting my bag on the dresser

top and opening it. He pulls out my toothbrush and hands it to me. "But I think you ought not to take anything else. Not just yet."

Again I nod in agreement, thinking how naked I feel without my shiv tucked in my vest.

"But it is good to see you presentable again, Miss."

I run my hands over my weskit, smoothing it down.

"You cannot know how good it feels to be clean again, Higgins, and to feel your kind touch." I sigh. "But I must be going. There is much to do. Can you have one of the men bring the bolts of white and black cloth down to the laundry? Good. And many needles and much thread. Scissors, too. I must get my girls out of their rags. Till later, then, and thanks for everything . . . Oh, and one more thing—if you could, have the Lady Gay handy during tomorrow's singing and dancing."

As we exit Higgins's cabin, I'm startled to see Captain Laughton standing at the long mess table, talking to First Mate Ruger. Upon seeing us emerge, the Captain breaks into a wide grin, while the First Mate dons a deep scowl.

"Ha!" barks the Captain. "I thought I heard the lovely tinkle of female laughter from in there, you dog! Doing a bit of early scouting of our tender cargo, eh, Higgins? Good man! Carry on!"

I quell my impulse to drop into a low curtsy and instead put on the scared big-eyed waif look and scurry away like any scullery maid who suddenly finds herself in the fearful presence of the high and mighty.

I feel Ruger's eyes burning into my back as I scurry, and I know one thing . . .

He ain't fooled.

Chapter 20

James Fletcher, Convict
Onboard the Ship Cerberus
London

Jacky Faber
Figment of My Fevered Imagination

Dear Jacky,

I have learned from a far-from-reliable source that instead of your being hanged, you have been taken for Transportation to New South Wales. I do not know whether or not this is true, but I choose to believe that you are still alive and will continue these spiritual correspondences.

Not only were the Frog and the Toad wrong in thinking that we should soon be joined by other prisoners, but they were also deprived of the satisfaction of soundly beating me in return for almost strangling the Toad. For as soon as we returned from the head, new guards appeared, and I was immediately taken off the Hulk and thrown into a cart with several others. The Amphibian Brothers were noticeably chagrined at being denied the opportunity to bloody me up some. As I was being hustled away, I wished them the worst possible fortune and expressed my fervent hope that they both would rot in hell very soon.

After a short ride through the seedier parts of the city—yes, I know, your "beloved old turf"—we arrived at the side of a fat merchant ship and we shuffled onboard, hands manacled, fetters on our feet.

"Name?" asked the dusty little man at the table at the head of the brow when it was my turn to stand before him.

"James Fletcher."

The man scratches my name into his ledger and smiles. "Ah, yes, our defrocked Royal Navy Lieutenant. We have heard of you. Welcome to the *Cerberus*. Behave yourself and you might live to see New South Wales."

I look out over the harbor and say nothing.

"Bo'sun, take him down to the maximum security cell and shackle him tightly. This man is not to be trusted."

Well, it's nice to get some sort of respect, anyway. The Bo'sun shoves his club into my back and says, "Git along, you."

I start toward the hatch leading down, but a man sidles up next to me—a scruffy little man who says, "Come down a bit, 'ave ye, Sor? Ain't likely to be bindin' up some poor cove t' the grating for a proper whippin' now are ye, Sor? Nay, ye ain't, and ye ain't likely t' be, since I'm the bloke what works the maximum security cell, and ye ain't—"

"Enough of that," says a man on the quarterdeck. I look up to see a man dressed as a Mate, or whatever they call the so-called officers on these scows. "No need for that. Just take him down, Weisling."

I survey the deck and call up to him, "No guns, Sir? How can you hope to defend yourself from pirates?"

"We will have an escort—a British Navy sloop of war."

Hmmm, I say to myself. *At least some protection there . . .* And then—

"James! James Fletcher!"

The call comes from the dock and I look to the Officer. He says, "Let him answer."

I am allowed to go to the rail. I look over to see that a coach has pulled up, and two men are standing beside it, gazing upward.

"James! Brother! Know that all legal efforts are being bent to overturn this miscarriage of justice!" shouts one, and "We shall not rest!" echoes the other.

"Thank you, Brother . . . Father," I say. The door to the carriage opens, and a woman gets out. I say one more word, but not to her.

"Jacky?"

"She has been sentenced to Life in New South Wales, and has already been taken off," says my father.

"Thank you, Father," I manage to reply. "That has removed a great weight from my mind."

The woman points a finger up at me and shouts, "If you had never laid eyes on that wretched girl, you wouldn't be having this awful trouble."

Yes, Mother, but I did . . .

I turn from the rail and say to the Bo'sun, "Take me to my berth, if you please." The brute grins and prods me along.

Before I go below, I ask of the Officer who had shown me some small degree of kindness, "Your name, Sir?"

"I am Mr. Hollister, Second Mate," he says. "Take him below."

He turns away and I am shoved toward a hatchway, where I duck, to enter the gloom of the hold. I climb down a ladder, go through a heavy door, and enter a cell. The room is roughly square, about twenty feet across, with a wide shelf running along the three sides away from the door. Attached to the bulkhead above that shelf are rows of dangling neck manacles, eighteen inches apart. The deck below is an open wood grating, and I hear men shuffling about below, their chains rattling. It does not take too much wit to surmise that this ship was once a slaver . . . and, in a way, it still is.

I notice that three long lengths of chain run along the deck in front of each shelf. I am put on the shelf and the neck manacle is put around my neck by the Bo'sun, snapped shut, and then locked. My ankle shackles are then attached and locked to the long chain at my feet. A few more cackling giggles from Weisling . . . *"Aye, and I heard yer little lady 'as been shipped off, too. My, my, I expects she's bein' rogered right now by two, maybe three, good honest jailers just like me . . . Now ain't that a fine thought, guv'nor? That little bitch finally gettin' what's comin' to her? Ah, yes, just think on it, guv'nor, just think . . ."*

Yes, Jacky, I recognized him right off as that low-life steward from the *Wolverine,* the one you named the Weasel and so forcefully put in his place. Then the outer door is slammed shut, and I am left alone to try to soothe my seething mind.

Oh, yes, Weasel, I will think, but what I will think on is just how much pleasure I will get from choking the miserable life out of you when it comes to that . . . And believe me, you little turd, it will come to that.

Enough. I lean my back against the wall and try to think as you would have thought, dear one, if you were the one incarcerated here. After all, you did escape from the brig on the *Wolverine,* and under my very nose, too. Could I hope to be as clever as you in this circumstance? I look about and try to think as you would. All right, then.

Item one: The long chains mean that we will sometimes have the neck manacles off and will be shuffled along with only the wrist and ankle shackles to restrain us—the line to the head, food lines, exercise times, up topside for some fresh air. After all, they don't want us to die, because they will be getting a head price for each of us delivered alive to the penal colony.

Item two: That idiot Weasel proudly carries the keys to our chains on his belt, thinking it enhances his status. Good. Let him think that.

Item three: That Mr. Hollister, the Second Mate of this bark, showed a modicum of kindness to me back there on the deck. Duly noted.

Item four: It seems that—

My thoughts are interrupted when I hear a great commotion outside, and the outer door swings in. The Bo'sun and two other hard-looking types muscle in a group of bound prisoners, men who are putting up a mighty howl.

"Go straight to hell, English scum! A curse on all of yiz, ye cowardly dogs! Aye, you and your whore of a mither, too! You may bind our hands but ye kin no bind our spirits, British pigs! Ye kin no hang us all!"

The men are clubbed as they are pushed in and manacled, but that does not diminish their voices in the least. They curse and damn their captors to the nether regions of hell and beyond. They seem oddly familiar to me . . . Then I spot a particular one in their midst, and all becomes clear.

That lad is Ian McConnaughey, and the other newly arrived Irishmen are former members of the crew of your late privateer *Emerald*.

What the hell . . . ?

Dearest Jacky, though I am suffering Durance Vile, I fear that you are suffering worse, and I cannot bear the thought. I can take the pain upon my own person, but I fear that the pain and anguish you are suffering is far, far more severe . . .

Jaimy

Chapter 21

Hooray, it's Saturday, which means holiday routine, and all are excited, especially me. *Wheee!*

I know, I know, Jaimy. What right have I to laugh and cavort about when I am condemned to life imprisonment in a far distant land? How could I possibly feel any joy, momentary though it might be, when I have no idea of the trouble you are going through? I know, I know, but it is my nature to be cheerful. And I realize, too, that if I curl up in a tight ball of misery, self-pity, and woeful silence, I will never get out of this mess, which means that I would never, ever see you again . . .

The Captain's table is being set up, and there will be singing and dancing after the noon meal, with an extra tot of rum for all, 'cept for the Under Sixteens—and except for me, too, because I have taken a vow to partake of spirits never again, Demon Rum having once almost been the ruin of me. But I start to think about getting into my wine stores, yes, I do, and I know where they are. The thought of a nice Bordeaux makes the spit well up in my mouth and . . . *Enough of that, you . . .*

• • •

Yesterday, my Newgate girls and I had been in a positive fury of sewing, getting us ready. After much discussion we decided the easiest, and quickest, way to dress ourselves appropriately would be to copy the serving-girl outfit that I'd worn at the Lawson Peabody School. The black skirts with matching vests and white blouses are easy to cut and to sew, and the tight barmaid/milkmaid costume shows that we know our place—no fancy Empire dresses here—and it sets us off from the other Crews, who tend more to the flouncy-bouncy sort of thing.

Another advantage of our new outfits is that the short skirts, which come only to the knee, are excellent for getting about the ship . . . and for giving a bit of a petticoat flash when that sort of thing seems called for. I'll not be pimping out my girls, but we are being taken to Australia as breeders, and I'll want them to make the best matches possible.

It is late June and the air is warm, so we won't need undershirts. There will be new drawers all around, though, with flounces, and we'll wear white mob caps with trimming of black thread to match the skirts.

It is a veritable orgy of cutting, tucking, and fitting. Mary Wade, being a former street urchin, is, of course, useless, so we use her as dressmaker's dummy. Esther, having been a milliner's apprentice, is expert in sewing. Molly and Ann and the rest bring what skills they have to the job.

While we were busy with the dressmaking task, I insisted on baths all around, but they didn't take much forcing on that. We finished and proudly pronounced ourselves ready for public viewing.

. . .

After the ship's crew, as well as the various ladies' Crews, have been given their food and drink, Captain Laughton comes out onto the deck, resplendent in a fine uniform of blue trimmed with white turnouts. He bows grandly to the cheers of his crew and sits himself down. Close by his left knee, a Judy of the Liverpool Crew places her bottom on the deck and leans her face against his knee. On his other side, a Lizzie, one of Elizabeth Barnsley's bunch, assumes a similar position. There are assorted Tartans about the table, as well, attending the Messrs. Seabrook, Gibson, and Hinckley. Apparently Higgins has done his job of procuring—or, rather, providing—appropriate company . . . It's all in how one says it, ain't it?

The army man, Major Johnston, is seated there as well, splendid in scarlet, with a pleasant look upon his face, although he does not appear to have an escort—at least not yet. He lets his eyes roam over the horde of females who come upon the deck. Then, when I bring my girls up into the light and array them along the left of the fore hatch, which will become the stage, I note that his eye has stopped its roving and has fixed upon Esther Abrahams, whose eyes are demurely cast down, easily radiant in her natural beauty. *Hmmmm . . .*

Higgins is there with his assistants, who put much wine about in front of the officers. G*rrrr . . . all of my best . . . Oh, God, there's that Madeira I picked up in . . . never mind . . . but grrr all the same.*

Oh, well, spirits are high and that's the way I like 'em. Higgins catches my eye and looks down at the fiddlecase next to the quarterdeck stairs. I nod.

After settling himself and getting some of my fine cheeses and truffles down his neck, the Captain calls out, "Shantyman! A song, if you please!"

The Shantyman advances to the foremast, head up, his stick before him. He has been onboard several days now and does not appear to need the arm of a guiding seaman. His stick raps against the foot of the foremast and he turns to face the drum that he knows will have been set there in front of him. He puts his hands on the drumhead and takes up the mallets he finds there and begins to pound out the basic rhythm.

One, two, three, and boom . . . boom . . .

I pull out my pennywhistle and get ready myself.

His voice rings out . . .

From Liverpool to Glasgow a-rovin' I went
To stay in that country it was my intent,
But girls and strong whiskey, like other damned fools,
I soon was transported back to Liverpool.

A great joyous cry goes up from Mrs. Berry's Liverpudlians arrayed to the starboard side—those of them who were not already by the side of some amorous seaman, that is—and all swing into the chorus . . .

So it's row, row Bullies, row!
Them Liverpool Judies have got us in tow!

This was the self-same song that I sang on the tabletop at Dovecote Hall that night after the triumph of the Sheik winning the race at the Downs, when we had this glorious ball and I was so completely happy and Clarissa Worthington Howe plied me with sweet Kentucky bourbon and I loved it and I loved her so much and then I disgraced myself before all and sundry with my drunken display and had to leave that lovely place under a cloud of shame.

Shaking those sorry thoughts out of my mind, I place pennywhistle to lips and play along with the very familiar melody.

The Shantyman, upon hearing the notes from my whistle, inclines his head toward me, the source of the new sound, smiles slightly, and then goes to the next verse.

> *I shipped on the Alaska well out in the bay,*
> *Waitin' for a fair wind to get under way.*
> *The sailors all drunk, and their backs is all sore,*
> *The whiskey's all done and we can't get no more!*

Groans from the crowd on the thought of no more whiskey, and the chorus is sung again, and it strikes me that many of the men on this ship have sailed with the Shantyman before and have formed a choir of sorts behind him and bellow out the well-known words with great gusto. The Crews pick up on the chorus, too, and, having some three hundred voices, untrained or not, singing in unison is something wonderful to hear.

The Shantyman swings in again, the *boom . . . boom . . . boom . . .* of his drum never wavering.

> *Now here comes our First Mate with his*
> *jacket of blue,*

A-looking for work for us poor sailors to do.
It's "Jig tops to halyards" he loudly does roar,
"So lay aloft, Paddy, you son-of-a-whore!"

That last line gets a roar of approval from many members of the Crews, and *"Yer all sons o' whores, you sailor scum!"* is heard shouted out, to laughter, from some lusty female throat. The Shantyman turns to my general direction and says, "So give us the last verse if you know it!"

Oh, I know it, all right, and I sing it out.

And now we've arrived at the Bramleymore dock.
All the fair maids and lassies around us do flock.
Our whiskey's all gone and our six-pound advance,
And I think it's high time for to get up and dance!

And at that I let my feet loose and, keeping up the tune on my pennywhistle, I dance all the way through the last chorus, ending on the *boom* of the drum.

There is great applause, and I take some of it for mine, and it warms me. Taking a deep breath, I then swing into "The Sheffield Hornpipe," and my bare dancing feet are joined by heavily booted others. The Shantyman motions to his man, and a fiddle and bow are put into his hands and he catches up the tune and then the dancing starts for real. And when it comes to dancing, I show 'em how it's done.

That double tot at noon along with that hearty dinner has certainly loosened up throats for song and given wings to dancing feet.

"Oh, capital! Just capital!" exults the Captain, rising to

his feet and dumping a miffed Lizzie to the deck. "More! More!"

The Shantyman puts bow to fiddle again and rips into "When You Are Sick Is It Tea That You Want?" with my tootling right along, playing a counter melody to his straight melody line. After a bit of that tune, he slips into "Dunphy's Hornpipe" and I do, too. He grins again, and I think he is testing me to see if I can follow along. Of course I can, and at high speed, too.

We end that with a flourish, and there is a great roar of appreciation for the now quite exhausted dancers and for the Shantyman . . . and me.

"*More! More!*" cries the Captain . . . *More music, more dancing, more rum, more everything!*

I bounce off the stage and dash over to the quarterdeck, where I flip up the lid of the fiddle case, and—*Oh, it is so good to see you yet again!*—pick up the Lady Gay and her bow and hurry back to the stage.

Mounting it, I begin playing opening notes of "The Leaving of Liverpool." It is a somewhat slower song, and it will give the dancers a bit of a break. Hey, if anyone knows how to run a set, it's Jacky Faber, by God. "Do you know it, Sir?" I ask the singer of songs who towers over me.

He does. He lays aside his drum mallets, throws back his great head, and applies his deep baritone to the song.

> *So fare thee well, my own true love,*
> *When I return, united we will be.*
> *It's not the leavin' of Liverpool that grieves me, love,*
> *But my darling when I think of thee.*

It is a lovely tune, telling of a poor sailor leaving his own true love far behind as he embarks upon a long ocean voyage. It's a song I have often sung to myself when Jaimy and I were forced to part yet one more time.

As I'm playing and the Shantyman is singing, I notice that the young Army major has risen from the Captain's table and has gone over to stand in front of Esther Abrahams. He extends his hand, and she, blushing, takes it and lets herself be led to the dance floor.

Hmmm . . .

He leads her in a stately dance—rather like the minuets I saw being danced at Dovecote. They look good together, and Esther positively glows. A concluding verse from the Shantyman.

> *The sun is on the harbor, love,*
> *And I wish I could remain,*
> *For I know it will be some long, long time,*
> *Before I see you again.*

The song is over, and while the Shantyman steps down to refresh himself at the Captain's table, I keep the fiddle going for the sake of the two dancers. I play a song taught to me at Dovecote years ago by Amy Trevelyne, and I sing it, too.

> *Drink to me only with thine eyes*
> *And I will pledge with mine.*
> *Or leave a kiss within the cup*
> *And I'll not ask for wine.*

They are a bit closer now . . . Another verse . . .

The thirst that from the soul doth rise
Doth ask a drink divine;
But might I of Jove's nectar sip,
I would not change for thine.

Closer yet. I figure I'll end this little set with "Those Endearing Young Charms," just violin, no voice.

Letting the last note trail off plaintively, I see that Major Johnston has released Esther's hand and is bowing to her. It is plain he has asked her something. She hesitates, then smiles and shakes her head, and goes back to her place with my Newgaters.

Good girl . . . Never pays to be too easy . . . Let him suffer a bit.

I'm about to play something else when I hear the Captain call, "You, girl, come up here!"

I put aside the Lady Gay to bask for the briefest moment in the applause from the crowd, and I give them a deep curtsy in return. Then I go to stand before the Captain's table. I put on the modest schoolgirl look, hands clasped behind me, my eyes cast down.

"That was well done, girl," says the Captain. "Do you play any other instruments?"

"The Spanish guitar, Sir, if it so please you."

"Hmm. Higgins, do we have such a thing aboard?"

"Yes, Sir," replies Higgins, standing by. "I believe there is one in your cabin."

"Ah, that thing leaning against the wall? Good," says

Captain Laughton with satisfaction, taking another slug of his wine. "Then you shall entertain us tonight in my cabin, if you will."

"Yes, Sir, I will."

Oh, yes, I will, indeed . . .

Chapter 22

I will not cry, I will not cry, I will not cry. I keep repeating this to myself as I rap lightly on the Captain's door, fiddle case under my arm. But my tears are in danger of streaming at any moment as I am escorted in by Higgins, and I gaze about *my* cabin. There's my cozy bed and lovely curtains, my guitar, my table, which is set for eight of whom I will *not* be one . . . and my bold pirate flag with its wicked, grinning skull draped on the wall. *Ain't feeling very bold and wicked now, are we, girl?* No, just suddenly sad at the utter loss of all that I hold so dear—Jaimy, my beautiful ship, my shipping company, everything . . .

Higgins senses my distress and quietly says, "Look at it this way, Miss. It's been less than a week aboard, and already you've wormed your way back into your cabin. Amazing work, even for you, I must say," and he gives me a "Chin up" look.

I sniffle and nod, thrust up the chin, and go to take my guitar from her cradle on top of the chest. Then I jump up and place my bottom on that same chest. I figure I'll be out of the way here, as befits my status as convict-musician.

When I had found the guitar that time we raided the outlaw and river pirate nest called Cave-in-Rock on the Ohio River, I had named her Rosalita because of her Spanish heritage and because of her warm, rosy hue. As I tune her up, I think fondly of Solomon Freeman, the runaway slave we'd pulled out of the Mississippi River. It was he who taught me how to coax melodies out of Rosalita, and I wonder how he is faring now, back in Boston. Pretty well, I suspect, knowing him and his talents. Ah well, that was then and this is now.

As I am figuring out my set for the evening, the door opens and the Captain, along with his guests for the evening, pour into the room. I pop to my feet and assume a low curtsy.

"Seats! Seats, everyone!" cries Captain Laughton. "Stand not on ceremony! Here's our good Higgins with the wine! And I see we are to have sweet music, too! Be seated all!"

There is the Second Mate, Mr. Seabrook, with a Tartan, whom I recognize as Betsey Leicester, on his arm, and there is the Purser, Mr. Samsock, with a girl I don't yet know, and there is the First Mate, Mr. Ruger. He does not miss my presence, putting his eye on me right away. I do not meet his gaze. The Surgeon Supervisor, Dr. Thompson, an open, jolly sort, whom I have not seen since our first day aboard when we were checked for lice and other afflictions, is also in attendance.

There are other girls, as well, including two for the Captain, who seems to like to take his pleasure in multiples—one I recognize as Sarah Acton and the other as Mary Mullenden, both Lizzies. Then, through the door comes Major Johnston, splendid in scarlet, who escorts Esther Abrahams into the cabin, to gasps of admiration.

Yes, the beautiful Esther Abrahams. Earlier, when my girls were getting me ready for my big debut in the Captain's cabin—brushing me up and dusting me off—I learned from Esther that, though she had refused the offer of jumping right then into the handsome Army officer's bed, she had not turned down his offer of a fine dinner in the Captain's cabin that very evening. *Smart girl*, I thought. *Why give up a perfectly good dinner?* I certainly wouldn't.

I had sent Mary Wade to find Higgins, to ask that I be given my black mantilla for tonight's performance and that Esther be allowed to wear my blue dress—the one I had sewn myself onboard the *Dolphin*. At the time, I had patterned it after a dress I had seen on a certain Mrs. Roundtree, a practitioner of a very old trade on the island of Malta. Being an impressionable thirteen-year-old at the time, it seemed like just the thing and I was right. It has served me very well whenever I felt that I needed to catch the roving male eye. Let Esther wear it now and see what happens with a certain red-coated major.

Since there are only eight places around the table, the girls are set on low stools, each to the side of her male host. Esther, however, is not so lowly placed, but is seated instead at the table, to the right of Major Johnston, and I notice a few covert glares of resentment from some of the working girls. *Suck it up, ladies*, I think with a certain maternal satisfaction. *Class tells.*

Lastly, Enoch Lightner, the Shantyman, enters, head high and regal, and without guidance. He apparently knows his way around this room now, for he makes his way to the foot of the table, touches the back of his chair to orient himself, and waits while Higgins pulls it out for him. Thanking

Higgins, he sits. His hand goes across the tabletop and locates his glass. I will find that on succeeding nights, that will always be his place.

As the glasses tinkle and food is served, I gather the mantilla about my face and quietly begin playing "Plaisir d'Amour," a French song that was supposed to be a favorite of the unfortunate Marie Antoinette, Queen of France. No words, just music, in a rippling-fingered style, and I am content in being only a good dinner musician, unobtrusive, in the background. I'm merely providing some gentle sounds to the general merriment and conversation, just as I had done back at the House of the Rising Sun in New Orleans. Thinking of that place, I do a bit of "The Young Girl Cut Down in Her Prime," and it seems to go over well, as I hear no complaints.

Things grow garrulous. "Do you have what you desire, Mary Mullenden?" roars Captain Laughton.

"Everything 'cept you, Captain," counters the resourceful Miss Mullenden.

I perceive that Higgins has been very judicious in his choosing of doxies for the cabin.

"Have you noticed, Captain, that half of our cargo is named Mary?" asks Mr. Seabrook.

"True, too true," retorts the Captain. "Go out at noon and yell out 'Mary,' and many heads will turn! Mighty ironic, I must say, considering the original Mary was a Virgin! Har-har!"

The Captain's witticism is roundly appreciated, and more toasts are proposed and drunk, and as the laughter increases, I turn to doing "Greensleeves" and then the "Willow Garden," which is one of the first tunes Liam Delaney taught me on the pennywhistle back on the *Dolphin*. As I am playing these numbers, I notice that First Mate Ruger's eyes do not leave me, and I do not like it. I shiver, as I have seen that look before and it never bodes me any good.

The good Captain gestures to Higgins, then nods at me, and a plate is brought over and placed next to me, and, "Thank you, Captain . . . Higgins . . . Oh, that is so good."

Licking the grease from my fingers, I launch into a Spanish piece, "Solo Tu." I am well into it when I hear the Shantyman call out, "Girl. That is very nice. What is the name of it?"

"'Solo Tu,' Señor . . . er . . . Sir," I say, momentarily forgetting where I am. "It means 'Only You.' It is a Spanish love song." I continue playing the melody.

"Are there words?"

"Yes, Sir."

"Then, sing them."

"Yes, Sir."

I continue fingering the chords till the melody comes around again and then . . .

> *Tú, so-lo tú*
> *Has llenado de luto mi vida*
> *Abriendo una herida*
> *En mi corazón*

There are several other verses, and I sing them as best I can. At the end, I draw a bit of applause from the table.

"Where did you learn that?" asks Enoch Lightner.

"In Havana, Sir. Last year. I performed it at Ric's Café Americano."

"Capital place, Havana!" exults the Captain. "We were there in '92. Remember, Enoch? Before this stupid war."

"Well I do, Sir."

"Prettiest whores in the universe, eh, what, Brother?"

"They were that, Brother," replies the Shantyman. He then adds graciously, "Present company excepted, of course." This is met with titters of appreciation from the ladies of the cabin. Then he asks me, "How many languages do you speak?"

"Aside from English, I speak French and Spanish, Sir. I have a bit of Latin, too, not much, and that's all."

At that, putting aside my guitar, I pick up the Lady Gay and lay bow to her to play "Londonderry Air" as softly as I can, for we are in a small space.

When I am done and am about to go into the next piece, the Shantyman again calls out, "Come over here, girl. Bring your fiddle."

I slide off the chest and go to his side. I feel all eyes in the place upon me.

He puts out his hand, and I place the neck of my fiddle in it. He grasps it and runs his fingers tenderly over her form. Then he extends his other hand, and I put the bow into it. He thinks for a moment and then begins to play.

It is not a melody with which I am familiar, but it is exquisitely done. I have not heard the like since Gully Mac-Farland, and I am shamed for having tried to play before him. I know greatness when I hear it.

After he stops, there is silence, and in that silence he asks, "What is her name?"

"The Lady Gay, Sir," I manage to say. "Gay is short for Gabriella, because she is Italian."

"Umm," he says, running his fingers over her form. "Yes, all the great ones are, aren't they?"

Thinking of Gully MacFarland's Lady Lenore, which had also been made by an Italian craftsman, I have to murmur in agreement.

"Is she for sale?"

"No, Sir, she is not. You have the power to take her from me, but I hope you will not do that, for she is very dear to me." I say that with a catch in my voice.

He gently places Gay and her bow on the table and says, "Come here," and he reaches out for me.

I step closer so that he can take me by the arm. Finding where I am in space, he then lifts his hand and places it on my head and then runs it down over my face, his fingers tenderly searching out the hills and valleys of my eyes and cheekbones, nose, mouth, chin, and jaw. His hand lingers on my neck and then proceeds down over my shoulders and then farther yet. I find I do not resent this exploration as he does not seek out the parts of me that males usually aim for when their hands start roaming, but rather confines himself to feeling the set of my shoulders and backbone and hips.

"You have a lot in common with your violin," he says, finally. "Taut. High-strung. Yet not lacking in curves. Have you been taken up by a man yet?"

"No, Sir. I am very young, and I'm not quite ready for that sort of thing." *Yes, Amy, I know. I hear you laughing . . .*

"What a bunch of horseshit!"

Uh-oh . . .

That sudden outburst came from Mr. Ruger, who is plainly well into his cups and can no longer contain his secret.

"Do you know just who that is?" he asks the table at large.

"She appears to be a rather small convict who is clever with musical instruments," answers the Captain, mystified.

"No, Sir. *That*"—and he points his finger at my face—"is the notorious pirate Jacky Faber, recently condemned for defrauding the King of his rightful treasure. She is extremely lucky yet to be alive and not to be swinging from some gibbet."

"*That* is a famous pirate?" says Captain Laughton, gesturing toward me. "Why, she scarce weighs seven stone. How can that be?"

I put on the woeful waif look, full bore.

"Yes, Sir," snarls Ruger. It is plain that he is not a pleasant drunk. "And I can prove it."

"What about that, my dear?" asks the Captain of me.

I look up through carefully tear-laden eyelashes. "Many false charges have been laid against my name, Sir, but please know that I would never do anything to harm you—nor this ship, nor to any upon her."

"My word," chortles the Captain, "then we must be very careful of this fearsome beast, musn't we? Oh, look at her! I am fair shaking in my boots! Har!"

Captain Laughton slams down his glass on the tabletop and covers it with his hand, so that Higgins cannot refill it, signaling an end to the evening.

He stands and roars, "Tonight to bed, and tomorrow Gibraltar, by God. And then won't all the Marys dance!"

Oh yes, we shall, Sir . . .

Chapter 23

James Fletcher, Convict
Onboard Cerberus
Dockside, London

Dearest Jacky,

I met some of your friends today, those of the Celtic persuasion, and I must say that I found most of them less than congenial.

Still struggling and protesting vigorously, they are thrown into the cell. Their feet are secured to the central chain and their necks to the bulkhead collars, just as I have been tethered. They eventually calm down.

"Wot's this, then?" demands a touseled-haired brute of his brethren, but with his gaze fixed upon me. He is tethered about three men down from me. "It looks like a bleedin' British officer, it does. And it fair turns me stomach to look on him, it does."

All eyes now turn to me.

"Go stuff yourself, mick, and sod off," I say, my eyes not leaving his. I know this will be an important confrontation, and I intend to play it to the hilt.

"Can ye reach him, Sean O'Farrell, and give him a few good ones for me and for Ireland?"

The man tethered next to me says he intends to do just that and twists on the bench to get me in range. But I lift my own manacles and spit out, "Fine, bogtrotter, come at me, and you'll crawl back to your filthy burrow with a few less teeth!"

With that, I gather all my strength and slam my wrist cuffs into his face.

The man, O'Farrell, grunts and sits back. I may not have loosened any of his teeth, but I certainly got his attention.

"How d'ye like the taste of that, potato boy?" I snarl. "Suck it up, Paddy, for I bet it tastes just like your mother's dirty teat."

"Wait a minute," says another voice, one with more reason in it than has mine. "By God, it's Mr. Fletcher."

I recognize the voice as that of Ian McConnaughey, whom I had met on several occasions in the past year at your London Home for Little Wanderers, and found a rather decent fellow—for an Irishman.

"Hello, Ian," I say, pushing off from the now bleeding O'Farrell and leaning my shoulders back against the bulkhead. "Good to see you again."

"*Mr.* Fletcher, is it, Ian?" spits out this Arthur McBride. "Just who the hell is *Mr.* fockin' Fletcher?"

"He's Lieutenant James Fletcher, Jacky's intended husband . . . or he was."

"Jacky? Our Puss-in-Boots?" McBride peers at me in the gloom and growls, "Well, cut off me balls and call me an Englishman, if you ain't right, Ian. It's him all right. And he's the sod what sunk our precious *Emerald,* ain't ye, *Sir?* Can't expect us to love ye for that, *Sir,* no, ye can't."

"Shove it up your ass, shit-for-brains," I growl. "I'd sink any ship afloat if I knew your sorry carcass was on it."

McBride chuckles but does not relent. "Because of you, I spent a year on the stinkin' *Temeraire* with the evilest Bo'sun's Mate what ever lived—swingin' his knobby at me, day and night. And you're to blame, too, for my good friend Kelly from County Kildare getting killed at Trafalgar, a fight that warn't even ours."

"I had many friends killed at that battle, as well. Do you hear me, whining bog man? Do you? Ah, but that's what the drunken Irish are best at, isn't it? Complaining about their lot and crying in their beer."

"Get him, lads!" shouts McBride, no longer chuckling.

Chains rattle and I get ready for the attack. "Come on, you low-life sonsabitches," I call out. "I've killed better men than you with one hand behind my back, and I'll make short work of you, too! Come on!"

"Wait! Leave off!" cries Ian McConnaughey. "He's all right! I know him! Let him be! Talk to him!"

The mob subsides, growling.

"How came you all here?" I ask in the ensuing surly silence.

"I came over to Waterford with Mairead, my wife, as you know," says Ian. "To gather the crew for Jacky's passenger ship the *Lorelei Lee.* She especially desired that I find as

185

many of her old *Emerald* crew as possible to staff her new ship. These"—and I am sure he gestures to the occupants of the cell, even though I cannot see it in the gloom—"are the greater part of that crew."

I had recognized McBride and others of your Irish crew, Jacky, from their brief time on the *Wolverine,* after sinking the *Emerald,* and their subsequent capture and impressment into the Royal British Navy. They chafed mightily under the British yoke, and Captain Trumbull wisely, I thought, decided to break them up and send them to other ships. He felt that they might prove more loyal to you than to him, if it came down to it, even though you were at the time confined below in the *Wolverine*'s brig . . . or so we thought.

"And what happened?" I ask.

"The night before we were to sail on the packet for London, there was a meeting of the Free Irish Brotherhood at Finnegan's on Water Street. We all went, thinking nothing of it, just a few pints and some patriotic songs is all, but the Brits stormed in and arrested us all for bein' rebels and traitors."

"And we weren't doin' nothin' like that at all!" says a young voice from the dark. "Just a few pints!"

"Right, Connolly, we warn't doin' nothin', but here we are, anyway, so put a sock in it," says McBride. "So, *Mr.* Fletcher, how come they got you here in this cell with us Irish scum, and not up in the Captain's cabin kissin' his hairy ass?"

"Because, Paddy, it is quite apparent that this is a special cell for convicts they consider especially dangerous."

"Then, why've they got a pantywaist like you in here with us real men?" Some snickers all around.

"Maybe they figure I revel in the stink of Irish feet," I say. "Or perhaps it's that they know I am a former Royal Navy officer, one who could captain this ship if it came to it."

"We could sail it, too," says another voice from the group.

"Aye, you can put up a sail and take it down, and you can steer a straight course, but can you navigate? Could you control a surly crew? Could you inspire them to follow your orders in foul and dangerous weather, or in a fight, or would you watch helplessly as things descend into anarchy and chaos?"

Mumbles and grumbles. "Aw right, for all it matters, we just elected you Captain o' the Cell, Fletcher. What is your first order, *Sir*?" mocks McBride, bringing up his manacled hands to knuckle his brow in false obeisance.

"Very well, men," I answer, ignoring McBride, and taking my election as some sort of small victory. "First we shall introduce ourselves. I am James Emerson Fletcher, late Lieutenant of the Royal Navy. You are . . ."

They hesitate, and then they call off . . .

"Ian McConnaughey, County Wexford."

"Daniel Connolly, County Clare."

"Padraic Delaney, Wexford."

Good Lord, Liam's kid!

"Sean Duggan, Waterford."

"Seamus Lynch . . ."

"Charlie Parnell . . ."

And finally . . .

"Arthur McBride, by the grace of God, County Wexford, Ireland. Damn your eyes."

"Very good, men," I say, intentionally being insufferably British. "Listen to me . . ." I lean into the circle of faces watching me and point to my ear and then to the gate and then hold that finger up to my lips . . . *They might be listening, lads, so we must be careful!*

Whispering now, I say, "If you ever again wish to see your Emerald Isle, you will do the following. Let no one know that you are all able-bodied seamen. Understood? Good. In the line for the head, and in the food line, talk to the others and find out which of them might be seamen— steady seamen, now, ones you could trust when it comes down to it. There's no head in here so they'll have to take us out for that and the chow line, too, if we're allowed to get in it. We'll have to see about that."

"What good is all this?"

"It might just be our way out of here, McBride," I snarl, wishing my hands were wrapped about his goddamned throat. "And another thing, we must act docile, such that they might let down their guard. Then maybe, in time, they might let us out into the general bunch of convicts. You don't need to act servile, no. Just be quiet and pretend that you are resigned to your lot. Got it?"

Some heads nod, but I sense that Arthur McBride's does not. "Fine, *Captain*. Let's just see where this leads."

"Where is Jacky, then?" asks Padraic Delaney.

"She, too, has been sentenced to Transportation," I reply. "She's out here with us. Somewhere."

"Ah," says Arthur McBride. "So let's go find our Jacky, so's I can have her back in my lap again where she belongs, squirmin' her little butt around in that way she does so well."

188

"Lay off, Arthur," warns Ian.

You are lucky you are out of reach, Arthur Focking McBride . . .

"Poor Puss," says Ian. "Poor little Jacky."

"You cannot imagine the depth of my anger," I say, seething.

"Oh, yes he can, Brit," replies Arthur McBride. "You see, they took his Mairead, too."

Wondering if the world has gone completely mad,
I remain,
Yours,

Jaimy

Chapter 24

It's morning and the Rock hasn't yet appeared over the horizon. It's a gloriously warm day, so to kill some time, I take a few of my braver Newgaters—Mary Wade, Molly Reiby, and Esther—up to the bowsprit for a bit of a toss in the spray. It's just like in the old days with Davy, Willy, Tink, and Jaimy, and yes, later with Mairead, too. And oh, it is so much fun! I bring these girls down because I know there will be those wild and merry dolphins all around. And sure enough, there they are, leaping about and making sport of our slow progress through the water. Slow to them, anyway. Actually, we're fairly ripping along.

Fly, Lorelei, fly . . .

"Look, Molly, there's one! No, there's five! Look how they jump! Aren't they marvelous!"

The thing of it is, there's a net spread out under the bowsprit to catch any unfortunate sailor who might slip and fall as he is tending the fore-and-aft sails way up forward, but that is not what it is for us. For us it is a safe and marvelous ride through the swells of the Atlantic as we approach the Rock of Gilbraltar, the gateway to the Mediterranean.

When a particularly large swell comes along, the *Lorelei Lee* goes bow under and we get dunked, only to come up sputtering and squealing with glee. The girls were quite fearful at first, but they got over it quickly, as they are a game bunch.

We're clad only in our undershirts and drawers, but considering what sort of ship we are on, it ain't much of a scandal. We ain't in much danger in the way of unwanted advances from the crew, since most of them seem now to have paired up with the dolly of their choice and are satisfied with their current condition. Besides, we're the youngest ones and not as full bosomed as the girls of the other Crews, and being quite buxom does seem to be the preferred shape in the way of a temporary wife. But the three ship's boys certainly seem interested in our watery antics as they lean down over the rail to peer at the four young girls frolicking about in soaked and clinging drawers.

"Stand up out of the water, Mary Wade," cries young Quist. "Let's see what you got!" His mates Denny Farley and Moe Suggins enthusiastically echo his request.

"What I got is not for you, boy, so now get on wi' all o' ye, and leave us alone," says the object of their scrutiny.

Mary Wade is certainly not another Joan Nichols, my Joannie who is back in Boston being made into a fine lady, just like I was. No. Though they both were street kids, Mary seems a lot tougher, inside and out. Joannie had a sweet self hidden beneath all that street gang roughness, but I don't know about this Mary. Course Joannie had never been condemned to die at age ten and then thrown into Newgate prison to await hanging, like Mary had been, either. That sort of thing tends to work on your mind and on your general outlook of life. We shall see.

Harry Quist does not leave . . . that is, not until First Mate Ruger appears at the rail. Then he and his mates vanish in a flash. Ruger stands regarding me with steady gaze and crossed arms. I do not acknowledge his presence and instead turn back to crashing through the next swell, and it's a good deep one . . . *Glorious!*

When I resurface, I see that the First Mate has been replaced up there by . . . what? . . . the Shantyman? He is surrounded by a mob of garrulous sailors, one of whom bears a length of rope, so I know what is going to happen next . . .

Over the past week or so on the *Lorelei Lee,* it has become a tradition, an initiation, like, for each man to be taken down, such that he can place his grubby hands on the chest of my beautiful figurehead and so become full-fledged *Lorelei* Mates in Good Standing, all rights and privileges therewith appertaining and all that. Most of the more able hands clamber over the under-bowsprit netting to accomplish this task, but some are less nimble and do not. Early on, the squalling young Ship's Boy Quist was bound about his hips and legs and lowered upside down to do the deed, which he eventually did with much relish.

It was Captain Laughton's own turn several days ago, so he allowed himself to be placed into a reasonably comfortable Bo'sun's Chair and lowered down in range of the quarry, where he did his duty with the *Lorelei.* He endured it all in good spirits and called it excellent fun—"Har-har! Just wait till we get all of you down to the equator when King Neptune himself comes aboard. Then we shall see, my fine laughing ladies. Then we shall see . . ."

But now, on this day, it is the Shantyman's turn. He, unlike Quist, is treated like an officer on the ship. The men would not think of touching him without permission, but it seems he has granted that, since he grins widely as he is bound up and put over. They treat the Shantyman much more kindly than they did Quist and his mates, and, indeed, even more gently than they did the Captain.

"Can't be a true member of the crew of the *Lorelei Lee*, Sir, if ye ain't touched the chest of the mermaid, now can ye, Sir? Careful there, Mr. Lightner, easy now."

Enoch Lightner is lowered within range of the mermaid and all her charms.

The Shantyman runs his hands over the *Lorelei*'s lower parts and then, to the delight of the seamen, starts to sing . . .

> *'Twas on the Good Ship Venus,*
> *By Christ, you should have seen us,*
> *The figurehead of a whore in bed*
> *And a mast like an . . .*

. . . and here he stops, for he has run his knowing fingers over the carved face of the wooden figurehead. Then he laughs and says, "Are you down there, Faber?"

"Yes, Sir."

"Ah. I thought I recognized your voice," he says, leaving his hands on the Lorelei's face. "And I think I'm seeing something else, too . . ."

Uh-oh . . .

And then I am saved, once again . . .

"On deck there! Land ho! It is the Rock!"

・・・

Later, when we have dried off and have gotten dressed, I climb into the rigging, and yes, it is the mighty Rock of Gibraltar that looms over us as we are warped in and tied up to the Mole, a long earthwork breakwater and pier. My girls below me on the deck are amazed at the massiveness of the thing and gape in wonder.

"Aye, ladies, it is not called the Pillar of Hercules for nothing," say I. "Is it not grand?"

They allow that it is, but then they see that there are at least four other ships—Royal Navy ships at that—tied up to that pier, and many sailors hang in the rigging of those ships and look avidly at us as we come in, all of our Crews festooned on deck and in our rigging. There are at least four hundred men on each of those ships—that's a lot of potential customers.

"But Jacky," says Esther, "all the other Crews will be out there making money, lots of it, and then, when it comes to the bidding for berths, we will have little. So we'll be tossed out of our berth, and I, for one, like the light and air up above. I sure don't want to go down into that dark hold."

"Steady on, Esther, we'll see what turns up. I have plans, trust me. The Newgaters shall not go down into the bottom of the hold," I say. *And as for you, Esther, you don't have to worry about going into any dark hole as long as you have young Major Johnston longin' after you.*

The *Lorelei Lee* is expertly brought into her berth under Captain Laughton's stern gaze, and as we are being tied up, he turns from his nautical duties on his quarterdeck to address his cargo.

"Ladies!" he calls. "We are in the port of Gibraltar! There are four Royal Navy ships moored about us here, as well. There is also a garrison of two thousand men quartered up at the fort. You see a long pier here that is called the Mole. You will be confined to that place, and there will be a guard placed at the end of that pier to insure that none of you leave it. The other ships moored here are the *Surprise,* the *Laurentian,* the *Indomitable,* and the *Redoubt.* I have been apprised by their captains that well-behaved ladies will be allowed aboard their respective ships for the three days we will be in port."

There is a general cheer at this, and not all coming from the *Lorelei Lee.*

"The under-sixteens, both male and female, are not allowed off," continues the Captain, once again occasioning groans from Quist and his lads. "And on Sunday morning, two days from now, when the ship's bell rings six times, everyone must be back aboard. Anyone late will suffer twelve strokes of the rod. Is that clear?"

"Yes, Sir!" is the general female chorus, eager to be off.

"Mrs. Barnsley, Mrs. Berry, and Mrs. MacDonald," intones the Captain. "Take care of your girls . . . and remember, madams . . . my twenty percent. And now, liberty call! And let Venus, Bacchus, and Cupid rule!"

And rule they do . . .

There is general riot throughout that evening and night. I counsel my lasses to lie low, so we gather down in the galley to sip strong coffee with Cookie and Keefe, telling stories of the *Bloodhound* and such. As the noise of the riot grows higher, I sneak out of there and down to a certain store-room, where I know the wine is stored, and though I could be whipped for it, make off with three bottles of the best, along with some select cheeses, and head back to the galley. Once there, we divide it all up, and Cookie adds some fresh and fluffy biscuits, so our magnificent feast is even finer.

A few more stories and songs and then we go down to our berth and turn in to our hammocks, while the sounds of merriment outside continue unabated.

"Good night, ladies," I say, burrowing my face into my pillow—yes, Higgins had gotten me one, bless him. "Think of how much better you will feel come morning than your wayward sisters."

Good night, Jaimy, I pray that you are safe.

Chapter 25

James Fletcher
Onboard Cerberus
Under way for New South Wales

Dearest Jacky,

It has been three days since I was first brought aboard, and now we are under way.

Large gangs of the the Great Unwashed of England, Scotland, Ireland, and Wales have been dragged aboard in chains, and the holds below are pure bedlam. I'm almost glad I'm confined here in maximum security with this pack of Irish scoundrels.

And yes, Jacky, your former associates have been treating me to many lively accounts of your antics in the Mediterranean and the Caribbean when you sailed with them on your *Emerald*. Ah, yes, many saucy tales of your dancing on tabletops and suchlike in low foreign dives. Some stories I believe, but some I ascribe to that Arthur McBride's apparent desire to piss me off as much as possible. We shall see . . .

One thing I know for sure is that if I ever again have to listen to a tale prefaced with, *Hey, remember the time our Jacky* . . . I shall lose all of my self-control and will wrap my chain about the throat of the taleteller and squeeze until nothing else ever issues forth from his lying mouth. Especially galling is their continued use of the phrase "*our* Jacky." I growl every time I hear it.

I know that Amy Trevelyne has written books about your exploits, and I know that I am featured in some of them. Yes, I realize that they are reasonably accurate, but I am sorry—I cannot bring myself to read them. Maybe someday, if we are ever together again and settled . . . Slim chance of that, I know, but still, one can hope.

The Irish lads keep up their spirits by singing—mostly in Gaelic, which is good because, if the meaning of the words were known, it would surely anger the guards. The songs lift my spirits as well as I lean back against the wall and listen, for I know you love these tunes, too, Jacky. I remember with pleasure hearing you sing some of them last year when we both sailed the Caribbean. Happy days, now, in retrospect . . . Happy, lost days . . .

Now that we are well away from the land and are not liable to escape, our neck manacles have been removed, giving us a bit more freedom of movement, which is welcome. As I had earlier surmised, we are taken down to the head each morning, and then we shuffle along to the mess hall. There are long tables and we stand at one of them where small buckets of slop are placed in front of us. We are given a short time to eat it—with spoons only, of course—and after the buckets and spoons are counted, we are led back to our cell. During that time, however, there are other prisoners with leg irons arrayed about the tables, and some conversation twixt them and the Irish lads goes on . . . good men . . . they are doing as they were told—finding out who's a seaman, and who might be trusted.

The Weasel, our cell keeper, has been joined in this task of guarding us by his two superior guards, the ones in charge of our entire hold. They wear the red coats of the Army, now faded and worn, but still they insist that we address them by their former ranks—Sergeant Napper and Corporal Vance. Filthy sods. They were undoubtedly drummed out of the corps, probably for sloth and cowardice, yet they still cling to some pathetic shreds of once honorable trappings. They both carry cudgels and use them without mercy. Several of the Irish lads receive thumps on the way to the mess line, but heeding my advice, they do not reciprocate in kind.

The Weasel especially enjoys tormenting me.

"How d' ye like yer fine life now, *Mr.* Fletcher, now that ye've been brought low? Would you like for me to shine your boots now, *Sir*?"

"What I really like, Weasel, is thinking about how much fun it will be in killing you, when the time comes," I reply. "Yes, that thought does bring me some joy."

Laughs and *Hear, hear!* from my cellmates at this.

"That time ain't never gonna come, and you know it!" hisses the Weasel. "You're naught but a dirty, chained-up convict now, and the rest o' yiz is filthy micks, and I'm the one with the keys! And don't ye call me that name again! That's what *she* called me back then. I had to take it from that mean little witch, but I ain't takin' it from you!"

"She named you well, Weasel," I hiss. "You slimy piece of dung."

The Weasel swings back his cudgel and lays it against the side of my head. Expecting it, I raised my shoulder and took most of the blow there, so it wasn't so bad, and it gained me a few points with the men I hope will end up serving as my crew.

Weasel . . . weasel . . . weasel . . . is whispered from across the room, coming from various lips, first here, then over there, and the enraged Weasel, confused, retreats from the cell. Derisive laughter follows him out.

I think you have lost the day, Weasel, and good for you . . .

Small victories, but still . . .

And so the days roll on . . .

Hoping things are better for you, I remain,
Yrs,

Jaimy

Chapter 26

We've had breakfast, then I seek out Higgins, who's gotten me some things from my seabag, and by noontime, I'm getting ready to go.

"Coo, Jacky, you can't go out there like that," warns Molly. "What will people say?"

I laugh and give her a poke. "We're on the *Lorelei Lee*, ain't we? You know this means that we'll soon be known as the most famous floating brothel that ever sailed the seven seas, so I don't think my costume preferences will ever be written down in the history of the ship. And wouldn't us Newgaters like a bit of money, so's we can buy nice things and maybe some good food now and then? You bet we would. And washing clothes and entertainin' strange men ain't the only ways to make money in this world. Now, Esther, my hair braided into a pigtail, if you would, so it'll be out of my way. That's it, thanks.

"Mag, you got your pouch? Good. You come with me. My cloak, Mary, thanks," I says, and I feel my cloak being put about my bare shoulders and snugged up around my neck. "You young ones, now, you can watch the fun from the rail. Come on, let's go and do it."

Our procession proceeds out on deck and advances to the gangway. There stands Mr. Seabrook as Officer of the Watch, with seamen Monk and Suggs loitering about, I suppose as the Bo'sun and the Messenger. Both of the seamen stand snickering and mumbling as we approach. For the hundreth time, I observe that this sure ain't the Royal Navy.

"What's up, then?" asks the Second Mate.

"We are going off, Mr. Seabrook, and consistent with the Captain's orders, we are allowed on the pier," I announce, nose in air. "And if you will, please, let us pass."

"And what are you going to do down there, Missy? Set up your own little crib?" he asks, with a mock salute. "I see no pillows and sheets."

"Nay, Sir, just gonna have a bit of fun, as you shall shortly see if you will let us go."

He makes a grand sweeping gesture of his hand as we descend the brow. I stride down the pier till I reach the spot of open water between the bow of the *Lorelei Lee* and the stern of HMS *Surprise,* where a ladder leads down into the water. Handy, that. The water appears clear of obstacles, but I shall have to make sure of that.

The Royal Navy frigate looms much higher above us than does the bowsprit of my, er, *the* brigantine *Lorelei Lee,* and although I cannot see on to the deck of the warship, I can certainly hear the sounds of merriment, both male and female. The bacchanalia continues full bore, but then I see several heads leaving the party and peering over the side and down upon me. I'll need more of them than that, though, I figure. *Well, it's showtime, mates . . .*

I whip off the cloak, fling it aside, and stand revealed in my swimming suit—yes, the very same one I had made last winter when I was diving on the *Santa Magdalena* in the Caribbean. And yes, right under the figurehead of the lovely *Lorelei*. And while it's true that this rig might be considered a bit scandalous back at Wiggins Pier in England, here, who's going to care? I certainly don't.

Rolling up the legs of my swimsuit bottom high on my thighs, I launch into my invitation for them to loosen up the coins.

"Ahoy, *Surprise*! I am none other than the right famous Jacky Faber, and I am here to play and dance and, yes, even to dive into the awful, scary briny for your pleasure!" I had thought about doing this bit as a Spanish girl—Hola, *all you pretty sailor* muchachos! Or maybe a French filly—Bonjour, mon jeunes marins beaux. *Toss zee coin and you shall see my* derrière-*in-zee-air as I dive for eet!*—but, nay, I decided to stick with the Cockney, as it might make them feel more at home, like. "Now, you foine British sea dogs, dig up some of your coins and get ready to toss 'em in that fearful water, then your own dear mermaid shall brave death and destruction to dive down and retrieve them!"

There are a few whoops and shouts from the deck of the *Surprise*, and I count that as good. However, to allow time for the word to get around that there is a very lightly clad female out on the Mole, I tiptoe over to the edge of the pier and pull my goggles down over my eyes.

"Spread the word, mates, and I'll be back in a jiff!"

And with that, I dive into the water. After all, I have to check out just what I am diving into, don't I? I certainly don't want to perish by slamming my poor head into some rock, or by getting tangled up in old discarded coils of rope, no, I do not.

Hmmm . . . The water is cool and clear—not Caribbean clear, but clear enough and that is good—and there doesn't seem to be much in the way of danger to a poor diver. Coo, there is, however, a good deal of rubble down on the bottom, well below the massive hulls of the ships moored here. I give a kick and go lower. *Hmmm* . . . There's some interesting stuff over there . . . Another kick and I drift over the detritus—old spars, chain, and amphoras—big jars with narrow tops and a handle to either side, which I suspect once held wine and olive oil during ancient times. There's a really good one right there . . . I swim over to it and rub the gray moss from its surface. Then I notice something writ in Latin, I think. Good Lord, this could have been here for a thousand years . . . from the times of the Romans . . . maybe even the Macedonians. I must come back later for that one. Gibraltar has been a Mediterranean port for a good long time, as I recall from Mr. Yale's history and geography lectures back at the Lawson Peabody. Poor man, so interested in antiquities and never able to see any, except for drawings. And here I am, floating above thousands of years' worth of the real thing. Funny how it goes . . .

Well, better get back up.

When I surface and climb up the ladder, I'm gratified to see that there are now a goodly number of sailors on the fantail of the *Surprise,* along with a lot of our own crew on the bow of the *Lorelei.* I can imagine why, as their own girls are out doin' business and there's naught for them to do but wait for their return.

I stand on the pier, lift up my goggles, tug at the bottom of my traitorous suit to pull it down over my bum, and call out, "All right, mateys! 'Oo's first? Step right up, now, not good to keep a mermaid waitin', y' know . . . She just might put a spell on ye."

"Here, girl!" shouts out a seaman from the warship. "See if ye can find that!" and with his thumb, he flips a coin in the air. It arcs up and then hits the water.

I myself arc into the water with what I hope is a graceful dive and grab the coin before it gets ten feet down. I pop back onto the dock, hold the coin aloft, and ask, "That fine show for just a penny? Come on, sailors, the honor of your *Surprise* is at stake! Let's up the ante a bit, shall we? At least several pennies at a time now, surely."

"I thinks I remembers that fine bottom, I do, and right fondly," announces Mick Richards, leaning over the rail of our own ship, his wide mouth in a leering grin. "And 'ere's a penny for the memory of it."

"And 'ere's one for me, too, Jacky lass," says Keefe, who stands beside him. The two coins hit the water, joined by two more from the *Surprise*.

"Thanks, mates! You're all good lads!" and I'm down under again, capturing all four pennies before they hit the bottom.

When I regain the pier, I no longer tug at the bottom of my suit, but instead let it crawl even further up the crack of my bum. I figure it's good for business, and from the shouts I hear, I believe I am right. As the coins come cascading down, I dive back in to scoop 'em up. Each time when I come back up on the Mole, I hand the coins to faithful Maggie, who tucks them into her bag—a purse that is beginning to look right pleasingly plump.

This time up, I see Mrs. Barnsley hanging over the rail of the warship. She tosses a coin onto the deck next to me and says, "There's a ha'penny, girl. Whyn't ye move it along, ye little tramp—makin' a spectacle o' yerself like that and interfering with our business."

I don't respond, but merely turn away and reach down to retrieve the lowly ha'penny from the deck behind me. I bend *way* over and stay there to give her a real good look at my wiggling bum, then I straighten up and loudly sing out a bit of a song.

> *I went to a tavern I used to frequent*
> *And told the landlady my money's all spent*
> *I asked her for credit and she answered*
> *   me Nay . . .*

(And here I fling the ha'penny back at Mrs. Barnsley)

> *Custom like yours I can get any day!*

Roars of laughter from the crowd, who know the "Wild Rover" song well. They raucously take up the chorus:

> *And it's no, nay, never,*
> *No, nay, never, no more,*
> *Will I play the wild rover,*
> *No, never no more!*

As we end off on a cheer, Mrs. Barnsley retreats from the rail in a huff. She never did like me much, and I'm certain she likes me even less now.

I continue to work this ship until it is almost time for lunch and a bit of warming up for me—the Mediterranean is warm, but not that warm—when Captain Laughton comes to the bow rail of his ship.

"What is this, then? Our little minstrel turned mermaid? Capital! Har-har! Here's a crown for you, then!" And he flips a full golden guinea over the side.

Well, that's some serious coin, I think, and leap down to snatch it up. When I grab it in my fist, I head back to the surface and see that another Captain is at his rail. It is the Master and Commander of the *Surprise,* a big red-faced man with long, flowing blond hair, and he is exulting . . .

"Gussie! You old reprobate! How the hell are you? Aside from the luck of having that gang of petticoats as cargo! And the fools of this world call *me* Lucky Jack! I fear I have now lost that title to you!"

"I am just fine, Jack! Good to see you!" replies our Captain Laughton.

"My God, man, I haven't seen you since the Battle of the Nile! And is that Lieutenant Lightner standing beside you? Yes, it is! Well met, indeed, both of you!"

"Well, you must both come on over for a spot of brandy! And dinner, too. Right now. Not a moment to lose! And here, this is for you, Miss," shouts this good Captain as he drops yet another full guinea into the water and, eventually, into my greedy hand.

I worked the *Surprise* for maybe another half hour, but then the cool water started to give me the shakes, so Maggie and I retreated to our berth. Huddled with my cloak about me and a mug of good hot soup—made special by Cookie— cradled in my hands, I soon warmed up enough to listen to the accounting of the money.

"Coo, Maggie," says Mary Wade. "There must be five quid there."

"Not nearly enough, dear," I say. "There's gonna be a lot more money made by the Crews this day. But don't worry. We shan't go down into the bilges. No matter what Mrs. Barnsley thinks."

"But how . . . ?"

"Not just yet, dear. Just a bit more of this grand stew and maybe a spot of wine, then I'll go back out to work the *Redoubt* and the *Indomitable*." The two are moored nose to tail, farther on down the Mole.

I get up and stretch.

"One thing I know," I say. "I'll sleep well this night. Let's go, Mag."

That, however, shall not be the case.

Much later, when we are wrapping up things with the *Indomitable*, and I am surfacing from my last dive, coin in fist, I see that a small cutter has slipped in alongside the *Lorelei Lee*. Do I remember someone saying we would pick up a few more female convicts on Gibraltar? I think I do, but I dunno—my mind is so fuzzy from the day's dives. I rap the side of my head a few times, to clear my left ear, and watch the poor wretches being brought onboard.

There are five of the usual drabs, heads down and weeping, and a couple more whores, heads up and cursing, but then there is one more . . .

Her head is up and her hands are bound, but she is not cursing, no. And from under her cap red curls spill forth and she is . . . she is . . .

Mairead?

Chapter 27

The instant I see that it is Mairead Delaney McCon-naughey, her own self, being brought aboard, I fly out of the water and dart up the *Lorelei*'s gangway and onto the deck where the new convicts are being entered into the ship's manifest . . . by John Higgins, of course.

I run to her and grasp her arm. She stiffens and then looks at me as if she expects to be hit. There are some bruises about her eyes. *Those sonsabitches . . .*

"J-Jacky? Is it you? How . . . ?" she asks, confused, her green eyes wide.

"Never mind that now, Mairead. We've got to get you settled," I say, looking over at Higgins. "Mr. Higgins. Can you have this one released? I'll take her into my Crew."

He lifts an eyebrow but does not display the slightest surprise, even though I know he recognizes the girl standing there, her ankles in chains. He lifts a finger and motions for her manacles to be taken off. When that is done, she collapses against me, sobbing.

"Oh, to see a friendly face, Jacky, you cannot possibly know . . ."

I embrace her trembling form and smooth the tendrils of her red hair from her forehead. "Things will get better, you'll see," I say, and lead her over to Higgins.

"Name?" he asks, coldly.

She looks at him and starts to greet him, but sees his warning head shake, and she whispers, "Mairead . . . Mairead McConnaughey."

"Age?"

"Seventeen."

"Place of birth?"

"On a farm in Bonnettstown, just outside Kilkenny, Ireland."

"Crime?"

She thinks on this.

"Uh . . . Rebellion, I think. I don't know . . . I wasn't doin' nuthin' . . ."

"That's what they all say," Higgins says dismissively. "All right, you may take her away."

As I lead her off, I ask, "The ones you were brought on-board with, are any of them your friends?" I ask, planning to go collect any who might have befriended her.

"No. I was put on that boat only last night. I know none of them."

Well, that makes things a bit simpler.

Sending Maggie off to collect my Newgaters Crew, so they can welcome their newest member, I take Mairead down to our laundry room. On the way, I bellow into the galley next door, "Cookie! Hot water for a bath and some of your fine soup! Coffee, too. And thanks!"

I sit her down next to one of the tubs and explain to her the lay of things around here, and she nods, taking it all in. I know her mind is reeling from all the recent events, but she seems to be calming down . . . now composed enough to ask me, "Why are you dressed like that, Jacky? And why are you all wet?"

"I have been diving for coins, Mairead, to make our Crew a bit of money so that we can buy some of the things we need," I say, taking her hand in mine. "There are two hundred workin' girls out there plyin' their trade right now, and if we are to hold our own, we must have money, too. Though not a hell ship in any sense, the *Lorelei Lee* is a pay-as-you-go ship, if you take my meaning. Ah, here's something to warm you."

She nods and says, "Well, with me own eyes I've seen you doin' a lot crazier things than that, and me, too. So I guess it's all good." Then she buries her nose in the mug of steamy soup that Mick has brought in. "Oooh . . ." She breathes out. "That's soooo good."

"Pretty thing, she is," says Mick, eyeing Mairead as he leaves to get the hot water for her bath. I give him a glare and he answers me with a shrug. *And not for you, Mick,* I snarl to myself. *She's a married woman and a good wife to her man, so lay off, swab.*

Keefe and Mick come in with the buckets of hot water, and we pour it into a tub with some cooler water and work up some suds. Then I shoo out the two men, and when all my girls are in and wondering at this new red-haired addition to our Crew, I shove the wedges under the door and get Mairead stripped down and into the tub. From the looks of her, after having been in the gentle custody of King George for some time, she is well in need of a good scrub down.

And when she is in the water and exclaiming, "Oh, Jacky, this is just so prime!" while I am running the soap through her hair, I continue to tell her the way of things—who to trust and who not—and then I demand of her just how she came to be here.

"Ian and I had gone off to Waterford to collect the crew for your ship, as you had asked in your letters, and when we were there, we met up with Arthur McBride and his boy-os, never a good thing in my estimation, but Ian wouldn't listen, and so the lads went off to a meetin' o' the Free Irish association or somesuch. I went with 'em and waited out in the coach, bitin' my fingernails. Then, what I feared most did happen. There was a great uproar and the police did come and the boys were hauled off to jail. And then me, too."

She pauses in her recitation, looks down at her hands, and then quietly says, "I'm sorry I showed myself so weak out there on the deck, Jacky, me bawlin' and all, but y'see . . . I've been feelin' right poorly sometimes lately. Mostly in the mornin' . . ."

Uh-oh . . .

"You see, Jacky, I . . . I am with child."

Oh, Lord.

That does it for me. The consequences of my actions come roarin' back at me, and I bury my face in my soapy hands, all my false bravado gone.

"Oh, Mairead, I am sorry, so very sorry. If it hadn't been for me and my foolish schemes, you wouldn't be here now. You'd be back at the Home for Little Wanderers, waitin' for the arrival o' your pretty little baby, and Ian would be standin' there by your side. Instead, you're here on a convict ship headin' for the other side o' the world, and for who knows what. And poor Ian's off, too, and . . . I've made such a mess of things."

My chest is heavin' for real now, as I keep rockin' back and forth, and my Newgaters gaze upon me with wonder at my distress.

"There, there, Jacky," Mairead says, taking my hand and holding it to her cheek. "No one knows the future. Only God knows . . . and maybe He ain't so sure sometimes. So don't worry yourself about it . . . Hush, now, girl."

And then, later that night, as we both swing in my hammock, my face buried in her mass of red curls, I think, *Yes, I am sorry for what I have done, but still . . . I have learned that my bold Irish crew is going Down Under with me, and I wonder . . . Can that be such a bad thing?*

Hmmm . . .

Chapter 28

I manage to arise the next morn—despite my anguished feelings of responsibility for having wrecked the lives of those most dear to me—and entrust Mairead to the gentle care of Esther Abrahams, who will see to her breakfast and show her about the ship. I then go topside to resume my diving bit. After all, I now have one more charge—one for whose current low state I am directly responsible—and this is our last day in this very lucrative port. So, guilt aside, money must still be made.

Yesterday I had given Mairead a set of my clean linen to wear when she arose from her bath. The clothes she had worn upon arrival, which were not in such bad shape, had been plunged into the bath water, scrubbed, and then hung up to dry. I am sure they are dry by now, should she want to come topside. We shall have to make up a Newgater's rig for her.

All right, then, out on the dock, down to the next ship, hands on hips, chin up, girl, and back into the game . . .

"Ahem! You sailors of the *Redoubt* and the *Laurentian*! I am Jacky Faber, famous in legend and song, as you well know, and I am here to sing and dance, and yes, even dive into Neptune's chilly waters for your manly pleasure! So free up your gold, mates, and I will give you a show!"

Coins are tossed, and I dive, scoop them up, surface, give the coins to Maggie and her purse, wait, and dive again . . . and again.

There are some surprises. When I'm coming up from one particular dive, after retrieving a shiny shilling, I hear from the deck of the *Redoubt* a shout from the man who had flung the coin, "Jacky! Come up here and I will give you two shillings for that one!"

As I clamber back on the dock, I call out to the man, "Why would you do that?" But a shilling is a shilling, all the same, and so, without waiting for the man's answer, I dart up the *Redoubt*'s brow and deposit the coin in the man's outstretched hand.

My question is echoed by others about me on that ship's deck—*Wot, Jim? Why not make 'er dive for it?"* and *"Roight, Jock, I like 'er much better drippin' wet. Make 'er put 'er little butt in the air to go down for her coin."*

The first sailor then puffs up and says, "Do ye jest, mates? Do ye not know that this 'ere little bit standin' in front o' ye, drippin' on the deck, is none other than the re-nowned Jacky Faber, none other than Puss-in-Boots of great fame her ownself?"

"Can't be 'er. She's dead—'ad 'er 'ead cut off by the Froggies."

"Nay, she ain't dead, Amos. She's right there! Show us yer tattoo, dearie."

I oblige the man by peeling down the top edge of my swimsuit bottom to expose my Brotherhood of the *Dolphin* tattoo.

"See that? It's 'er all right. Me own dad, Billie Barnes, sailed wi' 'er on the *Wolverine,* he did. Havin' only one leg now, poor soul, he's back in Bristol wi' his pipe and cup and 'is pension and 'is memories, but fer sure he's got that Vengeance-for-Puss-in-Boots tattoo big and bold on 'is arm, as do you, too, Lucas McCain—I seen it—and I know he'd appreciate a coin from the lass's very own hand, specially since she saved his own dear life from drowndin' one time. We shall 'ave it mounted and framed, then set up on the mantelpiece for all to gaze upon and admire."

Well!

After that, the coins fly right freely, and I reflect that sometimes fame ain't so bad after all.

Back down into the briny, you, and don't let your foolish head get swelled.

More of the usual coin tosses, and then, to warm up a bit, I take up the pennywhistle to play a few merry tunes and dance along with the melodies. Then, back with me into the salt. More coins, and then, another surprise . . .

Well, it ain't really a surprise, since it happens almost every time in situations like this. A sailor leans over the rails and pipes out, "Here's a whole half a crown, sweetheart," says a sailor on the frigate. "It's yours if you go down and get it *without* yer knickers and top on. Jes' like that girl there." He points at the *Lorelei* figurehead. "Who, by the way, looks a lot like you."

That proposition is met with cries of *"Hear, hear!"* and *"I'll add a shilling to that!"* and *"I will, too, and I'll double it, I will!"*

I was expectin' this, for it always comes. Just why they want a look at my scrawny self, I do not know, but they always seem to. *Men, I swear. But . . . that is a bit of money . . . and I am not very shy in that regard . . .* Then I look up at the rail of the *Lorelei* and there stands Ruger, who calls down, "And another half crown from the *Lorelei*," and I know I cannot do it because it will only cause me trouble on the *Lorelei* later on. I decide to make a joke of it.

"Sorry, mates. I'd love to do that for you if it would bring you some measure of joy. But y' see, I cannot, for the sea bottom is full of gnarly beasts and sea serpents, and I have to do battle with 'em every time I dive after the coins you so kindly toss. See the tooth marks on me ankle there? Those was put there by 'orrible sea snakes, which writhe and slither in their holes down there."

I point to a scratch on my leg that I had gotten from gettin' too close to a barnacle-covered rock.

"Y' see, mates, if I was to lose the next battle wi' them awful creatures, well, I certainly couldn't go up and stand in front o' Saint Peter at the Pearly Gates without me knickers on, now could I?"

Great laughter, and Mr. Ruger turns from the rail and disappears . . . for now, anyway.

The coins tumble down, and I go after them.

Later, when I'm having another dry-off pennywhistle, dancing-about-time, I hear yet another call from the deck of the *Redoubt*.

"Och, ye dance and play very well, Miss, and I have a fine guinea up here for you. But you must come up here to get it."

Hmmm . . . I'm thinkin', *I've already been up on that deck today and escaped harm . . . and a guinea is a guinea . . .*

I bounce up on the deck and look for the man, who, as I now recall too late, spoke in a distinct Scots accent . . .

Then I gasp as a man slips around the capstan and a large hand wraps about my throat, holding me fast in the shadow of the riggin'. A once very familiar face looms into my view.

"Gully!" I croak. "You!"

"Aye, 'tis me, Moneymaker. Yer old partner . . . and it looks like you're still makin' it . . . Money, that is."

"Let go of me, Gully MacFarland. One scream and my friends will come after me, they will. I'm part of Captain Laughton's cargo. I'm worth ten and six to him, and he would be *very* angry if you messed me about. Angry enough to have a pathetic drunk of a seaman strung up on the yardarm."

"Now, now, Moneymaker. I ain't gonna hurt you. Just wanted to thank you for getting me cleaned up and sober."

"Right, Gully. If you think I believe that for one moment, you've gone off your head!"

"Nay, nay, 'tis true. I'm a changed man, Miss. And listen to this: All of the Captains are meeting tonight for a last dinner on the *Surprise* before we all leave this port, and I'm to play for them. You, too, I hear. Why don't we put the old act together one more time? And then maybe we'll talk about the Lady Lenore."

There is a trill from a Bo'sun's pipe signaling the *Redoubt*'s crew to assemble.

"Gotta go, Moneymaker," he says, giving my neck a final squeeze. "See ya later."

And he is gone.

I stand astounded. The last time I saw Gully MacFarland was back in Boston when I had him tied to a wheelbarrow to deliver him to the Royal Navy for impressment, to this very ship here. This, after he, in a drunken rage, had slugged me so hard that I feared that I was going to lose my left eye. I did not lose my eye, but Gully certainly did lose his freedom . . . and his beloved violin, the exquisite Lady Lenore.

Imagine that . . . First Mairead, and now Gully MacFarland. Gilbraltar certainly has been a place of wonder for me.

It is evening, and we are in the great cabin on the forty-four-gun frigate HMS *Surprise*.

All five Captains are there, as well as some other officers. First Officers, mostly, but a few others, as well. One, I see, has on the uniform of Ship's Surgeon, and I also see Enoch Lightner being seated at the great table, and of that, I am glad. I am also happy to see that First Officer Ruger is *not* in attendance.

The glasses are filled and the dinner is served as Gully and I play softly in the background . . . softly, that is, till the food is eaten and the wine works its will, for then we are called upon for more lively stuff.

And we give it to 'em.

Gully has lost none of his touch with the fiddle. We'd had a bit of time to brush up on the old routines and had them down fairly well by the time we were called upon to play. Gully stands and we rip into "Billy in the Low Ground" and then "Morpeth Rant" and then "Handsome Molly," with me on the concertina and vocals.

We get great roars of approval and tear into the meat of our old repetoire, "John Barleycorn" and "Jenny Is a Weeper" and . . . oh, just all of them, and it is so grand to play them together again!

After the first time Gully's bow hits the strings of the Lady Gay—yes, I had lent her to him, for she was ten times better the fiddle than the poor worn and damp instrument he had—the Shantyman's head jerked up and listened. Though he said nothing, I sensed that he knew he was in the presence of a master.

The party got more and more raucous, and soon the table was bellowing out "Hearts of Oak" and "Rule, Britannia" and "God Save the King."

And later, of course, things got down and dirty, so we did "The Cuckoo's Nest" and "Captain Black's Courtship" and "The Spotted Cow." I couldn't believe it, but Gully did "Fire Down Below" and "The Parson's Little Daughter," and I accompanied him on the pennywhistle and, to my shame, on the vocals. The Shantyman added his deep baritone, too. Though obscene, it all sounded awfully good. Oh, well, when in Rome . . .

In the heat of the evening, the Captain of the *Surprise* offered to buy me, but good Captain Laughton demurred— *"Nay, Jack, she is a convict, not a slave, and I am bound by contract to deliver her body relatively intact to New South Wales . . . and, frankly, we have been enjoying her music too much to let her go. And by the by, Captain, did you know that she is famous? Yes, I am told she is. Seems she got in a bit of mischief with the Admiralty . . . Here, here, come over here, girl, and tell us something of yourself."*

I go over to answer their questions, playing the part of the demure and very misunderstood young thing—a poor girl buffeted about by the cruel winds of Fortune—and eventually I am let go. Then, sensing the party is winding down, Gully and I deliver our old closing song, "The Parting Glass."

Of all the money that ere I had, I spent it in good company.
And of all the harm that ere I've done,
Alas, was done to none but me.
And all I've done for want of wit,
To memory now I cannot recall.
So fill me to the parting glass. Good night . . .
. . . And joy be with you all.

A bow and a curtsy and we are off.

The next morning comes early—oh, much too early for many of us—but we rise up to do our duty. I know one thing full well, our laundry will be very, *very* busy this day.

There are shouts and many bells and whistles, flags are hoisted and shifted, and then the warships move off one by one—first the *Surprise,* then the *Laurentian,* followed by the *Indomitable,* and finally, the *Redoubt.*

As the warships wend their way out to the open sea, our own Crews festoon the rigging of the *Lorelei Lee,* waving them off by the flourishing of white petticoats.

When it is our turn, the lines to the Mole are loosed, our sails are ready to be raised, and we prepare to slip away from the land. From the quarterdeck, Captain Laughton calls out.

"*Shantyman!*"

Enoch Lightner advances to his spot in front of the foremast, behind his big drum. He raises his mallets, pauses, then brings them booming down.

> *There was a lofty ship*
> *From old England she came*
> *Blow high, blow low*
> *And so sailed we.*
> *She was the* Lorelei Lee
> *And the darling of the sea*
> *Down along the coast*
> *Of high . . . Barbar-eeee*

And so the *Lorelei Lee* and all upon her are off for the coast of West Africa. God save the ship. God save us all.

PART III

Chapter 29

**The Packet of Letters
Conveyed by Seaman Gulliver MacFarland
To the Reverend Henry Alsop
The London Home for Little Wanderers
London**

*Jacky Mary Faber
Onboard the ship* Lorelei Lee
*Gibraltar
June 1807*

*Reverend Henry Alsop
The London Home for Little Wanderers
Brideshead Street
London, England*

Dear Grandfather,

I hope that this letter finds you, and all of those at the Home, to be well and happy. To business first:

The man who stands before you, having given you this packet of letters, is a seaman named Gulliver MacFarland. I have given him permission to retrieve that old violin, which I left in your care, because it belongs to him. If the seal on this letter is broken, show him out and give him nothing, because I instructed him not to open any of the letters he carries. He is allowed that fiddle and nothing more. Though he might be charming in both appearance and speech, keep an eye on him while he is there and be especially mindful of any valuables the Home might have lying about, as he is not in any way to be trusted.

Our good Mr. Higgins has contrived to be on this ship with me, and he continues to be the kind protector of my undeserving self. He has sent a couple of letters of his own in this packet, one to Mr. Pickering in Boston, Massachusetts, USA, and another to a Liam Delaney in County Waterford, Ireland. In addition to your letter, I have enclosed two others: one to Amy Trevelyne in Quincy, which is about thirty miles from Boston, Massachusetts, along with another to Hiram Fletcher, Jaimy's father, who lives on Brattle Street, fairly near you. If you could forward them, we would be most appreciative.

I know that you are wondering at the disappearance of Mairead and her husband, Ian McConnaughey. Though it is not happy news, I hope it will ease your mind to know that Mairead McConnaughey is safe and by my side, onboard this ship, the both of us being condemned to the penal colony at New South Wales in Australia, me for life, she for seven years.

As for the condition of her husband, Ian McConnaughey, and my own James Fletcher, we know very little. If they could be included in your prayers, we would be most grateful.

Do not worry about us, Grandfather, as we are healthy and cheerful, and continue to bless each day that we are still on God's good, green earth and able to sail upon His mighty blue sea.

Your loving grandaughter,

Mary

Jacky Faber
Onboard the Ship Lorelei Lee
Gibraltar
June 1807

Miss Amy Trevelyne
Dovecote Farm
Quincy, Massachusetts, USA

Dear Amy,

A quick note, as we'll sail from Gibraltar in the morn and I must place this letter in the hands of Gully MacFarland (yes, that very same he) this evening, because we are performing together tonight in the Captain's cabin on HMS *Surprise.* His ship is headed back to London, so he will be able to convey these letters to Rev. Alsop at the Home for Little Wanderers and thence to you—an amazing piece of luck as regards the posting of letters in this whirly and confusing world, don't you think?

Where to begin? Well, yes, dear Sister, I have once again stepped in it, and landed in it good and proper this time. You will have undoubtedly heard from Ezra Pickering about my reversal of fortune, so enough of that. Suffice it to say that I have been condemned to the penal colony at New South Wales for the rest of my life. There are many in this world who say I certainly had it coming, and perhaps they are right. I don't know, as I never felt that I was all that bad. At least I shall nevermore bother the rest of the world with my troublesome presence, and, hey, I'll probably get to see my kangaroo, after all . . . and my Bombay Rat is another possibility, too, as we might be stopping in India on our way to Botany Bay. Don't know about the Cathay Cat, though, as China ain't on our route. Tell Dorothea that I have seen some wondrous birds so far and expect to see more on my way Down Under. I shall keep her and Mr. Sackett informed with detailed descriptions of the feathered creatures. The mail from New South Wales is sure to be slow, but it must exist in some way, that is, if money still talks . . . I am sure it still does and I am still capable of earning it in my various ways, you may be sure of that.

Thanks to Assistant Purser Higgins—and, yes, I am so pleased to have him along on this journey—I have gathered about myself a generally trustworthy group of twelve girls. The Newgater Crew we are called by the others because most of us have been recent residents in that foul prison, condemned to hang for petty thievery. I can't call my crimes petty, though, so I count myself lucky to have escaped the noose, one more time. We have cornered the laundry concession, and with my worthy Crew, we prosper to a small degree—not as much as the Whorey Crews when they hit a port, to be sure, but we get by. I chortle to think of you, dear Amy, as I am on this ship with some two hundred and fifty prostitutes, thieves, and other criminals. I almost wish you were here so I could watch your face! Remember that day in Boston when I said that my ship would never turn into a floating brothel? Ha! Never say never, indeed!

I have let it be known that I will be doing miniature portraits for two quid each, and I already have promises of two commissions. Thank God my good Higgins managed to preserve my seabag, so I have my painting tools, as well as all of my musical instruments. I know I mentioned it before, but I am so very lucky to have Higgins along on this journey—I cannot tell you how much.

I plan to do readings on the main hatch, admission one shilling each. I'll do *Robinson Crusoe, Moll Flanders,* etc., and some theatricals, to lighten the day-to-day tedium of the cruise—recitals of passages from Shakespeare, Marlowe, and Chaucer, even, for the risqué tales. The naughty bits of anything, be it song or story, are especially appreciated around here. Additionally, I have started a school for the young children aboard. There are twelve of them—seven girls, five boys—ranging in age from four to nine, and all seem to be taking to it quite well. We do reading, writing, and arithmetic. I am having the younger members of my own Crew—Mary Wade, Hannah Bolt, and Ann Marsh—attend as well. So you can see I am being kept quite busy, and that is all to the good, for we both know the Devil himself finds work for idle hands, especially these hands of mine.

As you've undoubtedly surmised, it is a pretty happy ship. In any other place, we would have been forced to do our work and warned to either produce or be flogged. Actually, and to my amazement, all of us ladies have been given a great deal of freedom on this trip, our Captain Laughton being a good and generous, if totally dissolute, man. Any thought I might have had of turning the crew or the Crews to rebellion would be quite in vain, as the men love their Captain, and the women aboard are resigned (and in some cases looking forward) to their fate. So I shall be going to New South Wales, make no mistake about that, dear Sister, for the once wily fox . . . or, rather, vixen . . . Jacky Faber has finally been brought to ground, good and proper.

As we are sailing down the west coast of Africa, we will be crossing the equator soon and I know a big celebration is planned. The men aboard cannot contain their glee. Alas, in all my travels I have not yet crossed that line. I am still a Pollywog, and must look forward to some abuse when King Neptune comes aboard and we Pollywogs are initiated into the ranks of the Shellbacks. Still, it should be jolly fun, for all that.

Well, I have gone on quite at length, in spite of myself— sorry about the jumble of words; my thoughts tumble about so—but no time for neat Literary Composition (belles-lettres), as Miss Prosser back at the Lawson Peabody would have it. I have ink spilled everywhere, but I have blotted it up and will manage to get this into an envelope. Please excuse the mess.

Do not be sad, dear Sister, at our separation, for as you well recall, a little of Jacky Faber goes a long way, and you've already had more than your share of that less-than-precious commodity. Please do not weep for me, Amy, as I am healthy and cheerful and look forward to tomorrow.

And if you feel so inclined, you might write to me care of the penal colony in New South Wales. You cannot know how much I miss your sweet company, and I will treasure any letters you might send to me. Please send me news of the girls at the School—I am sure Clarissa Howe is in a state of high rapture over my capture and debasement. Ah, well, let her have her fun. Regards to all my Sisters, both Upstairs and Downstairs, Clarissa included. Tell that Randall to be good— you might give him a peck on the cheek for me. I hope he and Miss Polly Von are getting on well, and I further hope you are being civil to our Mr. Pickering. Hmmm . . . ?

I live in hope of seeing your sweet face yet again,

Your loving Sister,

Jacky

Mr. John Higgins
Onboard the ship Lorelei Lee
Gibraltar, Spain
June 1807

Captain Liam Delaney
Bonnettstown
County Waterford, Ireland

Dear Captain Delaney,

You have perhaps heard that your son Padraic, daughter Mairead, and son-in-law Ian McConnaughey, were arrested in Waterford several weeks ago on the charge of sedition for having attended a meeting of the outlawed Free Irish Society. If not, then it is worrisome news that I bring you, and for that I am sorry. With Mairead's being condemned to Transportation to Australia for seven years, we can only assume that Padraic, Ian, and the rest of the Irish lads received similar sentences and suffer the same confinement.

The only good news I have to tell you is that Mairead is safe and here with us on the *Lorelei Lee*—yes, the very same ship that Faber Shipping was outfitting for passenger traffic when disaster struck. Miss Faber, too, had been arrested several weeks prior to Mairead's incarceration, and after being charged with too many crimes to enumerate, she was convicted and sentenced to life in the penal colony at New South Wales, and in a twist of irony, her ship was sold to the East India Company for the Transportation of Criminals. I will, of course, lend your daughter what help I can in my capacity as Assistant Purser of the *Lorelei Lee*. I hope that gives you a measure of comfort as well as the knowledge that Mairead and Jacky are locked in each other's arms in the bonds of mutual friendship.

I know that when you learn the particulars of the most recent unfortunate events concerning your family, you will rant and rave and wish nothing more than to have the satisfaction of wringing the neck of our impulsive Miss Faber for having been, we must admit, the root cause of the current mess. But, Sir, I beg you to put such violent thoughts out of your mind and treat Miss Faber as a wayward but loving daughter, as I know for certain that she considers you to be her temporal father with all her very full, generous, and loving heart. I know that you have looked upon her with great fondness in the past and I hope that affection will continue to abide in your breast.

That said, I would like to inform you of certain particulars. Although the loss of the *Lorelei Lee* was a grievous blow, Faber Shipping Worldwide still retains some assets. To wit, the *Nancy B. Alsop,* a two-masted schooner, sixty-five feet in length, with a beam of twenty-five feet. Although I am a landlubber by your standards, Captain Delaney, I have made several crossings of the Atlantic upon her and have found the *Nancy B.* to be a well-found, sturdy craft. Even though she is such a small ship, she is equipped with a generous amount of armament—both swivel guns and fixed cannons. For a generally peaceable person, Miss Faber does like to go about well armed in the world.

As First Officer and Vice President of Faber Shipping, I offer the *Nancy B. Alsop* for your use. I have already informed Mr. Ezra Pickering, Clerk of the Faber Shipping Worldwide Corporation, of my instructions in this letter and have requested that he restrain the various hotheaded young men who currently man the ship until he has heard from you.

Though I do not counsel any rash actions, I do want you to know that the schooner is at your disposal, should you desire to use her.

Enclosed you will find a draft on the Bank of the United States in the amount of three hundred dollars to cover your travel expenses, should you decide to avail yourself of this offer. More funds are available in Boston.

I am yr most devoted & etc.,

John Higgins

Jacky Faber, Convict
Onboard the Lorelei Lee
Bound for Botany Bay
June 1807

Mr. Hiram Fletcher
9 Brattle Lane
London, England

My dear Mr. Fletcher,

While I realize that I am not held in great esteem by you and your family, I do hope that you will find it in your heart to inform me of any news regarding your son James Fletcher, as I have absolutely no idea what might have befallen him since my forced departure from England's shore.

You may trouble yourself no more concerning any influence I might wield with Jaimy, since I have been condemned for life at the penal colony at New South Wales, and as a consequence, I shall undoubtedly trouble your family no more.

If Jaimy has been freed from confinement and exonerated of all the false charges brought against him, then I rejoice with you and wish for him a long life and happiness. I hope that he finds love with someone more worthy than I. But if Jaimy has yet to be freed, I despair and share your sorrow.

Either way, I would like to know. If you deign to inform me of this, I can be reached at the penal colony at New South Wales.

Praying for Jaimy's happiness, I am

Jacky Faber

Chapter 30

"Very well, ladies," says Captain Laughton to the various Crews arrayed before him. "The allotment of living spaces will now begin. There are four levels in the hold, the top one being the most desirable, having windows and sunlight, the second good air but no windows, and so on, down to the fourth level."

We are two full days out of Gibraltar and the Captain is seated at his usual table on the quarterdeck, flanked by the Purser and Mr. Higgins. Both Purser and Assistant Purser hold quills in their hands and bend over ledgers, ready to inscribe the amounts pledged. It is noon, the sun is high in the sky, the breeze is light but constant, the sails are full, and there are wineglasses and tankards all around. Although it is Wednesday, all aboard have been issued a double tot of grog in honor of the occasion. And yes, the Captain has a winsome Tartan on his knee. Does the man never tire?

My girls are all in our Newgaters' rigs—no stockings, of course, as it's just too hot, but still looking sharper than ever. We are arrayed up on the foretop, all laughing and chattering. There are only twelve of us, so there's plenty of room for us to sit on the foretop deck, our legs dangling over the side. I always like the superior position in a situation like this, lookin' down on all the others arrayed below. You can spit down, but they cannot spit up.

"And furthermore, there are some cabins available. They will have a flat rate of one full pound a month, each. Do I have any takers on those fine accommodations before we get to the larger auction?"

Hmmm . . . Heavy rent, I must say. The Captain may be corrupt, but he doesn't lack for sense; it wouldn't do for the three madams to start feuding amongst themselves, because it could get down and very dirty if one of them got private quarters and the others did not.

At this, the madams Barnsley, Berry, and MacDonald, dressed in their best, advance grandly to the table, like ships in full sail, to snap down their coin, and the amounts are entered in the ledger. Then they are given keys to their rooms, small cabins, which I know to be on the second level, below the officers' quarters, and *not* adjacent to the officers' mess . . . *and not quite what you fine ladies might be wishing for.* We shall see . . .

I do not advance to the table, though I have enough money to do so. The Captain notices this and calls out, "And nothing for you, Miss Faber, noble leader of the redoubtable Newgaters? No snug little cabin for you, our female Orpheus?"

"Beggin' your pardon, Sir, but no," says I, leaning over the edge. "Although your offer is charming, I prefer to cast my lot with my girls. They are loyal and true to me, and I shall be the same to them."

That gets a cheer from my Newgaters and some of the men, I notice, and some groans from the other Crews. *"Little prig . . . 'oo the 'ell she thinks she is, Saint Agnes or somethin'?"* is heard from the vicinity of Mrs. Barnsley, and *"Bleedin' little snot. We'll see about 'er sometime, we will"* echoed from near Mrs. Berry. Mrs. MacDonald says something in Scots Gaelic, but I don't quite get it. I do, however, earn a nod and a smile from the Captain.

Although I could afford the room, I don't want it just yet, as I don't want to be anywhere near that Ruger. I know those stateroom doors open outward, and I can't have that. My trusty wooden wedges would be useless in fending off unwanted intruders, of which Ruger would almost certainly be one. Right now, I feel safer with my Crew about me. Plus, I must care for my girls . . . and now Mairead, too.

"Very well," says the Captain. "Let us now bid on the lofts: The top level, currently being occupied by those called the Newgaters, is, I believe the prime residence space. Shall we start the bidding at ten pounds?"

"Ten pounds!" I shout, and a cheer is raised.

"Eleven!" cries Mrs. Barnsley.

"Twelve!" from Mrs. Berry, not to be yet undone.

"Thirteen!" says Mrs. MacDonald. Do I hear a slight reluctance in her thrifty Scottish brogue? I think I do.

"Fourteen!" That would be Mrs Barnsley again.

Seeing that the madams are now bidding quite briskly against each other, I drop out of the contest, shaking my head slightly when the Captain looks to me after each bid.

Mrs. Barnsley wins the top level with a bid of sixteen pounds. She looks up at me in triumph.

"Well, we'll be sure clearin' your lot out right quick, won't we now?"

I do not deign to reply. I only put on the Lawson Peabody Look and wait for the next turn of events.

"And now the second level, ladies. No windows, but lots of good clean air, and the finest of hammock hooks. Do I hear five pounds?"

"Five pounds," says Mrs. Berry.

"Six," say I.

"Seven."

I drop out at that. Mrs. Berry outbids Mrs. MacDonald and gets it for nine pounds.

"Looks like we're goin' down into the bottom hold." Molly sighs beside me. "A pity. Our old loft was startin' to look a lot like home."

"Don't worry, Molly, we're not going down there at all . . . at least not to sleep," I say. They all look at me. "Shush. I'll tell you later, after we are dismissed." I had thought this all out before, since I knew we would not have enough money to outbid the other Crews. No, there's much better uses for our money.

"It's your money, Jacky," says Maggie. "You're the one what dove down in the water for it."

"Nay, Mag, it's share and share alike in this gang. You all are pitchin' in to the sewing and the laundry, and doin' a fine job of it—and we all know there was a helluva lot of washing after the lusty frolics of Gibraltar." There are grunts of disgusted agreement all around. Ann makes a show of holding her nose and crossing her eyes.

"I'll continue to do my bit, too, in my own way," says I. "And all the coin will go in to sweeten the common Newgater pot."

Mrs. MacDonald, being Scottish and cheap, gets the third level for her Tartans. I only bid her up to three pounds.

"Will you bid anything for the bottom level, Miss Faber?" asks the Captain.

"Beggin' your pardon, Sir, but I believe I have gotten that fine space by default."

"Ha! Then you have it, Miss, for but a song, and I hope you enjoy. I hope you *all* enjoy! By and large, ladies, that was a very good auction," exults the Captain, richer by twenty-eight pounds. "We will do this again in another month, and we shall see who triumphs then. And take heart, ladies, there will be more ports of call and more opportunities to make even more money."

"Looks like you and yer crew is goin' down to the bottom of this bark with the rest of the rats," says Mrs. Barnsley. She grins and looks up at us, triumphant. "Just a pack o' thieves . . . and now you add traitors, too . . ." She looks pointedly at Mairead. "A damned bogtrotter, as well. You and your Newgaters are well named. Hope you'll all enjoy the lower deck. It should remind you all of home—both the bowels of Newgate . . . and focking Ireland."

Mrs. Barnsley has never concealed her dislike of me. I know she was jealous of my bein' able to wriggle my way into the Captain's cabin so soon—and maybe into his affections, too. Now, there's been many an individual Liverpool Judy, London Lizzie, and Scottish Tartan in the cabin, bouncing on various male knees, but the three Mesdames have not, and it rankles them to see me prancing in and out of there, like I half own the place—which I do . . . or did . . .

"*Erin go braugh!*" Mairead snarls, and goes to fling herself off the foretop. I manage to catch and hold her before she can leap down on Mrs. Barnsley, claws out and ready to do damage.

"Me and mine shall thrive wherever we are quartered, Mrs. Barnsley," I announce, "as we are secure in both our mutual friendship and our womanly virtue."

And the price for washing your Crew's filthy drawers just went up by half, you old bawd!

That gets the old bawd's goat.

"Listen, you little guttersnipe," snarls Mrs. Barnsley, pointing a threatening finger up at me, "you go holier-than-thou on me, and I'll teach you a lesson or two."

"Hey, hey, we'll have none of that, else we'll have to bring out the rod again." The Captain, being a generally easy-going sort, will not put up with a loss of good order. Only yesterday, two of the ladies—one Judy, a Jane Ellis, and one Tartan, Mary Davidson—had gotten into a fight, over a man, of course, and each had been punished by being stretched across a cannon, skirts hiked up, and given ten lashes of the rod over their very ample buttocks. Their howls were *quite* expressive.

"The darkness and gloom will be good for my snowy complexion, Captain Laughton," say I, getting a good laugh from the crowd. A week and a half out from London and I'm already tanned brown as a nut. The laugh eases the tension.

"Well said," replies the Captain. "Now, as for that song for your rent, perhaps it might be delivered by the newest member of your Crew, the lovely colleen with the flaming red hair?"

I pull out my pennywhistle and look over at Mairead. "It would be a good thing to do," I say.

She nods. In our hammock last night we had talked for a long while about our situation and had come to a joint conclusion: We can worry about our lads only so much, but we also know that they would want us to be cheerful and make the best of the lot that has befallen us. Then we fell asleep, wrapped about each other for comfort.

Mairead stands up and so do I.

"It will be 'Home, Boys, Home!' " she announces to the crowd, and to me she counts *one . . . two . . . three!* And we swing into it, she with voice, me with whistle.

Oh, well, who wouldn't be a sailor lad, a sailin'
on the main,
To gain the goodwill of his captain's good name,
He came ashore one evening at my own daddy's inn,
And that was the beginning of my own true love
and me. For it's . . .

"All you down there," I call out to those below. "Come join in the chorus and let's properly welcome our new lass aboard our *Lorelei Lee!*"

With great gusto they all—Captain, officers, crew, and Crews—sing it out.

Home, boys, home, home I'd like to be,
Home for a while in the old country
Where the oak and the ash and the bonny rowan tree
Are all growing greener in the north country!

Mairead goes into the next verse, while I toodle along. Although Mairead is not a large girl—not much bigger than

I—she has a powerful set of lungs and, when singing, is not at all shy of using them.

Well, he asked me for a candle for to light him up to bed,
And likewise for a handkerchief to tie around his head.
I tended to his needs like a chambermaid ought to do,
So then he says to me, now won't you leap in with me,
*   too. And it's . . .*

. . . the chorus, again, louder now, and . . .

Well, I jumped into the bed, making no alarm,
Thinking a young sailor lad could never do me harm.
Well, he hugged me and kissed me the whole night long,
Till I wished that little short night had been nine years
*   long. And it's . . .*

. . . the chorus, with all on deck joining in, and then Mairead crosses her hands over her belly and looks off with a rueful expression on her face as she sings . . .

Well, early next morning, the sailor lad arose,
And into my apron threw a handful of gold, saying,
"Take this me dear, for the mischief that I've done,
For tonight I fear I've left you with a daughter or a son."
*   And it's . . .*

. . . the chorus, with great laughter at Mairead's wide-eyed poor-maiden-finding-herself-suddenly-with-child pantomime, and then she sings the last verse . . .

Now come all of you fair maidens, a warning
  take by me,
And never let a sailor lad an inch above your knee,
For I trusted one and he beguil-ed me,
He left me with a pair of twins to dangle on
  me knee. And it's . . .

Home, boys, home, home I'd like to be,
Home for a while in the old country
Where the oak and the ash and the bonny rowan tree
Are all a growing greener in the north country!

I cap it off with a trill of notes on my whistle, and then we both bow. A great cheer for the two of us, and then the Captain rises and lifts his glass in salute to Mairead.

"Capital, just capital, my girls," he bellows. "Today, let the merriment continue with a double tot for all! Tomorrow, we shall be at Madeira Island, the Pearl of the Atlantic!" crows the Captain, holding up his glass for a refill. "The Floating Garden of the Sea!"

Huzzah!

Chapter 31

J. Fletcher
Cerberus
18 days out

Dear Jacky,

I hope you are as well as can be expected, considering our common circumstances.

Our days on the *Cerberus* are long—relentlessly, infinitely, tediously long—and the nights are even longer, and I fear you endure something of the same. Each day, at Two Bells in the Morning Watch, the long leg chain is untethered from its moorings at each end of our cell, and we drag it along to the head and thence to the mess deck to be given our slops. We are then taken up onto the deck for air and exercise. Do not believe, dear one, they are doing this out of any kindness in their hearts, for surely there is very little of that virtue contained in those dark places. No, for as they are being paid by the head of any convict who arrives in New South Wales alive and reasonably healthy, whichever wretch passes for the Ship's Surgeon must feel the exercising of us prisoners necessary to that end.

Out on deck, we are made to shuffle five times around the main hatch top, the one immediately forward of the quarterdeck, then it is back down into our hole. Being outside does lift our spirits a bit, and we are allowed to sing—encouraged even. The quarterdeck watch must get as bored with its lot as we are with ours and is glad to hear it. Plus, each of my pack of rascals seems to have an excellent voice. Something in the soil of Ireland, I suppose . . .

The time topside is beneficial not only to my body, but also to my mind, for it gives me a chance to size some things up. The state of this ship, for instance. It is a big, tubby merchantman that I will not dignify by naming it a proper brig. However, having three masts, with all sails square, I must call it a ship. Ship though it may be, it is certainly a seagoing wreck—sloppy and ill-kempt and an affront to any Royal Navy sailor's eye.

I note there are belaying pins sitting in holes drilled into the rails, as they should be, while others are just lying about the scuppers. There is the usual bunch of cutlasses chained about the foot of the foremast, as well. I note, too, the discontented, surly crew—I am sure they live only for their nightly pint of grog. I have heard no cheerful singing from them in the below decks, only the clanking of chains and the moans of the damned. It seems that only Napper, Vance, and the Weasel enjoy their work.

I am reminded daily of Dante's Inferno, and his various levels of hell. After some reflection, I put this particular hell at about level five. That time I spent in Pittsburgh's foulest prison in the rather dubious company of Mike Fink, which I had thought at the time was the worst of possible fates, pales beside this, and rates only a three, I believe. Actually, when I think of Sergeant Napper and Corporal Vance, I recall with some fondness the very large and very hairy Mr. Fink, King of the River, and our mutual acquaintance. He did, after all, wholeheartedly offer me his friendship—*Love her up good, boy, 'fore I come down and mess her up for good and ever, for the stealin' of my boat. After she's down at the bottom of the river with an anchor chain wrapped round her neck, maybe you and me'll bring my boat back upriver. Haul some cargo, buy us a coupla fancy ladies, have us a time. Whadya say, boy?*—and, I must admit, except for the prospect of your sad demise, a life on that river does not seem such a bad idea right now. *It's the only life for a man and you know it to be true.* Perhaps Mike was right . . . But I digress . . .

Now, the escort ship, which lies off our port side, that is another story altogether. It is a trim, well-maintained brig, sailed tightly in true Bristol fashion. It is Royal Navy, and looks it.

When on exercise drill, I find that Second Mate Travis Hollister often falls into step next to me for some conversation. At first I was surprised at that, but then I realized the cause—he and I are the only former Royal Navy officers onboard and the poor man must have lacked for nautical conversation, or intelligent conversation of any kind. Not that I have much to offer in that regard, but still.

It was he who told me something of HMS *Dart*, our well-armed escort.

"As you can see, she is a sloop-of-war, and is commanded by a Captain Adam Varga," he says. "They seem well turned out."

"The other officers?" I ask, thinking I might know some of them.

"I do not know."

"You do not go over to dine, sometimes? Is there not some common naval courtesy?"

"No, it's plain they hold us in the greatest contempt."

"Not you, too, surely?"

"They do not even know I am here."

I reflect that it must be difficult for him—to have gained his hard-won lieutenancy in the Royal Navy, served honorably, then not being able to secure a berth after Trafalgar, when Boney's fleet was destroyed with the help of such as he. It is ironic—you risk your life to save your country, and when you are successful, you find yourself out of a job.

I have thought and thought of ways of escape, but have so far come up with nothing. I lie back on my bench and muse on that.

Now, what would you do, Jacky? You who have escaped confinement so many times? Hmmm. Well, I imagine that first you would begin to charm your guards, right? Appeal to their male vanity, appeal to whatever protective nature might dwell in their bosom for a poor little girl so cruelly treated? Would you softly sing songs that remind them of their homeland and sisters and daughters so far away? Oh, yes, you would. Songs sung so softly and with such feeling that they would be lulled into reverie and sweet remembrance and inattention to their duty.

I fear, however, that Sergeant Napper and Corporal Vance would be somewhat immune to my charms in that way. *My* charms, yes . . . but maybe not the allure of some others. I have noticed during our exercise outside on deck that the eyes of the two brutes very often fall upon young Daniel Connolly, and then slide knowingly to each other's. I have seen sly smiles and nods pass between them.

You are shocked by that? Yes, well might you be, being a young girl and not exposed to such odious things, but such deviant lusts do dwell in the breasts of certain men. Connolly is an angelic-looking boy, well-formed, with curly brown hair and downy cheeks, hardly sixteen. He has not yet had his first shave. Although I shrink from such thoughts, I realize I must not, as I must use every device we can conceive of to triumph over our jailers. I would do you no good in the penal colony, Jacky, as a chained and dispirited convict.

However, we must have weapons, and sharp and deadly they must be. But we do not have them now, so we must wait until we can lay our hands upon such things.

In the dead of night, we whisper and plan. The lads speak of trustable cons who are also able seamen. Each of them reels off a short list of names:

"Matthews, Burke, Stackpole, all in third cell . . . They're all right . . ."

"And Hubbard and Elfstrom in the bottom crew. And Meehan, too. He's from Galway . . . He's solid . . ."

And so on . . . to the actual plans for the mutiny.

"We must get them through that door, and off their guard."

"How can we do that? They are very leery of us."

"I think I know how, but we must be patient . . . We must have weapons, and can do nothing till we get them."

"You noticed the cutlasses chained about the mainmast?"

"Aye."

"Napper will have the key to that on the chain he wears around his fat gut."

"Right. We'll have to get at that when the time comes."

"The Weasel will be easy . . . but Napper and Vance will not."

"Awful cozy with that Second Mate, ain't-cha, Captain?"

"He is a good source of information, McBride. And don't forget, if we succeed in taking over this ship, we've still got the Dart to contend with. She could blow us out of the water in a minute, and she is—"

There is a sudden rattling of a club against the bars of our cage.

"Awright, you scum, what youse whisperin' about in there?"

"Nothin', Corporal dear," pipes up Padraic Delaney. "Just saying our prayers is all, just like any good little Catholic boys. Come, lads, join me. 'Hail Mary, Full of grace, The Lord is with Thee, Blessed art Thou . . .'"

"Well, knock it off," growls Corporal Vance. "Bad enough we gotta haul stinkin' micks around w'out havin' to listen t' papist claptrap, too."

The men quiet down, but they are not done—not with me, anyway.

Presently McBride pipes up. "Will ye be tellin' us a joke now, Captain Fletcher, to be improvin' the morale of your present troops?"

"I'm not in the mood, McBride," I growl—plus I'm just not good at that sort of thing.

"Well, I'll be tellin' one then, Sir."

"Tell it, Arthur," urges another voice in the gloom.

"I shall, Daniel, I shall," says Arthur McBride, and he begins.

"One fine day last year as I was walking along a path in sweet County Cork, I happened upon a sleeping leprechaun, and I quickly snatched the little bugger up, you may be sure.

"'Och,' says he, rubbin' his eyes, 'I guess ye've caught me good and proper, and now ye'll get yer three wishes. But I gotta tell you, lad, that I'm a special kind of leprechaun, in that when I grant you a wish, yer worst enemy will get twice what ye wish for. Do ye understand?'

"'I do,' I replied.

"'All right, so what'll yer wishes be, boy-o?'

"Well, I think for a bit, and then I say, 'First, I'd like a million pounds sterling.'

"'It is granted,' says the little green fellow. 'But ye do know that yer worst enemy, Mr. James Fletcher, will get *two* million pounds?'

"'That's all right,' I says. ''Tis hard, but I can live with that.'

"'All right, done. What's next? Hurry up, I'm a busy elf.'

"'Now I'd like to have the renowned Miss Jacky Faber stripped down to her natural lovely self and put next to me in my bed, so that I might sample all of her lovely charms, at my leisure, for a whole week.'"

Uh-oh . . . low chuckles all around. I should have expected something like this.

"'That means that this Mr. Fletcher will have the delightful girl bouncin' in his bed for *two* whole weeks? Disgustin' to think about, but so be it,' I says firmly.

"'Done,' says the leprechaun. 'Now, what's yer last wish to be, knowin' as you do that Mr. James Fletcher will get *twice* what ye get?'

" 'Now,' I says, secure in my resolve, 'I wants you to cut off *one* of me balls . . . ' "

Great guffaws all around. Grrrr . . .

I will get him, count on it, Jacky . . .

Jaimy

Chapter 32

Madeira was indeed a pearl. I've traveled around some in this world, but never have I been in a more beautiful place—soaring cliffs, blue water and crashing surf, hanging gardens that assault the senses with their heady perfumes, and acres upon acres of the finest grapes. Porto Santos, too, was lovely in the extreme, and farther down, several hundred miles off the coast of Africa, there were the Cape Verde Islands, yet another of the ocean's jewels.

I, of course, did not get to see much of these fine Portuguese ports, being underwater most of the time, diving for coins. The sailors on the nearby ships were generous, and I did well. It is profitable work, and I find it great fun. Plus I got to practice my Spanish, as the Portuguese tongue is very similar.

"Hola, marineros! Tiren sus monedas en el agua, y para su placer, me zambullire para ellas," I call out from the dock, bouncing on my toes, my bathing suit bottom hiked up as far as modesty permits, and the coins do come raining down.

The Captain had put into those ports on the pretext of taking on fresh supplies—anyway, that is how he entered them in his logbook, Assistant Purser Higgins reports, but methinks the Captain did not so much desire oranges, lemons, fresh water, and such, as much as he wanted his good, honest graft—his twenty percent skim off the top of the Crews' take. He wanted to let loose his very accomplished female Crews on the male populations contained on these island paradises—and hey, what's a Paradise without a few hundred comely Eves? This journey might very well make our Captain Laughton very rich. I sense that he is certainly in no hurry to get to his final destination. And why kick a winning horse? ask I, in total agreement, as I'm not in such a hurry to get there, either.

We did, however, bring aboard many baskets full of the local grapes—and *many* barrels of the local wine.

The three madams dutifully handed over their tithes, and we departed for the Cape of Good Hope, the southern tip of the Continent of Africa. Yes, I had to hand over some, too. The Captain is no dummy, and what's sauce for the Lizzies, the Judies, and the Tartans, is sauce for us Newgaters, too.

About a week later, the *Lorelei Lee* ran into a bit of a problem. The Captain had put her in close to the African shore to take on water from the mouth of a river that had been spotted there. The water had been hauled aboard, and we were ready to resume our course to the Cape. Mairead, Molly, and I were lolling about the foretop, our stint at the washtubs over for now, when I heard the call from below.

"She won't come up, Sir," shouts the Bo'sun from the fo'c's'le. "She's snagged."

"Put your goddamn backs into it, you whore-son bastards," snarls Ruger from the quarterdeck. "All hands up forward." More men rush to join the others already straining at the spokes of the capstan wheel.

There is much grunting and cursing but to no avail—the anchor remains stuck fast. I run up and look down at the chain, vertical now, and quivering under the strain. The *Lorelei* is listing to the side in the vain effort to bring up the recalcitrant hook.

"How deep, Bo'sun?"

"Six fathoms, five, Sir!"

"Damn," says the Captain. "We may have to let it go."

No! It's my anchor, dammit! I paid good money for it, and I'm not going to lose it!

"Maybe not, Captain," I pipe up. "Let me have a look first. I won't be but a minute. Mairead, to me!"

We both plunge down to the laundry.

"My swimsuit, Sister!" I cry, peeling off my Newgater's rig as Mairead pulls my diving gear from under our bunk and tosses it out across our bed there, my solution to the living quarters thing.

No, certainly my Crew had not gone down to the bottom level, though we would continue to claim it as our own, since Mairead had won it with her song. Instead, we took the space we already had—to wit, the laundry, with its big open space, and its wide windows placed there for the dumping of the dirty water.

While the others below decks slept in hammocks, we now had beds, because I knew where spare mattresses were stored. Sheets, too. *"We shall live as queens, girls!"* I had announced when putting the plan into operation. And so we did. The forward wall of the laundry was a bulkhead—a moveable wall, which I had Mick and Keefe take down, revealing the storeroom that I knew was there. I asked the boys to remove the cordage kept therein and to stow it down on our fourth level, which they did with a minimum of cursing. *"Little busybody, does she think we're 'er bleedin' servants?"* Some small monetary inducements took care of that. Further bribes guaranteed that the Ship's Carpenter would collect enough boards to construct bunks for us around the perimeter of the space. Course, being no fool, I had cleared all this earlier with the Assistant Purser.

Since the door to the laundry opens inward, my trusty wedges see good service when we are snugged in for the night, protected in a way that the other Crews are not, be they on bottom level or top. I had the Carpenter cut the door crossways, Dutch door style, with a shelf on the bottom half for the receiving and delivery of laundry when we are open. That way we get the business, all neat, like, and keep out the rabble.

Busybody, indeed.

Being next to the galley is nice, too, for Cookie is generous, and Jezebel comes to visit us often. We have warm water and soap, and so we are clean. With some nice white muslin curtains fluttering merrily in the breeze, we count ourselves to be quite cozy and unwilling to change places with any of the Crews, and that includes yours, too, Mrs. Barnsley.

Guttersnipe, am I? Just you wait, you old sow . . .

"And what do you mean to do down there, Jacky?" asks Mairead, securing my back strap and sounding worried. She has seen me dive in the somewhat shallow waters of our past ports and wasn't all that pleased . . . *You could drown, Jacky, you could . . .*

But I didn't drown then, and I ain't gonna drown now. "I mean to see if I can do something about the anchor, Sister. Don't worry. It's only about forty feet deep. I've gone down that far many times. Let's go. Bring me a towel."

And then, goggles and swim fins in hand, I head back to the open air.

Gaining the deck, I plunk down on the planking, lift my right foot, and strap on the fin. Then I do the same with the left. Ain't very graceful, or ladylike, splayed out like that, but I don't hear no complaints. Then, goggles on and fitted to my face, I stand, and for the millionth time, tuck two fingers back to tug the bottom of my suit down over my bum.

"Well, it seems our little mermaid has turned into a frog," says the Captain, as I waddle over to the rail. *Very funny, Sir. You try walking in these things . . .* "I don't know what you hope to accomplish," he continues, "but you are welcome to try."

I nod and take three deep breaths, hold my goggles to my face, and then jump over the rail and into the water. It enfolds me, warm and clear, as I wriggle down into the depths, following the chain as it disappears into the blueness below.

Keeping a sharp eye out for any sharks who might be looking for an easy meal of tender maiden, I continue to go down hand over hand, grabbing the big links of chain to help pull me lower and lower. There are fathom markers every six feet . . . there goes four . . . five . . . now six . . . and there's the anchor.

Sure enough, one of the flukes is wedged deep in a cleft in a rock—a rock big enough that the lower parts of it are not visible. The *Lorelei* could pull on that chain forever and never gain an inch. The other fluke, however, sticks straight up, clear in the misty blue.

Hmmmm . . . Maybe that'll be the way of this little rescue . . .

I kick back to the surface.

"There she is!" I hear as my head breaks the surface.

"Thank God!" says another voice I recognize as Mairead's.

Hey, I was down less than a minute . . .

"Captain," I call. "Have the Bo'sun give me the end of a coil of one-inch line and maybe I can free our anchor! Put it under the rail, as you'll be taking a strain on it." *Wouldn't want to snap my beautifully varnished rail, would we?*

"Consider it done," says the Captain, and the bitter end of the coil comes snaking over the side, under the fragile rail. I grab the rope and stick it between my teeth, upend myself, and head back down. When I reach the anchor, I quickly slap a bowline hitch around the free fluke and then dart back up.

"Take a strain on the line, and if you feel it give, slack off and haul in the anchor," I gasp, a bit winded now. I wait till I see the Bo'sun and his men wind the line around the capstan head and begin to turn it. Then three more big gulps of air and back on the job.

I get down near the anchor and see the strain taking hold on the rope. It quivers and straightens out along its length, but still does not budge the heavy anchor.

Damn!

I kick over to the rope and lay my hands on it to give it a good shake back and forth. It is as unyielding as iron in my grip, but, nothing . . . *No, there! It's coming!*

I maneuver back out of the way as the anchor lifts, scattering sediment about as it breaks free. The rescue rope slackens, and the hook begins its journey up.

Hmmm . . . I've got some air left . . .

Ever the showgirl, I dart over to the anchor, slap my rump down on it, slide my goggles up onto my forehead so I'll look more appealing, and ride up in grand style. As the anchor breaks the surface, the entire crew sees me sitting grandly in the curve of the left fluke, ankles crossed, arm up in the air like any circus performer.

"Ta-da!" I shout, taking a half bow, as a mighty cheer erupts above me.

"Oh, capital, that!" chortles the Captain. "Just capital."

Eager hands reach down for me, and I am pulled aboard. Mairead comes over to wrap the towel about my shoulders as I toe off the fins.

"Our little tadpole has saved the day," announces Captain Laughton. "Or at least a very valuable anchor. Now, what will you have as your reward for that daring deed?"

I have been waiting for an opportunity like this.

"I wish no reward for doing my duty, Sir," I simper. "But if you could see your way clear, us girls would be most glad if we could see you brave men fire off those big scary guns, we would. Though we might tremble and cover our ears, still it would be a fine treat."

"Very well, then," says Captain Laughton, with a huge grin. "Let it be so. Today, for the ladies' pleasure, we shall exercise our mighty gunnery! Right after lunch! Mr. Higgins! If you please!"

• • •

"Jacky . . . Why did you ask for that as a reward for getting that anchor back? The shooting of those awful cannons? What profit is in that? Couldn't you have asked for something better?"

"Aye, Ann, but y'see, there is a method to my madness. We've got to find out just how expert the male members of this crew are in the firing of the cannons, that's why." I'm wriggling out of my swimsuit and about to slide into the warm tub to rinse off the salt. "We need to know 'cause the place where we are going will be swarming with pirates."

I put foot in washtub and then slide the rest of me in. *Ahhhhh . . .*

"But, Jacky, wouldn't it be better for us girls if pirates did take the ship? Then maybe they would treat us kindly, and we could escape this confinement?"

"Nay, Molly, you wouldn't escape. No, instead you'd be used in ways most cruel and then sold as a slave in North Africa. You do not know pirates as I do—for every gallant Flaco Jimenez and yes, even a Belle Jeune Fille Sans Merci, there are ten low and vicious El Feos. No, for now, dears, we're better off under John Bull's somewhat gentler yoke."

"And if anyone knows gunnery, it's this one," says Mairead, pushing my head underwater and preparing to soap it down.

I ain't got nothing to say to that, but I will be watching our lads very closely as they work their guns.

After I'm out and dried off and back in my rig, I call out, "Everybody lookin' sharp in their Newgaters' gear? Good. Let's go topside—heads up, chin out, eyes hooded, and shoulders squared. Let's show 'em. Proud to be Newgaters forever!"

"Very well, men," says Captain Laughton from his quarterdeck. "Let us show the ladies what we can do. Cast off the barrel on the port side. Guns two to twelve, prepare to fire."

I see matchlocks prepared, while men sight over the barrels. At least the guns had been left loaded. Powder prolly damp by now . . . They should be fired out every day, but I know that's not gonna happen—costs too much, and who knows where we might replenish our spent powder?

"Fire when they bear," shouts the Captain, and the exercise begins.

Pathetic, of course.

Number one fires . . . *craaack!* . . . and misses by twenty yards. That's all right. Let's just see how fast they can reload, because that will be the key to a close ship-to-ship encounter. I find out quickly: men stumble over each other clambering back up on deck as others careen down ladders to get more bags of powder. Both groups end up running into each other, both on the way down to the powder magazine and on the way back up, too.

What a mess.

Number four misfires, as does number six. Number eight manages to discharge its load . . . *craaaaaccckkk!* . . . but it misses by a wide margin, too.

The remaining port side guns do not do any better, and the starboard guns do even worse. Captain Laughton calls out, "Secure from the Exercise of the Guns. Well done! An extra tot for all!"

What? Well done? I am aghast, and struck to the core of my Royal Navy soul. But I hold my tongue, for what else can

I do? *Oh, well . . . sure hope we don't meet any well-trained, voracious, and merciless pirates.* It is a fervent hope, but I know it is a vain one, as well . . .

. . . and meanwhile, perhaps, I can manage to do a few little things . . .

Chapter 33

Jacky Faber
Onboard Lorelei Lee
Off the West Coast of Africa

Miss Amy Trevelyne
Dovecote Farm
Quincy, Massachusetts, USA

Dearest Amy,

I have decided, dear Sister, that I shall write you every so often to keep you abreast of my various doings on this journey to the Other Side of the World, should you be at all interested.

Our good Captain Laughton has promised that he will carry our letters back from Australia after he has dumped us off, and I believe he will be as good as his word in that regard—especially since he demands a full shilling per packet. That means, if I write to you now, you should get the letters, all in a bunch, in about, say, a year and a half. Not too bad, considering. Hey, maybe you can patch together another potboiler of a novel—however, nothing much in that sort of way has happened yet. But I promise to try to spice things up a bit in the coming days. You can count on me. If you would like to read these letters to the assembled girls of the Lawson Peabody, feel free. It would give me a feeling of some connection to my former schoolmates, whom I think of often and fondly, and it might give them some life lessons on how *not* to conduct oneself as a Young Lady abroad in this world. I am sure Mistress will second that. As will Connie Howell, I am sure . . .

It is noon and I am done with school for the day, having sent the little blighters off to play in the rigging, cautioning them to be careful of falling, and urging them to try to remember today's lesson on addition and subtraction. I've made up chips with addition or subtraction problems on the front and the answers on the back, like forty minus twenty on one side, and the answer, twenty, on the other, and told them to practice with each other when they are not working. If they get all of their answers correct upon my next quizzing them, they shall have their story at the end of class as usual. If not, then no story. I can be hard, I can, when faced with scholarly sloth. After class, the room is turned back into a laundry and my girls and I get to work, scrubbing away. You may tell Peg and the downstairs girls I am becoming quite the accomplished laundress. My love to all of them.

We have already visited several very exotic ports, and though we cannot wander far, still we have time to taste some of the wonders of the places. I am enclosing a watercolor of a very colorful little bird that lighted on our rail in

Cape Verde and sat there singing long enough for me to sketch it and to jot down its particular characteristics and colors. Please give the picture to Dorothea—maybe she can identify the pretty little creature.

My Newgaters have been joined by two more women from the other Crews, both mothers of kids in our school, making my Crew now number fourteen, not counting the kids. We voted on them and they were accepted. They are decent sorts in spite of their recent line of work. Hey, let any lady who would purse her lips and judge harshly these unfortunate girls—and that means you, too, Miss Trevelyne—let you get good and hungry sometime . . . or worse, watch your children grow weak from hunger, and we'll just see what sort of life you would sink to. Sorry . . . sorry for the rant, all of you, and sorry, Miss Prosser, for ending a sentence with a preposition. Enough of that. The children sleep with their mothers and have been warned that if they disrupt our sleep or the good order of our barracks, out they will go. They have been good. So far.

Several days ago, the Captain, at my urging, had the men drill at the gunnery, and though they did very poorly, I could not speak out about it, considering my station. After the exercise, Captain Laughton asked me my opinion and I replied that though it was wondrously exciting, perhaps things would go more smoothly if my girls and I could volunteer to be Powder Monkeys, as we are light in weight and small and quick and thus could free able-bodied seamen from that task and make things go more efficiently. He agreed wholeheartedly, and I went immediately below to inform my girls of just what I had volunteered them for.

"But Jacky," cried Molly, my bright-eyed fourteen-year-old horse thief, once again expressing doubt over lending any assistance to our captors. "Why should we do this for them? They are our jailers!"

"Because, Molly, I hear from Mr. Higgins, our Assistant Purser, that there is such a thing called a pardon, which the governor of the penal colony is authorized to grant to any prisoner, based upon sincere repentance and goodness of behavior." I placed my finger on her nose. "Believe me, Molly, Mr. Higgins is keeping a very strict account of every convict's behavior on this journey, and he will be entering your service to the *Lorelei Lee* in your own record, Miss Reibey, and you may live to be happy at that. Now stand still while Maggie measures you for your new uniform."

I have ordained that my Powder Monkeys be outfitted in clothing suited to the jobs they will be doing—light white canvas trousers and tops with modified mobcap, and hair done up in pigtail. It is a practical rig, and I believe it will instill some unit pride in my gang.

When all the uniforms were done and us girls dressed in them, I marched the Monkeys to the Captain for inspection. There were great hoots of hilarity all around, but I don't care—my girls looked straight and proud and smart as new paint. After Captain Laughton stopped laughing, he allowed me to assign the Monkeys to their stations and then drill them. We made a number of dry runs till they got used to the routes down to the powder magazine, and carrying up the five-pound cartridges of black powder.

The Captain was impressed enough with our good order that he called the men to battle stations and each gun fired off two live charges. Things went much better this time, with the help of my girls, and I pronounced myself satisfied.

When we secured from the drill, I left my monkey uniform on as I intend to adopt it as my everyday wear. Nobody said I couldn't, so on it stays. It is more practical than my dress, and cooler, too, to say nothing of being more modest when climbing up in the rigging. Didn't take Jacky Faber long to get back in trousers, did it?

I am called into the Captain's cabin virtually every night to provide musical accompaniment to his dinners. He has several of his officers in to dine at each meal, as well as various ladies, but one who is always in attendance is his good friend Enoch Lightner, a former Royal Navy lieutenant who had been blinded in battle. He has an excellent baritone voice and it is a pleasure to sing with him.

Well, time for me to blot and to file this letter and get ready to go to the Captain's cabin for the evening. You know, when I am in that space, I often think fondly of you, my dear Sister, and our last dinner therein. I hope this finds everyone well and happy.

I am,
Yr. devoted friend and classmate,

Jacky

Chapter 34

"Let all slimy Pollywogs who would have the courage to dare approach the great Lord Neptune, Ruler of the Seas and All Upon Them, and beg him for admittance into the Holy Order of trusty Shellbacks, do so now upon their unworthy knees!"

Yes, the *Lorelei Lee* is crossing the equator at noon today and the festivities, if they can be called that, are in full swing. Yes, I, too, am an unworthy Pollywog, and am on my hands and knees. I got close to crossing that line, that time back in the Caribbean, but not quite, and it does not do to lie to King Neptune. I may not be quite as superstitious as most sailors, but still, no sense tempting fate.

There is a ritual to this thing. The night before crossing the line, the uninitiated Pollywogs symbolically overthrow the rule of the tyrannical Shellbacks in what is called the Wog Uprising. Army Major Johnston, being the highest-ranking of those officers who have not yet made the crossing, becomes Lord of the Pollywogs and grandly directs that Captain Laughton be taken from his place at the head of his table and seated at the foot, where a flagon of ale is poured over his head. Wog Lord Johnston seats himself at the head with the Newgaters' own Esther Abrahams by his side as Queen of Wog-Revels.

The Captain takes all this with great good humor, roaring out his promise that all shall pay for this outrage. There is much *hoo*ing and hollering from us Wogs, and anyone who knows me knows I just love that sort of thing. *Let King Chaos rule! Hooray!*

It reminds me of the Pope's Day Riots back in good old Boston. I had such a roaring good time then, and I'm having a good time at this, too. I am afraid a good part of Jacky Faber's soul is pure, unbridled anarchist.

Yes, the Pollywogs do get to abuse the Shellbacks, and I get in my licks, believe me, but we must be careful in our abuse, for tomorrow the Shellbacks will take control again, and watch out, Pollywogs!

Kegs of good beer are cracked, meat is sizzled over the galley fires, and the carousing goes on far into the night.

The next day, the tables are turned. In the morning, no time is wasted—before any breakfast is served, roaring Shellbacks come through all the quarters, banging on pots and pans and demanding that all despised Pollywogs lay to the top deck to atone for their sins.

As the groggy and now fearful Pollywogs go up into the light, all of my girls, including me, are very wisely clad only in our underclothing, for I suspect that what will be coming will be, if nothing else, very wet and sloppy. *Things are going to get crazy, ladies, so best be prepared.* A few days ago the *Lorelei Lee* put in close to shore and loaded much slimy seaweed into her lifeboats. When I asked about the possible use of such vile stuff I was told, *Never you mind, Wog.*

"Get in a proper line, all you Wog Dogs! Now! King Neptune approaches!" This is roared out by the Shantyman, who stands beating a slow muted rhythm on his drum.

We get into some sort of a line and wait. I spot Higgins standing by the rail, serving tray in hand. I note that the *Lorelei* has been stopped and is dead in the water.

"On your knees!" thunders Enoch Lightner. "He is here! Well might you tremble!"

On cue, several seamen haul on a line, and a platform that hangs over the side is lifted level with the deck, and seated upon what appears to be some sort of throne is King Neptune himself. A great gasp goes up from the crowd. All fall to their hands and knees.

"WHO DARES? WHO DARES CALL UP MIGHTY NEPTUNE FROM HIS WATERY REALM?" bellows Neptune, waving the trident he holds in his hand.

It is, of course, Captain Laughton, himself, stark naked except for a crown made of rope entwined with seashell, sitting atop a grisly seaweed wig. Strands of that same gray-green seaweed are draped somewhat judiciously below his great bare belly, with some more hanging from his ears to suggest a beard. He wears a very fierce expression.

"It is a band of supplicants who have come to beg admittance to your kingdom, O Mighty Ruler of the Waves!" announces Higgins, handing the august King a goblet of wine.

"LET THEM APPROACH ME, THEN, TO KISS MY RING, BUT ONLY AFTER THEY HAVE PASSED THROUGH THE GAUNTLET SUCH THAT THEY MIGHT PROVE THEMSELVES WORTHY TO BE CALLED MY SONS AND DAUGHTERS!"

At the urging of several rough Shellbacks, the line begins crawling, rumps in air, toward the gauntlet, which consists of two parallel lines of twelve grinning Shellbacks each, and each holding three-foot-long sections of wet hose. There are about seven ladies in front of me, mostly Tartans. At the end, just before Neptune's throne, there are more Shellbacks standing next to tubs of foul-smelling seaweed. *Uh-oh* . . .

The first poor Pollywogs enter the gauntlet, and the hoses are swung and brought to bear upon shoulders, backs, and bottoms. Screams are heard, but laughter, too—they are not hitting hard.

Higgins, how did you manage to finesse this? You've never been below the line . . .

The first of the Pollywogs, a Tartan named Sarah Manning, has made it to the end of the hose-swingers, whereupon a mound of rank seaweed is placed upon her head. From behind me I hear the sounds of dresses being hastily pulled over heads. *Good idea, ladies, it's gonna be messy* . . .

The unfortunate Miss Manning is then lifted to her feet by two very courteous sailors and led grandly to stand before King Neptune.

"YOU MAY NOW KISS MY RING AND JOIN THE WATERY REALM!" he thunders.

The obedient Sarah bends down to kiss the ring, which is on the King's hairy big toe.

"WELCOME, TRUSTY SHELLBACK! YOU MAY NOW ENTER THE HALLOWED KINGDOM OF THE SEA!"

With that, the two formerly courteous Shellbacks pick up the very surprised girl and fling her over the side. The sound of her scream is cut off by the sound of a splash. There are cries of alarm down the line.

"NEXT!" shouts the King.

Are they crazy? These girls cannot swim! Some must surely drown!

Surely not. Sarah is soon spotted being put back over the rail, dripping but undrowned.

The blows to my back have continued unabated, but they are quite bearable. Or they were. Then my downcast eyes fall upon a particularly well-shined pair of officer's boots, and suddenly I receive a hard slap across my rear and cry out in spite of myself.

"Yeeow!"

I look up, shocked, and see that it is First Mate Ruger who has delivered the blow. *Of course . . .* He grins down at me and then winds up and gives me another sharp one.

Ouch! Please, not again!

Only the fact that the line moves relentlessly forward and takes me out of his range saves me from further pain. One more across the small of my back, then another on my legs, and then it's someone else's turn to crawl in front of that dirty bastard.

I feel with some relief the cool seaweed being applied to my head, and then I am led to the foot of King Neptune.

"HA! THE HALLS OF MY UNDERSEA GROTTO SHALL SURELY RING WITH MUSIC NOW. WELCOME ABOARD, MY LITTLE MERMAID!"

I kiss the ring, and then I see the blue water rushing up at me to cleanse me of seaweed . . . and fury.

Chapter 35

"Good soup, Cookie," I chirp, perched on the edge of a bench in the galley, bowl of tasty burgoo in my hand, Jezebel on my lap as usual. "How much pork we got left?"

"Not much, Jacky," he says, leaning over his pot of never-ending stew. "Things gettin' mighty thin. Maybe we can take on some meat when we get to Cape Town. Lots o' piggies there, I hear."

"Ummm," I murmur, swallowing the thick goodness. "Perhaps I should start up my miller business again." I stick my finger in my bowl and let Jezebel lick it off with her raspy tongue.

"Maybe. 'Specially when we gets on the other side of the world. No telling what we'll find there 'cept for the heathen Chinese and whatever the hell they got to eat."

Back on the *Bloodhound*, that vile slaver, Cookie and I had set up a bit of a mutually advantageous enterprise. I would procure the millers—from my very accurate archers, led by Katy Deere herself, best miller-murderer ever born—

and Cookie would roast 'em up for our delectation, keeping half of them for himself and his mates. The millers were actually recently deceased shipboard rats, nailed by Katy's arrows, but because the little rotters had been stealing our finest flour and grains, they were not at all disgusting. In fact, they were quite delicious. I remember them with a certain fondness.

Note to self: See to the construction of several bows and many arrows.

Mick and Keefe are there in the galley, too, and we talk over old times on the *Bloodhound* as well as our current situation. Mick has taken up with Isabella Manson, one of my Crew and a decent sort—neat in appearance and reasonably well-spoken, considering. They have taken one of the tiny cabins on the second level and are content. Surely the best berth Mick Richards has ever gained. He must thank his stars every single time that Isabella cuddles up to him in the dark of the night.

Keefe, strangely, has not yet taken a woman to his bed, in spite of the Captain's invitation for all to partake of the ocean of femaleness that exists on the *Lorelei Lee.*

"Our Keefe is shy, is all," pronounces Mick with a smirk. Isabella sits next to him with her head leaning against his leg, shelling peas for tonight's burgoo. Mick could have taken up with worse, I'm thinking.

"We'll see about that, Keefie," say I, ruffling his hair. "Jacky is on the case. She'll find someone who's right for you."

Hard to believe, but the rough, tough, and very weathered face of the seaman looks away and blushes.

• • •

Yesterday, I discovered that I need not have worried about anyone's drowning as a consequence of being pitched over the side and into the sea after kissing King Neptune's ring to become a Shellback. They'd provided for everyone's safety beforehand by rigging a square sail under the lee of the ship and out of sight of the fearful Pollywogs. They'd stretched it out so that it lay under the water to a depth of about five feet, thereby providing a safe pool of water in its belly. It is a thing often done in ships that sail in warm climes, to give the sailors a refreshing, safe dip. It certainly felt good to me.

After I hit the water and came up to clear the hair from my eyes, I saw Ann Marsh come flying down, then Molly Reibey, and then Esther Abrahams. And then, the over-thrown leader of the fore-doomed Pollywogs, Army Major Johnston himself, was tossed over. He had taken all this hazing in great good humor, bootless and stripped to the waist. A fine figure of a man, I noticed . . . And I also observed that he and Esther were not far apart during the whole ordeal. *Hmmm . . .*

By and large, we all had a hooting good time in the water, watching our astounded mates come flying down to join us in our watery hilarity.

Mairead was not subjected to the rougher parts of the ceremony because of her condition and all. I found out later that the Captain had ordered that all those who were with child to be spared the ordeal. I believe Mairead was a bit miffed at this—*"I'm as fit as any of ye! Why single me out?"*

And yet one other did not go through the line.

And how did you manage to avoid that Pollywog mess, Higgins? I realize that trial would have certainly been too

*much for your dignity to bear, but I also know you've never
been even close to the equator . . .*

"You do not know everything about me, Miss." He sniffed.
"If you must know, a short, private ceremony was held."

Higgins, you are a slippery one.

The hatch ports are open to let out the heat of the galley
stove, and we can hear the sounds of the normal routine
outside—the ringing of the bells of the watch, commands to
the sailors trimming the sails, and—

"On deck, there! Sail ho! Due east!"

I am on my feet in an instant, spilling poor Jezebel to
the floor in my haste. *This cannot be good!* Pausing only to
plunge into our quarters to grab my long glass and yell out,
"Powder Monkeys! On deck now. Take your stations!" I rush
out on deck.

A quick glance confirms that there is indeed a ship out
to our port side, its sails just showing over the horizon.
Throwing the telescope's lanyard around my neck, I leap
into the rigging, and in a moment I am standing next to the
lookout in the crow's-nest with my long glass to my eye.

It is not just one sail! There are three and they are corsairs!

"Battle stations!" I shriek, as I fly back down to the
quarterdeck. "Clear for action!"

As my feet hit the deck, I hear, "If you don't mind, Convict Faber, I will give the orders around here."

It is Captain Laughton, his own glass to his eye. Mr.
Ruger stands beside him.

"They are Arab pirates!" I cry. "I know, I have encoun-
tered their kind before! See that one there, he's flying the
Black Colors, under his masthead! And there! The others do

the same! They mean to frighten us into submission! They mean to take us!"

"They could be fishermen," replies the Captain, doubtfully. "Or they could be honest merchants."

"Fishermen do not come this far out, and if they are merchants, why are they coming straight for us? Oh, please, Sir, turn away and let us fly from them!"

"Oh, very well. Mr. Ruger, bring her right. Steer due west. We shall see if they alter course to follow us."

"Right your rudder, steady on course two nine zero," barks the First Mate. "Top men aloft to make sail!" He turns to me. "You. Get your ass off the quarterdeck."

Casting him a resentful look, I go down to the main deck to get my girls ready, while men scurry up the ratlines to trim the sails to the new course. When the *Lorelei Lee* falls off and comes to the new course, it is plain that the Arab ships do the same. There is no mistaking their intention now.

Corsairs—lanteen rigged . . . Not usually well-armed, but fast and full of fierce, cutlass-swinging fighters—they rely on their swiftness to get close to their prey so that their swordsmen can swarm aboard and overwhelm any resistance. What they lack in firepower, they make up in sheer numbers. Cannon and powder are costly, but desperate men who will fight for a share of any prize are not.

My girls, as instructed, are lined up down the centerline—Ann, Molly, Mary, and Esther will service the port and starboard guns, depending upon which side is engaged, and Mairead will handle the forward gun. I will be on the after nine-pounder because I figure that will be the one getting the most use.

"Steady, girls, steady," I say, hoping to soothe any anxiety they might have. "It will be all right."

As I expected, the order comes . . .

"Man the guns!" shouts the Captain. "Bo'sun, issue cutlasses all around. All women, get below!"

The Shantyman advances to the foot of the mainmast and sets up a booming, warlike rythym on his drum.

"Girls, stand fast," I say. Then I call up to the Captain, "Sir, we will need these Powder Monkeys if the pirates close with us. Things will get hot."

The Captain looks over at my girls, standing at their stations. "Very well. They may stay. All others below."

But there is one who attempts to slightly amend the Captain's order . . .

"Esther. Get below."

My eye catches a flash of scarlet, and I see that we are joined on deck by Army Major Johnston, and it is he who has spoken. He is wearing his sword and pistols and a grim expression. I'm thinking he's wishin' he had a squad of Redcoats with him right now, and I know he wants his Esther below and out of danger.

His Esther looks to me. I shake my head.

"Belay that, Sir," I say, puffing up. "She may be yours someday, Major Johnston, but she's mine now! Better she face her fate up here than to cower down below! All of you! Stand fast at your stations!"

Esther is allowed to stay. I turn to the business at hand. The after gun must be readied. I plunge into the Captain's cabin, expecting to find men manning the Long Tom . . . and I find none . . . Just the empty cabin.

I put my mouth to the speaking tube.

"Captain! Where is the after-gun crew?"

There is a pause, then . . .

"There was not yet a need to assign—"

"Well, there is a need now! Send down two strong men to help me!"

There is the sound of feet pounding, then Suggs and Monk enter the cabin.

"Stack the chairs in that corner!" I order. "Turn the table over and slide it on the bed!"

"But what . . ."

Christ! What a pair of dimwits!

"Don't question, just do it!" I snarl. "Then open the port! And be quick about it, lads, lest you wish to feel Arab steel across your scabby throats this day!"

They don't like it—taking orders from me—but they do it, and the nine-pound Long Tom lies exposed on its track in the rear position. I check it to see that it is still loaded, just like I had left it. It is. The gun had not been fired on those previous days of gunnery exercise. Why mess up the Captain's cabin for a mere drill? It had not even been assigned a crew. Well, it's got one now . . .

"All right, run 'er out."

The two men take the chocks from under the wheels and grab the lines that will move the gun forward. They pull, and the gun on its carriage lurches forward and pokes its nose out the port. The ropes are again tightly secured to take up some of the shock when the cannon is fired. Well, at least they know how to do that.

I peer out over the barrel at our pursuers—they're coming fast but are still out of range.

When I had outfitted this gun, I made sure that match-locks were lying by its side, and there they are . . . ratchet bars, too, and a ram and swab, as well as a rack of shot. I smile grimly to think of Davy when I see the "Kiss My Royal Ass" that he had painted on the butt end of the cannon all those months ago. Funny how things change . . .

I go back to the door and stick my head out and shout down the length of the ship. "Maggie! Mairead! To me! Powder! Lots of it! Go in relays! We must keep this gun going till the barrel glows red! Ann, bring me a bucket of water! Hurry, now!"

When the girls scurry back with the powder and the bucket, I go back to the speaking tube and put my mouth to it. "After gun ready to fire, Sir!"

"Very well, fire at will," comes the reply.

Once again, I squint out over the cannon. The lead pirate is staying off to the right, and my gun is pointing at nothing but open sea.

"Ratchet right as far as you can, Suggs . . . Monk, as high as she'll go."

They do it but it's still not enough. Back to the tube.

"Captain! If you could come a few degrees right till he crosses my sights!"

"That will lose us some headway," comes the reply.

"Aye, but I'll be able to lob a ball at him right down his nose, which might give him something to think about! After you hear me fire, resume your former course!"

"Very well. Right rudder."

The nose of the *Lorelei Lee* begins to swing right, and the barrel of the gun swings toward the target. That's it . . . Just a little more . . . There!

"Stand clear!"

I pull the lanyard and . . .

Crrraaak!

The gun bucks and leaps back, powder smoke fills the cabin, and I peer out to see what damage we might have done. The aim was true, but the ball falls far short.

"Reload! Swab!"

Monk plunges the swab into the bucket and then runs it down the barrel to cool it so that when the cartridge of powder goes down, it doesn't explode from the heat, peeling the barrel like a banana skin and killing us all with the hot shards thrown whistling into the air. "Powder! Wad! Shot! Ram! Stand clear!"

I sight again. Maybe he's close enough now . . . Maybe the first charge was weak from disuse, damp from lying unused in the gun all that time, maybe . . .

Crrraaackk!

Again I look out over the barrel . . . and wait . . . and there . . . Yes! We've hit him. He's staggered!

It looks like the ball fell amidships just forward of his wheel.

"Not so confident now, are you, Sinbad!" I crow. "Kiss my royal ass!"

"Reload! Swab!"

The swab sizzles as it goes down the barrel, but we dare not stop.

"Powder!"

Mairead drops her load into the mouth of the barrel and stands back as Suggs rams in the charge and then the ball and then the wad, and when I put the matchlock lanyard in Mairead's hand, I shout, "Give us some of that Irish luck, girl! Pull it!"

Crrraaaack!

Yes! A hit! His one mast shudders and falls as I run to the speaking tube. *Erin go braugh, indeed!*

"Captain! There's only two of them now! Swing to port and give them a broadside! Show them what we've got and they'll run! I know they will!"

I feel the ship turn while I'm running outside to see that the port guns are ready to fire.

"Steady, boys, steady! Not yet, hold on . . . Now! Fire!"

Cccraack! . . . Craaaack! . . . Craaackkk!

The guns spit out their deadly shot. Not that they hit anything, but that doesn't matter. What matters is that the scum realize that we are not helpless fishermen or coastal merchants.

"Gun crews, reload! Everyone else, to the rail! Wave your cutlasses above your heads as if you lust for nothing in this world but their heathen blood hot on your steel! Do it! Girls, too! Grab a cutlass and wave it!"

All go to the rail and do it, setting up a great *halloo* led by the Shantyman and his relentless drum . . .

> *There was a lofty pirate and he sailed upon the sea,*
> *Blow high, blow low and so sail-ed we,*
> *"I am a salt sea pirate, a'lookin' for my fee,"*
> *Down along the coast of high . . . Barbaree!*
>
> *For broadside to broadside, a long time we lay,*
> *Blow high, blow low and so sail-ed we,*

Till at last we shot the pirate's mast away,
Down along the coast of high . . . Barbaree!

Well, that ain't quite how it went, but for sure there's one lofty pirate who ain't quite so lofty anymore.

Look ahead, look astern,
Look to weather, look a'lee,
Down along the coast of high . . . Barbaree!

A great cheer goes up as we see the pirates fall off and turn away.

"Go straight to hell, you scurvy dogs!" I exult, as I see them cut and run. "Did you think we had no teeth?"

That's the last exulting I do for a while. As I am securing my girls from their duty, a hand comes up and clamps around my neck. It belongs to First Mate Ruger.

"Captain wants a word with you, Faber," he hisses in my ear, and hauls me up to the quarterdeck to stand before the Captain.

Uh-oh . . .

"You seem to know something of naval matters, Convict Faber. How is that?" asks Captain Laughton.

I stand at attention, gulp, then say, "Mr. Ruger has told you something of my past, Sir." Time for the woebegone waif look.

"Um . . . that piracy thing, which I scarcely believe, anyway. That does not explain how you seem so familiar with the workings of this ship."

I think on this and see no way out. With a great sigh, I

admit, "This ship was once mine. It was taken from me as part of my condemnation."

"Your condemnation?"

"The Crown seemed to think I purchased it with stolen funds. So they took her and sentenced me to life in the penal colony instead of hanging me."

"Do you think that was a fair trade?"

"I suppose so, Sir, since I stand here before you with my neck yet not stretched."

"From your past conduct, the stretching of that neck seems to be only a matter of time." This from Ruger.

"That may be so, Sir," I reply. "But I do try to be good."

That gets me a snort from Ruger. He reaches out and pulls my hair away from my face.

"You see that, Sir? That spray next to her eye? Definite powder burns. This girl has been around, trust me, and I believe her to be dangerous."

"Hmmm . . ." ponders the Captain. "That explains why the figurehead looks so much like you . . ." He pauses, hand on jowl, thinking. "So what are we to do? Confine her so that all ninety pounds of her cannot bring us to ruin?"

"She has brought others to ruin, Sir," persists Ruger. "And she—"

"Captain Laughton," I say, lifting my chin and putting on the Lawson Peabody Look. "I know that you were once in the Royal Navy. I myself was in that same service, first as a ship's boy, then as Midshipman, and finally as Acting Lieutenant. Do you know what it means when I swear on my honor that I will not do anything to harm either you or this ship on which we stand? Do you?"

"You may get down off your high horse, Miss Faber," answers the Captain, after some consideration. "We will take you at your word. Just behave yourself. Higgins! I need a drink! This has been hot work! Good work all of you, and an extra tot for all! Let's have a cheer, brave boys and girls alike!"

Hooorah! Hoorah! Hoorah!

Chapter 36

There is to be a grand night in the Captain's cabin, and both Esther and I are going. Mairead is, too—she and I as entertainers. Esther is guest, once again, of Army Major Johnston.

"How come we don't get to come?" Little Mary Wade pouts.

"'Cause you ain't fine musicians like our Jacky and Mairead," answers Molly Reibey for me. "And 'cause you ain't a rare beauty like our Esther, neither."

Our girls fix us up as best they can—hair is brushed, clothes cleaned and ironed—and we are off to the party.

"Cheer up, little Mary," I say as we leave. "You'll be a rare beauty someday, by-and-by."

When we join the party, Captain Laughton sits laughing with a girl on each hand, one of which, I am sure, will soon be on his lap, once he finishes downing his dinner, and one of which—or maybe even both—will share his bed this evening. Captain Laughton seems to have an endless appetite for virtually everything. I look over at that bed, *my bed,* and reflect that . . . S*top that, you. It will do no good.*

Mairead and I sit, with our instruments, on top of the bureau. It is a generous cabin, but space is limited and we cannot just stand about anywhere.

Esther sits by the side of Major Johnston, looking, I must say, radiant and serenely beautiful. Before the dinner is served, I notice that the pair is holding hands beneath the table and smiling into each other's eyes. Ah, yes, young love . . . beautiful to behold, no matter where it happens to blossom.

I think back to Mistress Pimm at the Lawson Peabody School for Young Girls and her saying to me, "All my girls make good matches."

Well, maybe I can look out for my own girls in that way, Mistress. It is true that while yours are fine ladies, mine are convicts, but still . . .

I strum my guitar softly in our corner, figuring I should lay low for a while, considering my rather bold actions yesterday—"Greensleeves," it is, with my own variations on the melody. Mairead trills softly along on her pennywhistle. *Let's get things off slowly,* I figure.

Everybody in this world has a set piece, a recitation they do when called up to offer something at a social gathering. It could be a song, a riddle, a rhyme, a poem, or a story. Anything that the performer thinks will please those around him, *and* give the person doing the thing a feeling of some pride and accomplishment.

I, of course, have many such things I am able to do, but when called upon this time, I once again recite "The Boy Stood on the Burning Deck," that poem depicting the heroic death of a thirteen-year-old boy who refused to leave his post in the thick of battle, that I know it will go over big with the officers . . . and with the Shantyman, who had lost his sight in similar heroics. He cocks his head back, as if in thought, and seems to like it.

Maircad pops off the bureau and delivers a fine rendition of "The Galway Shawl," her clear sweet voice, solo, unaccompanied by musical instrument, or even by me.

Mairead's own rare beauty has not gone unnoticed since first she came aboard the *Lorelei Lee* that day on Gibraltar. In this particular setting, I notice that sometimes Ruger's eye trails from me to the oblivious Mairead, laughing away at all the attention paid her. *Hmmm* . . . Well, maybe the fact that she is a married woman carrying a child will protect her from any advances on his part. I hope so.

"Mr. Higgins!" roars the Captain, through now with his dinner and leaning back in his chair. "Let us hear from you!"

Higgins has, of course, been in attendance as he always is, directing his assistants in the serving of food and the pouring of wine. After protesting that he is not worthy, he stands, puts his hand over his heart, and recites "All Praise to the Haggis," a Scottish poem he had apparently picked up in his travels in the north of England and dedicated to a particular savory dish made of sheep's pluck—the liver, heart, and lungs of an unfortunate sheep—cooked with onions and stuffed in that same poor sheep's stomach, baked, and brought steaming out to great acclaim from the lucky dinner guests. But not here, thank God. It is well known that the belly of Jacky Faber is made of cast iron, but the haggis goes a bit over the line.

Higgins bows to the appreciative audience while I make quiet gagging noises.

"Hey, Jacky, sometime you should try a plate of *she-nairuth,* or at least that's what we used to call it back on the farm," says Mairead, giving me an elbow in my side. "They're like oysters what never saw any sea."

And I do *not* want to know what they are, thank you, as I *have* heard of prairie oysters and their like, from my time in the wilds of America.

Mr. Gibson, the Second Mate, stands and gives us an excellent reading of "Band of Brothers," Prince Hal's exhortation of his troops at the Battle of Agincourt . . .

We few, we happy few, we band of brothers . . .
For he to-day that sheds his blood with me
Shall be my brother; be he ne'er so vile,
This day shall gentle his condition;
And gentlemen in England now a-bed
Shall think themselves accursed they were not here,
And hold their manhoods cheap whiles any speaks
That fought with us upon Saint Crispin's day . . .

Not a dry eye in the room. *Good job, Mr. Gibson.*

The dinner is cleared and the telling of jokes and poems and stories has wound down. Now the Captain cries, "Come, my girls, let us have something much livelier in the way of our entertainment!" He wipes his greasy lips across his sleeve, pounds the table, then hoists one of the nearby dollies onto his lap. "Let it be a fine fandango!"

I lay aside my guitar to pick up the Lady Gay, and launch into a few fast reels—"Haste to the Wedding" and "The Spotted Cow." Then Mairead and I do the comic-songs part of our act, to great hilarity. Then I say to the Shantyman, "A tune, if you would, Mr. Lightner, so that my friend and I might dance." He nods and I place the Lady Gay in his hands and he puts bow to her and rips out "The Liverpool Hornpipe."

A perfect choice.

We each put one arm across the shoulders of the other, lift our hooves, and proceed to tear up the deck.

"Bravo! Bravo!" shouts the Captain when we finish and take a bow. "Capital! Just capital!" Cheers and clapping all around, which warms my soul, and I can tell from the flush in Mairead's cheeks that it pleases her, too.

Later, as things are quieting down, I catch Esther's eye and wink. She nods in understanding as I begin Bach's *Minuet in G.* I get off of what passes for the dance floor as Esther and Major Johnston arise and join hands to begin the dance.

It is a slow, stately sort of dance, with much dignified posturing and bowing and curtsying, but by their looks and gestures, the dancers manage to get across their mutual affection. Their dance ends in a very un-minuet-like snug embrace.

As the last note dies away, Captain Laughton lurches to his feet, dumping a Lizzie to the floor. "A toast," he says, lifting his glass to the young couple. "A toast to the blushing bride and dashing groom, for tomorrow is their wedding day!"

"Hear, hear!" choruses the table, and the libation is drunk.

"A wedding, Sir?" asks the Third Mate, echoing my thoughts.

"Yes, Mr. Gibson, a wedding. Miss Abrahams has consented to be the wife of Major Johnston, but only on condition of being legally married, and the foolish man has agreed." Captain Laughton takes another pull at his wineglass and then continues. "Blinded by her beauty, no doubt, and I can't quite blame him. She is a rare jewel of a girl." He lifts that same wineglass to our Esther. "A jewel as well as a Jewess! Ha!" She blushes prettily and casts down her eyes.

"We'll do it up right, by God! In true *Lorelei Lee* style!" exults the Captain, pleased with his latest witticism. "You there, Faber. Look me up some verses from the Bible to read tomorrow! It reads for both Jew and Gentile all the same, right? Good. We shall have a proper wedding at sea, topnotch all the way! And now, more music! More wine! More everything!"

Chapter 37

The next morning comes early, as it always does after a night of riotous behavior, but by noon all have recovered . . . somewhat.

Higgins has seen to the placement of a lectern on the edge of the quarterdeck. When all is in place, he nods to the waiting Bo'sun, who blasts out on his pipe and roars, "All hands and convicts topside to witness wedding!" He bellows this with the same stentorian tone he would use to announce, "Witness punishment!" Maybe to him it is the same sort of thing . . .

Men and boys, women and girls, pour out from down below and array themselves about the deck. It is a great soaring day, all blue sky and brisk but gentle breezes—in short, a great day for a wedding.

When all are settled, Higgins goes to the cabin and brings out Captain Augustus Laughton, a bit unsteady on his pins this day but still in total command of his ship and all upon it.

I stand next to the lectern, put fiddle to chin, and play the "Wedding March." When done, I stand ready to hand up the Scripture. The Captain looks out over the crowd and begins . . .

"Dearly beloved, we are gathered here today to join in Holy . . . or at least . . . Naval . . . Matrimony . . . Major George Johnston of His Majesty's Eighth Grenadiers and . . ."

Here the Captain consults the piece of paper I had given him earlier.

"Uh . . . Esther Semple Abrahams. Will the two step forward and stand before me?"

Army Major Johnston and Esther Abrahams do, indeed, advance to the lectern, hand in hand. I have assigned Mary Wade as flower-girl-with-no-flowers, as there are none to be had, but she has been provided with sheafs of wheat to cradle in the crook of her arm. Second Mate Seabrook stands to Major Johnston's side as Best Man. Ship's Boy Darby Patton holds a pillow with a ring upon it. It's all a bit tacky, I know. *Sorry, but it's all I could put together on a moment's notice.*

I hand up the Bible to the Captain, with my handwritten script laid within. "Harken now all of you worthless sods to Scripture!" He picks up the paper and begins to read with great portentousness, his forefinger in the air.

"And the Lord God cast the Man into a deep sleep and, while he slept, took one of his ribs and closed up its place with flesh. And the rib which the Lord God took from the Man, he made into a Woman, and brought her to the Man. Then he said to the Man, 'She is bone of your bone, and flesh of your flesh; she shall be called Woman, for from Man she was taken.' For this reason a Man shall leave his Father and Mother and cleave unto his Wife, and the two shall become of one flesh . . . and what God has put together, let no man put asunder!"

Captain Laughton thunders out that last line in a voice worthy of Moses coming down from the mountain.

Yes, there was a Bible onboard the *Lorelei Lee,* so I got all that from it. Course, I fixed it up a little bit—it didn't quite flow, y' know what I mean? But I think I got the real sense of it, and I hope I will be forgiven.

There was an additional bit in Genesis at the end of all that—*"Both the Man and the Woman were naked, but they felt not shame"*—but I left that out, fearing that Captain Laughton would take note and bellow out, "LET'S ALL GET NAKED!" at the end of the ceremony. Although the command might have been carried out by all aboard if taken as a direct order from the Lord God Captain—and it does sound like fun—it might detract from the solemnity of the service, and I do want Esther to have her proper wedding.

"If any here have any objections to this union"—the Captain looks around—"let them speak now or forever hold their peace."

From the midst of the crowd comes, "Hey, Cholly, how comes ye don't want to marry me, all legal-like loike that gent there is gonna do wi' that girl?"

This is heard from elsewhere in the crowd, "'Cause you's a whore, Sheba, is why."

. . . And comes the answer, "And you's the bleedin' Pope, I suppose, Cholly, ever so true and faithful?"

"That I be, Sheba! Wham, bam, and thank you, ma'am. Thank you very much, very much indeed, my girl! When I leaves ye off in Australia, ye will 'ave a great big belly and me hearty thanks for a jolly ride! And if it's a boy, name 'im after me, and if it's a girl, name her Bertha, after me mum!"

"THAT AIN'T THE PROPER ANSWER TO THAT QUESTION!" bellows Captain Laughton, red in the face and disturbed by the ruination of his solemn ceremony. "It's rhetorical, like. And I'll have no more lip from any of you!"

Cholly and Sheba, whoever they might be, are abashed and quiet down.

The Captain gives a few *harrumphs,* then continues. "Very well. Now then, do you, Major Johnston, take Esther as your lawful wedded wife, to love and honor and all that?"

"I do."

"And do you, Esther Abrahams, take Major George Johnston to honor and obey and all that?"

"I do," responds the lass.

"Excellent. Now place the ring on her finger, kiss the bride, and . . . by the authority vested in me, I now pronounce you man and wife!"

The two lovers kiss, wave, and head below as a great cheer goes up from all.

The Captain then turns to those of us remaining.

"Every man on board now has taken unto him a woman, and that is as it should be!" he proclaims, grandly, his gaze falling upon all those assembled. "Higgins! A glass. Being a preacher is hot, dry work, by the living God!"

Higgins is right there with a brimming goblet of ruby-red claret.

"Thank you, thank you, my very good man!" He drinks deep and then furrows his brow in thought. He casts his eye upon his trusted steward . . .

"Hmmm . . . Yes, every man has taken a woman and maybe more than one . . . Ha! Except for you, Higgins, my good fellow. Tell me, why have you not yet done so?"

Uh-oh . . .

There are a few snickers from the crowd, but Higgins, composed as usual and with a slight smile on his lips, bows to the Captain and says, "Begging your pardon, Sir, but I merely wished to cast my eye over the entire . . . flock . . . as it were, so as to choose the one most suited to my taste and disposition."

"Disposition, my ass. Come, Higgins, you must pick a girl to bed. We must all do our duty to populate that continent. Surely one has struck your fancy. Choose now."

Do it, Higgins, do it! I think, imploring him with my eyes. *Else you will be in big trouble!*

"Very well, Sir," says Higgins, turning to survey the crowd. "I have considered, and, if it please you, I shall have *that* one, if she should so agree."

He holds out his hand to me. *Whew! Good move, Higgins!*

"Our little minstrel?" asks Captain Laughton. "Surely something a bit more buxom than that?"

"*Chacun a son goût,* Sir," replies Higgins. "Or, as the Chinese say, 'Every worm to his taste—some prefer nettles.'"

"Ha! Well said, Higgins, well said," chortles the Captain. "But I've heard that she has refused all comers. What if she refuses you? Hmmm?"

"Do you accept, Miss?" Higgins still has his hand out to me.

I hand off my fiddle to Mary Wade and step forward to take his hand and curtsy. Rising, I look into his eyes and say, "I accept."

I sense that Mister Ruger is glaring daggers at me. The Captain holds his hand to his chin and looks at us, considering.

"Hmmm . . . And how old are you, Miss?"

"I am sixteen, Sir. Seventeen in October."

"Well, then, I imagine it is all right," says Augustus Laughton, Lord of the *Lorelei Lee*. "Come over here and stand before me now." He holds his hand over our heads and intones, "The words from the Bible have already been said, so . . . by the authority vested in me as Captain of the *Lorelei Lee*, I now pronounce you man and wife!"

There is a cheer from the crowd, and the Captain roars, "The newly marrieds shall now repair to their bowers while we return to our revels! I like to run a happy ship, and by God, I cannot think of a happier ship than this one!"

Roars of approval from the crew and the Crews.

Minutes later, Higgins and I are at the door to his cabin.

"Will you carry me across the threshold, husband?" I ask, twinkling at Higgins and placing my hand upon his shoulder.

He laughs, scoops me up, and carries me into the cabin. He places me on my feet, and I squeal with delight in seeing my old seabag again. I kneel down to rummage through the dear old thing—my paints, my papers, my inks, my cosmetics. Yes, a little perfume right now, oh, yes! . . . And then . . . my miniature of Jaimy.

That cools my joy a bit.

"I'm sure he is all right, Miss," says Higgins, seeing what I hold in my hand and the expression on my face.

"Thank you for saying so, Higgins," I reply, returning the painting to the bag and rising to go sit on the bed. "Now, come over here beside me," I murmur. "We've got to make this sound good." I gesture toward the open porthole and then point to my ear. He nods in understanding—yes, they will be listening.

Higgins comes to sit next to me, and we have a raucous good time of bouncing up and down on the bed, making the bedsprings squeak and the bedstead thump against the wall. I add some feminine moans of ecstasy and cries of, "Oh, John, yes, oh, yes!"

Higgins adds a few low male grunts, and we agree that the job is done, and done well.

Afterward, he asks, "Can I get you anything in the way of a wedding present, Miss?"

As I lie back on the pillow, I think on this for a moment and then say, "You know, Higgins, my elegant little tub . . . I have not seen it for a good long while."

"Of course, Miss. I could not think of anything finer. I shall order it up."

He rises and goes out the door to see that it's done. I disrobe and duck under the covers, and I pull the sheets to my chin. Soon Mick and Keefe appear, full of smirks but also bearing the tub and buckets of hot water; and then Higgins returns and the bath is prepared.

"Har-har, she takes a bath and she's a virgin again, right, Mr. Higgins?" Mick chortles. Higgins forces himself to smile at that. Funny, but Keefe doesn't laugh, either.

When the two are gone, I slip out of the bed and into the tub, and Higgins's strong fingers are once again in my hair . . . *Oh, Lord, that is so good . . .*

Ahhhh . . .

Suddenly this lovely idyll is cut short by a ringing of the bell that hangs by Higgins's bed.

"Hmm," says Higgins. "I believe I'd best go see to the Captain. He was a bit into his cups rather early in the day, what with the nuptial celebrations and all. He will probably be needing his nap now."

"Go, Higgins, and thank you. I will be fine," I say. "Till later." I get halfway out of the tub to give him a peck on the cheek. "I could not be married to a finer man."

As he goes out the door, cheers are heard. *Men, I swear . . .*

The door is left slightly ajar, and I feel eyes boring into my bare back, eyes which I strongly suspect belong to Mr. Ruger. I continue to soap myself and to pay no attention to whoever is out there. No, I do not care. All I care about is this lovely, lovely bath.

After the boisterous festivities of the day, the evening is quiet. I expect everyone is quite exhausted. I know I am, that's for sure. I take a nightdress from my lovely seabag and crawl into bed.

I slip off to sleep, but I awaken when Higgins comes back into the cabin.

I turn over and slide over next to the wall. Higgins undresses, dons his nightshirt, and asks, "Are you awake, Miss?"

"Yes, Higgins."

"I shall sleep over here on the floor."

"No, you shall not, Higgins. You will sleep in here next to me, to keep me from the damp. I'll lie next to the wall, and you shall sleep on the outside so it'll be easier for you to answer the Captain's call, should it come."

He says nothing, but I feel him slip in next to me.

"Ummm . . ." I murmur and snuggle up next to him and settle in. After a bit, I whisper in the darkness, "Higgins?"

"Yes, Miss?"

"Is . . . is there anything I can . . . uh . . . *do* for you . . . husband?" I place my hand on his lower ribs. "We *are* legally married, you know . . . and there are some . . . things . . . that I have heard about . . ."

He chuckles, then lifts my hand, to place it higher on his chest. "No, Miss. I think it best that we keep our relationship on the platonic level. But thank you for the offer. Let us go to sleep now."

I nuzzle in closer and take a deep breath. "I do love you, John Higgins. You are my best and dearest friend."

The *Lorelei Lee* rocks us both into a deep and contented sleep.

Chapter 38

Mrs. John Higgins
Onboard the Lorelei Lee
Off the West Coast of India
July 1807

Miss Amy Trevelyne
Dovecote Farm
Quincy, Massachusetts, USA

Dear Amy,

Bombay! Can you believe it, Amy? We shall be in Bombay, India, tomorrow! There will be English ships there, and I shall be able to post my letters. Captain Laughton tells me that we English own the place—King Charles II got it as dowry from the Portuguese back when he married Catherine de Braganza. Guess the Indians didn't have much say in the matter, but hey . . .

I shall be able to look about for my Bombay Rat, whatever it may be, and wherever it might lie.

What news, then? Let's see . . .

The Captain has found out that I once owned this ship upon which we all now ride, but he seems to have gotten used to the idea; and now he even consults me on some things—like sail set and configuration and suchlike.

Enoch, the Shantyman—he who leads songs and beats out the rhythms to facilitate the work details, like raising and lowering sails, hauling anchor, and such—compliments me particularly on the design of my table, with its slots and depressions for all the dinnerware. Given his condition, he rejoices in always knowing where his food and drink lie. You would think a blind man would be messy in his eating habits, but he is not. A light touch of his forefinger on the contents of his plate tells him where and what things are. And for a rough, craggy-looking man, he is really quite kind and courtly, and congratulates me on my marriage to John Higgins, saying, "He is a fine man and I hope you will be very happy together."

Heavy sigh . . . Yes, dear, I know that news must come as a bit of a shock. I suspect this letter has fallen from your hand, and you are passed out on the floor. You see, it had to be done for the sake of Higgins's reputation onboard and for my own protection, too, and . . . uh . . . ask Ezra to explain, as he knows both Higgins and me.

What else . . . ?

Well, we have taken to playing at cards. There are endless games of whist, and I have become quite expert—and I don't even cheat. I usually partner with Higgins against the Captain and whomever he has invited to play. I take great pleasure in trumping Mr. Ruger's aces, and while I know I must be careful in that regard, it is satisfying to see his dark face redden. He is not at all pleased with my marriage to

John, as he had sort of staked a claim on me from the start. Why, I don't know—he is the high-and-mighty First Mate, and I am but a mere convict. There are two-hundred-and-fifty-odd women onboard from whom he could freely choose and yet he settles on me. Men, I swear . . .

Higgins opines that what one most desires is very often that which one cannot have. I don't know . . .

We have stopped at Mauritius and at the Seychelles and the Maldives—Oh, Amy, such wonders, such sights, such smells, such colors! If only you could be here with me to take it all in—not that I'd want you to be a convict, of course. I really don't think you're cut out for that sort of thing, but still, I would delight in your sweet company.

At each of those ports, we pursue our various trades—the girls of the brothel Crews plying their ancient trade; me diving for coins thrown from the decks of ships. Actually I am growing quite rich at it—and yes, Amy, I am wearing appropriate garb when I dive. Course I could make more by diving starkers, but no sense pushing my luck. Best leave that sort of thing to Barnsley and her girls. Besides, my swimsuit is skimpy enough to insure good tips.

I bask in Mrs. Barnsley's disfavor—she glares at me each time I waltz into the Captain's cabin for a night of cards and entertainment. I have noticed that when people like me, they tend to like me a lot, but if they don't, watch out for Jacky Faber. I repay kindness with kindness, love with love, but also hurt for hurt. I can be vindictive, yes, and vengeful, too. No, it does not say much for me, but there you are. When I catch Barnsley giving me the cold stare, I put on the Lawson Peabody Look, cock a hip in her direction, and stick out my tongue. *Old cow . . .*

Last night at dinner, Captain Laughton was musing on the fact that another convict ship with an escort left England shortly after we did, and he is surprised our wakes have not yet crossed, as both ships are taking essentially the same route to New South Wales. True, the ocean is large and our ships are small, but there are crossroads at sea, as well as on land.

Daytimes I fill my hours with drawing, painting, talking with my mates, and shooting rats. Yes, I have constructed a bow and manufactured a quantity of good-quality arrows and have gone hunting for the little grain-thieving varmints. I have access to the bottom deck, and my aim has become quite deadly, which is good, for our meat supply is running low and not always available in these tropical ports, where meat spoils so easily. Those of our sisters who were on the *Bloodhound* will recall how good Katy Deere and her Dianas were at bagging the creatures, and how good Cookie was at cooking them.

Being married to my dear John Higgins has many advantages, one of which is being allowed more freedom when we hit a port. I am, after all, married to the Assistant Purser, and so am accorded some respect for that. I have given my word not to try to escape, and I am trusted.

Well, time for dinner. The Captain calls and I must obey. *Tomorrow Bombay!*

Your Ever Devoted Sister and Friend,

Jacky

Chapter 39

⚓ "Come, Mairead, the Captain has given us permission to visit this great city in the company of my dear husband today, as Higgins is off to buy spices and other supplies for the Captain's table, and we"—I poke Mairead in the side and give her a wink—"shall see what we will see."

Mairead grins back as we advance to the head of the gangplank.

"You must be careful of her, Mr. Higgins," admonishes the Captain when we are on the brow. "You may be married to her, but she *is* going to New South Wales. The redhead, too. I know my duty, however distasteful it might be." He pauses, then adds, "And, furthermore, I have grown quite fond of both of them. Plus, there is to be a procession of some sort this afternoon, and I am invited to the Governor's box. I expect, Mr. Higgins, for you to attend me there."

Higgins bows and assures him his two charges will be good and careful, and that he will be delighted to view the procession in the Captain's company. And with a pair of delighted squeals from the two charges, we are off.

On the dock, Higgins greets a very dignified and proper Indian man dressed in Western style. He is a Mr. Rajeeb and has been hired to guide him about on the day's business. As he leads Higgins off into the teeming city, we follow meekly—well, sort of meekly.

Higgins had already checked with the other English ships in port to see if any had left England after us and perhaps had a copy of the *Naval Gazette,* so we could find out what happened to poor Jaimy, but alas, we were once again the most recent arrival.

Poor Jaimy, am I never to know your fate? Ah, well, perhaps it is best in not knowing, for I can always hope.

Mairead and I walk along, hand in hand, our senses reeling with the sights and sounds and smells and simply overwhelming nature of Bombay—we gasp out *"Look at that!"* and *"Oh, my God!"* There are huge, and I mean *huge* numbers of very exotic people—the men wearing loose white shirts and trousers—some with turbans, some not, some with full black beards, some with big, glossy mustaches. The women, many of whom are quite beautiful, wear brightly colored dresses that seem to be one long piece of cloth that is wrapped around their lower parts from ankles to waist, leaving the midriff bare. Above that, they wear a short-sleeved shirt that covers their shoulders and comes down to just below their breasts. The cloth that covers their bottoms comes up over their backs to hang over their shoulders. Their heads are uncovered, and their hair is put up in many becoming ways. They wear much jewelry—jangly bracelets about their wrists and ankles, many necklaces, and even jeweled pendants attached to their hair such that jewels hang across their foreheads.

I'm gonna like this place, I just know it!

The women have some dark cosmetic around their eyes, making their eyes seem even bigger and more luminous than they already are. I have *got* to get some of that!

I'm thinking about this when I feel something tugging at my skirt. I look down and see a little boy with impossibly big brown—nearly black—eyes. He has a mop of glossy black hair up top and wears what looks like a white diaper down below.

"Missy, Missy, Memsahib! You need guide! Ravi good guide! Speak good English," he implores, nodding, while still clinging to my skirt.

"You, boy! Go away! *Jaana!*" shouts Mr. Rajeeb when he sees the lad at my side.

"But he is so cute," I say. The boy's face shines a hopeful grin, his teeth amazingly white against the brown of skin.

"No, Miss. He is Untouchable! Dirty!"

"He looks touchable to me," I respond, reaching out my hand to tousel his hair.

Mr. Rajeeb spits out a long string of what must be dire threats in the local tongue, so the boy scurries away, looking disappointed and hurt.

"Come, ladies, please stay close," urges our guide, beckoning us along. We meekly follow. Sort of meekly. Too bad; I rather liked the little fellow . . .

I would have not thought it possible, but the teeming crowd seems to get even thicker as we go along until, as we round a corner and enter a market area, there is a loud clamor of blowing trumpets and beating drums and the mob presses hard into us so that Mairead and I are suddenly separated from Higgins and Mr. Rajeeb by a mass of pressing bodies. It seems to be caused by a procession of sorts.

"Look, Jacky!" exclaims Mairead in wonder. "It's an elly-phant!"

Sure, enough, high above the heads of the people, appears the head of an elephant, all brightly powdered and beribboned. It weaves its slow, ponderous way along the street and then disappears.

"Coo, imagine that," I breathe. "Jacky Faber from the slums of London and Mairead McConnaughey from the bogs of Ireland have gazed with their own eyes upon a real live elephant in its native land! Now all I need is my Bombay Rat and the visit shall be complete."

"Watch that 'bog' stuff, Brit," laughs Mairead, giving me an elbow. "But, aye, it is amazin'."

"Missy! Missy! Memsahib!"

I look down and it is our little lad again. I look about for Higgins and Mr. Rajeeb, but see them nowhere. Oh, well . . .

"Missies need Ravi now? He has much good English. Show ladies Bombay, get things for nice ladies, yes?"

"How is it that you know our language, boy-o?" asks the skeptical Mairead.

"Oh, Missy of Impossibly Red Hair, my mommy was in household of Big Mr. Elphy, big businessman. He good man. My mommy cleaned privies, other things. Yes, we Untouchable caste, but he good to us." Ravi's big eyes get bigger and then glisten with tears. "My mommy go to Brahma last year. Sahib Elphy gave me money for funeral. Mommy sweet. I know she come back as happy pretty bird that sings sweet."

"Your dad?" asks Mairead, softer now.

"No daddy."

"And Mr. Elphy?"

"Poor Sahib Elphy lose money. Have to close house and go away."

"Where do you sleep?" ask I, already knowing what the answer will be like.

"Under docks by big boats."

"And how do you live?"

"Ravi get stuff for sailor men—foods, clothes, trinkets, henna, hashish . . ." He looks up hopefully. "Hashish? Ladies want hashish? Got best! Can get finest kind hashish. You want?"

I smile and shake my head and think back to New Orleans and Mam'selle Claudelle's offerings in that regard— *"Oh, Precious, you must try this . . . It will make you feel so good . . . Breathe deep now, baby; it won't hurt you . . ."* But I did not snort in the line of white powder on the tabletop in that café, saying, *"No thanks, Mam'selle. I feel fine already . . ."*

"Anything you ladies want, Ravi can get—plus he keep dear ladies' precious bodies from harm—there are many bad men in Bombay! Assassins! Thuggies! Oh, Missies, you must be so careful—you must have Ravi to protect! Much horribles!"

"How much does this mighty Ravi protection cost?" The boy barely comes up to my waist, and I'm small.

"Only your sweet female companies, Memsahibs. And whatever bits you can toss to poor Ravi."

I laugh. "All right, Ravi, lead on and show us your city." He leaps in the air with a delighted *whoop*.

"What about Higgins and the Captain and all?" asks Mairead. "Won't they be worried about us? We are, after all, worth ten and six each—if breathing."

"And you a bit more," I say, giving her belly a light pat with the back of my hand. She is starting to show a little. "Nay, let them worry about us. I don't think Higgins will be overly concerned. He knows me, and he knows I won't leave my friends . . . or my ship. He knows I'll pop back up." I say this and give her a wink. "And, Sister mine, for the moment, we are free. Who knows if we will ever be able to say that again?"

She nods and lifts pale red eyebrows in agreement.

"Come, Missies, follow Ravi now. He show you city. Come, come . . ."

The crowd has thinned out a bit, so we are able to walk along, peering into market stalls at all the wonders offered there.

"Missy Memsahibs have money?" inquires Ravi, seeing our obvious interest.

I dig into my purse and bring out a handful of gold and silver coins.

"Put it away quick, Memsahib!" whispers Ravi, looking furtively around at the shopkeeps, whose interest in these two strangely dressed girls has suddenly sharply increased. Wares are handed out to us with ingratiating smiles and gestures.

"No take," warns Ravi. "First we must go to money-changers—do not worry. Ravi not let them cheat you. Come." He makes so bold as to take my hand and lead me on.

In a short while we pass a large churchlike building. I peer in and see a long hall, at the end of which is a statue of what looks to be a big-bellied creature with the body of a man and with the head of a rather jolly-looking elephant, all bejeweled and brightly colored.

"It is the god Ganesh," says Ravi, bowing his head. "He is good god." I give a little bow of the Faber head, too.

Mairead does not. "I would surely be excommunicated if I did that and the Holy Father found out that I bent my head to a heathen idol," she says, crossing herself and looking heavenward.

"The Holy Father is far from here, Mairead, so I would not worry," I reply, still looking inside at the intricately inlaid wall and the the plumes of incense smoke wafting about in there. There are worshippers inside, and they wave us in with smiles.

A supplicant comes out of the temple of Ganesh, wearing the robes of what I take to be those of a monk, and holding a wooden bowl. I open my purse again, to extract a small silver coin, which I put into his bowl. The monk smiles and puts fingers to forehead and says something softly before retreating back into the temple.

"He says, 'Thank you, kind woman-child. Your offering will feed us for three full days. Blessed be you and your children,'" translates Ravi. "It should bring you much good luck, Memsahib. Good karma."

"Well, I can always use a lot of that, given my nature," I say. "Press on . . . uh, what is word for 'boy'?"

"In Urdu, Missy? . . . *Larka.*"

"Well, that seems to fit," I say, grandly lifting a hand and pointing down the street. "Lead on, *larka.*"

We go on toward the moneychangers, wherever they may lie, and we come upon another temple—one that seems rather dark compared to the bright interior of the Ganesh temple. Again I peer in, and this time I see a statue of a woman, painted black, with many arms, the hands of which hold mostly cruel-looking weapons. Many skulls are festooned about. There are men outside the entrance, turbaned, with arms crossed across bare chests, great gleaming curved swords in their hands. They do not look at all welcoming. In fact, seeing us, they glower.

Ravi pushes us to the other side of the street, looking furtive again.

"What's going on?" I ask.

"Is temple of Goddess Kali," he says, nodding toward the dark temple.

"So?"

"Ganesh is good god," Ravi explains. "Missy Memsahib pray to Lord Ganesh for good luck. Kali sometimes good, sometimes bad . . . sometimes Goddess of Time and Renewal, sometimes Goddess of Death." The boy shivers. "Memsahib pray to Goddess Kali when she want some bad person murdered in awful way."

"Hmmm . . . Remind me to stay out of this Kali's way."

"Not always possible, Memsahib."

Wise advice, I am thinking.

We hear shouting, from one of the men at the temple gate . . . *"Ferengi!"* is shouted at us. *"Ferengi! Suar!"*

Uh-oh . . .

Ravi pushes us farther down the street, away from Kali's not very welcoming temple.

"What does *ferengi* mean?" I ask.

"Not nice word for 'person from away,'" says Ravi, looking worried.

"And *suar*?"

"Uh . . . it mean like oink-oink piggies. Not good. We must get dear bodies of Missies wrapped in Bombay ladies' cloths so they not be seen as foreigner ladies. Ah, here we are."

We find ourselves in a courtyard where men sit about cross-legged with bowls of coins in front of them. They have calculating machines—abacuses, I think—next to each of them.

I give Ravi a handful of coins from my purse, the fruits of my divings—English shillings, French francs, Spanish pesetas, and only the gods of money know what else—and he goes to work. There is much holding up of fingers from the men therein and much shifting of beads on the rods of the abacuses and much shaking of heads, but then some noddings and the job is done.

Ravi comes back with a much larger handful of coins, looking pleased. "I do not think you were bad cheated overmuch, Missy Memsahib."

He pours the coins into my hand. I give them to Mairead and then dart out my hand and grab his fist and untwine his fingers. Sure enough, a few rupees rest tucked between his fingers.

"Not beat poor Ravi, Memsahib, please!" he pleads, tears running out of his eyes. "Is mistake!"

He looks properly abashed, so I give his head a light rap with my knuckle and say, "Right. Just don't do it again. Do your job properly and you'll be paid."

Actually, I admire his entreprenurial spirit. When I was a street urchin, I would have tried to pull the same exact thing.

Right now, though, the lure of shopping calls, and wiping my forearm across my sweaty forehead, I say, "It's awfully hot. Let's see if we can get into something a little lighter."

"*Jee hann,*" says Ravi, which I take to mean yes. "Right this way."

We shortly find ourselves in a very hot, close shop, with a smiling, middle-aged woman very much in attendance. She quickly shoos Ravi off to a side room and divests both Mairead and me of our outer clothing. Soon we are encased in the most wonderfully colored saris. *Where do they get these beautiful dyes? I could surely sell cloth like this in Charleston, if not stuffy old Boston . . .* Further study is required . . .

After my bottom is well wrapped in a light orange and white sari with little green flowers all over it and a light chemise has been put on my top, the end of the sari cloth is placed over my right shoulder for me to use as head covering or veil, whichever I choose. My midriff is bare and I long for my old emerald to stick in my belly button, but hey, maybe I'll find something later that will serve. I look in the mirror and put on what I think is a sultry look. I like it a lot, but it is not quite perfect, yet . . .

I gesture to the woman by running my forefinger around my eyes.

"*Ah, kohl! Jee haan!*" she exclaims and reaches for a brush and jar.

When I look again in the mirror, my eyes have been ringed in dark, rich brown . . . *Now, that's more like it!*

I dance around the room as Mairead is outfitted in similar fashion. When she is done and all kohled up in the eyes, I exult, "Oh, your Ian should see his little *houri* now!"

Her face falls a bit at that, but I will have none of it.

"You *will* see your Ian again, I promise it! Now come, we will have some fun! Ian would want it, I know!" *And Jaimy, too, I hope . . .*

She nods, lifts her chin, and smiles . . . *Oh, Lord, those big green eyes ringed with darkest brown, against that red shock of hair . . . How perfectly beautiful.*

Back on the street again, gloriously decked out, we visit the market stalls to buy some cheap jewelry to festoon our necks and foreheads as well as our arms and ankles. Each purchase is carefully bargained for by our faithful Ravi, who carries the bundle of our former clothing and new purchases under his skinny arm. We buy ornate bottles of jasmine perfume and splash it liberally about ourselves, and for a few cents, I find a nice smoky green stone—*Yes, Memsahib, is fine jade, yes finest*—just the size for my belly button to complete my couture. Ah, yes, this rig is just right for sashaying about in this tropical clime, which I plan to do with gay abandon.

After a bit of this, Ravi wearily inquires, just as any male in the world who must accompany female shoppers would ask, "What Missies want to do now? Perhaps something to eat?"

I consider for a moment and then say with firmness, "We Missies want to ride an elly-phant."

Mairead jerks her bejeweled head around and looks at me funny. "We Missies do?"

"Yes, we do, Mairead," I say. "We may never get another chance. There are only kangaroos in Australia—and wallabies and koalas and wombats and such—but no elephants. Would you not want to be able to tell your child that he or

314

she was once rocked in the womb by the gentle sway of an Indian elephant?"

"Well, if you put it that way . . ."

Ravi himself is taken a little aback—but not for long. He puts chin in hand and does some quick calculations. Then he says, "There will be a great procession this afternoon. Will cost two hundred rupees for ladies to ride earthly manifestation of Ganesh. Ravi can fix. You still want?"

"Do I have that much?" I ask, thinking about the fistful of coins I got from the moneychangers.

"Yes, Missy Memsahib."

"Then, we shall do it."

"Jacky, you're spending all your money," warns Mairead.

"That's what it's for, dear Sister," I retort. "I'll dive again tomorrow and make some more. Now let's get something to eat. I smell delicious smells. Ravi?"

"Yes, Missy?"

"Find us something to eat."

"Oh, yes. What would Missies like?"

I look about and spy a large cow big as life, ambling down the street.

"There is a cow standing over there. Surely we can find a nice steak in some fine pub. I smell cooking fires," I say, lifting my nose and sniffing the air, catching a whiff of what smells like meat being roasted. The cow is white, very clean, and covered with braided tassels. There is a painted design on its forehead, and the horns are sheathed in bright embroidery. *Quite handsome overall, there, bossy. Our Jersey cows should get a look at you. They would be most jealous.*

"Steak?"

"Yes. Meat of that," says I, pointing at the cow.

The skin of Ravi's nut-brown face turns several shades paler.

"Oh, no, Missy Memsahib. Must not say, must not even think that horrible thing. Oh . . ." He shudders at my blasphemy and takes a moment to recover, his trembling hands clasped and clutched to his thin chest. "Sweet cows sacred to Brahma. She is called *gau mata*, Mother Cow. Never harmed. She give her milk and cheeses for us peoples to eat and her dung for fires and her urine for medicine. Much loved. She wanders where she will and people take good care of her, yes."

Hmmm . . . Be that as it may, all ye holy cows, but the Faber belly is still growling.

"Well, you Indians must eat something. And my throat is dry. Where's the nearest decent tavern? I'm buying."

Again he looks blank.

"Taverns. You know, beer, ale, wine," says Mairead. She lifts her hand and makes the universal tipping-glass gesture at her lips.

Comprehension comes and he shakes his head. "Oh, no, Missies, whiskies and gins not allowed . . . tsk, tsk . . . bad Missy . . . but come . . ."

Once again, he leads us on, and soon we find ourselves in a cozy little dive with people sitting cross-legged on the ground around low tables, eating out of big bowls. There is a fireplace in the corner where the food is being cooked. It all smells very good.

Ravi seats us at a vacant table and signals for the landlady. When she comes, he jabbers something at her, and she smiles at us—but not at him—and a big bowl full of food is brought and placed before us. A steaming pot of tea is also brought, with cups; it is poured and we drink. It is strong and very good, with overtones of vanilla.

"Ummm . . ." I say, putting down the cup. "Let's eat."

I look about for utensils, but see none.

Ravi motions that we should scoop up the contents of the bowl with our fingers. I look into it and see brown rice to one side and noodles across from that and a pile of cooked vegetables in the middle. I dig in.

Ummm . . .

"That is so *good*," I enthuse.

Mairead's fingers reach in to scoop up some for herself. She brings it to her lips and then licks off her fingers.

"Mmmmmm . . ." she says, and her eyes almost cross in the enjoyment of the food. "What is that strange flavor? I'm hopin' it's not something vile."

"Nay, Sister, it is but a spice called curry. I have tasted it before. Come, Ravi, have some yourself."

"Oh, no, Missies. Not allowed to touch."

I reach out and tap him lightly on the back of his head. "Eat or I shall not pay."

He surreptitiously reaches out and scoops up a handful of the food, keeping an eye on the landlady. I know that feeling, too, because when I was a penniless, dirty urchin on the streets of London, I, too, was not allowed in even the meanest of inns. Well, that doesn't go with me, now that I'm the one with the money.

I notice that we are watched closely, and that money talks, as it always does, in any language.

When we have eaten our fill, we lean back and notice that—surprise, surprise—entertainment is offered as part of the bill-of-fare. A man seated in the back begins to play a twangy kind of stringed instrument and two young girls arise and begin to dance. There is a tip bowl in front of them.

Their hips swing back and forth and their shoulders go up and down while their arms go out to their sides and describe sinuous arcs in the air. Their kohl-rimmed eyes look out all sensuous and inviting—inviting to what I don't know, but it sure is convincing. *Glad Davy and Tink ain't here.* At the tips of their fingers they have tiny cymbals that keep time with the music. I am reminded of that song those boys of the Brotherhood used to sing when they wanted to sound exotic—*"There's a place in France where the women wear no pants. And the dance they do is called the hoochi-coochi-coo."* All we need here is a snake charmer with his asp in a basket.

When the girls conclude and bow, I get up to place a coin in the tip jar and step between them, holding up yet another coin. *A sailor and his tin is soon parted* comes into my mind, but I banish the thought. I look to the player of the stringed instrument and nod, and he commences yet again.

The girls lift their arms and I do the same, and we begin. *Hey, I can do this dance. Did I not do something similar on that tabletop in Marrakesh? That dive in Algiers? Yes, I did, and yes I do.*

We do the moves together for a bit and then I motion for Mairead to come up to join us. She does and does a fine turn herself—no shyness in that girl, no.

The music ends, I drop the coin in the bowl, and all four of us bow. The patrons in the place nod in appreciation. I prefer outright applause, but I'll settle for that.

We pay the tab and head back out into the sun.

"Is time, Memsahibs," says Ravi. "We must go down to get in line for the procession."

"Very well," I agree. "Lead on, *larka* Ravi."

As we walk along, I recall again the sailors back at the Admiral Benbow in Cheapside, when I was but a street urchin, singing about Bombay Rats and Cathay Cats, and I wondered if I would ever see any of those wonders of which they sang. Not bloody likely, I had thought, but here I am in Bombay, after all.

"What is this karma stuff you talk about, Ravi?" I ask as we stroll along the bustling street. Ravi goes ahead, shooing people out of our way.

"Is way of living your life, Memsahib. You do good things, you get good karma. You do bad things, bad karma. Good karma is like Ravi helping Missies, bad karma is like Ravi trying to cheat Missy of money back at moneychangers. If Ravi get lots of good karma, he come back as something better when he die. You see?"

Hmmm . . . Not a bad concept for the conduct of one's life, I'm thinkin'—gold stars when you are good, demerits when you are bad.

"Sort of like us Catholics when we offer up some suffering here on Earth to lessen our time in Purgatory," murmurs Mairead.

"I suppose," I say, and then leave the field of religious discussion and head off into more mundane things.

"Tell me, Ravi," I ask, "have you heard of the Bombay Rat?"

He looks at me, perplexed.

"Rat, like big mousie, Memsahib? Many of those . . ." he says, crouching down and looking under a building to see if he can spot one of the little buggers and then point him out to me. Ah, yes, rats—Universal Citizens of the World—I've never been in a place where they were not found in great abundance and, unlike the rest of us, all speaking the same language.

"Never mind," I say. "It was only a line in a song."

"Missy sing pretty, I am sure, but perhaps you thinking of the Bombay *ghat*, Memsahib. Sounds alike to Ravi's stupid ears. We are going there now. Parade start there."

"The *ghat*?" I ask.

"Yes, Missy Memsahib. Steps that go down to the river Ulhas. The peoples wash clothes and themselves there. Ravi bathe daily in holy waters of Mother Ulhas. Him not dirty like that man say."

Hmmm . . . Do I sense some pride . . . and some resentment in our little lad?

"Here is *ghat*," he announces. "Parade will start over there."

We have come out of the teeming city onto a wide open space of steps—terraces, really—leading down to a wide, very brown, river. There are many women kneeling at the edge, washing, pounding, and wringing clothes. I see a line of elephants being readied for the procession, and I also see . . . *Oh, Lord* . . . That smell I had noticed before was not from some kitchen fires, as I had supposed . . . Oh no, it was not. There are racks of wood, some stacked up and ready, some burned out and smoldering . . .

Ravi notices my shocked look as I gaze out over the smoking funeral pyres.

"Yes, Missy Memsahib. Is also place to burn the dead. Good Mister Elphy give me money to burn my mommy right over there. Very sad, but she have much good karma, so she is all right I know."

And I thought the smell was of roasting pigs . . .

I look to Mairead, and she is a bit green about the gills, but she has seen worse, and she shrugs, then says, "Let us see to these elly-phants, Sister."

We draw near the line of the huge beasts and Ravi says, "Missies stay here. Ravi must fix with mahout. Missy give purse?" I flip him my purse and he catches it and bounds off.

"That's probably the last you'll see of *him* . . . and your purse," says Mairead. "Hope we'll be able to find our way back without him."

"Oh, ye of little faith," says I, basking in the sunshine and the wonder of the day and of the place. "Somehow I trust the little fellow."

Ravi goes over to a small, turbaned man standing next to one of the elephants and holding a long hook. We see Ravi talking to the man and then see the man shaking his head. Again Ravi speaks, gesturing toward us. The man looks over and holds up two fingers. Ravi nods and then opens my purse and carefully deals out coins into the man's open palm. The man closes his hand over the money and places a ladder against the side of his beast. Ravi puts his knuckles to his forehead, bows to the mahout, and runs back to us.

"Ladies, ladies, is all set! Come with Ravi!" and we duti-fully follow, with me saying, "I told you so," to Mairead, who I can sense is still withholding judgment on the lad as well as the plan for this afternoon's entertainment.

She looks even more dubious when we get up next to the elephant. The sheer hugeness of the creature is a bit intimidating, I must admit, but . . .

"Come on, Mairead," I say, putting a foot on the ladder. "Never let it be said that either Jacky Faber or Mairead Delaney McConnaughey ever quailed before a fine adventure!"

She laughs as she follows me up to climb into a boxlike thing, gaily decorated, of course, like everything else in this glorious land.

"Missies be good now," warns Ravi, who climbs up to sit on the animal's rump, behind our box. "Sit in palanquin and wave nice to the peoples."

He doesn't know me very well, does he?

There is a great fanfare of trumpets and cymbals and who knows what else and we are off!

The great beast ambles down the street, followed by at least twenty others, all covered in bright tapestries and carrying men and women dressed in their best—and their best is very, very fine. I wave at the crowd and the people wave back. There are people on the street, there are people hanging over balconies, people everywhere. I love it! Hooray!

As we progress, I take it into my mind that I would like to ride up with the mahout, who sits forward with his knees between the elephant's big floppy ears, and so I climb over the edge of the palanquin and step onto the animal's back.

"Missy! Be so careful! Is long way down! And if you fall, the next earthly manifestation of Ganesh might step on you, squashing poor Missy's body to something unsightly!"

"Don't worry, Ravi, I shall be all right!" Geez, compared to walking along the fore t' gallant spar in a living gale, this is nothing. And I do love being the center of attention, and this sure gets me there.

I drop down to sit and I can feel the elephant's shoulders working beneath my legs and hands. Such a wonderful thing . . .

We round a corner and up ahead I see that a stage has been set up off to the right, and I suspect some nobs will be on it and—Oh, my God, I am absolutely right!

There, in all his naval glory, sits Captain Augustus Laughton, resplendent in navy blue and gold, and standing behind him—oh, glory!—is none other than my good Higgins, looking splendid in white jacket with gold buttons and braid. He seems to be scanning the crowd, probably for me. *Never fear, Higgins, you shall see me very shortly.*

Next to the Captain sits an Englishman, also finely dressed, who has to be the Governor of Bombay, and next to him an Indian man, with turban, jewels, a big mustache, and a forbidding glare . . . the Maharajah, perhaps?

Well, stand by, gents, you're about to have a show.

I jump back into the palanquin, squealing, "Come on, Mairead, stand up! It's the Captain and Higgins up there! Let's give 'em a treat!"

Mairead leaps up, ready to go.

"Here's what we'll do. When we get up in front of them, I'll face them and you'll stand behind me. I'll begin to dance that Indian dance with the arms and all, and you'll put your arms out in the same way and we'll look like that many-armed Kali! It'll be great, and everybody will laugh and be gay!"

Our elephant pulls in front of the reviewing platform, and I stand with the end of my sari across my face as a veil. I can feel Mairead up against me, behind, laughing in anticipation of the coming stunt.

I start to move my hands in that sinuous way, snapping my finger cymbals as I do it. Mairead's hands at my sides weave about in the same way.

We must look just like that statue of Kali back there in that temple, I just know it!

When all the eyes on the reviewing stand are well fixed upon us as the incarnation of an Indian goddess, I whip off the veil and give 'em all my best open-mouthed grin.

"Ahoy, Captain Laughton!" I shout, throwing my arm around Mairead. "How do you like your little minstrels now?"

The Captain's jaw drops open, and when he recognizes us, he roars with laughter. "Capital! Oh, just capital!"

Higgins looks a bit relieved to see me, and then his look turns to one of concern. The Governor looks baffled, and the Maharajah looks positively steamed.

Uh-oh . . .

"Missies, oh, missies, you should not have done that thing! Kali's thuggees mad now!" pleads Ravi, jumping to the ground. "You must run, Missies! Quickly now, follow Ravi!"

I look out and see that we are once again in front of that dark temple, the one that holds the black statue of Kali, Goddess of Death, and the scimitar-wielding guardians of the gate to the place are now waving their weapons about their heads and screaming, *"Kali! Kali!"* and are rushing toward us.

Oh, Lord, what have I done now?

I slide down off the elephant's back and reach up for Mairead, but she is already on the ground and running after Ravi.

We pound off down the street in the general direction of the ship. The parade has stopped for the moment, the elephants standing quiet.

"Missies! Under here! Careful!" shouts Ravi, ducking under an elephant's belly. We follow—*Lord, look at the size of those feet!*—and emerge mercifully unsquashed on the other side of the parade and find ourselves at the mouth of a narrow alley.

"Here! Quickly!"

We run down the length of that, turn right on another street, through some laundry hanging on a line, the sounds of the pursuing thuggees giving wings to our feet.

Oh, why cannot I ever think before I act?

We dart through a doorway to a house, past some very surprised people, and out their back door.

"In here, Missies! Quiet now!"

We crouch in a low shed and wait.

Silence, except for our heavy breathing.

"Ravi think we have lost them."

He peeks cautiously out the door. After a few minutes he says, "Come. We are not far from your big boat."

Again we start running, and then suddenly we burst back into the light. It is the wharf and there is the blessed *Lorelei Lee*!

Sure is handy having a street-smart urchin around when you need one.

"Let's get back aboard, Mairead, and we'll—"

"*Kali! Kali! Kali!*"

I twist around and, sure enough, those crazy berserkers are coming at us screaming, "*Ferengi! Maarma! Ferengi! Maarma!*"

I know what *ferengi* means, and I strongly suspect that *maarma* means *KILL!*

"Faster, Mairead! We can make it!"

Mairead, however, is plainly winded, and slows, gasping.

"Ravi! Help me!"

The boy and I grab her arms and drag her forward toward the foot of the gangway. Gaining it, we push her up and onto the ship, and I shout up, "Sailors! Pull up the brow as soon as we are aboard!"

Mairead goes safely over the rail and I go to follow, but behind me I hear Ravi say, "Goodbye, Missy Memsahib."

I look back to see him standing at the foot of the gangway.

"Thuggees now kill poor Ravi for helping Missies. He go to Brahma to be with Mommy. Thank you, Missies, for fine day. Be not sad. This good karma for me. Ravi hope to come back as happy monkey to sit at Missy's feet to amuse you with high-jinkings. Or maybe sweet puppy dog . . ."

He kneels to accept his fate and looks up at me with those enormous brown eyes.

"Sweet puppy, my ass. Get up here, you little fraud!"

I go back down and grab him by his thick mop of hair. "Get yer skinny butt up here, you crazy little wog!" I shout, pulling him up the gangway and flinging him across the deck.

"Pull it up, mates," I cry, and they do it, leaving the thuggees howling below, waving their scimitars in impotent rage.

Uncomprehending but stern and suspicious looks from the quarterdeck follow us as we go below.

Oh Lord, in trouble again . . .

Chapter 40

"Thanks for not being too angry with me, Higgins," I whisper in the darkness of our room. I have my head on his shoulder and I'm running my forefinger through the whorls of fine hair on his chest. It is much too hot for me to wear my nightshirt, but Higgins insists upon wearing his. I swear, the man refuses to sweat. The cool bath I had enjoyed earlier had helped somewhat with the heat, but that benefit had soon worn off. Oh, well, better than being cold, I suppose.

"I don't know what comes over me sometimes."

"While I realize that it is youthful high spirits that rule your conduct, would it be totally out of the question for you to stop to think for a moment before plunging into action?"

"Please, Higgins, do not scold me, for I have suffered much this day."

A heavy sigh is all that is heard from my dear husband, John.

Earlier in the day, after the howling dervishes had been urged by the truncheons of the local police to leave the dock and return to their temple, Captain Laughton had come back aboard. And he was not a happy man, oh, no. He was, in fact, fairly steaming with anger. Mairead and I were made to come out to stand before him.

"I had to personally apologize to the damned Governor and to that goddamned jumped-up heathen of a Maharajah! Damn!" he roared upon seeing my very abashed self standing on the deck with Ravi wrapped firmly around my right leg, looking very fearful. My colorful garb hung on me limply and no longer seemed quite so gay and charming.

"Furthermore, we have been *invited* to leave this fine port immediately because of your conduct today! All hands make ready to set sail!"

There is a great groan from all about. No one is pleased—neither the Captain, nor his officers, nor the crew, and especially not the whorey Crews, as they had been doing a right brisk business.

"Beat the bleedin' crap out of her!" I hear Mrs. Barnsley shout. "Ruint our fun, she did!" cries another. "Flog the little twit till she's croakers!"

Somehow I don't think a simple heartfelt apology is going to serve here.

"Mr. Higgins," orders the Captain, pointing a stiff finger at me. "You will now take that wife of yours and give her a very sound thrashing!" The Captain turns and stalks off toward his cabin. "And when you are done beating her, you may attend me in my quarters. *I* will need a drink! A stiff one!"

Higgins, looking very stern, comes over to me, wraps his hand around my neck, and drags me off squalling to our cabin, banging me against several bulkheads along the way.

After I am flung through our doorway and land on the floor, I look up somewhat fearfully at Higgins. I know he is mad at me, so I really don't know what to expect.

"Get that goddamned garish whorish dress off of you, right this instant! Yes, the knickers, too! Bare your worthless bottom. NOW!"

I go to do it, but . . .

John, you wouldn't . . . would you?

No, he wouldn't. He takes his leather razor strop from the washstand and slaps it hard against his palm.

Slap!

"Take that, strumpet!"

He nods to me, and I take the cue.

"*Yeeeow!*" I scream. "Please, husband, no more, I beg of you!"

"No more? Hardly." Again the leather strap hits his palm.

Slap!

"Oh, Lord, help me!" I screech. "I shall die!"

"Nay, you shan't die, you little tart, not till I am done with you and your bottom is as red as a beet!"

Slap! Slap! Slap!

"Mercy, Sir! Please! *Ow!*"

Slap! Slap! Slap!

"*Yeeow!*" I howl. "I am undone!"

Slap!

"There," says Higgins, putting aside the strap. "I hope you took a good lesson from that."

I bawl away, crying out my supposed shame and pain.

"Be quiet, girl, and cover yourself," barks Higgins. "I must see to the Captain. And for God's sake, try to behave!"

With that, he stalks off.

Continuing to sob my theatrical sobs, I shed my sari and put on my powder monkey gear. When I've changed, I dip my fingers in our water pitcher and sprinkle some water on my face to resemble tears. Then I go back topside to look for Ravi.

Blinking in the sunlight, I see that we have already sailed far from the land, and we are headed south on a nice quarter reach, sails trimmed properly, and all is well. Good. Just the way I like it.

With my hands on my tail as if it burns from my recent beating, I head forward.

I do not go four steps before I feel a familiar form at my side, entwining his fingers in mine. I look down into those big brown eyes, brimming with tears.

"Ravi hear poor Missy screaming in much horrible pains," he whimpers. "Ravi sorry. Ravi cry, but could do nothing to stop beatings."

"Oh, don't worry about it, boy, I'm tougher than I look, and I've been beaten before," I say, giving his thin shoulder a shake. "Come, we must see what has befallen Missy Mairead in that regard."

We are heading toward the Newgater quarters when I hear . . .

"'Bout time . . ."

I turn to see that the madams Barnsley, Berry, and Mac-Donald are all seated at a table set up on forehatch and are playing at cards. They all grin broadly at me, happy in my recent comeuppance. It is Mrs. Barnsley who speaks first, of course.

"Wouldn't sit down, if I was you, dearie. You might fnd it a bit painful."

Gales of laughter from the other two.

I lift my nose and pass them by. *Grrrrr* . . . Let those old biddies rejoice in my apparent downfall. *We shall see . . . just you wait.*

We dive down to the quarters and find that Mairead has not suffered much. In fact, we find that she has been regaling all with the tale of the day . . .

"And then we got up on the head of the elly-phant and then Jacky"—there is much clapping and laughter from all my girls. Mairead still wears her sari and swirls about imitating the dance we did on the elephant's back—"why, here she is now!"

I bow and grandly announce, "And here is our bold champion who delivered us from the assassins of Kali!"

I push Ravi forward to stand before them.

"Oh, he is darling!" exclaims Mary Reibey. "Do you think you'll be able to keep him?"

"I don't know."

"Tell 'em he followed you home," says Mary Wade. "That usually works."

"All Missies very beautiful and kind," says Ravi, putting on the big eyes. "This poor *larka* thinks he has died and gone to heaven."

"We'll see about what kind of heaven you have landed in, boy," I say, "after we have secured your berth. Come with me."

I learn that Mairead had been spared harsh punishment because of her Condition and had been given only a few swats with a switch on the backs of her hands, as well as a stern lecture on the perils of falling under the bad influence of one such as me. She feigned contriteness and promised to be good. *I know the name of that tune, Mairead,* I think, and chuckle to myself when I hear of all this. *I have sung it many times myself.*

Although the others express great concern over my recent treatment, Mairead does not. I give her a wink and she gives me one back. She knows Higgins, and she also knows he would never hurt me.

After giving instructions for more appropriate garb for Ravi—I think our Powder Monkey uniform would be just the thing—he is measured, and I take him back on deck.

Nearing the quarterdeck, I spy Higgins emerging from the Captain's cabin and we go to him.

Ravi locks himself around my leg yet again.

"Oh, Missy Memsahib! It is the Sahib who did the beatings on your poor body!"

"Head up, Ravi. Stand straight. Things are not always as they appear."

The lad makes an effort to stand and not tremble and I say, "Higgins, this is Ravi. It is probable that he saved my life today, and I want to keep him. He has some English, so he will understand when you speak to him. Ravi, this is my husband, Mr. Higgins."

Ravi lets go of my leg and bows down and puts his forehead on the deck at Higgins's feet.

"Much congratulations and hopings of much marriage bliss, Big Sahib, and enjoying fine flesh of pretty Missy Memsahib, too."

"He has some English, Higgins," I snort. "But not a lot of sense."

"That could be said of others of my acquaintance," Higgins sniffs.

Though he faked the beating earlier today, I do think the sentiments he expressed at the time about my conduct were, indeed, heartfelt.

"Come on, Higgins, this lad could be—What the hell is *that*?"

Higgins follows my gaze skyward to the thing sitting in the rigging.

"It is a monkey. Mr. Gibson brought it aboard to provide him some amusement," replies Higgins.

"She nice monkey," offers Ravi. "Ravi meet before when Big Sahib beating on poor Missy."

"Oh. Well, anyway—"

"She's allowed ashore and she comes back in disgrace with a filthy wog in tow. To be expected, I suppose."

Uh-oh . . .

First Mate Ruger has appeared, cross-armed, on the quarterdeck, looking down upon me with displeasure. "If I had been given the task of whipping some sense into you, the job would have been done right, I assure you."

"He's not a filthy wog. He has bathed daily in the waters of Mother Ulhas," I retort.

"Well, get rid of him."

Ravi understands enough to again wrap himself around my leg, whimpering.

"If Mr. Gibson is allowed to bring a monkey aboard, I should be allowed my wog."

This conversation is interrupted by the appearance of Captain Laughton, who when apprised of the situation allows that Ravi can remain aboard provided I pay for his food and upkeep.

I agree to that, and me and my wog beat a hasty retreat and resolve to stay out of sight for a while.

The ship takes a gentle roll, and a light breeze comes in through the porthole. It rolls over Higgins and me as we lie abed.

Ahh, that feels soooo good.

I turn over and put my nose to Higgins's ear. I hear a well-bred sniff from my bedmate. "What *is* that smell?"

"What? Oh, yes . . . It's jasmine perfume. Do you like it?"

"Rather strong stuff, Miss, to have survived your bath," he says, disapproval evident in his voice. "I am sure that particular scent has *never* assaulted the senses in a proper English drawing room."

"Oh, but it will, Higgins, if Mother England succeeds in her plan to take over India, which seems to be her intent. All her young lasses will be wearing jasmine, if only to show their independence and anger their parents. Believe me, Higgins, I know young girls and their ways. That's why we've got to get in on it."

"In on what, may I ask?"

"Why, the trade to India and the East, of course—Japan, China, even. Faber Shipping cannot leave it all to the East India Company. Wouldn't be fair, them having it all."

"Might I remind the President of Faber Shipping that she has received a life sentence to the penal colony in New South Wales?"

"Yes, Higgins, but *you* have not been so condemned. Faber Shipping is now a thing that exists separate from me. I merely own much of the stock. You know that I always just wanted to have a small ship to take stuff from a place that had a lot of that stuff to a place that did not have a lot of that stuff and so prosper. It didn't work out quite that way for me. But there are a lot of people that depend on that little company, and I intend to see that it continues to exist. Faber Shipping must go on, Higgins, and you must be the one to do it in my absence. Say you will do it for me . . . for all of us?"

Silence . . . then . . .

"I will do what I can, Miss."

"Good, Sir John of the Strong Hand and Forgiving Nature," I say, snuggling in closer, now that a degree of coolness has entered our cabin.

"Ravi will be a very good addition to our company. Take him back to Boston, educate him—he is very bright, you will find—and in a few years, he will be an excellent liaison to India. He speaks the lingua franca after all, and he is a very cunning little fellow."

"Umm . . . My Errant Mistress is always thinking, even when she is being wildly irresponsible."

"I try to be good, Higgins," I say, for the hundreth time, nuzzling my nose behind his ear. "I do."

"I thought that being respectful of local customs was part of Faber Shipping Worldwide's charter."

I give him a glower in the darkness. "My good conscience was not with me."

"That is because you contrived to get yourself lost. You are lucky the Captain is of a forgiving sort."

"Forgiving? He had me beaten."

"The Captain has his vices, but he is not stupid. I'm sure he saw through our little farce today. He knew I would treat you lightly, but he did have to make a show of punishing you."

I roll over and sigh. "But, oh, Higgins, what a wonderful place! I would so love to visit again!"

"Well, at least you did not return with a ring in your nose."

"That *was* an option at one of the shops, actually, and I did consider it, Higgins, but I demurred. I heard Mistress Pimm whispering in my ear that it would not be at all . . . seemly."

"A wise decision, for a change."

I feel sleep coming and murmur, "Goodnight, husband. You do take such very good care of me."

Chapter 41

James Fletcher, Convict
Onboard Cerberus
Someplace Very Hot

Jacky Faber
Onboard another prison ship
Someplace as hot and as vile, I suspect

Dearest Jacky,

I hope you are well and in good spirits, but I am sorry to report that ours are beginning to flag. The treatment grows more savage by the day, the food worse, the water more putrid, the meat more rotten. I do not know how much more we can take. Twelve men have already died from the maltreatment, their bodies taken out of the foul hold and thrown overboard without ceremony.

I am glad, in a way, that these messages to you are of an ethereal nature and not written down on paper, as I do not like coming off as a complaining scrub—additionally, I would not wish to burden you with our trials, knowing full well that you have travails of your own.

I fear we grow dispirited, and I know we must do something, something to give us some hope. I wracked my brains over this and then I recalled those belaying pins I had seen during exercise, lying carelessly in the scuppers.

Considering this, I drew the lads about me last night.

"Boys. We have to take heart, else we must lie down to die dishonored deaths. We must gather weapons, however crude they might be. I am sure you have noticed the sloppy way of things up there . . ."

There are grunts of assent in the darkness. Many curses are laid upon the heads of our jailers, many imprecations cast as to the morals of their mothers.

I lay out my plan, concluding with, "We shall need a diversion."

"Oh, you want a diversion, Mr. Fletcher? Well, next exercise you'll get one, won't he, Arthur?" says Padraic. I sense him grinning in the dark. "We'll sing the good Sergeant and the fine Corporal a little bit of a song, won't we, Arthur?"

"That we shall, Padraic. Oh, yes, we shall."

I don't ask, for I know they will not tell.

The next day, after the morning swill, we are once again hauled up on deck for exercise and airing, and while we are shuffled around the hatch top, once again Second Mate Travis Hollister falls in beside me to talk.

"So, Fletcher, how are you holding up?"

"I am able to sit up and take nourishment, Sir," I answer, somewhat churlishly. "Thank you for your concern."

"Ah, well, cheer up, James, it shan't be too long now. We enter the Strait of Malacca in the Dutch East Indies tomorrow and should be at New South Wales within two months."

I still recall my old jailhouse partner Mike Fink bellowing at me that I should be able to do a mere two months' confinement standing on my head with my thumb up my rear . . . But never mind, Jacky. You should not be subjected to such crude talk.

"Yes. I can see from the angle of the sun that we are well past India. But thank you, Sir, for the more precise fix. It eases my mind a bit to know where we are."

What I am worried about is Hollister's presence at this spot right now. He simply cannot be here when I try for the belaying pin. I glance over at Padraic and catch his eye. *Not yet, lad, wait for my signal . . . If not today, then tomorrow . . .*

Just then First Mate Block climbs up to the quarterdeck and takes over the watch. Hollister leaves, and goes below.

With some relief, I nod to Padraic.

"Shall we sing a song, then, lads, to brighten our spirits this fine day?" he loudly asks. "And perhaps lighten the hearts of dear Sergeant Napper and Corporal Vance in the process? Of course we shall."

The Sergeant and the Corporal, clubs clutched in hand, listen to this without expression, and wait.

With that, Padraic Delaney begins.

Oh, me and my cousin, one Arthur McBride,
As we went a-walkin' down by the seaside,

Mark now what followed and what did betide,
For it bein' on Christmas mor-ning.

Padraic looks over at Arthur McBride, who picks up the tune.

Now, for recreation, we went on a tramp,
And we met Sergeant Napper and Corporal Vance
And a little wee drummer intending to camp,
For the day bein' pleasant and char-ming.

"Good morning, good morning," the Sergeant did cry.
"And the same to you, gentlemen," we did reply,
Intending no harm but meant to pass by,
For it bein' on Christmas mor-ning.

It appears the song's lyrics concern a recruitment detail trying to sign up poor hapless Irish youth for the battles in Portugal, France, and Spain. The Sergeant and the Corporal are beginning to look concerned, as Padraic picks it up again.

"But," says he, "My fine fellows, if you will enlist,
It's ten guineas in gold I'll stick into your fist,
And a crown in the bargain for to kick up the dust,
And drink the King's health in the mor-ning."

The Sergeant in the song continues his blandishments. Padraic lays it on thick . . .

For a soldier, he leads a very fine life,
And he always is blessed with a charmin' young wife,

And he pays all his debts without sorrow or strife,
And he always lives pleasant and char-ming.

I round the turn, my eye on a particular belaying pin lying in the scupper gutter.

And a soldier, he always is decent and clean,
In the finest of clothing he's constantly seen.
While other poor fellows go dirty and mean,
And sup on thin gruel in the mor-ning.

Padraic ducks his head and shuffles along, letting Arthur McBride take over.

"But," says Arthur, "I wouldn't be proud of your clothes,
For you've only the lend of them, as I suppose,
But you dare not change them one night, for you know
If you do, you'll be flogged in the mor-ning."

McBride plainly looks the two guards up and down in their now shabby red uniforms and presses on, his voice thick with contempt.

"We have no desire to take your advance,
All hazards and dangers we barter on chance,
For ye would have no scruples for to send us to France,
Where we would get shot without war-ning."

"Oh no," says the Sergeant, "I'll have no such chat,
And I neither will take it from snappy young brats.

For if you insult me with one other word,
I'll cut off your heads in the mor-ning."

The Sergeant and the Corporal make a threatening move toward Arthur McBride, and Ian McConnaughey takes up the next verse.

And then Arthur and I, we soon drew our hogs,
And we scarce gave them time for to draw their own blades
When a trusty shillelagh came over their heads
And bade them take that as fair war-ning.

And their old rusty rapiers that hung by their sides,
We flung them as far as we could in the tide.
"Now take them up, devils!" cried Arthur McBride,
"And temper their edge in the mor-ning."

Their clubs are out now.

"All right, that's it, you Irish bastards!" cries Sergeant Napper, lifting his truncheon and taking a savage swing at Ian McConnaughey's undefended back.

But Arthur McBride does not stop. He continues to sing, snarling the last verse right into the guards' faces.

And we havin' no money, paid them off in cracks.
We paid no respect to their two bloody backs,
For we beat them there like a pair of wet sacks,
And left them for dead in the mor-ning.

The riot is on.

Corporal Vance roars and hits Padraic hard on the side of his head, and he goes down, dragging Duggan and Connolly with him. Then, on cue, all the others fall as if a line of dominoes. I, too, hit the deck, as if dragged by the others.

"Dammit, no! Get them up!" shouts Mr. Block. "We cannot have this!"

But Vance and Napper are maddened beyond measure—again and again they lift their clubs to bring them down on the heads, shoulders, and backs of my poor lads—and the job gets done.

As I have been allowed to keep my boots, I have my trousers firmly tucked into the tops of them. Seeming to flail about helplessly in the melee, I lay my hand on a belaying pin and slip it down through the waistband of my pants and against my leg, where it rests secure and hidden. Yes, the job is done.

Order is restored when we are once again thrown down into our cell, with a promise of no food tonight and with many a bruise and bump to nurse.

But that is all right.

Later, in the gloom of night, I pull out the club and whisper, "Here. Pass this down to Duggan. If anyone can crack a skull with one swing of that, it is he." A satisfied grunt is heard from the massive Sean Duggan as he slaps the club into his palm. "Just bring 'em on."

"Just keep it well hidden, Mr. Duggan, and you'll get your chance."

A rather catchy tune, I must say. I hum it to myself, much later, as I search for sleep . . .

Oh, me and my cousin, one Arthur McBride,
As we went a-walkin' down by the seaside,
Now mark what followed and what did betide,
For it bein' on Christmas mor-ning!

Good night, Jacky. Although I find them somewhat rough around the edges, I feel you have chosen well in your friends.

Yrs,

Jaimy

Chapter 42

I have been largely forgiven for getting us kicked out of India, and I am soon back in Captain Laughton's good graces, if not Mrs. Barnsley's—*"Little brat gets away with everything, I swear,"* she grumbles to Mrs. MacDonald and Mrs. Berry, and they *tsk! tsk!* right along with the old biddy—as each night Mairead and I once again prance into the Captain's cabin for an evening of good food and revels.

As we sail on, Mr. Gibson tells me that we have entered the Strait of Malacca, because the islands of the Dutch East Indies will afford us some protection from high seas. That's good because after we had left India, we did encounter a storm of truly horrific proportions—a true cyclone—and the ladies of the *Lorelei Lee* finally got a taste of what the wrath of Neptune really could be like.

The storm worked up, and when it was upon us, hatches were battened down, and all, except for the watch on deck, were ordered below. As the poor ship was tossed about and groaned 'neath the fury of the wind and raging sea, I know there was many a wail of despair from those who thought their end had come, that they would surely drown. I am sure there was many a bargain made with God. I know, for I my-self have made many such bargains in the past.

At the height of the cyclone, I'd gone back on deck, in the lashing wind and rain, to help where I could. There I spied Enoch Lightner, the Shantyman, one arm around the mainmast and the other held high, his sightless eyes on the heaving sea, yelling.

Blow, winds, and crack your cheeks! Rage, blow!
You Cataracts and Hurricanos, Spout!

Mairead, who had come up by my side in this male-strom, shouted, "What makes him go on so?"

And I shouted back into the wind, "He may be blind, but he is still a sailor, and he is still a man. He'd rather die out here in the open than down below, trapped like a rat! Come, let's get him!"

She and I, with ropes secured about our waists, ap-proached him and tried to talk him down. He would not listen to me, but he did listen to her. I have noticed that they have become quite close in the last few weeks. After the sing-ing and the laughter in the Captain's cabin has died down of an evening, I often find her at his side, holding his hand and listening to his stories.

"Enoch! Please! Come down!" she pleaded, reaching out to him, rain streaming down her face. He continued to roar, shaking his fist at the wind.

Blow winds! Spout!
Till you have drench'd our steeples, drowned the cocks!
Singe my white head!

At last, grasping at his hands and placing them on her heaving breast, she coaxed him below.

Meanwhile, at Assistant Purser Higgins's suggestion, we have made a darling little white turban for Ravi, to go with a nice white shirt and blousy trousers. He looks absolutely smashing. All my girls are madly in love with him. He gets many hugs and kisses and pronounces himself to be in a place called Nirvana. We are thinking of getting him some white slippers with turned-up toes. Before his debut in the Captain's cabin, I put my thumb in my pot of red watercolor and smudge a dot of the color on his forehead, just between his eyes. He protests— *"No, no, Missy Memsahib, you cannot! Wrong caste! Is mark of Brahmin, not Untouchable!"*—I am, however, unmoved by that. *"You'll be whatever caste I tell you, Ravi. Consider it a promotion, you little twit! Hold still!"*

When we first had sent him in to wait upon Captain Laughton, bearing a small tray upon which rested a glass of Madeira, the Captain, upon seeing him standing there trembling in that outrageous costume, burst into gales of laughter, exclaiming, "Ha! Makes me feel just like a heathen Maharajah, by God! Capital! Oh, just capital!"

Ravi puts up with the trousers but refuses to wear the shirt, except when he's waiting on the Captain. I can't blame him—all the crew and half the officers go about shirtless because of the heat. Most of the girls, the younger ones, anyway, have dispensed with their heavy dresses and go about in drawers and chemise.

It's all right, though, for everyone seems to have settled down with mates. I have succeeded in getting Maggie and the shy Keefe together as much as possible, and that seems to be working out.

Cookie continues to take his pleasure where he finds it—trading favors from his kitchen for favors of another kind; but he seems content to spend most of his time in his galley with Jezebel, and Mick and Keefe, along with my gang and me on occasion. I do not allow any men into the New-gaters' quarters, so Cookie's kitchen has become sort of an informal meeting place for mixed company. Club Cookie it has come to be called, and Cookie rules his smoky kingdom of pots and pans and stove with an iron hand, similar to mine, and only a select few are admitted to his realm—a good policy lest some of the bawds get even fatter than they already are, as Cookie is a *very* good cook.

Mick is still with Isabella Manson, and he has expressed some resentment over the use of his Bella by other men when we are in a port of call.

"I knows they's all whores, but I don't know if I likes the idea of them other swabs gettin' on our girls. 'Specially, my Bella . . ." he was sayin' as we were hanging about the Club yesterday.

"Well, that *is* her profession, Mick," I point out. "You ain't the first one to amble down Bella's path, so to speak."

"I know, I know, but still, it causes me some . . . I dunno . . . some . . . unease."

Men, they always want it both ways. They want what the girls got and yet they want them to be good at the same time. I swear . . .

Some of the unattached women have made other . . . arangements. Most of the cabins are now occupied, and the

Captain is most appreciative of the rents. Love lives in many guises on the *Lorelei Lee*.

Ravi, aside from being the Captain's cup bearer and the darling of the ship, is also my arrow bearer—he holds my arrows for me when I am hunting rats in the bilges, and retrieves the arrows when I miss. He also holds a lantern up high so I can see the little buggers when they poke their noses out of their holes. While we lie there in the semi-darkness, waiting for a target, I regale him with tales of the Great and Terrible Katy Deere, Archer Supreme and the Bane of All Rats, with Her Fearsome Cohort of Deadly Dianas. I know he objects to this killing and trembles when he prays over each bloody body—*"Consider, Missy, that you might come back as such a mousie."* He is a very religious little boy and some of my so-called Puritan friends could take notice. But he does what he is told, even though he worries over my karma, as well he should, as it generally does need some serious tending.

The millers, as we sailors call 'em, are much appreciated in Club Cookie, and some have already graced the Captain's table—good fresh meat was very scarce in Bombay.

Another of Ravi's tasks is to look after Mr. Gibson's monkey, who has been named Josephine, after the Empress Josephine, Napoleon Bonaparte's wife. I suppose it's a mock upon both of them. I, who have actually met the Empress Josephine, think it's rather mean, as she had been very gracious to this sous-lieutenant, Jacqueline Bouvier, a mere messenger, when I had delivered to her the news of Napoleon's victory at Jena-Auerstädt.

• • •

After the excitement and terror of the storm, things settle back into their usual tedium—school, laundry, scrubbing of decks, and so on and on and on. To liven up the routine, I have, to Higgins's great dismay, restaged the little playlet I had written when Higgins and I were on the Mississippi, "The Villain Pursues Constant Maiden, or Fair Virtue in Peril." Higgins sighs and offers it up and is a good sport in reprising his role as narrator of the grand epic. Mr. Gibson plays Captain Noble Strongheart, the hero, and I, of course, play Prudence Goodheart, the virtuous heroine. Mr. Seabrook does an excellent job as the Villain, Banker Morgan, while the Captain graciously consented to act as my father, Colonel Goodheart. Consented? Nay, the dear old ham demanded to be included as part of the cast, bellowing out his part with great gusto.

Ship's Boy Harry Quist reluctantly plays the sickly Timothy Goodheart. He had to be bribed.

A dress was again constructed with weak seams, to be ripped off my quivering form by the lustful Banker Morgan. There was a great roar from the assembly as that dress was torn off, leaving me cowering in my chemise and drawers—always a high point in these productions.

All enjoyed our little drama, with hisses and boos and catcalls at the villain, cheers for the hero, gasps when my dress comes off, and calls of *"Get the snotty little bitch. Do her up good!"* from the likes of Barnsley and Crew.

And so life goes on. The hours turn into days, the days turn into weeks, and all the while, the sun blazes and the waves roll as the *Lorelei Lee* plows on and on through the wine-dark sea.

Chapter 43

"Fight!"

I'm lounging about up in the foretop with Ravi and Josephine, feeding her little bits of johnnycake from my fingertips, when I hear the fuss below.

I pop my head over the edge and look down. Violetta Atkins and Jane Wheelden have squared off against each other. Since I have recently started up a chorus, picking the best voices from all three Crews, I've become friendly with some of the members, so I know this Janey, who is a Tartan. She's a pretty good sort of person.

"You keep yer dirty hands off my Willie or I'll tear every hair outta yer filthy head, ya little slut!"

Christ! Fightin' over a man, of course . . .

"Oo are ye callin' a slut, now, ya bloody piece o' baggage!"

I can tell this ain't gonna be no simple exchange of curses, slurs, and threats. No, this is gonna be a screeching, hair-pulling, face-scratching, all-out brawl.

"Baggage, am I? Take this!"

Sure enough, the battle heats up.

I fly down to the deck and throw myself between the two combatants, both of whom have their fists clenched around the hair of the other, snarling.

"Stop it, you two! Right now!" I cry, putting a stiff arm on each chest and forcing them apart. "You'll be whipped!"

My restraining arms notwithstanding, the fight goes on, each girl glaring into the enraged eyes of the other. My feet lose purchase and we all collapse into a heap on the deck, fists and fingernails still inflicting damage.

"Please, girls! This is against the rules!" I gasp from underneath the heaving bulk of the two. "You'll be punished!"

Turns out they ain't the only ones to be punished.

Uh-oh . . .

First Mate Ruger has appeared on the battleground. With a certain amount of dread, I look over at his shiny boots standing within an inch of my nose.

"Bo'sun! Tear them apart and then bring them up before me on the quarterdeck! All three!" he roars.

I feel Bo'sun Roberts's hand clamp around my neck as I am put to my feet and dragged up before the one man on this ship who I know for certain bears me no goodwill.

"Fighting is not allowed on this ship!" Mr. Ruger roars. "You know the penalty!"

Janey, who stands on my right and who has obviously gotten the worst from the fight, says nothing, but only sucks in her breath in great gasps. Violetta, hauled up on my left, looks defiant. She has felt the rod before and does not fear it. But then her look of defiance fades as she hears Ruger's next words.

"It is apparent that a mere application of the rod is not sufficient to prevent this sort of altercation, as it has been tried in the past and been found wanting."

He pauses, peering down upon us with some satisfaction, as if he has been waiting for such a moment. Then he continues.

"Therefore, we must choose an alternate form of punishment. Bo'sun Roberts, rig up the dunking stool! Each shall get ten seconds under!"

"What? What does he mean?" gasps Janey.

"It means we are to get very wet, dear," I say.

There is a bustle of activity as the Bo'sun's Mate prepares the apparatus. A chair is taken and ropes are attached to it such that it can be hoisted on the end of a line that is fed through a winch, and then swung over the side and lowered. It is the kind of gear used when a sailor must work at a repair to the ship's hull when under way—a Bo'sun's Chair, it is sometimes called. That will *not* be the use to which this chair will be put today.

"What are they doing, Jacky?" asks the now quite subdued Violetta.

"We are to be dunked in the water, dear," I say.

Violetta makes a mewling sound, echoed by Jane. Both grab at my arms.

Had I any clothing on other than the light shirt and trousers of my Powder Monkey rig, I would be shedding it right now, but I do not. Oh, well, doesn't matter. Everything dries real fast in this heat, and I will, too. I stand and wait.

All this noise rouses Captain Laughton from his afternoon nap and he lumbers out on deck, rather grumpy, it appears.

"Do you mind telling me just what's going on, Mr. Ruger?" he asks, scratching his belly, blinking in the sunlight and gazing at the three of us standing there—two trembling, one not.

"Good afternoon, Captain," says Ruger with a certain smugness. "We have three malcontents here who are facing punishment for fighting. Since the rod was not sufficient deterrent, I have rigged the dunking stool to see how they like the taste of salt."

"Um," replies the Captain, not happy with this at all.

Looking at Janey's face, terror writ large upon it, I speak up.

"Captain, these girls are terrified. They've probably never had their heads underwater in their whole lives. If they go under for the ten seconds so decreed by Mr. Ruger, they'll panic and suck in a chestful of water. Then they'll die; and you will be out ten pounds six for each. Being dunked in the water is nothing to me, as you know, but not so for them."

Higgins has appeared on deck as well, looking mightily concerned.

It is apparent that the Captain is thinking furiously how to get out of this. On the one hand, he doesn't want to lose valuable bits of cargo; but on the other, he really can't countermand his First Officer's order. It would disrupt the way of things on the ship. So Ruger has put him in a tight spot, and I know he does not like it.

The Captain eyes the cowering Lizzie and Tartan and then addresses me. "You think that they might not survive?"

I nod. "Ten seconds up here is not long. Down there it can be an eternity."

"Hmm. Suppose you would take their punishment upon yourself? There are some who think you have not suffered enough for causing us to be booted out of Bombay. Will you do it?"

I pause, as if thinking, and then answer, "I will."

Of course I will—what's thirty seconds underwater to a mermaid?

"Very well, let's see this done, then," orders the Captain. So I go over to seat myself in the chair.

As my arms are strapped on to the chair and my legs fixed below, I hear Ravi whimpering, so I call out, "Maggie, see to Ravi, please. Make sure he doesn't do something stupid."

I am secured and the Captain says, "Are you ready?"

I nod, and I am jerked upward on the crane and then swung *way* out over the water, a good ten feet from the side. The water roils beneath me.

"Down!" is the command, and down I go. I suck in a big breath just before I hit.

The water is pleasantly warm and a nice shade of blue-green, I reflect, and then start counting out the seconds.

One, one hundred; two one hundred; three one hundred . . .

I can see the hull of my *Lorelei Lee* off to my left, but not much else. Oh, well, I should not have expected a show, as we are in very deep water.

Ten, one hundred; eleven, one hundred; twelve, one hundred . . .

At least I see no sharks, which is good, as my feet are rather exposed.

Twenty, one hundred, twenty-one, one hundred . . .

I'm thinkin' poor Ravi must be throwing a fit right now, poor lad . . .

Twenty-nine, one hundred; thirty, one hundred; thirty-one, one hundred . . .

Should be pulling me up about now . . .

Thirty-eight, one hundred; thiry-nine, one hundred; forty, one hundred . . .

Maybe I counted a bit fast. Slow down some . . .

Fifty, one hundred; fifty-one, one hundred; fifty-two, one hundred . . .

What's going on here? All right, what are you doing up there?

Seventy-three, one hundred; seventy-four, one hundred . . . Oh, the hell with it! It's over a minute, for chris'sakes! Are you trying to kill me?

I start to strain and buck against my bonds, but it does no good.

No, no, stop that! You're using too much air! Calm dowm! Don't panic! If you panic, you're done! Just wait, they'll pull you up!

But they don't pull me up, no. They leave me down here, and it seems it is their intent to kill me. Very well, I commend my body to the sea in which my body sits helpless and my soul to God.

I must breathe in soon; I must, I must. But I cannot, I cannot. If I do, I will die. But I ache to breathe! I do! I do! Please, God, I don't wanna die . . . I don't wanna die . . . I gotta breathe . . . I gotta . . . I . . .

. . . suck in the water . . .

Oh, it burns, it burns, Oh, Lord, I am done . . .

. . .

I come to my senses, stretched out, face-down over a barrel with Higgins pushing down on my heaving back. I spew out through my nose and mouth what seems like gallons of saltwater, and when it looks like I might live, Higgins scoops up my sobbing, gasping form and carries me down to our cabin.

"It seems, Miss," announces a furious Higgins, as he tosses me into the tub, "that the winch that was to draw you back up was jammed by what appears to be a splinter of some sort. It could have been a natural thing . . . possibly a shaving from a spar . . . Here, let me get that shirt off you . . . Or it could have been a knitting needle . . ."

I shiver as I sit in the empty tub, waiting for the warm water. *There are many in the Crews who knit . . . Could they really hate me so?*

I dimly sense Keefe and Mick bringing up the hot water, Higgins taking it from them, and then I feel it poured around me.

I lean back in this gentle, soothing, friendly water, and think back to the water outside.

"At least, Higgins, now I know what it's like to drown."

"Please try to put that out of your mind, Miss."

"I will try, Higgins, but—"

There is a light tap on the door. When Higgins opens it, I turn and see Mrs. Barnsley and Mrs. MacDonald standing there, with Mrs. Berry behind.

"Yes?" says Higgins, with a certain coldness. He has seen all three of these women at their knitting, their needles clicking.

"We've had our differences with your wife in the past, Mr. Higgins," says Mrs. Barnsley. "But . . . we thank her for standin' up for our girls. We just want you to know . . . We didn't have nothin' to do with what just happened to her."

Higgins nods and closes the door and I sink down in the tub.

"Well," I say.

"That may well be true, Miss, but someone on this ship wanted to take joy in your demise."

"Umm . . ." I say. "And I think I know who it is."

"I believe you are right, Miss, and I advise you to be *very* careful and—"

The door bursts open and Ravi sticks his head in.

"Missy Memsahib! Big Sahib! Two big boats out on the water!"

Chapter 44

Jaimy Fletcher
Bound to a Grating
Onboard the Vile Cerberus
In the Strait of Malacca

Jacky—

The leering sonsabitches mean to take young Connolly to-
day, and it is a damned shame! Too soon, too damned soon!

Sergeant Napper and Corporal Vance, emboldened by
their pummeling of us last week, have come to our cell door
to announce, "We need the convict Daniel Connolly for a
work detail!"

The boy looks up, his eyes big and full of fear.

We all know what kind of work will be involved—poor
young Daniel, taken in all his young innocence, and . . . No!
We cannot let it happen!

Padraic, Ian, and Arthur look over at me. They all stand
ready to prevent this outrage, even if it costs them their lives.
Sean Duggan begins to reach for the belaying pin entrusted

to his care. I shake my head at all of them. *No! Let me handle this!*

I have talked it over with Delaney, McBride, and Mc-Connaughey, and, yes, Connolly, too. We all agreed that we would use the boy as bait to get the miserable buggers inside the cell door, when the time comes. But right now, it is still too early. We have but one poor weapon—only Duggan's belaying pin, which he keeps hidden under his bench, secured there with pine pitch scooped up from the simmering pot in the galley, and thus the belaying pin is out of the sight of our jailers.

The cell door opens and Sergeant Napper and Corporal Vance swagger into our cramped space.

"Connolly. Let's go. You shall work for your burgoo this day," announces Napper. Vance chuckles obscenely, "Oh, yes, he shall—"

I stand and say, "He is too small for any work detail. Take me."

Vance looks me over. "Oh, you are pretty enough, Convict Fletcher, and maybe we'll take you out for a . . . work detail . . . soon enough." He sneers. "But you ain't half pretty enough compared to that boy . . . He's got a real fine tail."

That does it.

I lunge for Vance, bringing my clenched fists down on his face and, though hampered by my ankle manacles, I manage to shove my knee hard into his crotch. He cries out and falls. Sergeant Napper howls out, *"Riot! Cell number one! Riot! To me!"*

The Bo'sun and his men charge into the cell to club me down and then drag me up on deck. I am stripped of my shirt and tied spread-eagle to the main hatch grating. I had seen it done lots times, of course, to many a poor sailor . . . but it had never yet been done to me.

"Twelve lashes, and lay them on strong!" orders Captain Griswold. "Bring up the Irish pigs so they may watch and see what rebellion brings!"

The vengeful Corporal Vance has been given the pleasure of administering the strokes himself. Looking grimly gratified, he stands next to me with the cat in his hand. There is a lump on his forehead that is swelling up all purple and red. *Good for you, you piece of filth! I wish I could have damaged you more. Damn you to hell!*

The miserable Captain Griswold looks out over my assembled lads as they are led, chained at the ankles, onto the deck.

When all is in place, he says, "Lay on, Corporal Vance, and do not hold back!"

Vance rears back and delivers . . .

Through my pain, I dimly hear, after what I think is the sixth stroke . . .

"On deck there! Ship on the horizon! Due south! It's a brigantine flying British colors!"

What . . . ?

Having already suffered six lashes and been launched almost unconscious into a searing world of pain, I manage to collect what is left of my mind, grit my teeth, and try to rise.

"Hold there, Vance!" shouts Griswold. "Let us see what she is!"

I am left to sag in my bonds, halfway through my punishment.

I do not know if I welcome the interruption. I know it is weak of me, but in my pain, I just want it all to be over. I just want to crawl down to my burrow like any other beaten and wounded animal.

• • •

The instant after Ravi pokes his head in the door to announce the arrival of another ship on the scene, I am up, dried, and back in clean drawers and chemise. I have my shiv tucked into my waistband, which is hidden by my top. No telling; it could be another pirate. Higgins hands me my long glass as I whip out the door and run back up on deck and into the foretop, spyglass to eye.

I feel movement at my side and realize it is Mairead.

"What is it?" she asks. She is soon joined by Ravi, who looks anxious.

"Is bad people?"

"Don't know, Ravi. Two ships," I answer. "I see English flags, but it could be a pirate trick. I've seen it done before."

Hell, I've done it before myself, flying false colors to trick the unwary.

"On deck there," I call down to the quarterdeck Watch. "What do you think they are?" All below, Captain Laughton included, have long glasses to their eyes, trained on the visitors.

Mr. Seabrook drops his glass and looks up at me.

"We think it is an East India Company ship, just like us, carrying convicts to New South Wales. Her escort appears to be a Royal Navy sloop-of-war," advises Mr. Seabrook. "We are going to close with them."

Be careful, lads, you never know, out here on the wild and lawless ocean.

"Should we man the guns?" I ask, ready to assemble my Powder Monkeys in an instant.

"No," says the Captain. "I recognize the ship." He snaps his glass shut. "It is the *Cerberus*. Although there is very little love lost twixt Griswold, her captain, and me, we shall close with them for a gam. Must remember my manners. Right full rudder. Topmen aloft to trim sail."

The wheel is spun and the *Lorelei Lee* leans over, and the distance between the ships grows narrow.

"What's a gam?" asks Mairead. Josephine has joined us and leans her orange head against Mairead's shoulder, her long arms about Mairead's waist, content and seemingly oblivious to all this excitement.

"It's when ships out on the sea come together to exchange news. It's a whaler's term, but it goes for all seagoing vessels," I say, still looking at the approaching ships. "When you're out on the briny for a long while, all aboard hunger for news of what is happening in the rest of the world."

I know that others on the ships are looking at us, for I see the lenses of their long glasses flash in the sunlight.

Hmmmm . . . My ears are burning . . . Could it be that someone is looking at me? *Nah, it must be the sun.*

The escort ship falls off to wait several hundred yards off. Again the lens flash—seems to come from their quarterdeck. Hmmm . . .

We grow quite close to the *Cerberus* now, and the sails on both ships are slacked. Grappling hooks are thrown across, and we are drawn together. The mainmast spars touch, leaving a scant ten feet of water between our hulls.

"Ahoy, Captain Laughton!" cries this Griswold of the *Cerberus*.

"Ahoy, Captain Griswold," replies Old Gussie. "I trust you've had a pleasant voyage?"

"Not as pleasant as you, I see . . ."

Many members of the petticoat Crews are festooned about the decks and in the rigging.

Griswold continues. "So, why do you not trade several dozen of yours, for an equal number of ours? They are all going to the same place."

Captain Laughton spies me up above, and he calls out, "What say you, Jacky? What thinks our fierce little pirate? Should some of you ladies go off? I am sure there will be much profit to be made."

I gaze down at the *Cerberus*'s crew's lusty faces and say, "I think we are quite content where we are, Sir."

"Well, then, Captain Griswold, Mrs. Higgins has spoken, and you have your answer. You keep yours, and I'll keep mine."

"All right, but how about twelve of mine for six of yours?"

"Nay, Lemuel, a contract is a contract, and I wish to continue working for the good old East India Company. So let us peel off, Mr. Seabrook, and we'll continue on our way. Lemuel, I look forward to sharing a glass with you in Sydney. Cheerio."

I think I hear a growl from the *Cerberus*'s Captain.

"I see you have a man strapped to the grating," observes Captain Laughton, with scorn in his voice.

"Right. We are conducting punishment. That man led a riot, which we had to put down most vigorously."

"We do not often have to resort to that sort of thing here."

"True, but you have a much . . . softer sort of convict than do we. Sometimes these convicts of ours are much in need of . . . correction."

Man on grating? What . . . ?

I swing my glass over to look at the men gathered on the *Cerberus*'s deck, and . . .

My God! It's my old Emerald *crew! There's Arthur McBride, and Farrell, all in chains . . . and . . . there's Ian McConnaughey . . .*

I stand gasping.

Mairead looks at me curiously. "Jacky, what's the matter?"

Dare I show her? Yes, I must, I must . . . She has to know that he is still on this Earth and is all right . . .

I pass the glass to her and say, "Look down there . . . third man on the left, next to the rail . . . and steady now, girl."

Wondering, she takes the glass and holds it to her eye. As she scans the deck, I slip my arm around her expanding waist and wait to hold her fast for I know what is coming.

She jerks, and then screams, "Ian! Husband! Oh, Lord!"

Ian's head jerks up. "It's Mairead," he shouts. "Dear girl!"

She tries to free herself of my grip, but I do not let her go.

"Mairead!" I hiss in her ear. "You cannot go over there! You'll be in great danger! That crew hasn't seen a woman in a long time! They'll pass you around!"

"I dinna care! Ian's there!"

"And Jacky, too, up there!" shouts Arthur McBride, pointing a manacled hand up at us. "Fletcher! It's your Jacky!"

Fletcher? What . . . ?

The man tied to the grating lifts his head and cries out . . .

"JACKY!"

Jaimy! Oh, dear God, it's Jaimy!

I release Mairead, and she is off across the spar and into the rigging of the other ship, and then down the ratlines, and I am right behind her. We plunge down to the deck and head for our lads.

"Grab them!" shouts Captain Griswold, and rough hands are put on us. Enraged beyond all thought, I put teeth, fingernails, fists, and knees to good use and manage to get to Jaimy's side.

He lifts his face and whispers, "Jacky . . . I . . ." and he can say no more.

I cover his poor face with kisses and run my hands across his bloody back. "Oh, Jaimy, how could they do this to you? The bastards, I'll—"

Then I am torn away from him.

"Give them back, Lemuel," demands Captain Laughton, no longer bantering, as I am held back, panting, wild with fury. I hear sounds of struggle and Mairead screaming.

"But, Gussie, they came over of their own free will, didn't they?"

"Give them back, Captain Griswold," growls our Captain, tersely. "I remind you that we have guns, and you do not."

Captain Griswold considers this and wisely accedes. "Very well, keep your ship of whores. First, however, we have a bit of unfinished business. We were conducting punishment and now we shall let it proceed. Hold the female right there, so that she may clearly see."

I am held fast, next to the grating.

"Good. Now administer the remaining six lashes," says Captain Griswold. "And add six more for the interruption."

I am forced to watch as they do it. After they finish whipping him, and Jaimy's back is even more of a bloody mess, and I have vomited out the contents of my stomach, Captain Griswold motions to the men holding me, and sneers, "Let her go to give that bleeding carcass a goodbye kiss. She seems to be fond of it. It'll probably be the last one it shall get in this world."

I'm released, so I stumble over beside Jaimy and put my hands on him, to whisper in his ear, "I swear, Jaimy, by the blood that is on my hands, that they shall pay for this. I swear it!"

He looks at me through pain-crazed eyes but manages to nod. While I am holding him to me, I slide my shiv out of my sheath and down into his boot without anyone seeing. I can see he needs it more than I do.

"I repeat, send the girls back, Griswold. Mr. Seabrook, perhaps we shall have to man the guns after all."

"Very well, Laughton," answers Griswold. "Rest assured, though, that the Company shall hear of this."

Then he turns rudely away. "Throw the baggage over," he orders. "Here's two more of your poxy whores, Laughton, cleaner than when they arrived. Topmen! Aloft to make sail!"

As I am torn from Jaimy, I take one last look at his anguished face, and then I am thrown over the side. I hit the water hard, on my back, and as I resurface, I see Mairead come hurtling down.

The two ships throw off the grappling hooks and move apart. I swim over to the struggling Mairead and pull her to the surface.

Holding her, I tread water and manage to keep her face above its surface. There is the sound of a boat being lowered and men calling out to us. It is Monk and Suggs who haul us back aboard the *Lorelei Lee*, where we stand dripping with water, hatred, misery, and fury.

PART IV

Chapter 45

And so we plow on and on, out of the Strait of Malacca and into the South China Sea.

I've been a wreck for several days, but I get over it and try to lend Mairead some cheer—*"At least we know where our lads are, Mairead,"* I say, to give comfort to her as well as to myself. *"At least we know that, and we know we will see them again, since we're all headed for the same place. We'll figure out what to do when we get there. Now, come, let us be cheerful. We are expected to perform in the Captain's cabin tonight—shall we sing dirges, or shall we be gay? Good! That's my girl."*

Mairead's belly continues to swell. We have sewn her a new, more blousy, Powder Monkey top, and we make a great fuss over her. She smiles and often places her hand on that belly and looks off in the distance to where she last saw Ian, her husband and the father of her child.

Sumatra, Batavia, Malaysia, Borneo, Java . . . My mind spins with all the exotic places we have passed by and sometimes visited. Eventually, I am allowed out on land again, which I find most gratifying. I continue my studies of the local flora and fauna and am putting together a box of butterflies for Dr. Sebastian, as I know they are his passion.

We cross the equator again, but poor Ravi is the only Pollywog to be initiated. Since he is the only one, it is kept simple. He is made to kiss the Captain's ring, and then he is stripped down and a rope is tied about his waist. *"You sahibs going to use poor Ravi as fish bait? Oh, no, Sirs, please!"*

His tormenters are unmoved. *"Shut yer gob, boy. Even a heathen wog has got to rub the tits of the* Lorelei *or he hain't no true member o' the crew."* Ravi trembles but does it. Then he is dipped in the sea and brought sputtering back aboard, a newly christened Shellback.

We visit the port of Singapore at the lower tip of the Malay Peninsula. It used to be Portuguese, then it was Dutch, now it belongs to the East India Company, which is to say, the British.

We are in bed, preparing to sleep, when I ask, "Why was that place fought over so much, Higgins?"

"Probably for the crime of being a very nice little port in exactly the right place, from the powers-that-be point of view."

"But why so many overlords to that little port? Why did it change hands so much? Why did not one of them hold it?"

Higgins considers, and I know he is looking up in the darkness. Then he says, "From my reading of history, when it comes to lands and the people who live upon them, it is very easy to conquer those people when one has superior armament, more soldiers, and more will. But, on the other side of the coin, it is also very hard to hold those people and their ancestral lands beyond the initial victory. People never forget when harm has come to their native land and to their kin. I believe Monsieur Napoleon will someday find that out to his chagrin. As will our own John Bull."

"You are so wise, Husband John."

I hear him chuckle deep in the broad chest upon which my head rests.

"No, not wise. Not at all. I am merely an observer of things as they lie in this world."

"Do you observe me?"

"Oh, yes, Miss, I certainly do." He laughs. "And believe me, you are quite an education. More than all the kings and queens and all the would-be masters of the world."

"Me? Surely you jest."

"Who was it who brought down Troy, then?"

I give a snort at that. "Not me, but thank you, Higgins, even though you think more of me than I deserve. I am certainly not anything like *the* Helen."

"Till another such as she comes along, Miss, you will do quite nicely. To sleep with you now."

I snuggle in and sigh deeply, and Higgins knows what I am thinking about, yes he does . . .

"Miss, you do know what *could* have happened to Mr. Fletcher, back in London?"

"Yes, a firing squad on some quarterdeck if they had wanted to lend him some deference for his being Lieutenant in the Royal Navy and to accord him an honorable soldier's death, rather than hanging him in a rough, common, disgraceful noose. Yes, I know what could have happened, and I am grateful that it did not, in spite of what I saw that day. Yes, I know . . . Thank you, Higgins, for your comfort."

Good night, Jaimy.

Chapter 46

Jaimy Fletcher
Onboard Cerberus
No Longer Bereft of Hope

Jacky . . .

*Yes, my back burns, and it burns like a hundred fires, but
that is nothing compared to the fire in my heart, having seen
you this day. The pain of the lashes was lessened by your loving
touch, my raging mind gentled by your sweet kiss, my confusion soothed by your gift.*

What gift, you ask? In the gloom of our cell, after I had
been brought back down and all of our jailers had left, I
reached into my boot and drew out that lovely, deadly knife
that you had placed there, and held it up before my now
hopeful and ready crew—your shiv, with the cock's head
you carved on the hilt, grinning evilly at us. It seems to wink
at me and to ask, "How many notches are there on my hilt
now, Jaimy? Two, four, six? Will there be more?"

Oh, yes, there will be, count on it, Cock! The flogging was a cheap price to pay to get you. With you we can fashion more weapons, with you we shall throw off our shackles or die in the attempt!

Thank you, Jacky.
I am your bloody, but unbowed,

Jaimy

Chapter 47

At dinner this night, Captain Laughton waxes quite ribald about the whole incident on the deck of the *Cerberus* when I saw my Jaimy so cruelly treated.

"By God, Mr. Higgins," he chortles, his bulbous nose glowing bright red from the spirits he has already imbibed. "It would seem, from that heartrending display of young love to which we were treated, that your frisky little wife might have something in the way of a tempestuous past that perhaps did not include yourself? Eh?"

Great hilarity, with fists pounding all around the table. "Well said, Captain, and what say you, Mr. Higgins?" asks Mr. Gibson.

"Ah . . . ahem . . . well . . . yes, Sir," replies the impeturbable Higgins. He places a fresh glass of rum in front of the Captain, and another in front of Ruger, who takes it up and tosses it back without ceremony and without thanks to the server.

Hmmm . . . It appears to me that the First Mate has been getting more and more into his cups as this voyage progresses, and I believe I am not mistaken on that. After a few drinks, he grows surly and his gaze lingers on me . . . and, lately, more and more on Mairead, as well. I think only the Captain's presence prevents him from being more outspoken in his desires . . . his very base desires. *Hmmm . . . I don't like it . . .*

Higgins goes on. "It seems that most of the ladies aboard this ship would have quite a few interesting . . . items . . . to bring up in the confessional booth, should any of them ever have occasion to kneel in sincere contrition in that sanctified space . . . and my wife is no exception. But she has confided all to me—made a clean breast of things, as it were, and I have given her my forgiveness for her past actions."

"A clean breast! Contrition! Forgiveness! Har-har, Higgins, you slay me!" roars the Captain, his eyes squeezed shut in a state of high hilarity.

I work up a blush, lower the eyelids, and avert the eyes in a guilty sort of way and continue to quietly play my guitar.

As I strum away, keeping the sound of my instrument and voice well below the level of conversation, the talk at the table strays to a discussion of what we will find in New South Wales.

"Begging your pardon, Sir," asks Mr. Hinckley of the Captain. "What can our *ladies* expect upon arrival?"

Careful, Mr. Fourth Mate Hinckley, as there are none of us ladies who care to be sneered at . . .

"Well, I should expect there would be great rejoicing, but with Bligh in charge of the colony, I'm sure it will be a mess," Captain Laughton replies.

What? I am stunned.

"Bligh, Sir?" I venture to ask. "Surely not *the* Captain Bligh of HMS *Bounty*?"

"Aye," he says, shaking his good gray head. "One and the same." He pauses for a heavy sigh. "Poor old Bligh. Fortune never did smile upon that man. Despised as a tyrant, yet I know that he was not. In fact, it is known that he hired a fiddler, a seaman who had lost a leg in battle, to provide entertainment for his men on that ill-fated voyage when he suffered that mutiny . . . In the search for bloody breadfruit, of all things."

The Captain pauses for a long and most resonant belch.

"I've met him, you know," he continues. "Not a bad sort, actually. More sinned against than sinning as Gentle Will would have it. My take on the whole thing is that he was poorly served by his junior officers—that Fletcher Christian, for one . . . Met him, too . . . bleeding, preening, spoiled fop. If it'd been me, I'd have thrown that pampered, powdered ass overboard not two days out. But never mind about Bligh. Let us have a song, Mairead. 'The Galway Shawl,' if you please. Lend us some cheer, girl."

Mairead, after our duets together, has seated herself on the deck, by Enoch Lightner's side. He places his hand lightly on her bare shoulder and leaves it there. Hearing the call, she nods and rises, hands clasped in front of her, ready to sing for her supper, as it were.

"And if that was your young man we saw you clinging to that day, then be of good cheer yourself, for you shall surely see the young hound again," Captain Laughton continues. "And you may even prosper in the new land. I hear they give married couples, after they have served their sentences, small farms to work. Forty acres and a mule, I believe it is said."

"I hope it to be so, Sir," replies Mairead, head bowed, hands held in a prayerful attitude, waiting . . .

"I suspect mules to be a rather rare commodity in New South Wales, Sir," interjects Fourth Mate Hinckley, not very helpfully, I'm thinking. He is not often here, and plainly already halfway into his cups. *Be careful what you drink and what you say, Mr. Hinckley* . . . "I have heard they put convicts in harness and make them pull the plows," he continues.

"Hmm. That seems sensible, I suppose," muses the Captain, who then brings his gaze upon me. "How would you like to be put into harness to pull a plow, Mrs. Higgins?"

"I have been in worse conditions, Sir. I am little, but I am strong. And it would not seem at all strange to me, as nothing surprises me anymore."

"Ha! I bet not!"

"Perhaps forty acres and a kangaroo, Sir, would be more to the point," offers Mr. Gibson, who fancies himself something of a wit.

"Ha! Wouldn't that be a sight! A kangaroo pulling a plow! Ha!"

"I'm afraid it would be rather an uneven plowing, Sir— four big hops to one good pull. Would rather jostle the plowman, I suspect."

Ain't it strange how good wine and spirits make even lame jokes funny? And yes, with all the Mates in attendance tonight, including Army Major Johnston and his Esther, the cabin is quite crowded.

"How about a carriage and four, to bounce into town. Wouldn't that be a sight?" continues Hinckley.

Yes, things get rather bizarre in the way of mess table conversation when one has been at sea a long time.

"Could you see yourself outfitted for such a kangaroo saddle, Jacky?" asks the Captain.

"If such a saddle could be made, I would mount and ride him, Sir," I reply, secure in my ignorance. "Have you ever seen a kangaroo, my lord?"

"Yes, dear, I have. It was at a fair. In Cornwall," answers the Captain. "The beast was to box with a local tough. Actually the 'roo did quite well—knocked the country bumpkin down several times to the amazement and joy of all. 'Cept for the opponent, of course. He was quite mortified to be beaten by what looked to be a big rabbit."

I'm thinking back to Jemimah Moses and her tales of the wily Brother Rabbit, who outsmarted bears and foxes as well as country bumpkins, and wonder how she would voice Brother Roo. Hmmm . . . Food for idle thought . . . As a treat for the kids at my school—Lorelei Lee Elementary, as it is now called—when they have done their lessons well, I perform some of Jemimah's Rabbit Tales for their enjoyment. Course I can't do 'em as well as she does, but my young scholars seem to delight in them.

Mairead now sees her opportunity to begin her song, and she delivers "The Galway Shawl" a cappella, giving my fingers a bit of a rest, and she does it beautifully. I've never heard it better done. She even manages to smile while doing it, and it lights up the room.

As well you might smile, my redheaded friend, as it was not your lad we saw being beaten to a pulp. But no, stop that— snark back the sniffles and tears, girl, and get on with things. You know that Jaimy's alive and that's all you can ask for right now.

I am shaken out of my reverie by the Captain's request. "Come, Jacky," he says. "You have been uncommon quiet this evening. Give us something lively . . . something . . . new, perhaps? Something we haven't heard before?"

I think on this and then reach for my concertina.

"Actually, Sir," I say, "I have made up a bit of a shanty. I hope Mr. Lightner will forgive me my cheek in this regard."

The Shantyman grins and nods, waiting.

I pump up the bellows, run a few riffs, and then lift my chin and sing.

> *There was a wooden maid,*
> *And on her harp she played,*
> *It was the* Lorelei Lee *putting out to sea*
> *And they say she looks like me,*
> *Boys . . .*
> *She might look a bit like me.*

I drag out the "Boys . . ." somewhat to give it a bit of the Jacky Faber touch and to distinguish it from the rather naughty song from which I stole the melody.

"Har-har, that it does, dearie! A dead ringer for you, for sure!" chortles the Captain. Then I do the chorus.

> *'Twas on the* Lorelei Lee,
> *Two hundred girls and me,*
> *We sailed away, with a crew so gay,*
> *All up for a good long jour-ney*
> *Yes . . .*
> *Way up for a lusty jour-ney!*

There are roars of approval, and I keep the concertina going while I call out, "Beggin' your pardon, Sir, but might I use your name in vain, as it were, all in the name of good fun?"

"By all means! Sing it out, girl! Sing it out!"

I do the chorus again and all join in, and then, with some trepidation for what I am about to sing, I press on.

> *Oh, the Captain's name was Gussie,*
> *With the girls both brave and lusty,*
> *He had two full score, yet he cried for MORE!*
> *All on the* Lorelei Lee,
> *Boys . . .*
> *All on the* Lorelei Lee!

Out of the corner of my eye, I see Higgins wincing at this, but the Captain bawls out, "Yes, oh, yes! Capital! Go on!"

I do . . .

> *Onboard were two hundred dollies,*
> *All guilty of sundry follies,*
> *Gus inspected the lot and found them hot*
> *Down in their lower quarters*
> *Oh . . .*
> *Down in their lower quarters!*

Roars of laughter, another chorus, and I see the Shanty-man standing up and signaling for his turn.

"If you please, Miss, I have a verse to add to your fine tune."

I bow and say, "Of course, Mr. Lightner, lay on."

He throws back his head and belts it out.

> *When on that ship so grand,*
> *I got splinters in my hand . . .*

'Cause I rubbed the tits of that wooden bitch
From Dover down to Van Diemen's Land!

That, of course, brings down the house, with whistles and shouts of *"Bravo, Shantyman!"*

We end with another chorus, and then I bow my head humbly, knowing that I am a mere apprentice in the presence of a master of the craft.

The party roared on far into the night, but eventually it wound down and finally we took to our bed.

"Nice little . . . shanty . . . that," says Higgins in the dark. "I believe it to be on a par with 'The Villain Pursues Fair Maiden,' that notable . . . er, um . . . play of yours."

"Higgins, I've got to use what little wit I have," I huff, and face away from him.

"Do not take offense, Miss. We both know you possess considerable wit."

I roll back over. "All right, Higgins, I shan't because I cannot be mad at you. Good night, Husband."

"Good night, Wife."

We lie in silence for a while and then I whisper, "Higgins, have you seen the way Ruger looks at me?"

"Ummm. Yes. He has, in fact, offered me ten pounds for an hour with you."

"And what did you tell him?"

"That when I am tired of you, he shall have his pleasure. It seemed to satisfy him. For the moment."

"Very politic, Higgins."

"It was the best I could think of."

"And now his eye is on Mairead, too."

"It seems the man desires most what he cannot have. We must be very careful, Miss."

"We will try. Good night, Higgins."

"Good night, Miss."

I do not sleep at all well this night as I have an overwhelming sense of foreboding.

Chapter 48

Dawn comes early, as it always does to any band of very repentant revelers.

Yes, it does, but not so much to me, as I do not drink spirits and therefore do not have to face the iron fist of agony that lurks 'neath the velvet glove of silken and sweet libations, about which my sea dad Liam Delaney had warned me, very much to my benefit . . . or usually so . . . No, I pop out of bed full of self-righteous smugness, wash, and am refreshed and ready to face the new day.

Higgins, of course, has risen long ago to tend to the Captain's needs, which will surely include "a hair of the dog that bit him." That means, in common parlance, a good strong drink to ward off the dreaded and merciless hangover. Higgins has long since contrived a potion consisting of pepper, lime juice, horseradish, garlic, curry, and other spices he has picked up in these exotic lands, along with tomato juice, and lastly a good, stiff dollop of rum, and that concoction manages to get a grumpy Captain Laughton back on his feet again and in reasonably good humor.

"Good day, mates," I chirp as I skip into the galley, my trepidations of the night before completely gone in the light of a fine new day.

Mick and his Bella and Keefe and Maggie are therein, having breakfast, as are Mary Wade and Molly and a few other Newgaters. I had continued in my way nudging the shy Keefe and my Mag closer together, and they seem to be getting along quite nicely.

"Good day, Jacky," greets Cookie, handing me a mug of strong sweet tea.

Gratefully, I take it and slurp loudly at the cup and then pass the heavy mug down to Ravi, who is never far from my side. He sucks it in as avidly as I did. Jezebel curls up on my lap and I stroke her thick and glossy fur. I know she certainly eats well.

The talk turns to the day's events. It is a Sunday, so I can expect to be called upon for some entertainment. That's all right, that's my game, after all—rosin up the bow and all that.

"Captain wants to do the play again, so we gots to set up the stage," says Mick, his hand running through Bella's abundant black locks.

"Ah," says I. "Well, all right. We'll do it up proper then. It's always fun." *No matter what that Higgins says. Everyone's a critic, it seems . . .*

Captain Laughton dearly loves to do the silly playlet, and I have expanded his part considerably. The play now ends with him, a hand on both Goodheart and Strongheart, pronouncing that *"God's in his Heaven, all's right with the world!"*

Cookie chuckles over all this, knowing he has only to tend his stove and his pots.

"A few fresh millers might be just the thing for lunch, Jacky," he says, and I have to agree. I believe I'll string up my bow right away.

"Ravi, go fetch my bow and quiver, for a-hunting I shall go."

"Do you kill the big mousies again today, Memsahib, once more becoming Earthly Manifestation of Kali, Goddess of Death?"

"Yes, Ravi, Earthly Manifestation of the Minor God Pain-in-the-Butt. Yes, I do go to hunt the rats in the lower decks. Come."

"I have not heard of that particular deity, Memsahib," he says, doubtfully. "But you could come back as big mousie, Missy Memsahib, as I fear your karma points in that direction. And then you would feel the sharp arrow go into your dear side, oh."

"While I admit that would be uncomfortable, I shall chance it, boy. Let us go."

So after the hunt is over and several fat millers have paid the price of rodenthood, I give Keefe the job of making new arrows, as he is skillful with his hands. I think of Jaimy when I ask Keefe to do this, for *Fletcher* is the Old English word for "Maker of Arrows." Funny that, and quite fitting, I believe.

No, I hadn't lost the arrows down below in the hunt for the millers—Ravi had scampered down and retrieved those. No, 'twas the ones I had sent flaming aloft that I was losing at an alarming rate. I had taken to entertaining the Crews in the evenings, when the wind was light, by wrapping the ends of the arrows in burning pitch and shooting them aloft. Rather like fireworks, the spectacle was enthusiastically received by all. The Captain even said that he was pleased that he had been vindicated in appointing me Mistress of Revels, and I glow under his praise.

The play has just been performed again. The villain is killed, my dress comes off, but with virtue intact, and the Captain concludes with his final oratory, to great applause. Afterward he bows to all and then plunks himself down in his usual spot.

"Oh, capital, just capital!" he chortles from his throne on the quarterdeck, a new Lizzie on one knee, a new Judy on the other. He waves a finger at Higgins, who is approaching with a tray upon which rest three glasses of ruby-red wine. "You'd best watch your wife, Mr. Higgins. She tends to lose her clothes rather easily! Har!"

It is true; I have not bothered getting back in more formal rig. What's the point? Why bother?

The play now being over, Mick and Keefe are dismantling the stage so that the dancing may begin. When I come back out of the hold bearing my fiddle, hoots and hollers and applause erupt. I'm being carried into a lifetime of bondage, but for the moment, I suck it all in. I do love it so.

"You may rest assured, Captain," says Higgins, taking the tray and presenting the drinks to the Captain and his consorts. "That aspect of her character has been noticed and will be dealt with."

"Her character! Ha! You kill me, Mr. Higgins, you really do! Har-har!" roars the Captain. "I trust you will not beat her too harshly, as she is a brisk little thing and we would not want to break her spirit. The usual advice on moderation in all things should prevail—'A man should endeavor to beat his wife once every day, whether she warrants it or not.' Just once a day, now, Mr. Higgins, no more. And that should do the trick! Moderation in all things, Mr. Higgins. Moderation! Har-har!" He downs his wine and passes the glass back to Higgins. "Music now!" he roars. Captain Laughton is not a man to restrain his enthusiasms. "More music, more wine, more dancing, more merriment, oh, Lord, more—"

And that, appropriately, is his last word upon this Earth.

He gasps and slumps over.

Higgins, alarmed, rushes to his side and puts his palm to the Captain's chest.

"Quick! Get the Surgeon!" he shouts, and men run off.

When the Surgeon comes up from whatever hole he habitually hides in, he grabs the Captain's limp wrist, feels for his pulse, then shakes his head. There are wails heard from every corner of the *Lorelei Lee,* from Lizzies and Judies to Tartans, too . . . *Oh, no, not our dear Gussie!*

But it is true. Captain Augustus Laughton is dead.

It is hot, so funeral arrangements must be quick. The Captain's body is prepared and sewn up in canvas, then placed on a board. As the sorrowful bundle is quite round in the middle, it is impossible to mistake just whose corporeal remains are contained therein.

I assemble the Chorus and we gather about his bier to sing the Sanctus from Bach's B Minor Mass. I somehow think that Gussie would not at all mind being sung off to eternity by a heavenly chorus of thieves and whores. We then fall silent.

There is not a dry eye on the ship, save two, those of Mr. Ruger—now Captain Ruger—and he surveys all from his quarterdeck, but he does not come down to join us in saying farewell to our jolly Captain Laughton.

As I am the Mistress of Revels, it seems that I am also the Sayer of Words in sad times like these. I open the Book of Common Prayer . . .

> *Earth to earth, ashes to ashes*
> *Dust to dust,*
> *In sure and certain hope of the*
> *Resurrection into eternal life.*

Then Enoch Lightner goes to the side of our fallen Captain and puts his hand on his friend's now quiet chest. Tears are seen seeping from beneath the bandage that covers his eyes.

> *Go, Augustus, go off into the night, laughing.*
> *Give no thought to those of us left here in sorrow,*
> *Those who knew you and loved you.*
> *Go to God, friend!*

Then I step to the rail to say the old words, so often spoken at times like these.

> *We commend his body to the sea,*
> *And his soul to God.*

When I finish, I nod. The board is lifted and the body of our beloved Captain Augustus Laughton slides off into the sea. He died as he had lived, with a dolly on each knee, but, oh, how we hate to see him go.

Goodbye, Gussie . . . You were good to me and I shall never forget it. Requiescat in pacem, *Augustus Laughton . . .*

Chapter 49

Jaimy Fletcher
Onboard the Ship Cerberus
Armed, and Very Dangerous

Dear Jacky,

Yes, dear girl, thanks to you, we are armed, and not just me—all of us now have weapons.

Yesterday, when we were led on our way to the head, I spied a length of rope left carelessly lying in the passageway. I grunted at Ian and darted my eyes toward the coil of line. He understood instantly and contrived to fall against the others in the line and we all fell in a confused pile to the deck. *"We're sorry, Corporal Vance, yer honor, we're just so weak from cruel treatment that we cannot stand proper!"* from Padraic, and *"Get up, you worthless Irish scum! Get up or I'll beat you to your feet!"* from Corporal Vance. The rest of the Irish lads wail away in Gaelic, further confusing the scene.

The Weasel yells at us—*"Get up, you sorry lot!"*—and Corporal Vance and Sergeant Napper wade in with club and whip, and eventually we do stagger to our feet and get back into line. But not before I manage to get the rope wrapped around my waist and concealed by my shirt.

In spite of the near riot, we are taken up on deck for exercise. As we shuffle along, I look out on the horizon and see nothing.

The Dart *is gone!*

"Yes," says Second Mate Hollister, seeing me look around for the escort. "She is detached for three days—back to Singapore on some diplomatic nonsense. We have shortened sail so as to poke along until such time as she catches back up with us. Believe me, I do not like it."

So, it must be done now, while the ship is defenseless!

Later, we measure out the rope and find that we can apportion a bit more than two feet to every unarmed man— that being five of them, me having the shiv and Sean Duggan having the club. Each man wears his cord wrapped around his waist, waiting for the proper time—three and a half feet long with a good thick knot at each end. True, the garrote is a nasty weapon, but it is effective, and it is silent. A man may cry out if a dagger is thrust in his side, but no one cries out when in the hideous choking embrace of El Garrote.

"You know what to do," I whisper in the night. "One loop around the neck and then tighten with all your might. Clamp your knees about them as they stuggle but do not let them go till they go limp. Remember, very few of this crew has ever shown us a bit of kindness of any sort—it has all been kicks and curses and being treated like animals. Keep that in mind. Do not let the better angels of your natures rule. We must harden our hearts, else we be lost."

"My heart is hard as any stone, Fletcher, believe it," mutters McBride.

"So say you one, so say you all?"

There are grunts of agreement in the gloom.

"Very well, the die is cast. The escort ship is gone but will be back soon, so we must go tomorrow night after the watch changes at midnight. The men will be groggy from their beds and not paying much attention to things. We will either succeed or we will be hanged. So be it. Better an honorable death at the end of a rope than a lifetime of misery and shame."

The lads fall silent, but McBride is not yet done with me.

"That other convict ship, now, the one that had Ian's Mairead and *our* Jacky on it . . . Did you hear her Captain call *our* Jacky Mrs. Higgins? Did you hear that, now, Fletcher?"

Yes, I did . . . through all my pain, I did hear that . . .

"Come on, Arthur," says Ian. "We don't need this."

I calm myself and reply to the bastard. "I know John Higgins to be an honorable man. If she has married him, then so be it. Somehow I am not worried. I care more for her safety than for any other . . . insinuations . . . you might have, McBride. So how about keeping your thoughts to yourself?"

I hear him chuckle in the darkness. "Could it be that your little sparrow is sleeping in another's nest?"

"Believe me, McBride," I hiss. "When this is all over, we shall settle up our accounts."

"Fine with me, Brit. When the time comes, bring it on."

Oh, I will, mick. I will . . .

Our plan is laid and we are ready to go.
Wish us luck,

Jaimy

Chapter 50

Things are not good on the *Lorelei Lee*.

Ruger wastes no time in moving into my old cabin and assuming his place at the head of the table. In the beginning of the new regime, we have some music, but our hearts are not in it. When Captain Laughton left us, he took much of our joy with him, for he was the true Master of Revels, not me.

Ruger uses his new position as Captain to drink even more than he had previously, now being unconfined by any authority, and he is not a jolly drunk.

He hurls insults freely at those at dinner, gets sloppy with food, and spills drinks, and then blames Higgins for it. When Mairead and I sing and play, he cuts us off in mid song—*"Goddamn noise! Be quiet! Stupid drivel!"* Fewer and fewer people are invited to dinner and none really care to join. One night the Shantyman is missing—whether by his choice or Ruger's I don't know. Mairead and I exchange glances. We do not like this. What we like even less is that Enoch never again appears in the cabin.

Aside from a constantly changing girl from the Crews, who sits cringing by his side, the only two who are always there are Mairead and I, and we are there on his demand. After Higgins serves dinner, he is most often sent away so that Ruger can engage us more closely in conversation.

This night, Mr. Gibson is here, and not looking very happy. At Ruger's side is Mary Ann Anstey, a Judy. She doesn't look very happy, either.

I play quietly on my guitar and avoid Ruger's gaze.

It does me no good. After Higgins is sent away, Ruger calls me to him. I lay aside my guitar to go stand beside him. He points to the bed.

"You will stay here this night."

"I will not. I am a woman joined in marriage to my good husband, John Higgins, and I will neither disgrace him nor my vows by lying with you."

"We all know that marriage to be a sham."

"Do you, now? And how do you know that? Do you lie abed with us? Or do you listen outside our door, giggling in some vile perversion of true manhood? Do you?"

"Beware of mocking me, girl," he hisses, rising unsteadily to his feet. "It is a sham, I say."

"It is not a sham to me, Sir, and I mean to keep to my vows. If you force me, it will be rape, and the crime will be on your head. And believe me, the Company will hear of it."

"The Company? What do you think the Company cares about a condemned convict? It cares ten pounds six is what it cares!"

"Best kill me after you have had your way with me, then, for I *will* have justice."

His face contorts into a mask of drunken rage. He sweeps his hand across the table, scattering dishes and wineglasses to the floor.

"Get out of my sight," he snarls. Then he brings his hand up and catches me with the back of it. I cry out and fall back.

At my cry, the door swings open and Higgins is there, looking murderously at Ruger.

"Please, Sir! Forbear!"

Ruger is fairly foaming with rage.

"Get out! All of you leeches!" he roars. "Get out of my sight! Drink up someone else's wine! Get out!"

As the sorry company flees, I look back in the cabin and see that he has thrown Mary Ann onto the bed. Though you'd think women in her profession would be used to such things, the poor girl looks scared and beseeches me with terrified eyes. I am profoundly sorry that I cannot help her. *But just you wait, you . . .*

When I see Mary Ann the next day, her cheek is bruised and her left eye is swollen shut.

Mrs. Berry is mad, and even though she is not as outspoken as Mrs. Barnsley, nor as fierce as Mrs. MacDonald, the Madam of the Judies speaks up for her Mary Ann. She huffs up in indignation and faces Ruger from the main deck as he stands on his quarterdeck.

"Sir, please be more gentle in the handling of our girls, as they do not do well in suffering under such treatment as Mary Ann has received from your very hands."

He looks down on her with great disdain.

"Shut yer mouth, whoremonger. Do not ever forget that you are *all* nothing but convicts and subject to whatever punishment I deem necessary for the good order of this ship!" He jumps down to the deck, thrusts out the heel of his hand, and pushes her down.

"Oh! Please, Sir, I am but an old woman!" she cries, on her back with her skirts all ahoo.

"This is *my* ship now, and you will observe that proper discipline is being restored to this ship. No more foolishness. Holiday routine on Saturdays and Sundays is hereby canceled till every soul on this ship shows me proper respect! *Every* soul."

Here he casts his eye upon me, who sits in the foretop with Mairead.

"*Every* soul," he repeats. "And every body, too."

Things do not look good for us, be we Newgater, Judy, Lizzie, or Tartan.

Chapter 51

James Fletcher
Convict
Onboard Cerberus

Jacky,

There seems to be a bit of a celebration topside—apparently it is Captain Griswold's birthday, so an extra pint of rum has been issued to all hands. None was given to us convicts to drink to the Captain's health, oh no, but we wouldn't want to do that, anyway, as his good health is the last thing we would wish for that evil bastard. But I see this working in our favor, as the crew will be more groggy than usual and will sleep soundly. Tonight we go.

The bell rings eight chimes in the dark of night. We stir as we hear the sounds of the changing watch. The time grows near . . .

The Weasel comes by for his nightly round, and we know that Sergeant Napper and Corporal Vance will not be far behind. *It's time . . .*

"'Avin' a good evenin', scum?" the Weasel asks, rattling his club on the bars. "Sleepin' well, *Mr.* Fletcher?" He seems to be feeling rather good from his extra ration of rum.

I keep my eye on the pair of brass keys that hangs at his waist. He is not trusted with much, but he does have those—one key to open the gate, and the other to release our long, common ankle chain from its mooring, such that he can lead us shuffling on our morning visit to the head, and thence to the mess deck to be issued our slops. It's Napper and Vance who hold the keys to our shackles ... and to the cutlass rack. We must have all of those keys, else we are lost.

As planned, Padraic starts it up.

"I read a book once, Weasel," he says. "And you was in it."

"Wot? Wot book?"

"It was a book about the HMS *Wolverine* when our Jacky Faber and your own worthless self was on it. It was called *Under the Jolly Roger.*"

"So?"

"It was a good book. You should read it ... iffen you can read, which I doubt."

"So what? 'Oo cares?"

"Oh, we don't, Weasel, believe me," says Ian, picking it up. "We don't care if you lives or dies—in fact, we hope you does die—but others might care ..."

"Why?"

"'Cause there's a bit in there about how you liked smellin' girls' underpants, Weasel." Ian pauses. "How once when Jacky give you her clothes for cleaning, expectin' you to perform your duties like a proper steward, you took her knickers and charged blokes a penny to handle 'em . . . sniff 'em and stuff."

"That never happened! Lies! All lies!" cries the Weasel, pounding on the bars. The glow he felt from his extra pint seems to have worn off.

Open the door, Weasel . . .

"Oh? Sorry . . . you didn't know? Yes, you've gone right famous—the whole fleet knows about that. Do you really like that sort of thing, now, Weasel?" continues Padraic, relentlessly. "I, myself, have never been interested in that sort of thing, so's I wouldn't know. Sounds rather disgusting to me, actually, but there's no accounting for taste, is there?"

"You stop now, or you'll get it!"

Open the door, Weasel . . .

"What's it like? I heard our lass once dumped a full chamber pot over your head, too. How did you like the smell o' that? Pretty rich stuff, I suspect . . . eh?"

Open the door, Weasel . . .

"Stop it! Stop it!"

Open the door, Weasel . . .

But Padraic Delaney does not stop. He is his father's son, after all . . .

"I hear they call you 'Knickers Weisling, the Pride of the Perverted Patrol.' There's even a song about it. It's quite the rage in London. Want to hear it?"

"No! Stop! I'll get you!"

Open the door, Weasel . . .

Padraic Delaney lifts his voice and sings.

> *Oh, my name is Wei-se-ling,*
> *And on the* Wolverine *I did sing,*

I danced a gay gavotte for all that lot,
With a hat of the finest tin!
Oh, with a hat of the finest tin!

Low laughter from all the lads. Padraic continues . . .

Oh, with a chamber pot over my head,
Yes, a chamber pot over my head!
With that fine chapeau I did gaily go,
With a chamber pot over my head!
With a chamber pot over my head!

There is a curse and a rattle of keys, and . . .
The Weasel opens the door!
The cage door swings inward and the Weasel charges into the cell, fairly slavering with rage. Thinking us helpless, he lifts his club over Padraic.

"Sing about this, Paddy!" he hisses, and the club comes down.

But it is not Weisling's club that comes down. No, it is another, and it does not fall upon an Irish head. Nay, it is the belaying pin held in the fist of the mighty Duggan that comes down, and it slams hard down on Weasel's own worthless head. He drops like a stone.

"One down, lads," I whisper. "Two to go. Connolly, get ready . . ."

"Aye, Sir," says the boy. "I'm ready."

The Weasel is relieved of his keys and his limp body is shoved under a bench. We unlock the two ends of our common ankle chain and relock the front door and then sit and wait.

Presently Sergeant Napper and Corporal Vance approach.

"Where's Weisling?" asks Napper, looking about. He holds a lantern, which casts a dim light on all of us.

"Last we saw o' that sod, 'e was headin' for the crapper, clutching 'is miserable gut," says Arthur McBride. "Hope 'e dies o' the flux, I do."

"Shut yer gob, mick, or I'll come in there and shut you up for good, by—"

"Please, Sirs," pipes up young Connolly, in a whispery voice. "Some of the men in here have been right mean to me. Makin' me do stuff I don't like . . . awful stuff."

Connolly stops to give out a few boyish whimpers. In the gloom I can make out Napper and Vance looking sharp at one another. Young Daniel Connolly goes on . . .

"But you two gentlemen seem to be right kind . . . in that you bin offerin' me good food and suchlike . . . and I'm thinkin' maybe you kin be givin' me some . . . protection . . . like . . ."

I can hear Napper and Vance chuckling obscenely as they fumble for their keys in their haste to get at the boy. The key is inserted, the door opens, and the two red-coated would-be buggers stride right in.

"Come with us, boy, and we'll treat you right, oh, yes we will," whispers Vance. "Here, let's get that shackle offa you. There, how's that feel?"

"Oh, just fine, Sir . . ."

Corporal Vance looms above the boy . . . right next to Arthur McBride's seated figure. Sergeant Napper stands before me.

"That's good, boy, now . . . wait . . . What's this? Hey, Sergeant . . . this here chain is slack. What's goin' on here?"

That's the last question Corporal Vance asks of anyone upon this Earth, as McBride looms out of the gloom and loops his garrote about Vance's neck and pulls it tight. Very tight . . . As he does that, I steel myself and leap up and put my hand under Sergeant Napper's chin and jerk back his head. He tries to cry out, Jacky, but I draw your very sharp and deadly shiv across his neck . . . hard across his neck, hard across his throttle until I feel its edge grate against his neck bone.

The last sound Sergeant Napper makes on this Earth is a rather liquid gurgle.

I hold him till his struggles cease, and then I let him slip to the floor. Vance takes longer in dying. I hear McBride whispering in his ear as he slumps to the deck and gives up the ghost. "*'Tis me, Arthur McBride, who's killin' you. I want you to know on your way to hell that it was me who sent you there, you worthless piece of British crap!*"

"Quick now! Strip off their jackets!" I whisper, as I cut the ring of keys from Napper's belt and try one in my ankle shackle.

No, not that one, nor that one . . . There!

The shackle opens and falls off. I give the key to Padraic. "Free yourself and pass the key on. Lynch, hold on to the keys. You'll go to the cutlass rack and open it when the time comes."

I hear the muted rattle of the hated chains falling off.

Every man has been assigned a role in this venture and, as planned, McBride and McConnaughey struggle into Vance's and Napper's red coats. It will help us gain the quarterdeck. I put on my blue naval jacket, which I had kept rolled up to use as a pillow.

"All ready? All right, let's go."

Your knife clutched tightly in my hand, Jacky, I head up the passageway to the hatchway, followed by Niall Sweeney, Seamus Lynch, and then McBride, Ian, and the rest of the lads. I put my ear to the door and, hearing nothing out of the way, push it open and peer out. It is dark as pitch.

"Good," I whisper. "No moon. Black as pitch. Gentle breeze—means no topmen aloft. Sweeney, go!"

Niall Sweeney brushes past me, on his assigned task— to take out any bow lookout that might be posted. He goes forward, armed with both his garrote and the Weasel's club. Cruel work, but it must be done.

I look toward the quarterdeck. As my eyes accustom themselves to the dark, I believe I see only three heads silhouetted against the meager starlight. Probably the Officer of the Watch, the Helmsman, and the Bo'sun. I hope there is no messenger—I would hate to have to kill a boy.

"Lynch, go . . . Careful, now . . . Quiet . . ."

Lynch slips out, his bare feet quiet on the deck and Napper's keys clutched in his hand. Head down, he makes for the foot of the mainmast, where the cutlasses are clustered and chained.

"Now . . . Ian . . . Arthur . . . your turn."

McConnaughey and McBride stride out onto the deck, making no attempt to hide themselves as they make their way to the quarterdeck. As soon as they are out and, I am sure, spotted from the quarterdeck, I and the rest of the lads slip out and creep along the side of the main hatch, concealed from view . . . we hope. We each take a belaying pin from the rack on the rail and lean back against the hatch, waiting for our newly red-coated Irish boys to do their bit.

In spite of our very precarious state, Jacky, as I sit here in the dark, our various fates in the balance, I almost have to chuckle over how much this is so very like one of your own escape techniques. Ian and McBride are the Diversion, and me and my crew are the Boarding Party—the Dianas on this version of the *Bloodhound,* as it were. Hmmm. Well, let's see if I can execute this plan as well as you did yours. Yes, now I admit that I did finally read those damned books, and though I seethed over many parts but attributed many things to Amy Trevelyne's overheated imagination, I took lessons from them as well.

My, my, there's the Southern Cross up there . . . We must be below the equator. What, no ceremony for us poor convicts, Captain Griswold? Well, perhaps, if Neptune is willing, we shall have one after all.

Get your mind on the job, Fletcher—time for idle thoughts later.

Ian and Arthur approach the quarterdeck and are noticed.

"So, how are our animals down below, Sergeant?" asks the Officer of the Watch, who, I am relieved to see, is First Mate Block and not Hollister. "Do they rest easy?"

I am glad to see you there, Block—for if it comes down to it, I will kill you, for you have shown no kindness to any captives aboard this benighted ship.

"Aye, Sir, they do, they do . . ."

"Do I perceive that you might be a mite drunk, Sergeant Napper?" asks Block, a cold edge seeping into his voice.

"Oh, yes, Sir," admits McBride, climbing the quarterdeck stairs a bit unsteadily. "A wee bit, perhaps . . . in celebration of the . . . *hic!* . . . Captain's birthday, don'cha know." Ian is right behind him, equally unsteady on his pins.

While all eyes are riveted on Block, McConnaughey, and McBride on the port side, the Boarding Party and I creep silently over the quarterdeck rail on the starboard side. *Clubs, boys, if you can. No sense killing innocent seamen like ourselves, if we can help it. Let's go . . .*

"I think I must put you on report, Sergeant Napper," says Mr. Block. "Wait . . . you are not . . . Bo'sun! Sound the alarm and take these men!"

But the Bo'sun takes nothing except a hard blow to his head from Duggan's club, as we swarm over the quarterdeck. Block, shocked, goes for the speaking tube to alert the Captain, but I get there first and bring your shiv up under his ribs as hard as I can and twist it. He gasps and tries to shout, but I have my other hand over his mouth and he cannot. His hot blood pours over my hand, but I harden my heart and let it flow. After a moment he slumps to the deck.

The helmsman has long since been knocked unconscious by Duggan's club.

"Parnell!" I hiss. "Take the helm. Steer the same course till we see what's up!"

Young Connolly has already done his task in shoving his fist in the speaking tube and leaving it there so that the Captain cannot hear what is happening right above his head.

"Fletcher!" hisses Lynch from down below. "We've got the cutlasses! Here!"

The blades are passed up and all take one. I test the edge of mine and decide it's sharp enough.

"Quiet, all! There's still work to do! We must confine the crew!"

I leap off the quarterdeck to examine the doors leading down to the officers' mess and the crew's quarters and . . . yes! They both open outward!

"Duggan, to me!" I whisper more loudly than I wish. "Bring your club! And another belaying pin."

Mystified, he does it, and I grasp the pin and place it butt down on a bollard and lay my cutlass, blade aimed down, upon it.

"Hit it!" I order, and Duggan brings down his club, neatly splitting the belaying pin, top to bottom. As I knew it would, the pieces are wider at one end than the other.

Yes, my devious little girl, exactly like the wedges you used to great advantage at various times in the protection of your own tender self. You see, I did read, and I did learn . . .

I place one each at the bottom of the crew's hatchway doors and say, "Duggan! Pound them in!"

He does it and all is secure. They cannot get out.

We have the ship.

I stand on the quarterdeck and look off into the starry night. Looking again at the Southern Cross hanging low on the horizon, I button up my jacket and think on thee.

I put one foot to either side of the centerline so as to feel the action of the ship as you so often said you have done when in command of your own vessel, be she schooner, brig, or riverboat. This ship is not the sleek *Nancy B.*, no, but for now she'll have to do.

Ian McConnaughey comes up and stands next to me, looking off to the southern horizon, where he knows his lost Mairead lies somewhere over the sea.

"We have done it, Jaimy," he says.

"Aye, Ian, we have. Now comes the hard part . . ."

Off in pursuit of you, I remain,
Yrs,

Jaimy

Chapter 52

Thing have gotten worse.

Ruger has gone completely out of control. Maybe it's the drink or maybe it's something more sinister. I don't know, but something has ravaged his mind and havoc rules on the once happy *Lorelei Lee*.

Everyone stays out of his way. I haven't seen Army Major Johnston nor his wife, Esther, for days. The Shantyman appears on deck, but aside from some low conversation with Mairead, he sings no more. My Newgaters lie low, as does any member of the Crews who manages to avoid his grasp. Several girls have come back badly beaten and bruised from overnight stays in his cabin. He has taken to wearing two pistols in his belt, and well he might, for his own officers and seamen are not happy, either.

He remains relentless in his pursuit of me . . . and of Mairead, too . . . and I wonder at it. What kind of man would lust after a girl who is with child and already showing? Does he really have worms in his brain?

. . .

Sadly, all things seem to come to a head today. I have been idling in the foretop with Mary Wade and Molly, getting some sun and fresh air, all three of us in our light Powder Monkey gear. Ravi is there, too, with Josephine. He is scratching the little ape's belly, something she likes a lot. She leans back against the mast and grins her toothy monkey smile.

I see Mairead down below, standing at the rail, with her hand on Enoch Lightner's arm. 'Tis plain she has convinced him to come up for some air, which is good, for the death of his great good friend Captain Laughton and the turn of events on my poor ship have weighed heavily on him. Mairead has tried, over the past week, to lend him some comfort and cheer.

"Impossibly red-haired Missy to have little baby?" asks Ravi, looking down upon her. "Oh, what great joy!"

"Yes, Ravi, that seems to be the case," says I, indolent and drowsy in the warmth of the sun.

"Will baby have impossibly red hair, too?"

"Probably," I answer, thinking of the baby's father, Ian McConnaughey. He, too, has reddish hair, so—

There is a shout from below and we all, including Josephine, look down over the edge of the foretop decking. This is not a wise move, as things turn out.

The shout is from Ruger. He has come staggering out of his cabin, clutching a bottle, already drunk at ten in the morning.

He looks up and spots me right off. He may be drunk, but he is not blind.

"Get down here, you!" he shouts, pointing at me.

Uh-oh . . .

"Please, Sir, I'd rather not. Perhaps later, when you are more yourself . . ."

"Fine, I will . . . *urp* . . . kill your monkey first . . . and then your dirty little nigra boy—that will afford me some sport in your absence."

He draws a pistol from his belt, aims it at Josephine, and fires.

Crack!

"No!" I shout, pushing Josephine down, such that the bullet whizzes harmlessly over her head. She shrieks and heads for the high rigging. She may be an ape, but she knows things ain't right. "All right! I'm coming down!"

The shot brings all the officers up on deck, as well as most members of the crew. Army Major Johnston is there, with Esther behind him. Mr. Gibson, too, and Seabrook, and even the Surgeon, all trying to talk some sense into Captain Ruger. The three madams are topside, too—Mrs. Barnsley, Mrs. Berry, and Mrs. MacDonald—as well as many of their girls. Higgins appears and stands before Ruger. All look grim.

"I shall take your wife, *Mr.* Higgins, and I shall take her now."

"No, you shall not do that, Sir," retorts Higgins, and he does the unpardonable—he reaches out and pushes Ruger back hard against the rail. "Control yourself, Sir!"

"What? You place your hand on me, fancy man? On me, your Captain? That is a capital offense, as you well know." He lurches toward Higgins. "I sentence you to death!"

With that, he pulls out his remaining pistol and aims it at Higgins's chest.

415

"No!" I scream and leap over the side of the foretop, grab the buntline, and swing down to the deck and stand between them. "Here I am! Put that away! I shall go with you. Do with me what you will, but do not harm my husband!"

A sly smile creeps over Ruger's face.

"Good," he says. "That's what I like to hear. Get into my cabin. We shall have some . . . sport."

I turn to Higgins. "He is drunk, Higgins," I say. "I've handled drunks before. I will not have you killed for my sake. Let me handle this, please, John!"

I start in the direction of the cabin, but Ruger is not yet done out here.

Straightening up, about to follow me, he then notices Mairead standing next to the tall Shantyman, Enoch's arm about her shoulders. He points at her.

"That one, too. The one with the red hair. The three of us shall have a very gay time of it."

What? No!

The Shantyman's face shows that he knows quite well what is going on. "What? You would hurt her?" He pulls Mairead to him. "Stand behind me, girl!"

She does and he lifts his staff and swings it before him, saying, "Back off! Any who would approach us! Back off!"

"How wonderfully noble," snarls Ruger, hiccupping. He takes another swig out of the bottle. "But how stupidly pathetic as well. Bo'sun, take that poor excuse for a man and throw him down below decks. I am sick of him and his dreary songs."

But both the Bo'sun and Ruger underestimate the Shantyman. He may not be able to see like other men, but they find he is not without resources.

Smirking, Bo'sun Roberts strides up before the blind man and reaches out to grasp Mairead. His feet, however, scrape upon the deck. Hearing that, the Shantyman loops his staff around and places the club end of it on the deck before him and then slides it over till it touches the Bo'sun's foot. Knowing where Roberts's foot is, he can now sense where his head is, and with a mighty swing, he brings the club end of the staff hard against the Bo'sun's skull. Roberts does not cry out, for he cannot, being rendered speechless by the blow. No, he merely shrinks and crumples to the deck, and he does not rise.

"Against me . . . You're all against me . . . Always have been," hisses Ruger. He staggers against the quarterdeck rail. "Fancy airs . . . fancy music . . . fancy bitches . . . bunch o' crap, all of it."

He lurches upright.

"Take that blind bastard down, or by God I'll hang the lot of you! Do it! Now!"

It is Suggs and Monk who come forward, and each grabs one of the Shantyman's arms and drags him down to the deck. Suggs has a belaying pin in his fist and he swings it and brings it down on the back of Enoch's head. He does it again and again. "No, let him alone! Stop!" cries Mairead, lifting her hands to ward off the rain of blows, but to no avail. Suggs and Monk are on him, and they beat him till the Shantyman struggles no more. Then Suggs and Monk drag him down into the hold.

Ruger staggers across the deck and grabs Mairead by the neck.

"Now, my dear, let us go below."

I run across the deck and grab his arm and try to pull him off her, but he shoves me aside.

"Please, Sir! Let her be!" I plead. "Come, I will . . ."

He is relentless as he drags her toward his cabin door.

"But my baby!" wails Mairead.

"Your baby? Here's what I think of your baby!"

He swings his fist around and punches her square in the gut. She gasps and sinks to her knees.

There is a common gasp of horror from all onlookers.

"There. That should take care of that!"

"My baby! Oh, Lord, you have killed my baby!"

Mrs. Barnsley is aghast. "All my girls, get below! If he'd do that, he'd do anything! The man is mad! Get below, now!"

Mrs. Berry and Mrs. MacDonald shout to their women as well, and girls begin rushing out of the rigging, the upper deck, the staterooms, everywhere on the ship, and pour down the hatchway.

I rush to Mairead and lift her up. Blood is already running down the inside of her leg. Her face is a contorted mask of grief.

Oh, Lord, no!

Higgins is there and he sweeps her up in his arms and carries her to the passageway.

"Take her to our laundry!" I cry as I follow. I'm the last one down. "Lock the door!"

Ruger continues to stagger and roar outside.

"Goddamn 'em all to hell! Lock the filthy whores down! Lock 'em all down!"

Mairead, crying, is laid on her bed. It is immediately a bloody mess.

I find Mrs. Barnsley by my side. She has the other madams with her. All look grim.

"Let us handle this," she says. "We've seen all this before, and I'll wager you have not."

I stand back as they begin to undress the crying girl.

"There, there, dearie," croons Mrs. MacDonald. "There, there, you'll be all right."

"But my baby . . ." Mairead moans. "What about my baby?"

Mrs. MacDonald says nothing to that . . .

. . . but I do.

"That dirty son of a bitch is gonna pay!" I snarl, and rush to where my bow hangs on the wall. I nock an arrow and jump up on a bunk and look out forward. Good. He's still there.

Ruger leans up against the mast, his rage still not spent.

"Die, you miserable bastard!" I shout, and let the arrow fly straight toward his chest. "Die!"

Chapter 53

Jaimy Fletcher
Commander, at least for now
Of the ship Cerberus

Dear Jacky,

The sun is coming up now, as we complete our takeover of
the convict ship Cerberus.

After we had established ourselves on the quarterdeck
and made sure that the officers and crew were confined, we
set about securing our position. Rumblings and rattlings
started from those trapped below, but we paid them little
mind—they were well and securely confined.

I cracked on as much sail as we could to make all speed,
knowing as I did that the *Dart* was not far behind and could
cause us only grief should she arrive. With the added canvas,
the *Cerberus* did what she could.

Then there was the little matter of Captain Griswold—
ex-Captain Griswold, that is . . .

Stationing Parnell and Duggan to either side of the Captain's door, both armed with gleaming cutlasses, I go to the speaking tube and shout down it.

"Captain! Come quick! Warship on the horizon!"

Seconds later, Griswold comes charging out of his cabin, dressed only in his nightshirt, eyes blinking at the sudden light.

"What? Where . . . ?"

"Right here, Captain," I say, looking down upon him from the quarterdeck. He sees me, and then he feels the two cutlasses held tight against his neck.

"Take him down and tie him to a chair. We will need some information from him."

"What!" he sputters. "Why, you'll hang for this, who-ever the hell you are!"

"Please, Captain, I know you are in a state of shock at these proceedings, but a little more originality, if you please. As for who I am, I am Lieutenant James Emerson Fletcher, late of His Majesty's Royal Navy. You might recall you recently had me bound to the grating and given sixteen of the best." I pause to let that sink in. His face turns a satisfying shade of pale.

"Your servant, Sir," I continue, giving him a mock bow. "And as to which of us shall hang first, well, we shall see . . ."

I look up to the main yardarm, from which nooses would certainly dangle, and from which he would most surely be hanged. He gets the point, for just then the bodies of Sergeant Napper and Corporal Vance are brought up from our cell and tossed over the side, as is the corpse of Lieutenant Block.

Yes, Jacky, two more notches on your shiv, two more marks upon my soul . . .

The Captain sees, and his face goes even whiter, as he now knows we are serious about our business. My two stout Irish lads kick him back into what used to be his cabin.

Get in there, you!

Then I see that something else is brought up from our old cell, as well.

"Look what we have here!" shouts Seamus Lynch, triumphant, holding a groggy but plainly terrified little man by the neck. "'Tis the very Weasel himself, by the merciful God who takes good care o' his faithful servants, he does! Oh, it is to hell for you, Weasel, and very soon, too!"

Upon hearing this, the Weasel promply wets his trousers.

"What shall we do, Sir?" asks the delighted Lynch. "Throw him overboard, or string him up?"

The Weasel, his eyes rolling wildly, falls to his knees and pleads, "Oh, please, Sirs, no . . ."

I consider this, and look over the side of the ship and say, "Yes, both those suggestions would be most entertaining, and he certainly has it coming to him . . . And I see we have some rather large sharks following in our wake . . . That could be fun, watching those brutes tear him apart, limb by limb. But no, not just now. Let him live for a while yet. He might prove useful."

"Useful?" asks Lynch, dubiously, ready to lift his club and to cheerfully spill the Weasel's brains out over the deck. "How?"

"Well, for one, he will know where the armory is, such that we can arm ourselves properly with pistols and muskets.

Those below are getting restive, you might note. There are more and more sounds from below, and a whiff of grape-shot in their faces just might calm them down."

Heads nod, and the wisdom of this is generally acknowledged.

"Now, the Weasel, being what he is—a dirty little rodent—will know where *everything* is on this ship." The Weasel, still on his knees, his eyes wide and pleading, nods vigorously to this. "Would you not want a spot of wine or rum this evening to celebrate our victory? How long has it been, Lynch? Some good food for a change? Hmmm?"

There is general assent to that notion. *Wine? Rum? Good food?*

There is now a heavy pounding from the inside of the hatchway doors. The crew grows restive.

"Weasel, if you value your life, lead on to the armory."

He does it, taking a key from the ones that Napper wore on his belt. Soon we are all armed with primed pistols and muskets. The guns feel splendid tucked into my waist as I advance to the door behind which sits a very unhappy crew of seamen.

"Let us out! Let us out now, else we shall take all of you and throw you into the sea!" comes the cry from the other side of the door.

Idle threats, lads, will do you no good . . .

I draw one of my pistols and put a shot through the door, at just about waist high level. I hear a sharp cry of pain from within.

"Who speaks for you?" I demand. There is a pause, then . . .

"I do. Second Mate Hollister."

"Ah, Hollister. This is Fletcher, now in command of this vessel. I know you to be an honorable man, unlike most on-board. Rest assured you will not be harmed if you follow instructions. My intent is to put you and your crew off in one of the lifeboats. We are not far from land, and you should be able to make landfall within hours of being cast away. Where you will land, I do not know just yet, but I will be consulting the charts in Griswold's cabin."

"What of the Captain?"

"He is not yet dead, Mr. Hollister, but Block, Napper, and Vance are," I say. "Now, everyone settle down and perhaps all remaining will survive this day. But know this. My crew and I are desperate men. We are preparing a lifeboat, and we will put you in it so you may sail away. If you do something stupid, like setting fire down below, then we will be off in that same boat and all of you will perish most horribly. Understood? Good. Quiet, now."

During my confinement I have had a lot of time to think of various eventualities . . .

"All right," I say, going back to the quarterdeck. "Sweeney, take the watch. Steer the same course till I figure out just where we are. I'll be below. Delaney, McBride, McConnaughey, come with me."

We go down into the Captain's cabin and find that Duggan and Parnell have, indeed, tied him very securely to a chair, using their garrotes. Handy things, those. They also have stuffed a rag in his mouth to shut him up.

He looks at me as I enter, his eyes wild. I ignore him for the present.

We will get to you later, Captain Griswold, count on it.

I go to the chart spread out on the table. There are lines of position laid out upon it, and from them I deduce that we are about fifty miles off to the east of a place called Sumatra, and somewhat north of the port of Batavia.

I have heard of Batavia, and, even though it is held by the Dutch, it just might suit our interests.

After all, I say to myself with a bit of regret, *we are no longer British.*

I occupy myself with going through the Captain's papers, and I discover something that strikes my interest. All the prisoners onboard this ship are to be delivered to the penal colony at New South Wales, commanded by Captain William Bligh.

Imagine that, old Breadfruit Bligh himself. This gets better and better . . .

"Take out his gag," I order, and Ian pulls the cloth from Griswold's mouth. He sputters for a bit, but with a swat from the back of McBride's hand he becomes right docile.

Holding a paper before me, I ask of him, "Tell me, Griswold, have you ever met this Captain William Bligh personally? Ever raised a glass with him?"

"No. Never."

"Hmmm . . . And the payment for the delivery of the convicts . . . How is that accomplished?"

"Go to hell, you blaggard!"

I look off out the open door.

"Is the noose ready at the yardarm, Ian? The proper knot?"

Ian nods. "Yes. Duggan is quite expert at knots of that sort."

"Good. We'll want that done right. Royal Navy, drum rolls and all . . ."

Griswold turns yet another shade of pale and says, "The Commander of the Company ship is paid by a draft upon the Bank of England with delivery of each live convict."

"Well, well," I say. "I'd rather have cash, but we can work with that. Now, where is your money?"

"What?"

"Yes, Captain, your money. You must have some. We will need to purchase some gunnery. You'll admit this ship is woefully underprotected."

"I have no money."

"Of course, you don't. You are but a simple merchant captain, doing your job. I accept that."

I neaten up the papers, lay them aside, and say, "We have no more need of him. Take him out and tie him to the grating. Strip off his shirt. He gave me sixteen, McBride ten. So give him twenty-six . . . and since yesterday was his birthday . . . give him one to grow on."

"How—how can you do that?"

"Simple, Griswold. Tit for tat, simple as that."

"You would torture a man to gain information?"

"Oh, no, Captain. I am a Lieutenant in the Royal Navy . . . or at least I was. I am a man of honor. I would never torture a prisoner," I say. "But I will mete out deserved punishment. Take him out!"

The Captain struggles and then sags in the grasp of Ian and Arthur.

"All right," he says. "Under the floorboards. Over there."

Well, all right . . .

"Thank you, Captain. That makes things easier. Take off six lashes for good behavior, making it an even twenty. We'll have Duggan swing the cat, as he's the strongest."

Griswold is hauled out cursing me to hell and back again. Soon he is not swearing, however—he is howling.

The old crew of the *Cerberus* is taken out of the hold at gunpoint and forced into one of the two lifeboats. They are given some food and water and advised to steer east.

"Goodbye, Mr. Hollister. Good sailing to you. You were a decent sort and I thank you. Captain Griswold, I hope you took a good lesson from today's events. To wit, *be careful whom you whip*. Farewell. I wish you all a safe voyage."

The Captain glowers, wrapped in his bloody shirt, as they are cast off, and we see them no more. Then we change course and set sail for Batavia.

When we are off, I turn once again to the business of running the ship.

"Ian. Start bringing up the prisoners we have designated as trustable. Don't let the other convicts know what's going on. We don't want trouble from them—not yet, anyway. Padraic, make sure all locks are secure . . . Oh, and have the Weasel set to work cleaning the stinking uniforms of Napper and Vance. We shall need them for deception purposes. McBride, take three men and—"

"And just what, *Sir*." McBride sneers, his arms crossed on his chest.

Uh-oh . . . Here it is . . . And I've got to do this now, or I am the Captain of nothing . . .

I grab McBride by his collar and shove him backwards, hard. He stumbles, but does not fall. He puts up his fists.

"All right, McBride, up on the main hatch. Me and you. Let's settle it. Now."

He grins and climbs up on the hatch. He motions me to follow.

"You don't have to do this," says Ian. "We—"

"Oh, yes, we do," say Arthur McBride and I together in one breath.

"What will it be, guv'nor? Swords?"

"No, McBride. I am a trained Naval officer, and you are a lowland Irish bogtrotter—the fight would not be fair. I would run you through in an instant, and as attractive as that notion is, I will not do it, being a man of some honor."

"What, then, Mr. Honorable Brit?" says McBride, rolling up his sleeves.

"I know your kind would prefer shillelaghs, but I will not sully my hands with crude dumb cudgels," I say, leaping to the hatch top and rolling up my own sleeves. "Nay. It shall be fists . . . with no holds barred. Last man standing will be the Captain. Agreed?"

"Oh, yes, agreed," says McBride, getting into a crouch. "Come on, *Sir*. Let's see what you're made of."

I know that McBride is tough, but I am tough, too. I have been toughened as a ship's boy, kicked about by rough seamen, and as a midshipman, heir to all the kicks and blows the senior middies could pile on. And have I not "rassled" with the mighty Mike Fink on the banks of the Mississippi! Yes, I have. And did not Beatty and McCoy pay the price for crossing me? Oh yes, they did, and now they rot in hell for it. So come on, McBride, you low-life Irish swine. I ball up my fists.

As I expected, he charges in low, head down, in hopes of knocking me off my feet. I jump back, swing, and hit him high on his cheekbone.

Yeow! My fist vibrates with the pain. I realize there's no sense in hitting him in the face—the hardheaded mick is undoubtedly used to that. I'd probably just break my hand. No, go for the body. Catch him in the lower ribs.

While I'm thinking this, he swings his right and catches me above the eye, rocking me back and opening a cut on my forehead. Blood trickles into my eye.

Seeing this, McBride grins and drops his guard, pulls back, and launches a broad roundhouse that would surely end this fight and my leadership if it were to land.

It does not land. I stick up my left forearm and stop the swing. His midriff is wide open, so I bring my right around and slam it into his lower ribs.

He gasps. I hit him again in exactly the same place, trying to bury my fist as deep in his gut as I can.

Take that, you ignorant son of a bitch. Yes, and here's another one for Jacky. And yet another for that damned joke . . . Laugh at this, why don't you?

His mouth is open, trying in vain to suck in air. Unable to catch his breath, his face turns bright red and he sinks to his knees.

I stand over him, victorious, my fists still clenched. I could now destroy him. But I do not. Instead I extend my hand.

"I am the Captain. Ian McConnaughey shall be First Mate, Padraic Delaney Second, and you, Arthur McBride, shall be Third. Duggan will be Bo'sun. Shall we all now get to work?"

He reaches up and takes my hand, and I lift him to his feet. "Thank you, Captain," he wheezes. "Third Mate it is."

When the day's work is done, the table is set, the wine opened, and the rum poured, we have a fine celebration in the cabin . . . *my* cabin now.

During the conversation, Padraic asks, "Should we change the name of this bark? Hard to love that name."

I lean back in my chair and motion for the Weasel to refill my glass, then say, "I had thought about that, but since we are now plainly a pirate ship in the eyes of the civilized world, perhaps the name is appropriate."

"What does it mean?"

"In Greek myths, Cerberus was the fierce three-headed dog, servant of the god Hades, who guarded the gates of the Underworld."

"Ha! Seems right to me! Right piratical!" says Duggan, pounding the table.

"So say you one, so say you all?"
Done!

Till Later, Jacky,

Jaimy

Chapter 54

No, unfortunately, I had not managed to kill that unspeakable spawn of hell. Ruger had lurched sideways at the last moment so that my arrow only grazed his neck, pinning his shirt collar to the mast. Before I could loose another shaft, he had torn away and disappeared.

But a truce of sorts is now in effect onboard the once happy *Lorelei Lee*. It has been negotiated between Messrs. Seabrook and Gibson, the Surgeon, Major Johnston, and myself. I refuse to talk to Ruger, that miserable fiend, and he stays mainly in his cabin, almost certainly drunk. When he does appear, he wears his sword and pistols.

The agreement is this: We shall proceed to New South Wales, which is only about three weeks off, should the wind and weather be kind. Once in Australia, I will be tried for the attempted murder of Captain Ruger and he shall be brought to account for the murder of Mairead's child.

Why do the *Lorelei Lee*'s officers talk to me at all? It is simple. Barricaded with me below are Higgins and Ravi, along with Mick and Keefe, neither of whom want to give up their girls, and they do owe me some loyalty. Then there is Cookie and the galley, as well as the storerooms that hold the food . . . and the wine and rum. All three of the female Crews are with me, too.

Furthermore, I have my bow and many arrows. They know I could sting them at will and make their lives miserable. Should they attempt to charge our hatchway, many of them would certainly die, and no one wants to die for Captain Ruger.

Furthermore, I have a dozen torch-tipped arrows, and the bucket of pitch sits by the galley stove, just waiting to be lit. I could set the sails on fire, and then none of us would be going anywhere.

The powder magazine is down here, too, and without powder, the ship is defenseless. I had rigged up a small bag of powder with a six-inch fuse that I lit and threw out at their feet as talks were beginning. It flared up with a fine flame and was most impressive. Negotiations proceeded quite quickly after that.

Should the crew hold to its side of the bargain, the three madams and I have agreed to let the "wives" of the crew gradually return to their former cozy berths. So far the officers have held to that bargain. Major Johnston was delighted to have his Esther back, I know that for certain.

I, however, do not venture out, not having complete confidence in the truce. In fact, I have fashioned another weapon, because if I'd had my shiv, I would have gutted that Ruger right then and there for what he did, by God. But I did not have it, as I'd given it to Jaimy. So to take its place, I'd sharpened the small end of my pennywhistle with Cookie's whetstone and rubbed till it was sharpened to a point—not much of a weapon, but if it's shoved up hard under someone's chin, well, it just might get their attention. And it still plays just fine. I have put my forearm sheath back on, and I wear the whistle there, under my shirtsleeve.

I sit by Mairead's side and put a cool, damp cloth to her forehead. She lies on her bed, covered with a clean sheet, her hair combed and fanned out on her pillow. Barnsley and company did a good job. I notice with some relief that a degree of color has been restored to Mairead's face.

"There, there, Sister, you just rest now," I say. "You'll be—"

She reaches up and takes me by the wrist and looks off over my head. "What was my baby? A boy or a girl?"

I swallow hard and decide to tell her.

"Mrs. Barnsley says it was a boy."

Her eyes fill up and tears pour out over her cheeks. My eyes, too, are crying, to see my dear friend in such distress. I wipe away her tears and then mine with the cloth.

"The poor little thing . . . to never see the light of day . . . to never be at my breast . . . to never know his dad . . . to never be baptized," she whispers, her eyes full of anguish.

I take her hand and put it to my lips. "Please, Sister, think of the paintings you have seen in church, the statues . . . all the happy little cherubs flying around the heads of the saints, around the Virgin herself. Think of that."

She nods, squeezing her eyes shut, grasping my hand ever the tighter.

"Pray with me, Jacky," she whispers.

"I will, Sister."

She pauses, collects herself, and then begins . . .

"Hail Mary, Full of grace, the Lord is with thee . . ."

Yes, and with your little boy, too, Mairead.

"Blessed art thou among women, and blessed is the fruit of thy womb, Jesus. Holy Mary, Mother of God, pray for us now and at the hour of our death . . ."

Amen.

We are quiet for a bit, and then I say, "Mairead. When you are up to it . . . Not now, no . . . But when you are . . . Enoch Lightner has lost hope in living. He has lost his great friend Captain Laughton and he has seen—no, heard—you've been abused most horribly, and he was unable to prevent it. If, soon, you could see him and lend him some comfort . . ."

"I shall see him now," says Mairead, releasing my hand and throwing back the sheet that covers her. She rises and looks about for the Shantyman and sees him lying in a bunk not far away.

"I will go to him now."

"Are you up to it, Sister? It's only been two days."

"I am up to it." She even manages a smile. "Know this, Brit—they grow us up strong on the hard green turf of Ireland."

She stands, steadies herself, and then walks to his side and sits on the edge of his pallet.

"Come now, Enoch," she says, placing her hand on his shoulder. "You must regain your spirits, for the sake of us all. Here, a cold cloth for your brow . . . I see you have received a wound there, and I fear it was in defense of my poor self. Let me take off your blindfold such that—No, no, Enoch, you need not hide your eyes from me."

It is late afternoon and I sit with Higgins, looking out through the starboard laundry window. We sleep down here

434

now because I feel safer here. It is not very private, but we manage to work things out. We have taken a corner bunk and hung a drape over the front of it, and it serves for the marriage bed. Ravi, too, is here, at my feet. He witnessed all the happenings of the other day and is terrified of Ruger and does not like going topside, but he did, nonetheless, manage to creep out to retrieve my seabag from our old stateroom . . . and to coax Josephine down from the mast-head. So we are a complete, if rather bizarre, family group.

"What do you think they will do to Ruger?" I ask, already knowing the answer. I hand Josephine a piece of ship's biscuit and she takes it gently from my fingers. As she chews, I give the dome of her orange head a bit of a pet. She blinks her wise eyes and seems pleased with her lot.

Higgins sighs, and I know I will not like his answer.

"Probably not much," he says. "He could claim it was an accident, that she was disobeying a direct order from the Captain of the ship. At the most, he will be charged with simple assault."

"Simple assault? He murdered Mairead's child!" I say, incredulous.

"As the law sees it, the baby has to be born before it becomes a person. Therefore, no person, no murder."

"Fine law," I say, seething. "Made up by men, no doubt."

"Ummm," says Higgins.

"So they'll let that bastard go free, and hang me from the nearest tree for trying to skewer the son of a bitch."

"Do not despair just yet, Miss. Others have tried to hang you before."

"Hang Missy Memsahib?" cries Ravi, looking very alarmed. "Hang her dear body from tree? It cannot be. It—"

"On deck there!" comes the call from the lookout out-side. "Sail! Big one! Two points abaft the port beam! Heading right for us!"

We all fly to the port window and gaze out.

Could it be Jaimy's ship again? Hope surges . . .

Chapter 55

A ship on the horizon? Could it be Jaimy?

I leap for my glass, which dangles from the wall of our makeshift homestead, and rush to the port side window and put the glass to my eye. I see a massive sail that seems to be made up of many battens, looking for all the world like a woven rush doormat. I lower the glass and note that the First Mate is there, glass to his own eye.

"Mr. Seabrook! What is she?" I call.

"Lookout reports it is a strange craft, hull already up over the horizon. I suspect it is a Chinese junk. It looks like it has eight—no, ten—masts, so it's got to be a big one." He sounds worried.

"Surely it cannot harm us, Sir. The *Lorelei Lee* is armed!"

I know, for I armed her, and armed her well.

"Aye," he says, folding his glass. "And so are they. And they carry up to a thousand heathens, every one of them carrying a broadsword . . . and they are coming on fast."

A thousand? Good Lord!

Mr. Seabrook is soon joined by Mr. Gibson. "Get the *Captain* out here, Gibson," he says, not bothering to hide the contempt in his voice. "We have the sea room. We shall try to run. Have the Bo'sun pass out cutlasses and muskets." A man is sent to rouse Ruger from his den.

Damn! They're gonna need more than that! They'll need powder and shot and my Powder Monkeys and me as well, for who can aim the guns better than I?

"Mr. Seabrook! Mr. Gibson! I must come out for the sake of the ship! Will the truce hold? Will you defend me?"

They know exactly what I mean by that, as Ruger has just emerged from his lair, disheveled and looking about, confused. Befuddled or not, he does wear his sword and pistols.

Seabrook touches the butt of the pistol at his belt. "Yes, we will defend you," he answers.

"Come, girls, to me!" I shout to my Powder Monkeys. "Let's go! Mick! Keefe! Follow me!"

We remove the wedges, throw open the latches, and burst out onto the deck.

"Monkeys! Powder to all the guns! Molly, to the stern gun! Quick! Ann, to starboard! Maggie, port guns!"

Mairead! Damn! You shouldn't be here! Not yet!

But she is, and she goes down to the powder magazine like all the rest and comes up bearing the bags and the shot.

"What's going on?" Ruger mumbles. "Why are the whores out?" He casts a bleary but wary eye, no doubt remembering our last encounter when I did my best to kill him.

"Chinese junk, Sir. A big one. Probably a pirate. And we need the girls to carry powder. He should be in range of the after gun very soon," announces Seabrook, nodding to me.

I need no further encouragement.

"Mick! Keefe! To me!" I cry, tearing down into the Captain's cabin. "Free up the gun!" I shove Ruger aside on my way.

The lads do it, throwing over tables and chairs to expose the gleaming brass of my nine-pound Long Tom lurking beneath. It's still got the name painted by Davy Jones on the butt end, Kiss My Royal Ass. They haul it back on its carriage and open the gun port. Maggie brings up the powder bag and we ram it in, followed by the wad and the nine-pound cannonball. The gun should have been left loaded, but plainly it wasn't. Stupid Ruger . . . I pierce the bag and set the matchlock in the touchhole. The gun is ready to fire.

I peer out over the gun at our pursuers.

Good Lord, there must be at least a thousand of them, in the rigging or leaning over the rail of the thing, waving gleaming swords and howling for our blood.

"Put her amidships and crank her up three notches, lads!"

They do it. I know the junk is still out of range, but maybe this'll scare 'em off. I pull the lanyard.

Crrrack!

The gun bucks back and I look out over the smoking barrel.

Hmm . . . The shot is a good hundred yards short. It does *not* scare them off.

"Keefe!" I shout. "Crank her up as high as she will go! Reload!"

The gun is made ready and we fire again.

Crracckk!

It is no good. The shot again falls way short, but still . . . the junk slows its progress toward us.

I wonder why . . .

I do not wonder long. There is a flare from the junk and a rocket goes skyward, trailing sparks.

"Reload, lads!" I shout, and run back out on deck.

We watch the rocket rise, then we hold our breath as it falls, twenty yards to port. Immediately thereafter, two more rockets are launched.

So. That is the way of it. They will stay out of the range of our cannons and continue to rain rockets upon us until such time that they score some hits and then we will be lost.

"Man the hoses," orders Mr. Seabrook. "If one of those rockets sets our sails afire, we are done." Heads nod and orders are given and the hoses are pumped up and ready.

Which is good, for the next rocket lands square on the fantail and sets up a fierce flame.

"Damn!" says Mr. Gibson. "It's phosphorus! It'll eat right through the deck. Douse it! Now!"

It is done, but we all know that the Chinese have many more rockets.

"If we turn to port and give them a broadside . . ." ventures Mr. Gibson.

"No," says Mr. Seabrook. "If we do that, they will still be out of range and then we will have lost headway, so they will swarm all over us. Look at them! The heathen devils!"

The junk is close enough for us to see the Chinese swordsmen crowding their rail. We can hear them screaming, as well.

Ruger, for his part, stands weaving on the quarterdeck, sword in hand, shouting his defiance to the enemy. While the other officers stand calm, ready to accept whatever Fate has in store for them, he does not.

"Away, you heathen devils! Monsters!" he roars. "Spawn of Satan, away! Back to your hellholes. Back, I say!"

Fat lot of good that will do, you sorry excuse for a man!

The junk stays just out of range and continues to pepper us with those soaring missiles.

Oh, Lord, this cannot end well, I know, and to have come all this way to end up either burned alive or to be enslaved by some Chinese pirate, my inner coward wails.

No, this calls for desperate action . . . from me.

I have a plan and I resolve to carry it out, shoving my sniveling cowardly self back down. *No, you idiot,* she wails. *Are you out of your mind? Run and hide! Run!*

Run where, self? I ask.

She whimpers but does not reply, so I turn to the First Mate . . .

"Put in the small boat," I say. "Attach a long thin line to it—at least fifty yards long, with more standing by."

Seabrook cocks an eye at me.

"The Chinaman is trying to burn our sails," I answer, trying to keep the coward's quaver out of my voice. "Fine. We will burn his first. Ravi, my bow, my arrows, and the bucket of pitch. Have Cookie light it off. Now!"

He scurries off while the little rowboat used for painting the ship's side is put in the water, with a rope ladder leading down into it. Ravi returns with my gear and I order him into the boat—he is light in weight, and I need him. He doesn't look happy, but he does it. Then I follow him down.

Ruger looks confused and not at all happy to see me with bow and arrow in hand, but the other officers know my intent.

"All right," I say, when I'm settled on the middle seat. "Let out the slack. Keep doing it till you see me hit their mainsail." The line tied to the bow of the boat is loosened and my fireboat begins to drift back in the wake of the *Lorelei Lee*.

Ravi sits in the stern, scared but ready to prepare the arrows when I call for them. I keep the bow hidden down under the gunwales so the enemy will not see what I plan.

We draw closer, and I know we are spotted, as I can see the reflections of lenses pointed at us. Perhaps they will think me an emissary sent to parley . . . or perhaps sent to offer a surrender to their tender mercies, for which pirates are not well known.

Think again, Chinaman. We are close enough now . . .

"Ravi. Give me one."

The boy dips the cloth-tipped end of the arrow into the burning pitch and hands it to me. I grab it by its shaft, nock it, pull back, and let it fly. It arcs up and . . . misses the sail. It falls onto the deck of the junk and I cannot see what damage it inflicts. Prolly not much.

Damn!

"Ravi! Another!"

He dips and hands me the flaming arrow. I nock and fire . . .

Hooray!

This one hits dead center on their mainsail. *That* gets their goddamned heathen attention. Immediately there are men in the rigging, with some jabbering away as others carry buckets of water.

No hoses, you devils? Well, too goddamn bad . . .

It does seem that their sails are made out of woven mats of some sort—reeds or grasses or something. Whatever they are made of, my airborne torches fire them up quite nicely.

"Another, Ravi!" I crow out, triumphant.

"Good shootings, Missy," he says, handing me another arrow with a flaming end. I take it and let it fly . . . and fly it does . . .

Another hit! Katy Deere, you should see your Sister now!

We are a mere fifty feet from the huge junk now. I fire away at will and soon I've got their mid sail in flames and then the after sail, as well.

Ha! The Lorelei Lee *is saved!*

But, as happened many times in the past, my triumph is short-lived. While I have one arrow left, I suddenly find that they have many, many more arrows, as I see a flock of them come winging our way.

I hold my breath and . . .

. . . most miss, but one arrow does thud into the seat next to me. Ravi trembles, his black eyes wide with fear and looking to the heavens. He whispers, *"Happy puppy, happy puppy,"* over and over. His back is to the junk, so he cannot see the arrows coming toward us, and perhaps that is best for the little fellow. *Happy puppy, happy puppy . . .* Other arrows fall close, but I am a small target and the junk is large.

I loose my remaining arrow, setting their topsail aflame.

We have done our job. More arrows fly at us and do us no harm, but I know they will soon get lucky. I lift my arm and signal to the *Lorelei Lee* to pull us back.

But she does not pull us back. No, the rope goes slack and the *Lorelei Lee* gets smaller and smaller on the horizon, while the Chinese junk looms ever and ever bigger.

Ruger has cut our line! He's running! We have saved the ship, but we ourselves are doomed! The cowardly bastard!

My heart sinks. We are undone.

The arrows from the junk stop coming at us—they know we are adrift and helpless now. I put down my bow and wait for capture and certain death. I wrap my arms around Ravi and he continues to murmur his mantra . . .

I add mine . . . *Lord, as I am coming to you, please make this hapless girl welcome. I promise to be good . . . and yes, happy puppy is good enough for me, too . . .*

Chapter 56

A hook is put down into our little rowboat and we are hauled alongside the massive junk. I had not realized the sheer size of the thing before, but I do now. Not that it matters, as I will certainly be dead soon. I know that for sure because all I see about me are furious faces—Chinese faces, with shaved heads and pigtails, looking like demons, all waving curved swords and screaming at me. Can't say as I blame 'em, for I had set their ship on fire. I'd be rather mad, too.

I know I'm going to die, and I only hope it will be quick. *I'm so sorry, Ravi, for getting you into this . . . I hope it will be quick for you, too.*

There is a ladderlike thing that is attached to the side of the ship, and men clamber down it and rough hands reach for us and we are dragged onboard. I cannot see what happens to Ravi, but I am put on my knees before . . . what . . . ?

That matters to me less than the fact that someone grabs me by the hair and stretches out my neck and I feel the cool steel of a blade laid upon it. I shiver at the touch.

This is it. Yes, Lord, I am ready. Goodbye, Jaimy . . . I hope . . .

The blade is taken from my neck and I know it is being raised high above my head.

. . . I hope you have a lovely life, Jaimy . . .

"*Cheng Pao! Ting! Zhi!*" shouts a woman's voice.

I sure as hell hope that means "Stop!"

Apparently it does, as my hair is released and I can lift my still-attached head to gaze stupidly upon the one who gave that order.

It is a small, very young woman. She is dressed in loose yellow and green pantaloons, shirt, and vest. On her feet, which are very close to my nose, are elegantly brocaded slippers. All of her clothing fairly shimmers with richness, which pales beside her own personal beauty—her rather exotic beauty. Above her dark, almond-shaped eyes, she is half bald, her forehead shaved, leaving her long black hair at the back of her head to be plaited into a long pigtail. The only thing out of place in the little-china-doll image is the hilt of the two-handed broadsword that sticks up over her right shoulder. That and the rather stern look she fixes on my poor quivering self. Can't blame her for that, for I did a lot of damage here. The fires are mainly out, but the smoke still drifts all around us.

Next to her stands a very large Chinese man in the process of re-sheathing his sword, probably the man who was about to take my head. Men come up to jabber reports to the large man, but from the deference shown to the girl, she is the one most definitely in charge.

In one fluid motion, she reaches back, grabs the hilt of her sword, whips it out of the sheath strapped to her back, and brings the blade around in a wide arc to rest against the side of my neck.

I gasp with the sudden swiftness of it all. My poor neck feels very tender and bare next to the steel. Though the touch is light, I can feel that the blade is razor sharp.

She stares at me down the gleaming shaft of her sword.

"*Suk naai!*" she snarls.

What does she want? How do I handle this? Is it—

"Cheng Shih wishes to know who you are."

What? English words? Here?

It is then that I notice a man standing slightly behind the female creature. He is plainly European and is dressed in the habit of a monk—black cassock with hood laid back from his head, a large golden cross dangling from his neck, and a hempen cord about his waist.

A Catholic monk on a Chinese junk? What? Is he here to give me last rites? Is that it? My mind, what's left of it, reels . . . I grow more and more confused.

"Cheng what? Who . . . ?"

"Cheng Shih is the commander of this ship . . . and her entire fleet as well," says this monk. "It would be best if you answer her question."

"My . . . my name is Jacky Faber and in England I was born. I am a convict heading for New South Wales. My ship has many such convicts, and we only ask to be left in peace. Where . . . where is my little boy?"

Oh, there you are, Ravi. Newly released by his own captor, Ravi grabs the opportunity to wrap himself around my waist.

The monk turns to the woman and rattles off a few sentences, which I assume to be Chinese. She grunts and looks me over, touseled head to bare foot. Then she steps back, and with the same fluid motion she had used to draw her sword, she whips it back into her sheath and turns around. Embroidered on the back of her emerald green garment is a large golden dragon, its mouth open and spitting bright red fire. The Lady of the Dragon issues an order, my arm is taken, and I am dragged off toward a hatch. My fear, which had left me for a moment, comes flooding back.

"Is she going to have me killed?" I ask of this holy man, who follows close behind us.

"If she were going to kill you, you would be dead already," he says mildly, as if he would have watched me having my head cut off back there on the deck with a certain calm equanimity. "No, she wants me to find out more about her new captive. You see, she has seen many such as he"—he gestures at the dark and wide-eyed Ravi, and then looks at my sandy blond mop—"but she has never seen anything like *you*. And I believe she is . . . intrigued."

We are taken below to a small, plain room that contains a low bed, a desk, and several chairs. Since there is a golden crucifix above the bed, it is not hard to figure out that it is the friar's room. The one who had me by the arm—an evil-looking brute stripped to the waist, with long, thin mustaches that hang way down past his chin—tosses me to a chair. Ravi tries to crawl up into my lap, but I tell him that he must sit on the floor beside me. He does.

The cleric takes a seat behind the little desk. On it is paper, quill pen, and a little jar of ink. He takes up the pen, dips it in the ink, and then looks at me.

"I am Brother Arcangelo Rossetti, Society of Jesus. Translator and advisor to Cheng Shih. Your name again?"

"Jacky Faber. Baptized Mary Alsop Faber." Might as well let him know I'm a Christian of sorts. Might help. It doesn't.

"Hmm. Catholic?

"Church of England."

"Ah, a heretic. Age?"

"Sixteen."

He writes all this down and then leans back in his chair. "Very well. Now tell me of your life and how you come to be here. Go slowly, as I am Italian and my English is—"

"We could speak in French, Sir . . . or Spanish, if that would be more comfortable for you."

He cocks an appraising eyebrow. "Spanish, then."

And so I tell him of my life. I give a concise history, switching from Spanish to French to English when the need arises, and we get along in all three languages. He professes disbelief in a lot of it, but I assure him it is all true, no matter how strange.

Finally, we end up in the present day.

"Two hundred and fifty women, all prostitutes?"

"Most of them. Not worth much, even as slaves," I say, hoping to prevent further pursuit of the *Lorelei Lee*.

"Hmmm . . ." He ponders all I have told him.

"Perhaps you will now tell me something of her?" I ask.

He considers, puts his fingertips together, and begins.

"Cheng Shih is without doubt the most successful pirate in history. She is twenty-three years old. At age sixteen she was a prostitute in one of the floating brothels on the Zhu Jiang—the Pearl River. Already famous for her beauty and cultural accomplishments, she met the pirate Zheng Yi and was married to him at the age of seventeen. Together they amassed a mighty fleet of ships. When Zheng Yi died in a typhoon, they had a total of one hundred ships.

She took over the leadership after his death, instituted new rules and regulations, and the fleet now numbers in the hundreds."

"*Hundreds?*" I manage to gasp.

"Yes, and thousands of men."

"Good Lord. *Thousands?*"

"I see you are impressed, seeing as how you, in your own rather colorful life, managed to procure a fleet of . . . what . . . ? *Two?*"

I nod. "But how did she do that? A common prostitute?"

"Believe me, she was not a 'common prostitute.' Unlike our own European dens of iniquity, in China, and Japan, as well, girls in that particular profession are trained in art, music, and dance. True, it is still prostitution, but the girls are very refined. I have seen the floating brothels of Guangzhou, and they are quite impressive—a thousand floating lanterns set out upon the water at night, gentle music drifting over all, with the heady smell of jasmine and incense. Actually, very nice . . . in a heathen sort of way. They call it the Willow World, a place where the gentle reeds bend easily and with grace."

Brother Arcangelo looks out over my head in a dreamy sort of way.

Hmmm, Brother . . . Have you been tempted? Have you fallen for the charms of the Orient?

"But how could she hold something like that together?" asks the ever practical me.

The priest shakes his head and brings himself away from the floating Willow World and back into this little cabin.

"Ahem. Well, she has established a system of rules and regulations that endear her to the populace. She does not allow abuse of captives—the penalty for raping a female hostage is death. Any Chinese seaport town that welcomes her troops is treated well. Otherwise, watch out—heads fall and ears are cut off. The captains of her far-flung fleet may plunder Vietnam, Korea, and Japanese ports as they will, but they have to obey the rules and they must pay her tribute. You see how it works? It is actually a well-regulated economy, of sorts—a government in all the usual ways, except that it floats. Additionally, she has married Cheng Pao, the big man you might have noticed before, and he is Zheng Yi's adopted son, further cementing her control on her floating empire. Now, if you will excuse me, I must report to Cheng Shih. There are cups and plum wine on the shelf there. You may refresh yourself. Your throat must be dry after that rather fanciful story you have just told."

"Wait," I say. "If you have any pity in your heart for this poor heretic, please tell me what the Chinese words are for *good day, please,* and *thank you.*"

They are *nei ho mah, cheng,* and *doh je.*"

He does not repeat them, but I nod my thanks and run the words over and over again in my head.

And I do take a taste of the plum wine and give a bit to Ravi, as well. He probably figures there is alcohol in it, but he does not seem to care. I don't blame him—we have both stared Death in the face today, and that grim figure still lurks about, waiting for his chance . . .

After a while, Brother Arcangelo returns and beckons for us to rise and to follow him. Which we do.

I am led into an incredibly sumptuous room that is sure to be the cabin of the pirate queen. Rich silks hang from the walls and there are painted scrolls and strange musical instruments that I would love to get my hands on. There is a bed, of course, with silk drapes that hang all about it, and many plump pillows. Over and over the golden dragon theme is repeated. I am directed to a spot on the floor and made to sit down upon it.

"Best be prepared to put your forehead to the floor. Cheng Shih is expected momentarily," says the priest. I nod, sit back on my haunches, and wait.

"Hush, Ravi," I say to the quivering lad, who huddles next to me. I put my arm across his shoulders. "We are still alive, and we should be glad."

From behind me I hear a rustle and look around to see Cheng Shih emerging through a beaded curtain from yet another room. I put my head to the floor and push Ravi's down as well.

Cheng Shih and Brother Arcangelo converse for a while, and then he says, "Stand up," and I do it.

"*Nei ho mah, Cheng Shih,*" I say, respectfully.

She is surprised, but, I can tell, not overly impressed.

Cheng Shih brings her face close to mine, her dark brown eyes peering into my light brown ones. Only slightly taller than I, she walks slowly around me, giving me a poke here and there. She runs her fingers through my hair. I'm sure she is checking my roots to see if my hair is dyed. Satisfied that it is not, she speaks again to the monk.

"She says she does not believe your story. She says you are a liar and she does not like liars."

Uh-oh . . . I can imagine what she does with people she does not like. Think, girl!

I do think, and I come up with a way to prove at least one thing: that I can dive.

"Brother, do you have a coin I can borrow? I will demonstrate something."

His eyebrows go up, but he does produce a silver coin from his purse and hands it to me.

"Now, if you could ask Cheng Shih to go outside with me."

She considers and then nods and goes out the door, followed by the cleric. When their backs are turned, I quickly dig into my money belt and take out a coin similar to the one given me. I stick Brother Arcangelo's coin in my mouth, tuck it beside my back teeth, and go through the door.

Back in the daylight, I'm glad to see that the sails are still slacked for repairs and we are dead in the water. Spotting a likely opening in the port side rail, I go for it. The others follow close beside me. I look down at the waves and begin disrobing.

I pull off my shirt in one swift movement, step out of my trousers, drop drawers, and stand naked on the deck.

The Chinese are not immune to gasping, I notice.

The coin, which I had held clenched in my fist, I hand to Cheng Shih, who appears slightly astounded. Putting my toes on the edge of the deck, I say, "*Cheng Shih . . .*" and gesture for her to toss the coin in the sea.

She looks me over one more time and then flings it over the side. I take a deep breath, wait a moment to let the coin sink a bit, and then dive in after it.

I hit cleanly, hoping I am graceful, and then kick down to a depth of about twelve feet. I have no intention of chasing that coin—*Neptune, if you are down there watching this little drama, you are welcome to it*—no, I plan one of my usual tricks, similar to the one I pulled on the crew of the *Excaliber* that time back in good old Boston.

The hull of the junk looms beside me. Diving down a little farther, I turn and swim under her—the draft is only about fifteen feet, and the beam of the craft is a mere thirty feet or so. The ship is very long but not so very wide and I am able to slip under her easily.

Coming up on the other side, I surface quietly and put my hand on the ladderlike grating that I had noticed when we were first brought aboard. I rest for a bit, and then wait a little bit longer, to make certain that all on the ship think me drowned for sure.

Reaching into my mouth, I pull out Brother Arcangelo's coin and clamp it between my lips. Then I climb up and, hooking a leg over the rail, gain the deck.

All the others are at the other rail, gazing down at the water.

I pad as quietly as I can across the deck and stand behind them.

Yes, there are a few astonished *Hai!*s from assorted personnel about the rigging, but neither Cheng Shih nor Brother Arcangelo seems to notice.

"*Nei ho mah, Cheng Shih,*" I say.

She whips around to see me standing there looking, I hope, like any wet and comely mermaid—minus the green fishy tail, of course. For that, my pink one will have to serve. I hold up the coin and put on my foxy grin.

The shock on her face is slowly replaced by a smile. She reaches out and takes me by the hand and leads me back into her cabin.

It's been a wild day, but I think I have done myself a world of good. Hope so, anyway . . .

Chapter 57

A grinning Chinese man comes toward me, brandishing what looks to be a very sharp razor. I shrink back against the bulkhead.

"Do not worry, Miss. He will not hurt you in any way," assures Brother Arcangelo, again scribbling away at his desk. "It is only Chi-chi. He is a eunuch, and he is here to make you more . . . presentable . . . for Cheng Shih. Go with him, please."

Presentable? Where have I heard that before . . . ?

With Ravi at my heels, I follow the creature out the door, down a passageway, and into yet another room. This one is bare except for several benches and a large tub full of hot water. It is plainly a bathhouse, and it is also plain the Chinese have a much higher opinion of cleanliness than do my fellow Europeans. Chi-chi gestures for me to disrobe, and, what-the-heck, I do it. He holds out his hand to guide me into the bath, and I slide in.

Ahhhh . . . Now this isn't so bad . . .

Ravi stands by, his dark eyes wide.

"Get in here, Ravi. It ain't the holy waters of Mother Ulhas, but it'll do for me and you."

He shyly complies, dropping clothing and crawling in with me. He may not be completely at ease, but at least I have not heard "happy puppy" for a while. I position him between my knees, facing away, and dunk him under.

Chi-chi hands me a cake of soap and I apply it to Ravi's head.

"Missy Memsahib! Please! Ravi's eyes stinging so bad . . ."

"Oh, hush up, boy, and enjoy. Not long ago you were asking your heathen gods for deliverance from gruesome death and here you are now, still alive and being scrubbed by a reasonably handsome maid."

I lather up his shiny black hair, dunk him again to rinse, then wash the rest of the slippery little fellow.

"Out with you now, lad," I order, giving his little brown rump a light slap on its way out. Chi-chi hands him a towel and he wraps himself in it. "My turn now." I lean back and luxuriate in the warm, sudsy water. *Ummm . . .*

My Chinese attendant begins with my hair, first taking it out of my pigtail and washing it, his fingers working wondrously soothingly at my scalp. That done, he takes scissors and trims my forelocks down to stubble, back to a line running from my left ear across the top of my head to my right one. Yes, my poor hair does seem to suffer a lot as I travel this world. It's a wonder it even bothers growing back in after so many shearings. Then he soaps me up again and brings that wicked razor to bear and renders everything up there smooth as . . . as . . . as an eggshell, I decide, after he is done and I reach my hand up to place it on my now naked skull. *Ah, Higgins, you should see me now . . .*

Chi-chi chatters away in a very high-pitched voice as he goes about his work, and I understand not a word of it. He shaves around my ears and the back of my neck. Then he has me stand in the tub and takes his razor to the rest of me—legs, armpits, and . . . other parts as well . . . *Too bad . . . I sigh to myself . . . But, hey . . .*

Then I am dried, powdered, pampered, perfumed, and dressed in new clothing. Silken drawers, silken pantaloons, silken shirt, all bound up with a silken sash wound about my waist. All bright yellows and reds, cool whites with bold slashes of deepest black. By this time, my hair, what's left of it, is dry enough to be braided into a pigtail. Chi-chi takes me to a mirror and I regard myself. I am astounded. I twirl around to make the silks swish about me.

Tonda-lay-o, Queen of the Ocean Sea, indeed. Well, it is what you wished for, girl, and now you've got it—Bombay Rats and Cathay Cats . . . and all the rest . . .

Chi-chi is finished with me now and he takes me by the hand to lead me out of the bathhouse, but he does not take me back to Brother Arcangelo Rossetti's room, oh, no, he does not. He takes me to Cheng Shih's cabin and opens the door.

I enter and see that she is seated on a cushion before a low table. There is another pillow beside her and on the table there is an elegantly shaped bottle and two ornate cups.

I enter and go to my knees before her. I put my forehead to the deck.

"*Nei ho mah, Cheng Shih,*" I say. And then, in English, "I hope my appearance pleases you."

In spite of the language barrier, I think she catches my drift. She puts her hand gently under my chin and lifts my face and smiles. Then she points to the cushion beside her and I rise and go to it. I sit down.

Cheng Shih gestures to Chi-chi and he pours two cups of the dark purple liquid. She takes hers and lifts it to her lips. I do the same with mine. It is very good. I like it a lot. I take another nervous sip. Soon I am less nervous. When she puts her hand lightly on my arm, I do not flinch nor pull away.

I look over across the room, at her bed. I know that her sheets are of the finest silk, and her bed will be very soft . . . and I know that I will sleep there this night, and many nights after.

So, Jaimy . . . I am now . . . well . . . the pet . . . of a notorious Chinese pirate. Imagine that . . . Little Mary from the slums of Cheapside, now dressed in silks and satins. What a strange and wonderful world. I hope you are well and in good spirits, love, and, as for me . . . I am . . . not so awfully bad off . . .

Worry not for me, dear one, but only keep yourself safe . . .

Love,

Jacky

Chapter 58

James Emerson Fletcher
Commander, the Pirate Cerberus
Becalmed in the Java Sea

Jacky Faber
Somewhere, as always,
Up ahead of me

Dear Jacky,

The damned wind will not blow.

We lie dead in the water, well to the south of Batavia,
where we had hoped to put in to buy arms and otherwise
equip ourselves for our final push to Australia and wherever
else this ship will go. My men go about the decks, sweating
in the heat, their lips pursed, trying to "whistle up the wind."
That old superstition doesn't work, at least not this time.
The air lies fetid and still all about us. I am reminded of the
Sargasso Sea, through which I once sailed, and, if memory
serves, so did you.

We have brought up fifteen more men from below, trustables, to help us man the ship, and they have worked out well. Those remaining below have been told their rations will improve now that we have taken over, and there will be a daily tot of rum, as long as the stores hold out. They are mollified, grateful even, after the treatment they have received so far, but it is hot down there and I fear that gaol fever—typhus—might soon rage.

Oh, for a cool breeze, Jacky! Some of that good old damp London foggy mist!

The Irish lads are hot to take some prizes—born pirates, all of them—but until we can arm ourselves, no prizes can be taken. We can do nothing but sit here in the sweltering heat. Captain Griswold's gold stash will hold us in good stead if we could just get to port!

I worry about our situation—we have spotted some strange-looking craft off on the horizon. They appear and then they are gone. One of the men brought up from below, who has been in this region of the world before, believes they are Chinese junks. Why they come to gaze upon us and then disappear, I do not know. But I do not like it.

I am sure you are already in Australia, or at least close to it, and for that I am glad. It will afford some protection for you at least.

Meanwhile, we look out for better weather.

Hoping you have winds more fair . . .

I am,
Your most loving, devoted & etc.,

Jaimy

Chapter 59

"What does *Ju kau-jing yi* mean?" I ask of Brother Arcangelo. We are out on deck, waiting to be called in to Cheng Shih's presence. "She has taken to calling me that, is why I ask."

It is a beautiful day and I gaze up at the set of the huge sails. I have been here about a week, and I continue to marvel at the skill of these Chinese mariners. The ship's name is *Sheng Feng,* which is *Divine Wind,* and she is fast, for all her size. I think the *Lorelei Lee* could take her in a race in a good stiff breeze, but it would be close.

"It means 'little round-eyed barbarian,'" replies the priest.

"*Barbarian?*"

He laughs. "To the Chinese we Europeans are *all* barbarians—they call us 'hairy apes'—very clever apes, to be sure, but apes all the same. You must remember that their culture is a lot more ancient than ours."

"Umm . . . and what does Chi-chi's name mean?" I see the chubby little eunuch hovering by Cheng Shih's door, waiting for the summons.

"It means, well . . . 'Silly-silly' is as close as I can translate it."

"Poor fellow, to have such a name . . . and to have had that awful thing done to him."

"You mean the castration? Let it not bother you, dear. It is done to them when they are very young—most don't remember it being done. We have them in Italy, you know—the *castrati*, they are called. If a boy is found to have a fine voice, then *snip!* and his life is set for him. They are used for choruses and as soloists; they are singers with high, pure voices powered by massive grown-up lungs. I have heard them—they are quite impressive."

"I don't like it. There's plenty of good music around without doing that to little boys. It's . . . it's barbaric, is what it is," I say, running my fingers through Ravi's black locks. The boy stands by my side, attentive, as always, to what is going on. I have found, from the times he has sung along when I play my pennywhistle, that he has an excellent high soprano singing voice. But to preserve that voice in its present state by . . . No, I cannot even think of it.

I look over to see that Cheng Pao, Shih's husband, is standing on the quarterdeck, gazing down upon us, arms crossed on his chest. His eyes meet mine and then he turns and says something to the men there with him. All erupt into laughter.

My ears burn a bit, like they always do when I know I'm being talked about.

"Tell me, Brother, why does Cheng Pao not get angry over my enjoying his wife's company and not him?"

"He probably thinks it's a harmless bit of sport. Believe me, if he thought otherwise, there would be great trouble."

Brother Arcangelo chuckles. "It could be that the poor man welcomes a bit of a rest from the side of his fierce bride. I am sure you have found her most . . . energetic?"

I nod. She is that.

Early on I played the big-eyed fearful little waif when alone with Cheng Shih—it seemed to please her to take pity on her winsome captive and treat me gently. For all her reputation as the most fearsome pirate that roams the China Sea, with me she is kind. I am reminded of Mam'selle Claudelle, sort of . . .

I have learned many new Chinese words in my time with her—words for love . . . kiss . . . touch . . . soft . . . beloved . . . tender, words like that.

She has bestowed on me many presents—silk dresses, slippers, fine pieces of carved jade, and even a sword and scabbard like hers, and some instruction in how to wield it. The hilt is wrapped in gold thread, and the blade is of the sharpest beaten and tempered steel. I am amazed.

In return for this generosity, I do what I have always done when presents need to be given and I have the ways or means to procure them—I paint miniature portraits. There are plenty of watercolors, brushes, and fine paper aboard. Yes, they are a cultured people, and, as a matter of fact, Cheng Shih herself is quite good at painting. She has given me a fine painting of a fanciful fish that I shall treasure as long as I'm around to treasure things. I have done a portrait of Cheng Shih and she pronounced herself delighted with it and now demands one of me. There is a mirror in her cabin, and I am to start on it this very afternoon, after lunch.

"Why do you think she enjoys me so, Brother?" I ask of my companion.

He looks off, considering. "It seems that you do intrigue her, as your head is still on your neck. I think she finds you fascinating for being so very different from Chinese women. The way you carry yourself, the way you laugh and smile . . . and the very obvious fairness of your skin and hair."

He considers further. I reach up and put my arm through his and stand close to him. I have become quite fond of Brother Arcangelo Rossetti, as I have found him to be a good and kind man.

"For another instance, you should know that Chinese women are very modest when it comes to exposing their bodies," he continues. "From your diving performance on your first day here, you do not seem to share that modesty. I know you shocked Cheng Shih to her core."

"It seemed a wise thing to do at the time. I did have to prove myself."

"Perhaps. But anyway, you have only to look at Chinese art—very seldom will you see a nude female portrayed. Unlike us Italians. Have you ever been to the Vatican, child? No? Well, I can tell you the walls are virtually covered with nude bodies gamboling about . . . and that is a church, not a brothel, no matter what you heretics might say or think. Ah, here is Chi-chi. I believe we are being called."

Cheng Shih sits on an ornately decorated cushion, and I lie next to her with my head in her lap. We have already eaten of the rice, meat, and vegetables—all of it wondrous good— but she enjoys putting sweetmeats to my lips and giving me little sips of plum wine from her glass. I do not find it at all unpleasant—hey, I could be in a tub of boiling oil instead of lying here, dressed in fine silk, and being fed treats from the hand of a beautiful Chinese woman. Yes, my head could be resting on a chopping block instead of reclining here on her lap, jasmine perfume swirling all about us, and her fingers— her very knowing fingers—gently tracing the lines of my face. No . . . I ain't complaining.

Presently, Cheng Shih places a kiss on my smooth brow and murmurs something to Brother Arcangelo.

"She says it is time for you to do the portrait of yourself. She wants to see how you go about it. Observe your technique, as it were," he says, motioning for me to get up. I suppress a groan of pure laziness—yes, I quickly grow very used to luxury—and rise.

The colors, brushes, and papers have been laid out on a small table in front of a mirror. There is a chair and I place my silk-covered bottom in it. I regard my image in the glass. *Oh, Jaimy, if you could only see your girl now.* Then I set to work.

First I lay in the basic shape of my head with light pinkish-brown, and then put in the background colors— reds and yellows from the drapes hanging behind me. Then I put in some of the darker planes of my face, neck, and hair. The shadows in my eye sockets, alongside my nose, under my chin and lower lip. I think she is rather amazed at the speed with which I work—hey, spend a lot of time painting portraits of squirming children and you learn to be real fast.

At length, I sit back and say, "It is now blocked in, but I must let it dry for a few moments before I put in the details, or else it will blur."

Brother Arcangelo translates and Cheng Shih takes her hand from my shoulder where it had been resting and pours another cup of that delicious plum wine and hands it to me. *Too much of this and I ain't gonna be paintin' nothin',* I'm thinking.

"Thank you, Beloved Shih," I say as I take a very cautious sip. That is how I have been addressing her in Chinese. She beams. Her little European trifle is learning to speak a cultured language, imagine that.

As the painting dries, I cast my eyes about the room. There are various decorations—painted screens depicting great battles and lissome maids with fans and fancy hair, figurines, and a squat statue of a little fat man.

"What is that?" I ask of Arcangelo.

"Ah. That is a statue of the Buddha, the Great Teacher," he answers. "One of the major figures in Oriental religion."

"He seems rather pleasant enough. Is that Cheng Shih's religion?"

"No, actually she is, like most Chinese, a Confucian. She keeps that there to remind her of a debt unpaid."

I lift my eyebrows, in question, and he turns and murmurs something to Cheng Shih, I guess keeping her informed of what we are talking about. Nobody likes to be left out of a conversation, and we certainly don't want to get *that* one mad.

"*Bueno.* Here is the story. Last year, we visited a town on the coast of Java. As their town was being sacked, Buddhist monks residing therein succeeded in making off with an enormous statue of great worth—the Golden Buddha. They got it on a ship and were bound away, their sacred idol safe, they thought. Alas, they were wrong, as they were soon overtaken by the *Divine Wind.* Seeing that their efforts were in vain, the would-be rescuers of the Buddha threw him

467

overboard and, in true Buddist monk tradition, all the monks threw themselves in after it to perish. I think they were smart to do that, as Cheng Shih was furious and she would have had them all killed in horrible ways. Attempts were made to raise the Buddha but all proved fruitless. It was just too deep—at least thirty-five fathoms down. Several divers died trying to get down to the statue, and others refused to go. Cheng Shih eventually gave up on it, but did mark the spot with bearings and buoys, and then she sailed off, fuming. She is still angry now. After all, it's a very valuable prize—solid gold and studded with jewels, and all that."

The painting is dry enough now to resume work. I pick up the thinnest of the brushes and begin tightening up the forms, firming up the overall structure and putting in the details. All the while I am thinking . . .

There it is . . . a way to free myself, free Jaimy, and get my Lorelei *back. Now, just how to present it to Cheng Shih . . .*

I blot the last strokes and hold the painting up to Cheng Shih. She clasps her hands in delight. To while away the afternoon, I take out my pennywhistle and begin on "The Sally Gardens," to lend Cheng Shih some enjoyment and to calm my churning mind.

In bed this night, with Cheng Shih lying beside me asleep, I think on my plan and go over it and over it in my head. Tomorrow, I will present it to her.

Wish us luck, Jaimy . . .

Chapter 60

Hai!

Her sword comes whipping out of its sheath and slashes down toward my head. I reach back with both hands and grasp the hilt of my own sword and barely get it out in time to parry her attack.

We are on the main deck of the *Divine Wind*.

She smiles and withdraws her blade, slowly circling around me, the tip of her sword describing small circles in the air. She looks for an opening, then . . .

Hai!

Leaping in the air, she strikes. I do not get my own sword around in time and she lays her blade against my neck.

"Xian! Hao!"

She laughs and returns her sword to the scabbard that is strapped to her back. I ruefully sheathe mine, too. In this particular discipline of Oriental sword fighting, the object is to draw your sword, strike, and then resheathe in one fluid motion as your opponent slumps to the ground in a pool of his own blood. It is very elegant to see, but very difficult to do.

I bow low to her in defeat.

"She has just complimented you on how well you are coming along," says Brother Arcangelo.

"*Doh je, zhong ai de Shih,*" I say, bowing low. Then I take a deep breath and say, "I have a request to make, Beloved Shih. Please. In your cabin."

The priest, looking a bit perplexed, passes it on. Cheng Shih looks at me, nods, and strides off. I do *not* think she is pleased. I follow her to the cabin.

Once there, she sits on her cushion and signals to Chi-chi for a cup of wine. *One* cup of wine, not two.

Uh-oh . . .

I immediately fall to my knees and put my forehead to the floor at her feet and begin to speak.

"Beloved One, I thank you for all the love you have shown me, an uninvited barbarian, since first I came here. I arrived, intending to do your ship harm, and yet you took me in and treated me with kindness . . ."

Brother Arcangelo drones on behind me, translating my words.

". . . and now I want to ask of you a favor, one that is well within your power to grant. And if you grant me that favor, I will bring up your Golden Buddha for you."

That gets everybody's attention, for sure.

She reaches out her foot and puts her toe under my chin to lift my face. I take this to mean I can sit back on my haunches. I do it and continue.

"You see, there are two British ships out on the China Sea, probably very near here . . ."

Cheng Shih says something very tersely at this and Brother Arcangelo informs me, "Yes, she has scout ships out and she has heard of these."

"Good. You see, one of the ships, my *Lorelei Lee*, has a . . . device . . . on it that will allow me to go down to get the Golden Buddha."

There is sharp intake of female Chinese breath on this.

"It is on the very ship you attacked on the day I came aboard the *Divine Wind*. You already know that vessel is very well armed—I know because I armed her—and if you were to attack straight on, there would be much bloodshed on both sides, and I have many dear friends on that boat as well as on this one. Plus, in a heated exchange, the ship might well go to the bottom and the device would be lost and you would never, ever, bring up the Golden Buddha."

"So how is it to be done, gaining this magic machine?" she asks, doubt plain in her voice. From her tone, I know what she says, even without Brother Arcangelo's translation.

I scooch over next to her, pressing my advantage.

"There is another British ship out there, a convict ship, that carries no gunnery—it is the *Cerberus* and is but a simple convict ship bound for South Australia and is completely helpless." I let that sink in and then continue. "However, the two are known to each other, and if you were to take the unarmed ship, the *Cerberus*, first, we could fill it with your men in disguise and come up next to the unsuspecting *Lorelei Lee*, in the guise of friendship, throw over the hooks, and take her, with little or no bloodshed." *I hope no bloodshed . . .*

Cheng Shih fixes me with a shrewd look and speaks.

"She wishes to know what shall be your reward for this?" says Brother Arcangelo, looking like he'd like to know the answer, too.

I put my forehead to the deck and and begin my plea.

"Beloved Shih, there is a young man held captive on the *Cerberus* along with many of my friends. He and I were pledged to be married but cruel injustice pulled us apart, and I want him back so much, so very, very much . . ."

Cheng Shih's eyes narrow.

"Yes. Go on," murmurs Brother Arcangelo.

My eyes are tearing up now, but I gulp and press on.

"If I succeed in bringing up the Golden Buddha for you, will you give me back my ship and my young man and . . . let us go?"

The tears are coming on strong now as I lift my face to hers.

"Please, dear one. You have your ship . . . I just want mine. I love you, Beloved Shih, but . . . but . . . I want to be with my people . . . with my man, my friends, and with my ship. You have shown me that you have affection for my poor self. If you could grant this wish—"

Cheng Shih gets to her feet and stares down at me. She spits a few clipped words to Brother Arcangelo, and then turns her back on me and stalks off toward her cabin. On the way, she calls out something to Cheng Pao, standing on the quarterdeck. He in turn bellows out an order and men fly up into the yards and the rudder is put over. We are changing course.

Brother Arcangelo gives me his hand and lifts me off my knees.

"He is turning in the likely direction of those ships. He will send out scout ships. It will not be long till they find them," he says. "Cheng Shih agrees to take those ships, and if you manage to bring up the Buddha with that wonderful device, she will free your lad"—here he pauses—"but she said nothing about letting *you* go."

Oh.

I follow her and stand outside her door. I give a light tap, but I am not admitted. No, I am forced to stand there for at least an hour.

Then the door suddenly flies open and Cheng Shih's hand shoots out and grabs me by the wrist and yanks me in. Her face is stormy, and in her other hand she holds a thin, whippy switch.

Uh-oh . . .

She points to the deck and snarls, *"Fu! Dai niu!"*

I drop to my knees before her. She puts her hand on my neck, forcing my upper body down, leaving my rump in the air.

Target in position, she strikes . . .

Yeeow!

Once, twice, and yet again. I howl out in pain.

"Please, Beloved Shih! Yeoow! Oh, God, it hurts! Please stop!"

She stops all right, but not before she's given me an even dozen and my shrieks are heard from one end of the *Divine Wind* to the other. The thin silk trousers provide my poor tail no protection at all.

When it's over and I lie bawling in a corner, she stands over me, wagging her finger and spewing out a long diatribe, detailing no doubt the shortcomings of my unworthy, ungrateful, unfaithful self.

I lie there weeping for a good long time, but eventually Chi-chi brings in lunch and Cheng Shih relents and calls me again to her side, and it is she who gently applies a cool ointment to the red marks on my poor abused bum.

It doesn't look like she'll let me go, Jaimy, but at least you shall be freed and that will give me great joy . . . wherever I might be in this world . . .

Please be safe . . . Soon, Jaimy, soon . . .

Chapter 61

James Fletcher
Captain of the Wretched Cerberus
Still Becalmed

Jacky Faber
Most probably in New South Wales
Australia

Dear Jacky,

Yes, we are still virtually becalmed, ghosting along on the slightest of breezes, our sails hanging slack. We desperately need fresh water and food, as well as armament. I hate sitting here helpless, knowing that if the Dart shows up again we will be taken, and all that we have fought for will be lost.

At least I now have paper and pen with which to record my thoughts in case one day you should want to read them.

The convicts grow more restive by the day. All the trustworthy ones have been released from confinement, for there is much nasty work to be done in caring for the basic needs of said convicts. It might bring a smile to your face to know that we have the Weasel here—yes, old Weisling from the *Wolverine*—and we put him to the absolutely worst tasks. Serves him right. He was one of our guards before we revolted and escaped our confinement, and he was unspeakably vile in that position, but he is paying for it now.

At least we have not yet had an outbreak of typhus, thank God, but it is only a matter of time if our condition does not improve. For once, dear one, I do not wish you were here by my side, for if the gaol fever does come, then I would fear for your—

I must put down my pen for a moment, for Padraic has put in his head to announce that there is a ship out on the horizon, coming toward us. More later . . .

I must write in great haste now, Jacky, as that ship, a huge Chinese vessel, is bearing down on us fast. They have no more wind than we, but they have put out their long sweeps and are rowing ever closer to us. We have no such oars. I go now to see that the men are armed as well as we can be, for we are sure to be boarded. I am afraid it will be just swords and cutlasses, but we will make a fight of it.

This might well be my last message to you, Jacky. It is my most fervent hope that you have a long and happy life. Please remember me as one who did love you.

With Love,

Jaimy

Chapter 62

The *Cerberus* lies ahead, bobbing in the slick swells, its sails hanging slack. I am crouched by the rail of the *Divine Wind,* hidden from view of any onboard that ship, as we are rowed ever closer. It has been decided that I will stay hidden in case that miserable Captain Griswold should spot me with his long glass and remember me. I am sure anxious eyes are upon us. I have certainly got my own glass trained on their quarterdeck. I see figures in navy blue jackets moving about, but I cannot yet make out individual faces. I do, however, see the flash of steel in their hands.

Cheng Shih, every inch a commodore in complete command of her fleet, stands next to me as does Brother Arcangelo. Cheng Pao, looking fierce, stands in front of his horde of howling swordsmen, ready to swarm aboard. It did not take long for the *Divine Wind*'s small, fast scout ships to find the hapless ship, and now she lies before us, easy prey.

I put down my long glass to give my eye a rest. I am nervous, of course, and hope that all goes well. I tell myself that Jaimy will be below with the rest of the convicts, so he should be out of danger. I cannot spare too much sympathy for Griswold and his crew, not after the way they treated Jaimy . . . and Mairead . . . and me . . . so, if they suffer, so be it. I am dressed for battle in a very nice bottle-green tunic and matching trousers. All silk, of course, with gold thread, and a golden dragon now adorns my own back . . . and oh, yes, my neck as well . . .

It was the morning after the switching of my somewhat innocent tail, when, as I was out of the bath and into my robe, Chi-chi came into the bathhouse bearing a tray that held what I saw to be thimble-sized bowls of intense color . . .

What . . . ?

. . . and a needle.

Uh-oh . . .

He was accompanied by Brother Arcangelo.

"What's going on?" I asked of the priest.

"Cheng Shih has ordered it," he replied. "Do not worry. It will not hurt much. Chi-chi is quite expert, I am told. Please pull your hair to the side, Signorina, so that he might work."

I take my hair and lift it and place it on my shoulder, exposing my neck and . . .

Yeeouch . . . !

It is true, Chi-chi is good at his job and it was soon done. With a skillful positioning of two handheld mirrors, I was able to admire his handiwork.

It is quite handsome—a golden dragon on a field of green with black detailing and some red in the claws and fiery breath. 'Course I thought it might be better presented on a flag or a picture, rather than on my neck, but, hey, so it goes . . . My hair, when let down, will cover it anyway.

"So that means she owns me, Brother?" I asked, somewhat sullenly.

"Well, yes, I suppose," he replied. "But it also means she is extending to you her protection, which, in this part of the world, is no small thing."

"All right," said I, twisting my neck and admiring my new tattoo, "then I shall look on it as such."

My sword is strapped across my shoulders, and I find its presence and the feel of its snug harness reassuring, even though Cheng Shih has forbidden me to go over in the first wave of boarders.

Cheng Shih is dressed in an identical outfit. She has forgiven me, but she has not mentioned my petiton for release since the day I broached the subject with disastrous consequences for my backside. I don't mention it again.

Our rowers are expertly bringing us in on the starboard side of the *Cerberus*, and I again bring the glass to my eye. *Damn.* The convict ship's spanker hangs down on the stern, obscuring the quarterdeck, so I cannot see those upon it. We are very close now, less than twenty yards and closing.

The *Cerberus* rolls over a swell and the spanker swings to the port side, exposing those on the quarterdeck. I give it another look and focus on the blue jacket who seems to be in charge.

Wait a minute . . . That's not their Captain . . .

Oh, my God! It's Jaimy . . . and there's Ian . . . and the others! They must have mutinied! They'll be slaughtered!

I gasp and jump to my feet.

"Cheng Shih! The command on that ship has changed! I must go over first, alone, or there will be great bloodshed!"

Brother Arcangelo quickly translates. She looks dubious. The hooks are ready to be thrown.

"Please trust me! I'll . . . I'll stay with you forever, Beloved Shih!"

She fixes her gaze upon me, then nods curtly. I turn and dart to the head of the boarding party and stand in front of Cheng Pao as the ship's sides meet.

I leap over the rail and run up to Jaimy.

"Oh, Jai—" I begin, overcome with joy at seeing him.

But he does not see me. Oh, no. What he sees before him on his deck is a pigtailed Chinese pirate in strange garb with a shaved head and a sword on his back.

"Damn you to hell, you heathen son of a bitch!" he yells, and swings his sword at my neck.

Without thinking, I reach back with both hands and grasp the hilt of my sword and whip out my blade. I barely get it up in time to stop his deadly swing.

The swords clang together, hilt to hilt, and I hiss, "Jaimy! It's me! Jacky!"

His wild eyes try to focus on mine.

"What . . . ?" he asks, amazed.

"Jaimy! Yes, it is me! You've got to put down your sword. Come on, Jaimy," I plead. "You're stronger than I, and I can't hold you off much longer!" My arms are beginning to quiver under the strain of keeping his blade from my neck.

Recognition dawns and I feel the fighting spirit ebbing from him. He realizes that it is, indeed, me.

"Ah, Jacky, what the hell now."

"Sheathe your sword, Jaimy—your life depends on it!" I step back and whip my own sword into its scabbard. In exasperation, he flings his to the deck.

"All of you! Put your weapons away!" I shout to the others standing about. "There are maybe twenty of you and a thousand of us . . . er . . . them! You have no chance!"

I feel Cheng Shih come up next to me and stand silently.

"This is Cheng Shih. She is the commander of these ships and many more. She is not here to take you or to kill you. We have a bargain. You will benefit! Ian! Padraic! Sheathe your swords! Now!"

Ah, good. They are doing it.

"Now, bow down low. Be respectful. Easy now."

I look over at Arthur McBride. He is not bowing down. No, he is standing there grinning at me as if he were watching some comedy instead of just being delivered from certain death.

"Arthur! Damn you! Bow down to her!"

With a smirk, he does it.

Jaimy steps toward me, and I step back.

"Don't come any closer to me, Jaimy," I say. "Please. I beg you. This is Cheng Shih. She is the Admiral of this fleet. I . . . I am her . . . pet. She is very possessive of me, Jaimy, and she is very dangerous, so be very, very careful."

Cheng Shih has come up by my side and is eyeing Jaimy very suspiciously. She knows who he is and what he means to me. *Be very careful, Jaimy, she could have her sword out and at your neck before you could even blink.*

Brother Arcangelo is translating all that is said, as well he must. I just hope he's putting the best gloss he can upon it.

"You are her 'pet'?" asks Jaimy, perplexed. "What does that mean?"

McBride's grin only gets wider.

It means I get petted a lot, Jaimy. Now hush!

"Not now, Jaimy," is what I say to the confused lad. I generally revel in astounding Jaimy, but not just now. "We have bigger things to discuss. We must have a parley and I think refreshments would be in order."

Brother Arcangelo comes up and whispers in my ear and I nod.

"Captain Fletcher, Admiral Cheng Shih invites you and your officers aboard her ship to talk about our plans. As you are not captives, you may keep your swords," I say. *Fat lot of good they'll do you should you draw them over there, but nobody knows like the Chinese how face must be saved—even the face of a smelly barbarian. I choose not to inform you that the Chinese do not like being on your ship because it stinks too much.*

"Bring a bottle of Madeira if you have it," I say, following Cheng Shih back onto her ship. My own nose is offended by the smell of the *Cerberus*. Hmmm . . . Perhaps I am turning Chinese . . .

A low table is set on the deck of the *Divine Wind,* and we array ourselves around it—Cheng Shih on a cushion at the head, with me beside her on the deck, my legs pulled up under me. Jaimy is at the foot of the table, with Arthur McBride and Ian McConnaughey to one side and Padraic Delaney to the other. They sit cross-legged on the deck and I know they are uncomfortable, but so be it . . . and it is so *good* to see them all!

Cheng Pao stands to the side, his mighty arms crossed on his chest, making it plain he does not sit at the same table as barbarians.

A young Irish-looking boy bounds onto the deck of the junk, looking wildly excited—and well you should, lad. You would never find this kind of exotic adventure back in Limerick. He carries stemmed glasses and pours out the wine, placing the first in front of Shih, then one before each of the rest of the company.

Cheng Shih does not reach for hers and I know why. I reach for it instead, and put it to my lips to sample it. *Yummm, it is very good.*

In Europe, this would be a breach of etiquette, but not here. One does not become a pirate queen by allowing herself to be poisoned.

I offer the glass, proven to be unpoisoned, to our hostess. "Here, Beloved Shih, taste it. It is from the barbarian lands, but it is very good."

She smiles and takes the wineglass, looks at its curious—to her—shape, and takes a sip. She smiles and nods, and takes this opportunity to stroke the back of my neck and pull me to her. She puts a light kiss on my forehead. I do *not* look over at Jaimy.

Then she says, "*Siu.*"

I begin . . .

I tell the lads of the Golden Buddha, of the bargain I have struck with Cheng Shih, how we will use the *Cerberus* to sneak up on the *Lorelei Lee* and take her, then use the diving bell that rests in her bilges to raise the golden statue. The Golden Buddha will bring such great pleasure to Beloved Shih that she will allow all of them to go free and be on their way. I tell them of how we on the *Lorelei Lee* had been so kindly treated by our dear Captain Laughton and how sad we were at his death. Then I recount the reign of terror that

Ruger had instituted after our poor dear Captain had died and he had taken control . . .

Then, I must tell it. . . . All this time, Ian McConnaughey has been looking at me, imploring me with his eyes . . . *Tell me of my Mairead!*

I beckon for him to come up and sit beside me. Shih looks at me with question in her dark eyes, but does not interfere.

When he settles in, I take his hand and say, "Ian, I must tell you this . . ." and tears come from my eyes, and he looks stricken. "No, no, I am sorry, no . . . Your Mairead is well, but . . ."

Then I proceed to tell him of Ruger's vicious attack upon his girl and the loss of her . . . and his . . . baby.

His face turns ashen, then hardens.

"Ian, I know," I whisper. "I know . . ."

But then Cheng Shih reaches out her hand and says something . . . and Brother Arcangelo Rossetti translates it for her into the English that Ian will understand.

"Know this, young foreign man, when the time comes, it is you who will kill him. I promise it!"

Chapter 63

"How does that feel, Jaimy?" I ask, massaging the muscles of the back of his neck. We are in the washroom of the *Divine Wind* and Jaimy is in the tub. I kneel by the side if it, having just finished washing and rinsing his hair. When it's wet, the white streak in his glossy dark mane stands out all the more bright and sharp.

His lovely eyes are closed. He does not reply, but only gives out a low animal moan of pleasure. I believe that all thoughts of violent mutinies, troublesome Royal Navy escorts, and unruly Irish crew members are erased, for the moment, from his now relaxed and easy mind.

Cheng Shih has allowed me to do this—under the merry but watchful eyes of her faithful Chi-chi. I'm sure he has been ordered to make certain we don't end up doing anything too frisky.

In the days since we took the *Cerberus,* we have had each of her officers over for a bath, while their uniforms are taken off to be cleaned, as they are rather rank, especially to my newly tuned nose.

Ah, yes. I am, indeed, becoming Chinese in that way.

Ian McConnaughey submits to being put in the tub and having his head scrubbed by Chi-chi, Ian's mind being on other, more vengeful things. However, when Arthur McBride's turn comes, he demands girls to do the job, and several are found onboard the *Divine Wind*—in the laundry, the storerooms, the usual places where one finds girls on any ship—and given new duties.

Grinning broadly, and aided by his new, giggling female attendants, McBride drops clothing and climbs into the tub, lighting his pipe and leaning back in complete piggish male contentment. All the Chinese are very curious about the tobacco he uses, having never seen the vile weed before, and McBride is generous in passing out Captain Griswold's considerable stash of the stuff. Pipes are loaded, packed, and lit, and soon many of the Chinese who partake of this treat are sick, throwing up over the side. But others continue to smoke the stuff.

One time I had gone into the washhouse with Chi-chi to carry in more towels and such and I found Arthur within. I have this image, which shall stay with me always, of Arthur McBride in the tub with his two big feet propped over the side, a dreamy expression on his face, two giggling girls on either side soaping him up, and his popping open an eye and saying, "Ah, 'tis our own dear girl, herself, appearin' out of the mist. Come over here, Jacky Faber. Drop yer silken garb and please to slip in here beside me now."

I did *not* accede to the rascal's request.

When Jaimy is off the *Cerberus*, Ian McConnaughey takes command, and I know he is bending on every scrap of canvas possible to get to his Mairead . . . and to Ruger . . . as quickly as he can. The doldrums have lifted and all ships plow along at a nice clip.

"Chi-chi, the eucalyptus oil, please," I say, reaching out my hand toward the bottle. He does not have to know the language to catch my meaning, and he places the jar in my hand. Chi-chi, I'm finding, is quite bright, and I'm learning elemental Chinese from him. Surprisingly, he is also literate and can read and write the complex calligraphy of their language. I guess nothing but the best in the way of eunuchs will do for the mighty Cheng Shih.

Taking the bottle, I pour some of the liquid onto my hand and then apply it to Jaimy's back. I put down the bottle and begin massaging the oil into his muscles.

"You like, Mr. Pretty Barbarian Man, Sir?" I croon in a high singsong voice. "You like when Jak-ki cow-child move fingers like this? Or like this? No? Yes? No?"

He laughs and reaches around and takes me by the wrist.

"Yes, Jacky, cow-child, I like it very much. Now give your barbarian a kiss."

Well, we cannot do that, sweet barbarian . . . Chi-chi would see and report. But we will do this . . .

I know that I'm risking a switching for this, but I say, "Make room, Jaimy," and I loosen the ties of my robe, slip it off, and drop it into Chi-chi's hands. A quick leg over the edge of the tub and I slide my own slippery self in next to Jaimy.

Ummmm . . .

"Sort of like our lovely hammock back on the dear old *Dolphin*, eh, Jay-mee?" is what I say, snuggling into his side. "'Cept it's a little more wet."

"It is that, Jacky." He laughs, his breath coming a bit fast. "We only lack Davy standing over us, calling us a pair of sodomites."

Recalling that magical time in our youth, when we were just kids on a wounded British frigate, cast adrift with not much of a future to hope for, I sigh and trace my finger down through the center of his brow, down his nose, over his lips and chin, and down to his throat.

"Mmm, it's so good to be here beside you, love," I murmer, luxuriating in the warmth of the water and the feel of his body here next to mine.

Oh, yes, Lord, thank you for this gift . . .

He in turn lifts his own right hand and places it on the part of my head that is bald and leaves it there.

I have noticed that whenever my head has been shorn, various males of my acquaintance seem compelled to place the palms of their hands upon my bare skull, and I think I know why . . .

"Yes, Jaimy, I know what you are thinking . . . and believe it or not, it is true. Under your hand is a mind, a person, a brain. I know it is sometimes hard for you to believe that, but it is true. And that which is under your hand loves you very much."

With that, I squirm around and place myself between his legs, my back toward him. Taking the bottle of bath oil from Chi-chi, I hand it to Jaimy, saying, "My turn now, dear one."

He applies the fragrant oil to my back and rubs it in with his long, strong fingers, and I moan with pleasure at his touch.

Purrrrrrr . . .

"Oh, yes, right there, Jaimy. Oh, yes, that is so nice . . . so nice . . ."

After several moments of exquisite pleasure, I feel him move my pigtail to the side and *uh-oh . . . back to reality . . .* as I know he is looking at the new addition to my bodily splendor.

"What is this, then?" he asks.

"It is the mark of Cheng Shih," I say. "The Mark of the Golden Dragon."

"So you are her slave, then?"

He has tensed up—I can feel it.

"No, Jaimy, it just means that she has . . . given me her protection."

He is silent, and he has stopped massaging my back.

"Will you be with her again, tonight?" he finally asks.

I sigh and say, "Yes, Jaimy, I will."

Another silence . . . then . . .

"You have made yet another bargain for my safety, haven't you, Jacky?"

I don't reply for a moment, then I reach back and pull his arms around me, across my chest, and push myself back against him.

"Jaimy, love, you must learn to live in the moment. We must take what we can get in this world."

"But . . ."

I wriggle my bum a bit. That should ease his mind a tad.

"Look, Jaimy, in this case, she is justified. I did try to burn down her ship. By rights she should have killed me. And she did not."

"Because she wanted to . . . use you."

I whip around in the bath to face him.

"*Use me?*" I ask. "Just how does she use me, Mr. James Emerson Fletcher, Man-of-the-World-Who-Knows-Everything-There-Is-to-Know? Hmmm?"

He looks off, uneasy, and says, "You know . . ."

Uh-oh . . . The male mind must be set at ease.

"No, I *don't* know." I put my palms to either side of his face and look into his eyes and say with all sincerity, "Believe me, Jaimy, Chinese women are very reserved and very . . . shy about some things." *A lot more shy than a certain Mam'selle Claudelle de Bourbon back in New Orleans, that's for sure.* "And she might look like a heathen devil, but to me she is very kind." *Mostly,* I'm thinking, remembering that switch. "And very proper, too. Now just pet me, Jaimy, and put everything else out of your mind."

I turn around again and feel his strong hands on my back.

Oh, yes, Jaimy, just like that . . .

I lean back against him and feel his arms encircle me again . . .

Ummmmm . . .

No, we did not come together as one in that lovely tub, James Fletcher and I. That would have been awkward and probably gotten the both of us beheaded. No, when I go to the marriage bed, be it legal or not, I want it to be made up with the finest silk sheets on a day that is perfectly beautiful, with the windows open and a gentle breeze blowing and the birds outside singing a glorious song. That's what I want for *that* day.

On *this* day, however . . .

The door bursts open and Ravi rushes in.

"Missy Memsahib! Come quick. We have found our dear ship!"

Chapter 64

Once again I am crouched, hidden behind the main hatch of the *Cerberus* as we approach the unwary *Lorelei Lee*. Except this time, it is Jaimy who stands up on the quarterdeck as I lie here below with my Chinese cohorts, ready to spring. Our boarding party lies out of sight of those on the *Lorelei Lee*—me, Cheng Pao, and a dozen of his best swordsmen, and Cheng Shih. We will board the *Lee* in that order, right behind Ian McConnaughey, who stands ready at the port rail of the *Cerberus*. The *Divine Wind* lies over the horizon, with other ships of Cheng Shih's fleet. We are arranged such that I might point out Ruger to Ian and possibly talk the other officers out of a pointless fight—I would hate to see them hurt.

Oh, yes, and there are some one hundred Chinese swordsmen down below decks as backup. I hope they will not be needed.

"Two thousand yards," says Jaimy, up near the wheel, splendid in his clean blue Royal Navy jacket, his glass to his eye. *Ah, how good to hear his voice.*

So, knees up, rump on deck, back against the hatch, sword across my back, I wait . . . and hark back to our lovely bath this morning . . .

I had turned again in the bath. "What is . . . or was . . . your plan, dear?" I asked as I lay my head back against his shoulder. "After you so heroically took over the *Cerberus*?"

"My plan? It was to arm my ship at Batavia, get down to New South Wales, offload that stinking mob of worthless convicts, collect the head price on each of them, then get the hell out of there to come looking for you. That was my plan . . . Till you and your heathen horde came along."

"The head price?"

"Yes. The ten pounds six bounty paid for any convict delivered alive."

"But how—"

"Captain Bligh, the governor of the penal colony, has never met Captain Griswold. I planned to stand in for him and take the reward."

I twist around again, sloshing water to the deck, and grasp him by the shoulders, looking into those beautiful gray eyes. "Why, Jaimy," I say, giving him my best, delighted open-mouthed grin. "That is a scam worthy even of me! I am so very proud of you!" Then I hug him to me. "So romantic—the fearsome pirate Captain Jaimy Fletcher, the Scourge of the South China Sea, come lookin' for his lady love, lost somewhere on the great rolling sea!"

Jaimy gives out with a gentlemanly snort. "Some fearsome pirate—a tub of a ship without a single gun."

"Well, you did look rather romantically piratical the

other day, your face a mask of menace, your mighty sword raised above my poor head."

"To think I tried to kill you back then, not knowing . . ."

"Aw, go on wi' ye, Jaimy," I say, giving him an underwater elbow and a quick kiss on his cheek, knowing full well how he dislikes it when I put on the Cockney accent. "And, luv, ye didn't even come half close to splittin' me poor bald noggin!"

He laughs, placing his hand once again upon that bald head.

"And Higgins, now," says Jaimy, looking off. "How goes he?"

Hmmmm . . . He must have heard . . .

I pull away from him a bit, put my finger on his nose, and look him in the eye.

"You are my own true love, Jaimy, and I mean that with all my heart and soul, but John Higgins is my best friend in this world and if—"

He laughs and pulls me to him. "Do not worry, dear one, I could never be jealous of our good John Higgins, no matter what."

I think to give him my "In spite of what all has gone on, I am yet a maiden" speech, but, no, I do not. He must take me as I am, or not take me at all.

"Well, good," I say nestling my face into that spot where his neck meets his shoulder.

He is silent for a bit, plainly musing about something. Then he asks, "Why do you think the Dragon Lady is so . . . taken with you?"

I ponder this, then reply, "I think she finds me . . . fascinating . . . because of the way I look—my hair, my skin, and all. She calls me her Golden Child when she is in a good mood. She calls me Little Round-Eyed Barbarian at other times because, I suppose, my eyes are not slanted like hers or any other Chinese woman's eyes. And because I *am* a barbarian, from her point of view. She seems intrigued by accounts of my exploits—it is plain that Chinese women do not generally act as I do."

"Nor most English women," says Jaimy with a bit of a laugh.

I give him another poke with my elbow and signal Chi-chi, who comes over with another pitcher of hot water and pours it in.

"Ahhhhh . . ."

"I am what I am, Jaimy," I say, luxuriating in the warmth and the closeness of his body. "Maybe Cheng Shih sees a little bit of herself in me. I don't know . . ." Then I give out a low chuckle. "Just wait till she gets a look at the *Lorelei Lee*'s figurehead when we catch her. Ha. You, too."

"What do you mean?"

"Never mind, dear one. Now, where were we? Oh, yes . . ."

Ummmmmmm . . .

I did not get switched today for my conduct in that tub—nay, just a very stern look from Cheng Shih. My robe wrapped around me, I threw my nose in the air, put on a partial Lawson Peabody School for Young Girls Look, and she let me get away with it . . . for now . . .

That was this morning. This is now—and now we must all, whether we be Chinese, Irish, or Brit, take the *Lorelei Lee.*

"One thousand yards," says Jaimy.

By his side is Padraic Delaney, looking noble, and Arthur McBride stands there, too, looking down at me. I had heard that Jaimy had given him a good thrashing when he took over the *Cerberus*, but it's plain that the lad never learns.

"Five hundred yards," comes the countdown from the quarterdeck. The *Lee* looms closer.

I look down at my shiv, once again tucked in my belt. Jaimy gave it back to me yesterday, saying he and the Irish lads could not have accomplished their escape from the hideous hold of the *Cerberus* without that blade. I don't doubt it. The cock's head I had carved on the handle those many years ago looks up at me as if to say, *How many more notches in me now, Jacky, me lass? How many dead men on a poor shiv's hilt?*

Be quiet, you, is what I say, shoving him down deeper into my belt, his face against my belly, shutting him up.

"One hundred . . . Prepare to board."

I wait . . . wait . . . wait . . .

And when I hear the thump of the sides meeting, I jump up and shout, *"NOW GIVE ME BACK MY GOD-DAMN SHIP!"*

Ian is already over the rail as I lope along his side. There, on the quarterdeck, stand Mr. Seabrook and Mr. Gibson, both wearing expressions of extreme shock. They had expected a simple gam twixt two English vessels, and what they get is a swarm of Chinese pirates bent on their destruction—that, and one very angry Irishman.

"Wait! All of you!" I cry. "Seabrook! Gibson! Put down your arms! There are just too many of them! You cannot win! You will not be harmed! I am your own Jacky Faber and I promise you this!"

They stand immobile, unable to move. Then their drawn swords point down to the deck. They know that they are lost.

"Which one, Jacky?" asks Ian at my side, his voice cold.

There is one who has not lowered his sword and it is Ruger. He stands, his sword in his fist, his eyes wild. He had expected a gam with Captain Griswold of the *Cerberus*, further expecting, I know, to be able to trade some of his female cargo for money, whiskey, or who knows what—the same trade Captain Laughton had refused all those weeks ago. *Well, it ain't gonna happen, Ruger. You will get something else, you cur.*

"That one there," I say, reaching back and whipping out my sword and pointing it at Ruger.

"You," says Ruger, fixing his eye on me. "No . . . not again . . ."

But he need not be concerned with me. Ian McConnaughey steps up and puts his sword in Ruger's face. "You dared to put your hand on my girl."

Ruger, realizing his peril, retreats a step, and then swings his sword wildly at Ian's head. Ian easily parries the blow, bringing his own blade back and then slipping it into Ruger's belly.

Ruger drops his sword and sinks to his knees and hangs his head, sobbing, "Mercy . . . please . . ."

"Ian! Dear husband!"

Both Ian and I look over to the hatchway and see Mairead standing there, her arms out.

Ian steps away from Ruger, his anger spent, and Cheng Pao, taking this as a signal to end things quickly, whips out his sword and swings it, taking Ruger's head off in one clean stroke. The sword goes back in Pao's scabbard before Ruger's head hits the deck.

All is silence. I feel Cheng Shih come up next to me, and I know I am expected to do something . . . and I do it.

Ruger's head lies at my feet. The eyes blink once, then cloud over. I resheathe my sword, then lean down to grab a fistful of hair and lift up the head. It is surprisingly heavy, but I carry it over and present it, dripping, to Mairead.

"Blood for blood, Sister," is all I say. I feel Cheng Shih's arm come circling around my waist, making me steady.

Mairead nods. "Blood for blood."

Then I throw the vile thing over the side and she runs to her man and wraps her arms about him.

Blood for blood, indeed . . .

Chapter 65

Once the last trace of the hated and hateful Ruger has gone over the side, I leap to my quarterdeck and put one foot to either side of the centerline, just the way I like it, the better to feel the movement of my glorious ship. *Oh Lorelei, I thought never to see you again!* Then full of pure joy, I lift my voice.

"This is Captain Faber . . . *oh yes it is!* And I have the con. Mr. Seabrook, you are now my First Mate and you are relieved of this watch."

He looks about him at the crowd of heavily armed Chinese that has just swarmed aboard, and nods. He shrugs and says, "Captain . . . uh, Faber, indeed, has the con."

And, oh! It feels so good!

"All topmen aloft to make sail!" I bellow, bouncing up and down on my toes. "Right full rudder! Helmsman, follow that junk!"

The *Divine Wind* had been signaled after the *Lorelei Lee* was secured, and she has joined us, pulling to the head of the formation, with the *Cerberus* and the *Lee,* side by side, behind her. We have been joined by another ten of Cheng

Shih's ships, which fall in aft and to either side. Nobody's going to mess with her fleet, that's for sure . . . least of all, us.

I am still sucking in great gulps of glorious free air when I hear . . .

"Welcome back, Miss," says my dear, dear Higgins, joining me on the quarterdeck. "Lovely outfit, quite exotic—and your hair . . . Well, what can I say?"

"Good to see you, too, Higgins," I say, my face beaming out my joy at seeing him again. I take him by the arms, go on tiptoes, and plant a good one on his cheek.

"Umm, I must say, Miss, that in spite of my usual optimism concerning the state of your health when you have gone missing, this time I rather despaired of ever seeing you again. In this world, anyway."

And can you be misting up a little, Higgins, even you?

"Ah, well, Higgins, you have seen that I do have a way of bobbing back up," I say, snorting back a tear of my own. "Sort of like a cork."

"Indeed, Miss. Ah . . . do I see your Mr. Fletcher standing on that deck over there?"

I look over to see Jaimy standing on the quarterdeck of his ship.

"Yes, you do, Husband."

"Hmmm. Well, I certainly wish him the joy of his command, and since he is here, I believe I must regretfully give up my wife," he says, musing. "And since we are very near some Muslim lands, I believe I will use their method in solving this particular marital problem."

He places his hand on my smooth forehead and intones, "I divorce thee, I divorce thee, I divorce thee. There, it is done."

"So I'm a single girl again?"

"Just so, Miss."

"Thank you, Higgins. I did enjoy being wife to you. I hope I was a good one," I say. "Now permit me to introduce my friend and protector Admiral Cheng Shih and her translator Brother Arcangelo Rossetti, Society of Jesus."

I notice the *Divine Wind* has turned east and I give the helmsman a significant look and he understands, adjusting his course to follow in the wake of the junk. Cheng Shih is plainly wasting no time at all in getting us back to where the coveted Buddha lies.

Higgins bows low and gets a slight nod of the head from Shih and a decent bow from Brother Arcangelo, who has been translating in a low murmur ever since he came aboard. I know that she is a bit puzzled over the "husband" thing, but I'll explain later.

"Higgins, some refreshments for our guests, perhaps? In my cabin, if you would."

Higgins has miraculously managed to remove all traces of Ruger from my cabin. The windows are open, the breezes blow through the thin gauzy curtains, and there is none of his stink in the place. It's all just so lovely—*so* good to be back in my very own lovely cabin again. I fling myself across my bed and revel in my return.

The table is set by—*the Weasel? Himself? How can it be? Oh, this is so delightfully rich!* And Higgins sets out a fine spread. After asking him to arrange a meeting later with me and the officers—and with Mrs. Barnsley, Mrs. Berry, and Mrs. MacDonald—I settle in and show Cheng Shih around my cabin and show her something about our food, our drinks, and our ways. She examines all the relics I have collected in my travels—my scrimshaw, my amphora, my figurines, and such. I play my guitar for her. And my fiddle. My concertina, too. And she is pleased.

Afterward, we go back on deck and Cheng Shih and Brother Arcangelo return to the *Divine Wind*. I know that she has business to conduct with the captains of her fleet. Duty calls all of us, even Chinese pirate admirals . . . but, she will be back, I know.

As I look out over my deck, I see that Mairead, having finally unwrapped herself from her Ian, has brought up Enoch Lightner from below. He appears on Mairead's arm and holds his face up to the sun, which he cannot see, but which he can certainly feel.

"Shantyman!" I call out upon seeing him. "Sing us away to Mindanao!"

He does.

Chapter 66

Soon after we had gotten under way, bound for the resting place of the Golden Buddha, cheer returned, full force, to the decks of the *Lorelei Lee.* All the girls, Newgaters and Crews alike, were soon up from their confinement below, and the decks and ratlines were festooned with white petticoats to the wonder, I am sure, of our Chinese escorts.

Cheng Shih has forbidden any contact between my Crews and hers—the penalty being loss of ears. Pretty wise, I'm thinking. But no matter—my girls get plenty of action with the crew of the *Cerberus,* said crew being delirious with lusty joy at the marriage of our two vessels. Naughty boys. Wait'll I tell your mother, Arthur McBride. And Padraic . . . tsk, tsk . . .

Small boats steadily ply back and forth between the *Cerberus,* the *Divine Wind,* and the *Lee.*

On that first day, back in command of the *Lorelei,* I assemble the officers to tell them of my plans. But first, I meet with the Mmes. Barnsley, Berry, and MacDonald.

Higgins again sets out a nice spread, and I know the madams are pleased to finally be in the great cabin—even if I'm in it, too. They make a show of fine elegance by lifting their wineglasses, with pinkies extended, and sipping delicately from the contents, while nibbling delicately at the cakes, cheeses, and sweetmeats laid out. Ravi, dressed in full Sinbad rig, goes about refilling glasses as needed.

I put myself back in my Royal Navy Lieutenant's gear for these meetings, deeming it more appropriate than my silken dragon costumes. After all have tasted the bounty of my table, I begin . . .

"Here it is, ladies," I say, leaning back in my chair with a certain air of arrogance. "It is your choice. Do you and your girls wish to return to England, go on to the colony in New South Wales, or be put off in a random port? We are right now off the coast of Java."

I am fully aware of my appearance and position of authority, and how it must gall them to see me here, offering them terms. *Suck it up, ladies.*

Hardened veterans of Life's hard roads that they are, they do just that. The three madams consider, confer, have a lot more of my wine and foodstuffs, and then Mrs. Barnsley speaks up.

"Ain't nothing for us back in England—they'd just send us back again, and I for one am heartily sick o' the sea. And we sure don't want to be dropped off just anywheres," she says, thinking of the very fearsome-looking Chinese swordsmen who strut about our deck. "No, we'll take our chances in Australia—least we know the men there is decent British criminals." So the matter is settled.

The ladies are ushered out and the remaining officers of the former convict ship *Lorelei Lee* are invited in. I rise to meet them, knowing that this will be a very delicate meeting. I need these men, and I do not know if they will agree to serve on what they will now consider to be a pirate. We shall see.

"Good day, gentlemen," I say, as Messrs. Seabrook, Gibson, and Hinckley file in. "Please be seated and refresh yourselves." They look at me somewhat dubiously as I stand, not quite five feet of me, drawn up at attention in my naval rig—snug blue jacket with gold buttons and braid, and lace spilling out of my collar and cuffs, tight white trousers, and shiny black boots—but they go to their places and sit. I march to the head of the table and place the Faber bottom in the Captain's chair, fold my hands before me, look about at all, and begin.

"Sirs, let us speak plain and see if we can come to a common accord. I would like it very much if you gentlemen would continue in your current posts, as First, Second, and Third Mates. I value your seamanship and your ability to run a tight ship—men with such skills as yours I am sure I would not be able to find in Botany Bay, and I do not want my *Lorelei Lee* sailed by untested officers."

I pause to take a sip of my wine and to let that sink in.

"If you accept my offer, you will continue to draw your pay as employees of Faber Shipping Worldwide, as well as receive a generous share of the head money we expect to get when we deliver the convicts. If you decline my offer, you will be put ashore with said convicts to languish until such time as passage back to England can be arranged. You would be penniless, and I fear the accommodations in the prison colony might not be to your liking—very short rations, indeed."

"But what of . . . legal considerations?" asks Mr. Seabrook.

"Ah. You worry that someday you might be brought up on charges of being members of a pirate crew and party to a mutiny, as well you might. But look at it this way," I say, ready to make my case. "The *Lorelei Lee* was once mine, owned by Faber Shipping. It was then owned by the East India Company and used as a convict ship. In that capacity, she was captured by a Chinese naval force and then returned to me, in exchange for services about to be rendered."

They are attentive, and I go on.

"So you see, gentlemen, in each of those changes in ownership, *mutiny was never committed.* You are all merchant officers, not Royal Navy, and so you will simply continue to serve your ship in all honesty. Should the ship subsequently be involved in something . . . well . . . irregular, you will be held blameless. It will all be on my head."

Mr. Gibson still looks unconvinced, and I do not blame him—a man has only one neck and he hopes to never let it be caught up by the hangman's noose. "I don't know . . ." he says.

I give that a bit of thought and then say, "If you are worried about future retribution, then let us seal this pact with the traditional Pirate's Choice—join with us, stand onboard as brothers, or else walk the plank."

With that, I rise to go pick up the pistol that has been placed upon my sea chest. Coming back to the assembled company, I place the barrel next to Mr. Seabrook's temple. He starts, but does not move.

"Do you, Mr. Seabrook," I ask, "agree to follow me, else your precious life be forfeited?"

He nods. It is plain to all at the table that the pistol is not cocked. They do not know that the gun is not loaded, but I do. I go next to Mr. Gibson and point the pistol at his forehead.

"Do you, Mr. Gibson, agree to continue to serve upon the *Lorelei Lee,* upon pain of death?"

Another nod.

"And finally, young Mr. Hinckley, do you also agree to turn pirate on the salt sea and serve both me and my ship?"

"Oh yes, Miss Faber," vows the young boy enthusiastically. "I really do."

"Good," I say, lowering the pistol. "That should satisfy any Court of Inquiry. Should you someday come up on charges, you can truthfully say that you were forced at gunpoint to join the merciless La Belle Jeune Fille Sans Merci, and you will be acquitted. So. We are agreed?"

Nods all around, especially from the grinning Mr. Hinckley. *Ah lad, nothing like the promise of a little adventure, is there, young sir?*

"Very well," I say. "The matter is settled. Now this is what is going to happen. We will proceed to a spot off the coast of Mindanao, where Admiral Cheng Shih has marked a place where there is sunk a large golden statue—a Buddha, as it were. I will dive down and get that statue for her, and when I do that, Cheng Shih will release the *Cerberus* and the *Lorelei Lee.* Captain Fletcher of the *Cerberus* has already indicated his intention to deliver most of his cargo of convicts to the penal colony at New South Wales. I have spoken with the leaders of the girls upon this ship and, given several options, they elected to also go to Australia, as have my Newgaters."

I pause for breath, then continue.

"After the two human cargos have been placed on Australian soil, and the head price collected, the *Cerberus* and the *Lorelei Lee* will depart, the former under the command of Captain Fletcher, to wherever he directs her to go, and the *Lee* back to her home port of Boston, under the direction of John Higgins as Commander and Mr. Seabrook, here, as Master. This ship will then resume her duties as flagship of Faber Shipping Worldwide. Each of you gentlemen can expect to continue gainful employment in your present capacities at that firm."

"Captain Fletcher?" asks Mr. Gibson, his eyebrows raised. All here know of my connection to Jaimy.

"I am hoping that someday Mr. Fletcher will consent to sail his ship under the Blue Anchor Flag," I say primly. "But we shall see about that. Any other questions?"

"But what of you, Jacky ... er ... Miss Faber?" asks young Mr. Hinckley, with, I think, real concern in his voice.

I take a deep breath. "Do not worry about me, Mr. Hinckley. Cheng Shih has indicated that she does not want to let me go, and I did make a bargain in that regard, and so I must stay with her. Any other questions?"

"But can we not help you in that regard?" asks Mr. Gibson.

"Just look out there, Sir. There are at least twenty of Admiral Shih's ships out there, each one full of Chinamen and all armed to the teeth."

There are no further questions.

But joy and cheer does return to the *Lorelei Lee,* even if, for me, it is a bittersweet time, knowing that soon all will sail away, and I will remain. But, hey, I will abide, and I will see what happens.

Just like in the old days, when we had good Captain Laughton with us, we put on musical shows, and this time we invite our Chinese allies over to watch. Cheng Shih is especially delighted when I play my fiddle and dance at the same time, yes, that nails her pretty good . . . as does our little play "Villain Pursues Virtuous Maiden." She claps her hands in joy over that one. Brother Arcangelo tells me the play is similar to many in Chinese culture—simple plot, much overacting, broad gestures, garish costumes, some action, and a happy ending. Cheng Shih, Admiral of the South China Sea, fairly shrieked with delight, covering her mouth and collapsing in uncontrollable giggles when my tearaway dress came off.

Yes, and Ravi was reunited with Josephine and me with my Newgaters—Mary Wade, Molly, Maggie, and the rest. Ian and Mairead were given a cabin on the *Lee* and they are in it quite often. Ian does have duties other than that of making another Irish baby with Mairead, he being Jaimy's First Mate over on the *Cerberus,* but still, he manages to get over here quite a bit. I think Captain Fletcher is being kind to him in that regard.

Me, I don't get to see Jaimy at all. Ah well, I know he is busy. So am I.

Yes, we sailed, we sang, we danced, we ate, we drank, and we got to that spot off the coast of Mindanao where rests the Golden Buddha.

Chapter 67

When we came upon the buoys marking the spot, and Cheng Shih's navigators took bearings and assured us we were in the right place, I left the deck of my *Lorelei Lee* and said to Higgins, "Please, John, my swimming suit, if you please. And my goggles and fins, too."

He is not all that happy to do this. *Please be careful, Miss . . .*

Oh, bother, Higgins, you know I always am.

Soon I am rigged up to dive, and I step out onto the deck of the *Lorelei Lee.*

Cheng Shih is waiting by the diving bell, which has been placed on the deck, ready to go. Seeing me dressed as I am, she immediately orders every male to face away. The Chinese sailors do it, as they are the only ones who understand what she says.

I figure I'll do some exploratory free dives first, and so I go to the rail. Cheng Shih watches, I believe a bit fearfully, as I adjust goggles, tug down bottom of suit, and dive in.

The water is clear—not Caribbean clear, but clear enough, more green than blue—and I can see my way.

I grab one of the marker buoy lines and head down.

Hmmm . . . Nothing yet at about one hundred feet, but then I didn't expect anything. I mean, Cheng Shih would have had some pretty expert divers working on this thing. No, so back up to prepare the bell.

As the bell is being readied, there is an unlooked-for setback. From behind me I hear a thud, a cry, and a splash, and I turn to see that Chi-chi, who had been lurking nearby, attentively awaiting any order from Cheng Shih, had been struck and knocked over by the boom as it was being swung over the deck to pick up the bell. I look over the side just in time to see him and the soles of his slippered feet disappear below the surface.

I wait a second to see if any will go to his aid. None do.

Damn! At least this time I'm dressed for it. I arc myself over the rail and dive into the water.

The water, although not as clear as those blue-green Caribbean waters, is clear enough for me to see him sinking down, down, ever farther down into the depths, his pigtail sticking straight up from his head, his arms and legs thrashing about in panic.

What no sailor—be he Chinese or Brit—seems to know is that if you have a lungful of air and hold it tight within you and stop struggling, you'll bob right back up to the surface. 'Tis plain that Chi-chi, also, does not know that, for he flails away in vain, sinking ever lower.

I follow the stream of silver bubbles that leads down to him, grab his pigtail, then kick hard to bring us both back to the surface. When he hits the air, he sputters and coughs, and pukes up great quantities of saltwater. His eyes roll about wildly, but he seems all right otherwise. I get us to the ladder that's rigged on the side of the *Lorelei Lee,* and hands reach down to pull him aboard.

I expected some expressions of joy at the rescue of what has to be a valued servant, but I hear none. Instead Cheng Shih lets fly a string of Cantonese invective, pointing an accusing finger at Chi-chi, who stands there trembling, very wet and very abashed and sheepish.

Hey, it wasn't his fault, I'm thinking, getting ready to climb into the bell. *Leave the poor guy alone, for heaven's sake.* Course I don't say that to Cheng Shih, who seems right steamed.

She ends with *"Meng chi jyut! Suen ta!"*

Chi-chi bows to her and then comes to stand next to me.

"What's going on?" I ask of Brother Arcangelo. "What did she say to him?"

"She called him a stupid, ignorant, clumsy worm," he replies. "And she directed him to go to you."

"To me? Why?"

"Because, my dear but inept student of the world's philosophies," sighs the indulgent churchman, "the Chinese have a belief that if you save a person's life, you have interrupted his karma, his destiny, and are therefore responsible for him the rest of his life."

What?

"It is true, Miss. He is now your slave. Cheng Shih has given him to you."

"But I won't have it," I say, aghast. "I am against slavery in any form."

"If you refuse, they will merely throw him back in the water to complete his karmic journey to the bottom of the sea."

I throw up my hands in exasperation. I will never understand *anything*. "Let's get to diving. That's something I know about. Karma, indeed!"

I go over to the bell. Higgins, with towels at the ready, stands nearby with Ravi, regarding poor Chi-chi standing woefully next to me, then casts his eyes upward toward Josephine perched in the foretop and murmurs, "My, my, Miss, how your tribe doth increase."

I cut the ever-so-droll Mr. Higgins an evil glance and readjust my goggles.

My diving bell is hoisted off the deck and I go to get under it, but Cheng Shih grabs my hand and looks in my eyes. She seems anxious and looks dubiously at the bell with its many signal lines trailing out beneath its bottom edge.

"I'd rather have you, Golden Child, than any ten Golden Buddhas," she says. "Do not do this, dear one."

Brother Arcangelo barely finishes translating this when I squeeze her hand. "Don't worry, Beloved Shih. I will be all right. We have a bargain and I must do my part."

I plant a kiss on her cheek and give her a rakish wink.

She lets go my hand and I get under the bell and onto the seat.

Let's go.

Hello, Bell, it's been a while since we've explored together, hasn't it? Good to see you're still in fighting trim, strong of iron wall and thick of glass window, protecting my frail self down here in the awful depths, eh?

The bottom of the diving bell is, like any ordinary church or tower bell, completely open, and I can look down through that opening, past my dangling feet, as if through a clear lens. Professor Tilden, the supposed man of science who first convinced me to go down in this rig, maintained that it was the atmospheric pressure that kept the water out of the bell. Well, it keeps it out to a degree, but the deeper you go, the more the water creeps up the inside, the air inside being compressed, you see. Me, too, it seems—compressed, I mean—as I found out that time when I swam up to the surface outside of the bell after being so compressed, resulting in great, stupid, glorious rapture, and then great pain as the gases compressed in my body elected to bubble out through my joints. The bends, it is called, and Dr. Sebastian, my good friend and scholarly associate, said I was lucky to have survived. Believe me. I am much more careful now.

The surface of the water below my dangling feet, which started out a scant few inches above the bottom edge of the bell, is now about eighteen inches below my toes.

As the bell sinks, with me tucked inside, I think on things . . .

After I bring up the Buddha, the terms of the bargain will have been met, and the Lorelei *and the* Cerberus *will sail off—with all my friends, and yes, with Jaimy, too, and I will be left behind on the* Divine Wind *with Cheng Shih . . .*

I look out and all is just green beyond my window. It is bright but grows darker as we go ever downward.

Thinking of Jaimy gone brings a tear to my goggled eye. *But hey, maybe I've already caused enough trouble for the poor lad and maybe he'd be better off with someone else—someone who isn't in trouble all the time, someone who would be content to stay in that rose-covered cottage while he is off at sea, a loving soul to raise his children and wait longingly for his return from the merciless ocean. Someone . . . but, sadly, not me. Yes, I'm sure that would be best.*

I squeeze my nostrils together and blow to clear my ears of the increasing pressure. Swallowing helps, too. I work up a gob of spit, swallow it down, and am rewarded with a click in each ear . . . Good . . . Hmmm . . . Still just green out there in the South China Sea . . .

But I cannot feel too sorry for myself . . . for did I not sign on for a life of adventure when I first set foot on the Dolphin *back there on that dock in London? I did, so maybe being the treasured possession of a female Chinese pirate is part of that adventure . . . And after all, as companion to Cheng Shih, I shall see wondrous sights—China itself, and maybe the Great Wall, and Japan and Korea, and don't forget my Cathay Cat, no, don't forget him, nor the Kangaroo, nor any of those figments of my overactive imagination, and there will be other, even more magical things . . .*

I lean back and wait as I go ever deeper.

. . . But not to see Amy again, nor Randall, nor any of my friends at the Lawson Peabody School, ah, that will be hard, indeed. But, hey . . . wait a minute, Amy—that day when Randall came back to us, all resplendent in his new U.S. Marine uniform—did not that goose walk over my future grave, making me shudder? Yes, it did, and is that not proof that I will

someday return to Dovecote, if only to be put in the ground? Or is it just a silly superstition? I don't know, I—

Wait! The bottom is coming up!

A waving field of sea grass suddenly appears below me, I reach for the STOP signal cord and give it a hard yank. The bell stops its descent about twenty feet above the bottom and hangs there slowly swinging about.

Well. Time to have a look about, eh?

I adjust my goggles to fit tighter about my eye sockets, check the straps on my foot fins, take three deep breaths, holding the last one, and then slip out under the lower edge of the bell.

The bed of sea grass extends in all directions, with a patch of bare sand here and there. Small fishes dart about . . . some bigger ones, too, but none so large or so fierce as to cause me worry. I give a kick and float out over the slowly undulating seaweed.

Nothing to be seen, yet. Everything is relatively flat, unlike that place off Key West, with its chasms and drop-offs, where at last I located the Spanish treasure galleon *Santa Magdalena,* the source of all my riches and all my current trouble. It wasn't the *Magdalena*'s fault, though. It was due to my inherent and all-consuming greed . . . *But never mind, girl, that's done with—keep your mind on your present work.*

The expanse of grass seems endless, and I fear that we shall go through a long process of exploring the bottom, bit by bit, by moving the position of the *Lorelei Lee* a small degree each day. But wait, over there's the line of one of the marker buoys that were dropped on the day the Buddha first took his salty dip. Must check, but first . . .

Back to the bell for some quick breaths, and then back out again to follow that buoy line to see where it might lead. Putting my hand upon it, I see that the other end of the line disappears into an especially dense thicket of grass. Testing it, I feel that it is still securely held by whatever weight was attached to it. That weight turns out to be heavy enough to support me as I go, hand over hand, down the length of the line.

I feel a sudden surge of underwater current, and the grass parts beneath me and . . .

There you are, you sweet thing.

The Buddha smiles beatifically up into the light, glowing all golden and beautiful. And, oddly, it does seem that enlightenment of some sort streams from his calm and benign countenance. He appears to be just as happy down here in the depths as up there in the air. I feel the same way, too, sometimes. There is a serenity down here beneath the sea, all clear and bright, that I often do not find up there, and I like—

Oh, never mind what you like, girl, just get on with it.

I give him a pat on his shiny bald head, and then kick back to the bell. Once in it, I pull the UP rope, and I feel the bell slowly rise. I will need about two hundred and fifty feet of half-inch line. That'll be strong enough to get him to the surface, where stronger ropes can be attached to haul him aboard. No longer is it a problem of finding—now it is a problem of simple salvage.

As I sit on the bell's bench, waiting to again join those in the upper world, a grin spreads over my face, and I'm thinkin', wouldn't it be a great joke on Cheng Shih, when the bell is pulled onboard the *Lee,* for me to flop out of the bottom of the bell, limbs all ahoo, water streaming from my mouth, seemingly dead and drowned?

No, it would not, says my bottom, damp but comfortable on the bell's bench, remembering the cruel switching it got the last time I angered Cheng Shih. *No, it is not wise to tease the Dragon Lady.*

And so I don't do it. Instead, when the bell is swung back over the *Lorelei Lee*'s deck, I spring out, yank off goggles, toe out of swim fins, and submit to being wrapped in a large, soft towel by Higgins. A hot cup of tea is put in my fist by Ravi, and I receive a very warm look from Cheng Shih, who I know despaired of ever seeing me alive again.

I issue orders for the proper line, and invite Cheng Shih down into my cabin for a bit of lunch . . . a private lunch, just the two of us.

After said luncheon, I squirm back into my swimming suit and head out to complete the job.

The coil of rope has been prepared and I slip back under the bell and sit myself down. The bell and I are lifted, and down we go again.

The descent this time seems quicker, and I am soon hovering above the lovely Buddha. I look about for the proper place to loop the rope about his holy form, but can find none. His neck is too fat and thick to put a noose about it. It would slip right off and would not be very respectful of a major religious figure. No, it will have to be something else . . . Ha! His left foot extends out from under his loincloth, and that will have to be it. I wrap the bitter end of the line around the chubby foot, slap on a few half hitches, and jerk the line twice.

The rope goes taut, and the Buddha begins his return to

the temporal world—upside down, to be sure, but still beaming his light upon all about him.

I nip back into the bell and watch him ascend into the light.

The job is done, the bargain made.

Chapter 68

The Golden Buddha now sits placidly on the deck of the *Divine Wind*. I stand on the deck of the *Lorelei Lee* with Cheng Shih standing beside me, both of us dressed in rich silken jackets with golden dragons on our backs. James Fletcher stands in front of me and we are holding hands and saying goodbye. Small boats are moored alongside with crews ready to take Jaimy back to the *Cerberus* and me and Cheng Shih and Brother Arcangelo back to the *Divine Wind*. All our crews stand in the riggings, watching. Above us, at the masthead of the *Lee*, a dragon pennant flies, all splendid in green, red, and gold. A similar one snaps at the main mast of the *Cerberus*. Cheng Shih has given those to us to guarantee safe passage for our ships through the waters controlled by her mighty fleet.

I, of course, am crying.

"Goodbye, Jaimy," I say, looking into his eyes for probably the last time. "Perhaps it's better this way. Maybe it was never meant to be . . ."

His face is dark with anger and frustration.

"Jacky," he says, his voice thick with stifled rage. "Surely we must be able to—"

"Look out there, Jaimy. There must be fifty of her ships lying not two hundred yards off. We wouldn't stand a chance. Think of your ship, your men," I say, sniffling.

"My men will fight for you, as will I."

"I know that, Jaimy, but it is no use. There are the women, the children, to consider. She is letting everybody go, everyone 'cept me, and I think that's a fair trade. And . . . and think of the fine adventures I shall have, the places I will see, so do not pine for me." I gasp for breath. "I love you, Jaimy, and I know you love me, too, but I want you to go on with your life . . . I do . . ."

I turn to Cheng Shih, tears streaming down my face.

"Please, Beloved Shih, may I kiss him goodbye?"

Her dark eyes look into mine and she shakes her head.

"*Fau!*" she says, and turns from me.

What? She says no to such a simple thing? How can she deny me that little thing when she says that she loves me?

But she is not doing that at all. I look at her face and see that a tear glistens in her own eye. Visibly trying to control herself, she looks at me and says something to Brother Arcangelo.

"Cheng Shih wishes to say," says the priest, "that you may go with your young man. She does not wish to cause her Golden Child, the one who has brought her much joy, such great unhappiness."

Stunned, I drop to my knees before her. "Bless you, Beloved Shih! You shall forever rest in the heart of this unworthy one!"

She puts her hand on my head.

"*Joi gin, ju kau-jing yi,*" she says softly.

Brother Arcangelo does not have to translate—I know what she has said.

She then turns and walks away in a rustle of silk and a whiff of jasmine perfume. Cheng Shih, Admiral of the China Sea, goes down into a waiting boat, and is gone.

Brother Arcangelo follows, but before he goes over the side, he smiles and says to me, "*Buon giorno, Signorina Faber.* It has been both a pleasure . . . and an education." He nods, blesses me, and then I see my unlikely friend, the Italian Catholic priest, Arcangelo Rossetti, Society of Jesus, no more.

Amazed, I stand on my deck for a moment and then fling myself on Jaimy, giving him the kiss of his life. Then I pull back and exclaim, "Jaimy! Get back to your ship! She is letting me go! Let's get the hell out of here before she changes her mind!"

Jaimy stands on his quarterdeck on the *Cerberus* and I stand on mine on the *Lorelei Lee*. Both ships have all sails up and drawing, and we are close enough so we can hear each other call.

"To Australia, Jaimy!" I shout, waving my hand above my head.

"To Australia, Jacky!" shouts Jaimy. "I will join you in Botany Bay! And, by God, you shall then be mine, in all ways!"

"Yes, Jaimy, oh yes!" I reply. "And you *shall* have me in all ways . . ." I chuckle to myself. "*If* you can catch me," I cry. "For I shall beat you and your gang of Irish scum down to Botany Bay, or me name ain't Jacky Faber! Then we shall see about who has whom!"

Cheers from the lads on both decks.

I plant my feet on my quarterdeck and shout, "Sail on, lads, and let the *Lorelei Lee* show them her tail!"

I shout down to my crew, and then I sing out . . .

"Shantyman, sing us away!"

Enoch Lightner advances to his drum and commences to beat a slow march upon it, and, as the *Lorelei Lee* heels over into the wind, he sings out . . .

> *So heave away, my bully, bully boys!*
> *Haul away, haul away!*
> *Heave her up and don't you make a noise.*
> *We're bound for South Austral-lia!*

PART V

Chapter 69

"At the risk of sounding portentous," remarks Higgins, who stands at my side as we watch the Crews prepare to debark. "Could we be witnessing the birth of a nation?"

The Lizzies, the Tartans, and the Judies, with the Madams Barnsley, MacDonald, and Berry at the lead of each of their Crews, wait for word to head down the gangplank in a state of high hilarity, and, yes, I believe, into history. The men on the land below can only gape up at them in complete astonishment.

"I believe we are, John Higgins," I say. "Hey, you put boys and girls together and how can you miss? It's all biology, my good sir . . . biology and a bit of time . . ."

Higgins gives a hint of a dry laugh at that. He stands on the deck of the *Lorelei Lee* dressed as her Captain. He could not impersonate our late Captain Augustus Laughton—no, Old Gussie was too well known about the various fleets for that to be pulled off successfully, and our good Captain had to be listed among those who had died on the way here, along with several of the older ladies of the Crews, a sailor who had been swept away in a storm, and a certain convict named Mary Faber, who had died of Unknown Causes. No, instead, Higgins poses as Acting Captain Ruger, and we all hope to get away with the sham. We stand and wait, with bated breath, to see if Jaimy can pull off his part of the deception. I myself stand on my quarterdeck, dressed in my Creole ship's boy costume—ragged trousers, short curly black wig, straw hat, and pipe clenched in teeth—as Ship's Boy Jacques Bouvier, Messenger of the Watch. I certainly could not impersonate any Captain, living or dead.

No, of course I did not race Jaimy and his *Cerberus* to this spot. My *Lorelei Lee* is much too swift for that to be any kind of contest. Plus, Jaimy's ship had no armament, and we could not leave him sailing alone, helpless. No, we sailed in concert down the west coast of Australia. Did we get together, he and I, during that time? Closely together? Alas, no. We were both much too busy for that. No, we communicated only by signal flag, as we needed to get down to the penal colony as fast as we could, bending as much canvas on the slower *Cerberus* as possible. Jaimy is woefully shorthanded on his ship and is finding it more and more difficult to handle his unruly cargo. I have given him Suggs and Monk, but that's about all I can spare. My Crews are pretty much satisfied, but still . . .

And, actually, we are not in Botany Bay. That is a bay a little to the south of here that had originally been designated as the site of the penal colony but later deemed unsuitable, not having a proper safe harbor. No, we are in Sydney Cove, New South Wales, the site of the permanent colony. It has good, protected moorings, lots of sea room; it's just not as poetic sounding as Botany Bay.

When we came to this place, the *Lorelei Lee* stood in first, followed by the *Cerberus*. Then the *Lee* gave out a lusty, rolling, twelve-gun salute, which, I am sure, got the attention of the inhabitants.

Ah, yes, I do love a bit of a show. True, but I also wanted to let them know that we were armed and could do them great damage should we choose to do so. That stockade wall over there, for instance . . . Several well-placed shots and the confined prisoners would pour out of the breach . . . Wouldn't want that, Captain Bligh, now, would we? I am sure those prisoners are not in the best of temper, hmmmm?

We had arrived at the penal colony together, held a conference by signal flag, and agreed that Jaimy would go in first to present his cargo for payment, with us to cover him with our guns. Upon our anchoring, he immediately took leave for the shore and has been in the Commandant's headquarters for a good hour now, and I grow ever more fearful. *What if he is taken? He is still a convict after all . . . and so am I . . .*

There are other complications to this. There always are. I had lowered a dory for Major Johnston, such that he could go in to assume command of the red-coated garrison, which he did, leaving his Esther to join him later, when all was set and safe. He soon found out, however, and had informed us as well, that the colony was seething with fury and on the edge of open rebellion and it was up to him to handle it. In short, Captain Bligh had cut off the rum ration to everyone, convict or garrison guard alike, and the place was in turmoil.

Damn! Has that man no sense? First the mutiny on the Bounty, *and now here, too?*

I hold my breath and keep my long glass trained on the colony's headquarters . . . *Come on, Jaimy, you can pull this off . . . and, yes! There he is!*

I let out my breath upon seeing him. Through my long glass I see him return to his boat. He knows I am watching, so he waves an envelope in triumph over his head, and the boat heads straight for the *Lorelei Lee.*

"All right, Higgins," I say. "It is our turn. If there is the slightest bit of trouble, I shall turn this place into a raging inferno! I will not lose you for all the money in the—"

"Please hush, Miss," says Higgins calmly, smiling that little smile of his. "Was I not trained in the finest thespian tradition by none other than Messrs. Fennel and Bean? Never fear. All shall be well." And he goes off, with the manifest of the surviving convicts, all in good health and a good many pregnant, to present the bill to a rather harried Captain Bligh, Commandant—at least for the moment—of the British Penal Colony at New South Wales. I continue to hold my breath.

Mr. Seabrook assumes the deck as Captain Fletcher of the *Cerberus* comes aboard. Jaimy and I go below and into my cabin. We are instantly locked in an embrace and it is oh, so good!

He leans me back and my straw hat falls off my head, as does my curly black wig. He reaches back and grabs my thick pigtail and pulls my head back, making my mouth fall open . . . and upon that open mouth he plants a kiss, yes, a kiss to make up for all those kisses never delivered over our star-crossed years. *Oh, yes, oh . . .*

There is a ringing of the ship's bell, and then a discreet knock upon my door.

"Missy Memsahib?" I hear Ravi say. "Sahib Higgins returns in boat."

I struggle out of Jaimy's grasp and say, "There are things that need to be done, dear, just wait . . ."

I put my wig and hat back on, and again go out on deck—*Ravi, see that Mr. Fletcher is made comfortable and has refreshment*—just in time to see my dear Higgins come up over the brow.

He catches my eye and then taps his vest, wherein lies, I know, yet another check drawn on the East India Company.

Joy!

"Higgins," I say, putting a kiss upon his cheek in my relief at seeing him back. "So soon?"

"Captain Bligh was . . . preoccupied, to put it lightly."

"The Rum Rebellion . . . yes, I know. The poor man just does not know how to handle people. But, no matter. Please join Mr. Fletcher in my cabin. I'll be in directly . . . I must say goodbye to my girls."

He bows and goes below.

I proceed to the brow and signal to Mr. Hinckley that all may depart. The Bo'sun puts his pipe to his lips and blows long and hard, and there is a great cheer as the Crews begin to go off.

Mrs. Barnsley leads the way, of course, followed by her "gels," and then the Tartans and the Judies descend to the waiting boats. My Newgaters are the last to go.

"Goodbye, Mary Wade," I say to the youngest of my crew, and hug her to me. "I am sure you will do well here. And Mary Reibey, please steal no more horses, and Ann, oh, I hate to see you go, but it's all for the best, you'll see."

I had seen to it that each of my Newgaters now carries a bundle containing a fresh dress, clean linen, soap, brush, and a small packet of money to start them off in their new life. Two pounds six, which is more than they had when they came onboard my ship, that's for sure. I also begged Esther Abrahams Johnston to look out for them till all are settled, she having some influence as wife to the Garrision Commander. She said she would, and I believe her.

"Goodbye, Esther," I say, clutching her hands. "Go now to your husband. He is a good man and you shall be a good wife to him, I just know it." She nods, turns, and is gone with the rest.

Wiping the tears off my cheeks, I turn to the next to go, only to see that just as I had expected, I'm losing two more of my crew. I hate to see this pair go, even if they are the most hapless of sailors.

"I likes me Maggie, and she says she likes me, too, so I'm sticking with her," says Keefe, his seabag on his shoulder and his arm around my good friend Mag, who grins at me as I place a goodbye kiss on her cheek. We all stand at the brow as they go off.

"Didn't we have some times, then, Jacky, didn't we?"

"Yes, we did, Maggie, and there's better times comin', you'll see," I say, tearin' up even more than usual in times like this.

"They say they'll give us free colonists some land and a plow, some seed and a mule," says Mick, standing by his Isabella. "So we'll give farmin' it a shot. God knows we wasn't very good at bein' sailors. Plus Bella here is with child, which she says is mine, so we've got to see what the little blighter looks like, eh?"

"Indeed, Mick. Goodbye to you both. I know you shall prosper." I plant a farewell kiss on his weathered cheek, and they all go off to follow their destiny . . . their karma, as I am beginning to see it.

Cookie, however, elects to stay onboard the *Lee*.

"The ladies was lovely and I know I'll never see their likes again," he says. "But I was born at sea and I reckon I'll die there, too."

Jezebel also elects to stay.

When I've see them all off, good and proper, I return to my cabin, where Higgins, Ravi, and yes, my dear Jaimy, looking absolutely lovely in his captain's gear, are therein. True, he might now be a pirate in the eyes of Mother England, but he still looks grand.

"Please sit, everyone," I say, and doff both wig and hat. "And let us lift a glass or two in celebration of our new freedom . . . and maybe in our new wealth. Higgins, what have you to report in that regard?"

Ravi places a glass in front of me, and Higgins pulls an envelope from his vest and hands it to me.

"I have here a check drawn on the Bank of the East India Company in the amount of four thousand, six hundred pounds sterling," says my good Mr. Higgins.

"Not a bad haul, considering," I say, handing the check back to him. "We shall be able to meet the payroll of Faber Shipping Worldwide this pay period, I believe, Mr. Higgins."

"Even so, Miss," agrees Higgins. "And a good deal left over. We should tender our heartfelt thanks to John Bull and the East India Company."

"Yes, we shall, Higgins," I say with some satisfaction. "I think they both will, indeed, regret the day they sent Jacky Faber in chains to Botany Bay."

Higgins laughs. "I am sure they will, when their bespectacled accountants, hunched over their ledgers, run their ink-stained fingers down over their columns of figures . . . and wonder just where in the world a large amount of money went missing."

"Serves them right," I say. "They had it coming . . . And now, Captain Fletcher, how did the *Cerberus* fare?"

Jaimy pulls out his own check and looks at it.

"Five thousand, three hundred and sixty," he says. "Not bad."

"Not bad, indeed, dear," I say, growing serious. "But now I must talk to Captain Fletcher . . . alone . . ."

All rise, except for Jaimy, and they bow and leave. When they are gone, I go and place myself in Jaimy's lap. After I place a good one on his lips . . . *oh, yes* . . . I commence with what I've got to say.

"Jaimy. We need to think clearly about some things. This place is in turmoil, and for us it is dangerous. There is no food, no supplies, and Major Johnston reports there is a rebellion brewing over the cutting off of the rum ration.

And you and I, and your Irish crew as well, are all escaped convicts . . . Mairead, too, and Ian, and all the rest . . ."

I pause for breath and nuzzle my face into his neck. "We must run."

"We must run, Jacky? After all this?" he says, running his hands up my back. "No, I won't have it. We have two ships—pirates, I know—but I have gone through too much to be denied now."

"I know, dear, but we must think," I say, breathing heavily into his ear. "Your ship is unarmed and helpless. You must run up to Batavia—there is an English bank there—and deposit that check, then spend every cent of it on guns for your ship! Every cent! Arm yourself to the teeth!"

"But—"

"Please, Jaimy, listen to me. If we tarry—and you know I want to so very much—we might be lost. And to have come all this way only to fail . . . I couldn't stand it. Be off, love, and be safe. I'll meet you south of Batavia, off a place called Singapore. Then we can relax our guard and enjoy peace . . . and each other. Please, Jaimy, fly away! The Golden Dragon pennant will protect you on your way there."

I give him a packet containing that flag . . . and one other.

"One kiss, love, and off! Please tell me you will!" I plead.

He does, though it tears my heart out to see him go.

I watch the *Cerberus* raise the Golden Dragon pennant, drop the mainsails, catch the wind, and then heel off. Flying also is the other flag I had made for him on the way to this place.

No, it is not the blue anchor of Faber Shipping, no. I know he is not yet ready to fly *that* flag. It is the Jolly Roger, just like mine, flapping all bold in the wind.

Might as well be hanged for a wolf as for a sheep, I always say . . .

Chapter 70

I'm lolling about on my foretop, thoughts of the future slipping in and out of my mind as the *Lorelei Lee* pounds up the Strait of Malacca, heading north. We expect to rendezvous with the *Cerberus* in a few days, maybe even sooner.

I stretch out lazily in the sun and gaze up at the flags snapping in the breeze above me, the roguish Jolly Roger grinning above the Golden Dragon pennant. When that dragon flag waves, it looks like the dragon's tail is twisting on itself, over and over, in the wind. Very effective, and very beautiful, and I reflect on how very clever are the Chinese. I am clever, too, in my own way, and had several copies of that pennant sewn up on our way down to Botany Bay, just in case I add any more ships to my fleet.

Another lazy stretch and a heavy sigh. Ah, yes . . . *Here, Josephine, a bit of a scratch behind your ear? Feels good, doesn't it?* I'm dressed in my cool Chinese silks and Josephine is clad in her natural reddish hair and both of us are content to be just sinfully slothful on our perch aloft on this perfectly beautiful day. *Ummm . . .*

My sluggish mind tells me that once I meet up with Jaimy again, we'll have to decide where we are going to go and what we are going to do. Shall we stick around in the South China Sea, raiding a town here and there for plunder and supplies? When Jaimy arms the *Cerberus,* we will be a strong fighting force. But no, that doesn't seem to be quite the way to go. The shipping and the seaports we have seen around these parts seem rather poor and meager, and I really don't like that sort of thing anymore—taking other people's stuff and all—since I find I don't like it when people take my stuff, no, I don't. I think of the recent loss of my precious *Lee,* and how I had ached until she was returned to me. I pat her smooth foretop deck beneath me. *Never again shall you slip away from me, I swear it.*

Down below on the main hatch, I hear Ravi going over English lessons with Mr. Lee Chi . . .

A . . . Bee . . . Ceee . . . Dee . . .

Ah . . . Bay . . . Chee . . . Day . . .

No, no, Sahib Lee . . . A . . . Bee . . . Ceeeee . . . Deeee . . . Like that.

Ravi is patient and Lee Chi is coming right along. Both Higgins and I agree that he will be a valuable asset to Faber Shipping when we open up the China trade. Yes, we've changed his name a bit, thinking "Silly-silly" was just not a fit appellation for an employee of said august corporation. After much gesticulation and sign language, we discovered that originally his family name had been Lee, so we combined it with Chi, and we went with that. Mr. Lee has been instructed in other things, such as how I like my bed made— nice and tight, with the corners folded in just right—so has relieved Ravi of those duties, freeing him up for other pursuits. As soon as Lee Chi has learned enough English to understand that he is no longer a slave but rather an employee of Faber Shipping, he will be informed of his new role in helping us open up trade. Till then, hey, he is an excellent servant, and I can appreciate that, having been one myself.

Lee Chi, has, in fact, just this morning drawn a bath for me in my lovely little copper tub, and has washed, combed, and rebraided my pigtail. He has even given my head a bit of a shave as I intend to keep it in the Chinese style for as long as I am in these waters. *And oh, how I would love to prance into the dining hall of the Lawson Peabody School for Young Girls coiffed and attired like this! Would that not be a howl? Oh, yes!* I allow him to take his razor to my armpits and touch up my lower legs, as well, as I will soon be entertaining Mr. James Emerson Fletcher and I will want to be at my smooth best. However, I do instruct Lee Chi and his razor to leave my nether part alone.

I have to chuckle at that, and Josephine notices and looks at me curiously—very perceptive monkey that she is—and then I have to laugh again over one thing that was especially amusing on that otherwise very tense day back there at the penal colony. As the *Cerberus* had been discharging its cargo of convicts, one of that number who was struggling mightily had to be taken off bound and gagged. The guards who took custody of the unfortunate man were informed that he had gone insane on the way there, the poor man being convinced that he was a legitimate member of the ship's crew and not a prisoner. He was written into the manifest as one Thaddeus Stevens, who had been transported for life for the crime of forgery, but was, in fact—heh-heh—

the poor Weasel. *Ha! Let's see the creepy little bastard talk his way out of that one!* Plus, Jaimy got ten pounds six for his wormy hide! And they say that James Emerson Fletcher does not have a sense of humor! Ha!

Ah, yes, and about Jaimy . . . I did hustle him off quite briskly down there 'round Botany Bay, with the excuse that he must immediately arm his *Cerberus,* and, of course, Higgins saw right through me, as usual, smiling his small smile as he set out my lonely dinner that first night away. Our other dinners on this trip have been joyous, with Messrs. Seabrook, Gibson, and Hinckley in attendance in my cabin, and with the Shantyman to provide music and laughter, but it wasn't quite the same without good old Captain Gussie, he having passed on to a place hopefully joyous enough to contain the spirit of that happy man, and Mairead, back on the *Cerberus* and bedded up with her dear Ian, and all the members of the Crews right now spreading the joy of their presence through the colony at New South Wales. Still, we maintain our cheer as best we can.

"All right, Higgins, you see right through me, as always," I had said, poking at my otherwise delicious dinner.

"Whatever do you mean, Miss?" he'd asked, knowing full well what I meant.

"Yes, I sent poor Jaimy off with only a kiss or two, when he had every expectation of . . . you know . . ."

"I had no notion."

"Of course you didn't, my ever present mentor. Of course, you didn't . . ."

It's at least five months back to the Atlantic, and maybe I don't want to be with child during that time. Maybe I want— Oh, I don't know what I want. Everything is just so damned complicated. I don't know . . . Maybe I'll just relax and let my karma take me where it will . . . Maybe I am turning Chinese, after all . . .

I turn my head to watch the shore of Sumatra slipping past, several miles out to the west. That shore is quiet, unlike the Australian shore we had left on our starboard side not many days ago. That place had constantly reverberated with low, weird humming sounds that I knew came from no human nor animal throat. There were drums, also, and buzzing noises, and I had a strong suspicion that the local inhabitants were expressing their joy over the prospect of John Bull setting up a colony on their land—the same so-called joy that Tecumseh and Chee-a-quat and his people felt when it happened to them, I suspect.

I look up again at the dragon pennant twisting in the wind and think back to the parting with Cheng Shi. After our ships drifted apart, I had looked back and noticed her standing on her quarterdeck, looking back at me. I stood there myself until such time as the *Divine Wind* slipped beneath the horizon. It was the least I could do for her. *Joi gin, Beloved Shih.*

I settle back against the mast. *Complicated, complicated, everything is so damned com—*

"On deck there!" shouts the lookout, high in the mainmast. "Ship. Flying English colors! Two points off starboard bow!"

Boooooooommmmmmmm . . .

The sound of cannon fire rumbles across the water.

In an instant I roll off the foretop and hasten down to stand next to Mr. Hinckley on the quarterdeck, my glass to my eye. *Can it be Jaimy, come to the rendezvous?*

No, it is not. It is that damned annoying *Dart*, the Royal Navy sloop-of-war assigned to guard the *Cerberus* on its way to Botany Bay. *Why the hell does she have to turn up now?*

"Beat to quarters!" I cry. "Man your stations, man your guns, but do not yet open your gun ports!"

I peer again at the *Dart*. She had hidden behind a headland, which is why we didn't spot her right off. *Damn!*

"All stations report manned-and-ready," shouts Mr. Hinckley, looking rather pale. He is a good lad, but he has never been in pitched battle before.

"Good, Mr. Hinckley. Stand ready. I do not wish to fire on a British ship. But, by God, before I go back into captivity, I'll fire on King George himself, I'll—"

"He is signaling, Miss," says Mr. Hinckley, his eye to his glass. We have been joined on deck by Mr. Seabrook, Mr. Gibson, and Mr. Lightner. "It is a blue pennant with a white stripe. What can it mean?"

"It is the Numeral Two Pennant," answers Mr. Lightner, the only Royal Naval officer aboard, except for me, and I am not all that good at the meaning of the signal flags. "It means he requests a parley."

Another flag races to the top of the *Dart's* mast top.

"Red pennant, with white stripe," reports Mr. Hinckley.

"Plain text to follow," translates the blind Mr. Lightner.

"There's an H flag," says Mr. Gibson. "I do know the alphabet flags . . . yes . . . and there's an E . . . and an L . . . and yet another . . ."

"*Hell?*" I say, mystified. "What could that mean?"

"There's more . . . an O . . . and now a P . . . and there goes a U . . ."

"Hellopu?" I wonder. "It sounds rather . . . East Indian . . . I don't know . . ." I look to Ravi, but he shrugs and shakes his head.

"He's hoisting another one . . . It is an S . . . And there's another one, the same . . ."

"H-E-L-L-O-P-U-S-S," repeats Mr. Hinckley, mystified.

Yes, they are confused, but I am not. No, I stand astounded, for I know what the flags say . . .

Hello, Puss . . .

Chapter 71

A boat is lowered from HMS *Dart* and is rowed over to the side of the *Lorelei Lee*. A ladder is rigged over the starboard side, and in a very short time, Mr. Joseph Jared steps onto my quarterdeck. There have been times in my life when I have been very glad to see this rogue, but this is not one of them. Right now I stand astounded . . . and somewhat worried.

The boarding party is bristling with pistols and cutlasses, but Jared is armed only with his cocky grin . . . and a courtly bow.

"So good to see you again, Jacky," he says, gazing in open amusement at my silken garb, my shiny smooth head, and the Chinese sword strapped to my back. "And Mr. Higgins, too. It has been a long run from the old *Wolverine* to here, has it not?"

"Indeed it has, Sir," says Higgins, returning the bow. The other officers say nothing, but I know they, too, are extremely concerned by the arrival of a well-armed Royal Navy ship while they stand onboard a ship flying a pirate flag.

"Good day, Mr. Jared," I say, as coldly as I can. "May I present my officers . . . Mr. Seabrook, First Mate, Mr. Gibson, Second, and Mister Hinckley, Third." Each bows in turn. "And my Sailing Master, Mr. Lightner."

Jared acknowledges each, casting a wry eye at me when he nods to the plainly blind Enoch Lightner.

"Gentlemen. I am Lieutenant Joesph Jared, Commander of HMS *Dart*, at your service."

Commander? How did Joseph Jared, whom I first met as a common seaman onboard HMS Wolverine, *end up as Captain of a Royal Navy ship? And here, of all places?*

"Well, then, Captain Faber, might we repair to your quarters?" he asks me. "We have much to discuss."

"Like what, Captain Jared?" I ask.

"Oh, the terms of your surrender, and all that . . ."

"My surrender? You will note, *Mr.* Jared," I spit out, my look as steely as I can make it. "I have not yet hauled down my colors . . . nor have I given you my sword."

He nods, looking at the hilt of my sword that rests behind my right shoulder. "Impressive weapon, that. However, I do not think it would stand up to the cutlasses of the hundred men I have aboard my ship, all of them trained British man-of-war men. Come, Puss, a glass of wine between old friends? There is never an excuse for bad manners, you know."

I thrust my chin into the air and turn abruptly away. "Very well. You may follow me down into my cabin. Mr. Seabrook, maintain the ship in its current state of readiness. If that ship fires on us, fire back. Mr. Higgins, please have Ravi bring down some refreshments."

I lead the way into the cabin, and I hear Jared's footsteps behind me. As soon as the door is closed, I feel an arm around my middle, and I am twisted around to face him.

"Ah, Puss, it is so good to see you!" He plants a kiss on my forehead and then grabs my pigtail and pulls my head back and then puts one on my open mouth. A part of my reeling mind reminds me just how handy randy males are finding the convenience of my pigtail—jerk on her pigtail, her mouth opens, just like that. *Sort of like a pump handle, rather,* I'm thinkin' . . . But then I ain't thinkin' no more . . .

"And here's some colors we can think of taking down," he says, his voice thick with passion, and he hooks his thumbs in the waistband of my colorful silk trousers and begins hauling them southward . . .

Oh, Joseph . . . I—

The door opens and a wide-eyed Ravi, little white turban and all, comes in, bearing a tray with glasses upon it.

"Is pretty Missy in trouble with Big Mister from other boat?" asks the lad. "If so, Ravi has sharp knife here in belt and will—"

I withdraw my tongue, collect my senses, and push Mr. Jared back.

"No, Ravi, it is all right . . . But you should learn to knock. Please, Mr. Jared, be seated." I gesture toward my table, and Captain Joseph Jared sits down, as do I.

Ravi places the glasses in front of us, then stands back. I reach for mine, but Jared stays my hand.

"Just a moment there, Puss," he says.

He reaches out and switches the glasses. "Excuse me, Jacky, but I do know you and I do not want to wind up drugged, bound and gagged, and headed for a very poor berth on some Chinese junk bound for Shanghai. Considering how you are dressed, I imagine you could arrange that quite easily."

He takes a long drink out of the glass.

I smile what I hope to be my new, inscrutable Oriental smile, and say, "Mr. Jared, if you really knew Jacky Faber, Golden Child and Little Round-Eyed Barbarian, then you would know that I would have drugged *both* glasses and then just *pretended* to drink out of mine."

I look at him over the brim of my glass, my lips only touching the rim.

He looks dubiously at the remains of his wine, and then tosses it back. "Well, if it is to be some miserable rice-boat, then so be it."

"Do not worry, Mr. Jared, the wine was not drugged," I say. "But we must get down to business and there are things what must be discussed."

"Like what?" says the grinning rascal, gesturing for Ravi to refill his glass.

"There are coincidences and then there are coincidences, but this is just too bizarre. Yes, the Royal Navy and the seagoing brotherhood is small, but still it is a very big world and a very broad ocean. So how came you to be here?"

He settles back in his chair and begins . . .

"Well, Puss, it was like this. I was in London when your trial was being held, and I was apprised of your probable death by hanging when I was approached by Captain Hannibal Hudson, who is, I must say, a very good friend of yours. That good man stood up for you at the trial, as you know, but he advised me to keep silent, figuring my testimony as a mere warrant officer would mean nothing. 'Wait, wait, Joseph,' he said, 'and we might yet do her some good' . . ."

Another sip, another look around my cabin . . . and at my bed . . . and he continues . . .

"Leaning very heavily on his political contacts, he prevailed in preventing you from being hanged . . . And believe me, Miss, that took some effort on his part, as your past transgressions against the Crown . . . Well, never mind. Suffice it to say, Captain Hudson called in many markers, you may be sure."

Good Captain Hudson, I do owe you my very life.

"Anyway, knowing that you were to be transported to Australia, and that HMS *Dart* would escort the *Cerberus* down to the South China Sea, he figured that if I were placed as an officer on that small warship, I might be on hand to keep an eye on you."

"And so?"

"And so, the good Captain arranged for me to stand for my Lieutenancy Tests, which I passed with flying colors, all the questions being oral, and did I not know seamanship better than any wet-behind-the-ears squeaker of a midshipman? Of course I did."

"And so?

"And so I was appointed First Mate upon the *Dart*, Captain Wallace commanding, all to keep an eye on you."

"And so . . ."

"And so the good Captain Wallace perished of a fever on the way here, and Joseph Jared, son of a tailor, becomes Commander of His Majesty's Ship *Dart* . . ."

It seems that this little cruise was rather hard on captains, I reflect.

"And so, it worked out, as here I am, and there you are . . . looking lovely, I might add . . . Rather exotic, but it adds a bit of spice—"

"Spice for you, Sir, but not for me," I say, looking away.

"But, Puss, why so cold? It is not like you at all."

I rise to my feet, all hot. "You fired on my ship, Jared!"

"Oh, come on, Puss, that was a warning shot. I only fired to get your attention. If I had actually wanted to hit your pretty little ship, we'd be standing in waist-deep water right now. So get over here and sit in my lap, where you belong."

"I shan't. I am promised in marriage to—"

"Oh, yes, the oft misplaced and much confused Mr. James Fletcher. Just where is that poor man now? I expect he has been deposited as a convict in New South Wales . . . That was the sentence laid upon him."

"Umm . . ." is all I say to that.

Joseph Jared rises, stretches, and then lifts me up again.

"Let me go, Joseph," I say, not very convincingly.

"But you are my prisoner, Jacky, and as such, I have . . . privileges."

"What?" I exclaim, as my feet are lifted off the floor.

"Of course, Jacky," he says. "You are an escaped convict, and I suspect you have misappropriated this ship—something I know you are very good at."

"You say you know me, Joseph Jared," I say, fuming. "And you may, indeed. But I also know you, and I know you will not force an unwilling captive."

"True," says he, flinging me onto my bed and then looming above me on hands and knees. "But we have many miles twixt here and England."

547

He brings his face down to mine and places his lips on my forehead and . . .

Oh, Joseph . . .

And . . .

BOOOOOOMMMMMMM . . .

The broadside rolls out across the water.

Jared sits up in bed and looks out my window.

"Damn!" he says.

I look out, too, and there stands the *Cerberus*, bristling with twenty guns to each side, all trained on the now tiny *Dart*.

I get up on one arm, grab his collar, and grin into his face.

"Just who is captive of whom right now, Mr. Joseph Jared?"

Hmmmm . . .

Chapter 72

It is what Mr. Yancy Beauregard Cantrell, renowned Mississippi gambler, used to call a Mexican stand-off . . . all participants involved standing with guns pointing at one another's heads, waiting for someone to make the first deadly move.

I sit at my table in my cabin and counsel calmness.

In attendance is Captain Jared of HMS *Dart*, Captain Fletcher of the pirate *Cerberus*, and Captain Faber of the pirate *Lorelei Lee* . . . that being me.

Also all about are Mr. John Higgins, my officers from the *Lee*, and the *Cerberus*'s First Mate, Ian McConnaughey.

Yes, it is very crowded in here.

"Gentlemen, please," I say. "We must come to some sort of agreement. Captain Jared, you may speak first."

Jared stands and says, "Most of you are escaped convicts. I am honor bound to take you back . . ."

That gets him a low growl.

". . . however, I am open to suggestions."

John Higgins, as always, the very soul of reason, speaks up.

"I know, Mr. Jared, how deeply you hold your concept of honor as a Royal Navy officer. However, consider this— your initial duty was to escort the *Cerberus* to New South Wales and back to England. Is that true?"

Jared nods. "That was our mission."

Higgins fusses with some papers on the tabletop, then continues.

"The *Cerberus* did, indeed, go to Australia and did discharge its cargo of felons as ordered. It is now ready to go back to England, under your protection, as per your original charter."

Ian McConnaughey stiffens a little at this, but with Jaimy's elbow in his ribs, he says nothing.

"Now, as to the *Lorelei Lee*," says Higgins. "I believe, Captain Jared, there is nothing in your orders concerning that particular craft. Is that true?"

Jared considers, and then nods. "True."

"Well, then, this is Faber Shipping Worldwide's modest proposal—that we all proceed back to European waters. Once there, the *Lorelei Lee* will go back to her home port of Boston, and the *Cerberus* will go into British waters, and any disputes between their respective captains will be settled there, and in an honorable fashion. Captain Fletcher has begged Captain Jared to grant him a period of time upon their arrival to effect a clearing of his name from false charges laid against it and to call out, on the Field of Honor, several personages whom, he says, in the vernacular of the American West, 'need killing.' Those two persons being a Mr. Flashby and a Mr. Blifill. Captain Jared has granted that request and wished Captain Fletcher godspeed in pursuit of that goal."

Higgins again pauses and looks about. He clears his throat.

"Ahem. There are further considerations. It is a long way back to England, and we are a formidable force—three swift ships, trained crews, and sixty-two guns, with powder and ball to match. It is to be expected that we will encounter many French and Spanish ships, and we are still at war with those nations . . . Prizes, Sirs . . . Many rich prizes . . ."

There is a low growl of avarice all around the table. Jaimy looks at me, and then at my bed. I return his warm look . . . Then I see Jared looking at me in the same way . . . *Complications, complications . . .*

I stand and say, "So we are all agreed, gentlemen?"

All stand in agreement.

"Then lift your glasses and let us drink to our common enterprise."

Hear, hear!

As we are again seated, Ravi comes up to me and tugs at my sleeve. "Missy Memsahib . . . must talk."

"Not now, Ravi," I whisper to him. "Just serve the dinner." I note that the air in here is getting rather close.

"But, Missy," he persists, and points to Lee Chi, who stands nervously in a corner. "Sahib Lee teach me some of his words . . ."

"Yes, dear, go on," I say, knowing that the little fellow will not relent.

"He say *tai* means 'big' . . ."

I nod at that, anxious to get back into the high hilarity of the evening, however hot it is growing in here.

". . . and *phoon* means 'wind.'" Here he fills his cheeks and blows out little puffs.

"So?"

I look up at Lee Chi and he points outside and says one word.

"Typhoon."

Uh-oh . . .

Apologia

(Author's Note)

To the people of Australia:

It is my hope that you will not mind my having some of your founding mothers jump through fictional hoops. To wit:

The names of the female convicts in this novel were taken from the manifest of the *Lady Julianna*, a convict ship that left England bound for New South Wales in 1790. Conditions on that ship were very similar to those on the *Lorelei Lee*, including the lax attitude toward coupling amongst the crew and the girls and the plying of their ancient trade in various ports.

Yes, Mary Wade—condemned to hang at age ten—as well as Molly Reibey, sentenced to the same fate at age thirteen for stealing a horse as a prank, lived on in the colony.

Mary Wade, at the time of her death at age eighty-two, had three hundred direct descendants. Today, they number in the thousands.

Esther Abrahams, who married Major George Johnston, became the first First Lady of Australia, when he later became Governor. Their manor house still exists.

Cheng Shih? At the height of her powers, she had a fleet of four hundred ships and seventy thousand men, making her, without doubt, the most sucessful pirate in all history.

Later in life, she received a full pardon from the Chinese emperor and spent her last years running the finest gambling house and brothel in Canton.

When she died, at age sixty, it is reported that among her effects were many fine things . . . Curiously, there was also found a small portrait of a young girl in Oriental dress, but obviously European, smiling a very un-Chinese-like open-mouthed smile. Underneath it is written the inscription, in English,

To Beloved Shih . . . Your little round-eyed barbarian,
Love,

Jacky